Wild Eyed Southern Boys

Wartime Druid Saga, Volume 1

Shawn McGee

Published by Assetstor, 2023.

WILD EYED SOUTHERN BOYS

First edition. April 11, 2023.

Copyright © 2023 Shawn McGee.

ISBN: 979-8215444634

Written by Shawn McGee.

Chapter 1—Stone Mountain

Like most of us, people have chased me off of property with a shotgun or a rifle firing behind me—but today was different. The first rifle shot at me took a chunk from a beautiful red cedar and the shotgun blast took a branch of golden leaves from a bald cypress. The rifle and shotgun blasts came from a priest in a black clergy shirt and a cardinal wearing a black cassock with a red sash and skull cap.

Even though I live in a carry state, I carried nothing for self-defense. Luckily, they didn't get a good look at me and I ran away before they shot again.

I picked up a couple of broken sticks from the packed dirt path and tossed them to the side. Beginners tripped on these and it ruined their experience of the outdoors, and it didn't slow me in the least. Orange tape on the pine tree to the right marked this trail and was easy to pick out. My nervousness, mixed with my post workout shake, had caused me to stifle a belch.

You're doing great, Corey, don't lose focus now. Old Donnie was my mentor and supported me like few others, so his voice stayed in my head.

I didn't think the priests got a good look at me when they shot at me. I ducked off the trail to my hidden pack and changed shirts to a red one and wore a hat. Today needed to be about blending in with crowds and hiding. I even wore tennis shoes and missed out on my direct connection to the Earth. I brought no weapons, and only wore my camping waist pack.

My arms ached, since I spent three hours practicing stances, blocks, and strikes with, and without tonfa. Rachel had no one to train but me—again, and she spent the time exposing each of my weaknesses in stances. If it were an actual fight and not just that karate stuff, I'd take a shot or two from her and use my size to win. But Rachel kept my best interests at heart and if I didn't listen to her, I'd pay for it. Plus, truth be told, her training had done wonders with my skills.

We kicked off our plan for me to hunt as a loner and I took ownership of this plan and made a risky first step. As long as the clergy didn't get a good look at me, or identify me outside of my magical signature, escape remained possible. Rachel waited in the parking lot to hide my license plate by tailgating me when I drove off.

Early November in Atlanta kept me from sweating and the trees here had not turned colors like in North Georgia near the cabin.

My primary job is to read the <u>Abernathy Book of Gargoyles</u> to discover when a gargoyle can escape the Realm of Darkness back to Earth. I draw a circle and provide a portal inside of it. With druid magic and the information in the book, I bind it to my circle, then banish it again for hundreds of years. That's the way druids worked for thousands of years.

The Abernathy's were the only druids to survive the Catholic church's raid using the Roman armies. I'm the first druid that is not an Abernathy in fifteen hundred years, and the church wants me dead. The church was a term we used to describe the enemy. The Curia of the Catholic church contained an ensconced group of magicians and that's who I fought. They promoted a Priest to a Bishop then assigned him to Atlanta for the first time in history. This past year, he closed in on me, and now it was time for drastic action.

The small gargoyle I banished this morning caused no problems and arrived immediately. However, the church waited for me near my location and sprinted to me when my magical signature broadcast. The Curia kept meticulous records of gargoyles like the Abernathy's and knew when a gargoyle is due. Since a gargoyle has specific conditions to be met, the church can watch the sites close by that qualify. The Southeast is big enough that they normally aren't this close. Today, they were on me like bugs on a bumper and nearly put a bullet in me. I already had one bullet wound. I didn't need another.

Fortunately, Stone Mountain contained thousands of squirrels and enough squirrels gathered around to see a druid, that I asked them to delay the two without putting themselves at risk. The Animal Domain was one of the four magical Domains granted to me and animals recognized me.

Two large racoons played in the area and joined in because they thought attacking the two sounded fun. I couldn't admonish the trash pandas when they helped me.

I skidded down a hill and kicked off a rock and leaped through branches to land back on the main trail. Passing a patch of intrusive eastern honeysuckle, I fought the urge to convert the damn carpetbagging species to the natural coral type. But more magic was a bad idea when I had a head start on my pursuers. With my pack yanked above my belt by my shoulder straps, I placed my feet carefully around the groove in the dirt from hikers and saw the parking lot.

Stone Mountain's services team removed the Halloween decorations from last week's celebration. I scoped out this site on the thirtieth and banished a gargoyle on Halloween thirty miles from here. Today, the workers at Stone Mountain Park decorated for Thanksgiving. I stepped off the path onto the pavement and weaved my way around a large stack of decorations on the ground, just past the pools of standing water. Past them, I merged into groups forming to climb Stone Mountain together.

The chance that anyone else of the thousands of people visiting Stone Mountain today used magic or even access to learn magic was insignificant. Five years ago, this part of reality was not part of my life. Five years of training later, people believed I was a soldier and avoided me.

Combat training and magic from my Plant, Animal or Earth domains gave minor effects and weren't always beneficial. I called those minor powers, but with Old Donnie's training, I learned to use them effectively. My friends made fun of me for having plants, animals, and Earth as domains.

Old Donnie had protection and weather. His grandfather mastered healing and stone. But all those Domains were minor compared to the power we had with the Circle Domain.

If I spent the ten minutes to initiate a circle and bind it to something—well, I was something else. This wasn't bragging. Even Old Donnie said circles like mine hadn't existed in centuries. I felt like a proper hero when I initiated a circle.

Crossing over the train tracks for the park's train, I scooped up three crushed plastic bottles on the ground and threw them into the recycling bin. I merged with another group, walking into the parking lot to hide in the crowd. Bile rose in my throat from the panic, so I calmed myself by reciting the instructions from Old Donnie—God rest his soul.

Circle castings take ten minutes and blast out a magical signature. This is because our circles touch the Fey realm. You create a link to the Fey realm with your personal signature. The stronger you make the link or the longer you use it—well hell, some sort of residue is leftover. Just because we can't see it doesn't mean others can't. The church has sensors around the south and can pinpoint one in minutes. They contact underlings to look for us at that location. If they are close, then learn to dodge bullets.

I debated whether to use my long, dark hair to cover enough of my face to avoid AI versus looking different from the other hikers. Deciding to stick with the plan, I left my hair in place to blend. The full parking lot contained plenty of people milling around or walking about. Even if no one watched the security cameras, the church gained access to the tapes.

I used the term AI, Artificial Intelligence, to discuss any of the fancy computer stuff the church used on video recordings or other data. As a college dropout, I understood none of it. Old Donnie had paid an AI specialist to fly in from California last year to give the three of us a lesson. I didn't understand half of what he said, but I memorized 'best practices' and did my best.

The key fob popped the trunk on the red Mustang GT to get me access. This was Miles' car and when the AI examined tapes from the cameras of parked cars from multiple gargoyles banishing's, changing vehicles helped us hide.

Rachel parked a few rows from me and waited for me in my van. She'd be hiding my license plate from the cameras. I would miss my two friends on banishing, but it was important I learn to become a loner.

I'd miss Rachel. We'd been so close since high school and developed what our mandatory high school therapist called a codependent relationship. I didn't know about that. It's just I wasn't complete without her nearby.

Our problem that led to talk of me becoming a loner started with how much time they wasted joining me on hunts. As a druid, only I could banish gargoyles. But, in situations where the supernatural creature became loose, or priests tracked me, his hunter skills and her fighting skills were invaluable. But I needed to learn to work alone because in cities with cameras and artificial intelligence watching us, working together put us in more danger.

Today, the wind blew my sweaty hair that stuck out from my hat enough that trying to position it would look weird. I replayed the cameras in my head for this location. Two monitored security cameras on poles in the corners of the parking lot and one more at the entrance building. After taking a long drink of water, I started the engine. I slid the messenger bag with the book of gargoyles and the druid book from under the passenger seat and placed it next to me.

While only druids saw the book of druid spells, the Abernathy Book of Gargoyles was a big old fancy dark leather-bound tome from old times and people may try to steal it. Both books measured sixteen inches by twenty-eight inches. The druid book weighed twenty pounds and had a red leather outer shell. The book of gargoyles contained thousands of Fey enchanted pages, was three inches thick and weighed fifty pounds. I owned a messenger bag, that was always with me, that held a hundred pounds of giant books.

I made a show of putting on my seatbelt and refrained from taking off my hat or putting on sunglasses. This is what we called hiding in plain sight. I heard Rachel's van start up after I revved the engine like we planned.

Once ready, I eased out of the lot, and the white van got right on my butt. *Breathe easy.* I drove the twenty-five miles an hour down the long winding entrance road and exited past the ticket booth with its camera. Rachel tailgated me the entire way. I would not speed in the park and risk getting a ticket that documented my presence. Stone Mountain sold yearly passes. I bought two—one in my real name, Coire Norwood, and one in my fake identity, Tyler Nash.

Today, I checked in with the Coire Norwood pass since I'd be traveling using the Tyler Nash ID. Fake IDs confused the heck out of me. I labeled phones, wallets, and boxes for things like passes, credit cards, and other legal papers separately. But this is what my mentor taught me to stay alive.

The left turn I made at the stop sign brought me onto the main road, and I drove the thirty-five mile per hour speed limit in third gear to hear the engine rev to remind me to keep the speed low. The van turned right, and she left for her day. Her advice stayed though, *be a loner, not lonely.*

PHASE ONE OF MY ESCAPE succeeded, and it allowed me to relax slightly. I put my hand on the cooler in the passenger seat to remind myself not to get pulled over. There were a few long necks for my friends in the cooler. Rachel and I drank when we weren't working, which unfortunately wasn't that often.

This batch of beer I brewed was good, and I wasn't sure what my next changes should be. As a druid, you think I could brew the best lager known to mankind.

After a mile, I took the hat off, slicked my hair behind me, and took off my red t-shirt. I put on my sunglasses and turned onto the perimeter. Shirtless, wearing sunglasses, and driving a Mustang, I downshifted into third and entered the highway and merged into traffic. Atlanta may be a modern city, but people like me still fit in. A few easy shifts later, the RPMs wound down, and I cruised and checked for cars in my rearview mirror, not just for the police, but for anyone tailing me. Finding none, I eased the car into sixth gear, took my foot off the accelerator, and hit the cruise when I slowed to sixty-five.

My back collected sweat against the leather seat, but I ignored it since I grabbed the Georgia Thunderbolts t-shirt for my third shirt. I bought it last February, which was the last normal month for us. My favorite memory was when I took Old Donnie to see the band. He spent a wild year as a roadie in the seventies and loved Southern Rock. He told me after Georgia Thunderbolt's concert he gained hope for the future. I pinpointed that evening, heck, that whole week, as the happiest I had ever been.

Everything was perfect then. I had not met Rebecca, Old Donnie was still alive, and my friends and I spent time together having fun. The new Bishop hadn't focused on us. Heck, if you told me the sun shined brighter, and the grass was greener, I'd back you up.

According to the clock in my dash, it had been forty-five minutes since I sent the gargoyle back to his realm. Finally, I reached under my seat and pulled out my torc. I didn't want to wear it on camera because the ruby and blue emerald in the open parts made it easy to identify me. The smooth metal on my neck made me whole again. I kicked off my shoes just in case the church was desperate enough to release a captured gargoyle after me. Plus, being manmade, the shoes bothered me.

This week was the craziest week for gargoyle returns I'd experienced in the past two years, and my plan contained no margin for error. It was unfortunate the church predicted the location for my first banishing in this plan, but if I escaped, no harm, no foul.

This morning's gargoyle preferred landmarks and Metro Atlanta had plenty, but the priests waited for me in Stone Mountain Park. Downtown locations for the binding had easy highway access. I thought the church expected me at locations with direct highway access.

Druids learned to banish unnatural and supernatural creatures to other realms. I could banish anything to the Realm of Darkness. If I ever failed at banishing a gargoyle, the church negotiated with it for freedom and then the gargoyle would help the church do evil. That's why I needed to hide. They used computer people, bounty hunters, trained priests, or gargoyles to come after me. Heck, they still had access to Snake-Hunters, the beings created with the demon Patrick, which eradicated the old religion from Ireland.

Now, with Old Donnie dead, they could eradicate all druids permanently. Rachel was kin to Old Donnie and would be next on the bishop's hit list, then her brother and sister. If the bishop killed me and my three friends, gargoyles would soon take over the Earth, under control of the church. It weighed on me how I was the last hope for humanity. A dumb twenty-four-year-old piece of white trash.

Traffic was normal for a Tuesday after rush hour. It was close enough to the holidays that people took vacation days, but not enough to thin traffic. Right before spaghetti junction, I cut back over to the right lane, took I-85 north, and entered the highway at the speed limit.

According to my book, the next gargoyle appeared tomorrow, and I needed to banish him just after midnight because Italy was his last location, and that was ten hours ahead of me. This morning's gargoyle had been from Lisbon, Portugal. That was only five hours ahead of Eastern Standard time. I'd learned more geography fighting gargoyles than I ever did in school.

I wasn't the best of students and I knew I'd never be a college person, but Rachel and I took a few semesters and dropped out together. That was before I was the only person banishing gargoyles and we started acting like adults.

I'm not sure why eight gargoyles are scheduled to return this week, but since I was the only person on Earth sending them back to the realm of the dark, focusing on this and nothing else became my priority. I once asked Old Donnie what the end goal was with the gargoyles, church, and the realm of darkness.

Corey, this is one time you are thinking too much makes sense. I got no idea. My grandfather died in 1893 and he never figured it out either. I stop gargoyles cause I've seen them rip down a building, tear a locomotive from its track, and wade through a crowd of people killing. If you find out why the church wants them, you're a better man than I. Until then, let's keep banishing.

An hour had passed since this morning's priests did not identify me. Only two creatures had innate abilities to track me. A hunter, like my partner Miles, tracked any ally. Second, and what I worried about, was a gargoyle released by the church. If they released a gargoyle, they knew I was within ten miles, its maximum range. It performed supernatural sniffing of Fey creatures and humans with an attachment to the Fey realm. I had a permanent attachment to the Fey realm just by being a druid. Supernatural creatures sensed me from a handful of miles away because of that link.

I figured the church calculated my next location for this next gargoyle in either Atlanta, Charleston, Winston-Salem, Birmingham, or Greensboro. My plan took me to DC next. Then my plan had me putting miles between myself and home. This would cross up the church and give me cover for years. Old Donnie and I never left the Southeast. I may not be the sharpest spoon in the drawer, but if we never left the Southeast, leaving it would confuse my enemies. Let's see that new bishop track me if he watched the entire country.

I plugged in my ten-year-old music player, which Rebecca teased me about by calling it my collection of mix tapes, as if I was old, and not twenty-four like her.

Crap—Rebecca. Rebecca was so far out of my league that restaurants would try to seat us separately. But when we were together, she was nothing like that. She was funny, real, playful, and caring. *Dammit! Stop thinking with the wrong head, you are escaping enemies.*

Since Rebecca didn't know I hunted gargoyles, she thought it weird I had few items with location tracking. One of the many things she thought was weird about me and led to the breakup. Not wanting to date a honkytonk fighting man was another. What made me sad was while her description used to be correct—that one time she saw me square up in a bar, I was innocent. I confronted a vampire to stop him from feeding, but I couldn't explain it to her.

I should have known she'd leave me. Even though beauty wasn't her best feature, she was beautiful. She was smart, competent, and interesting, and liked me for me. I was dumb to fall in love with her. What's strange is I felt her love for me. But my pathetic ass fell in love with each of my three girlfriends. Haley in High School was my first love, and she went away to college. Tiffany, I broke her heart when I found out what being a druid entailed. Rebecca broke my heart. This one hurt. *Stop thinking about ex-girlfriends! Stay focused!*

Lonesome hours of driving meant music would not keep my brain alert, and reminiscing about ex-girlfriends wasn't helping nothing, so I ran through everything Old Donnie tried to teach me. He told me the most important thing was to stay alive and stay hidden. He taught three other people in his career and they all died, along with their spouses, to a gargoyle or priest. In one hundred and fifty years, Old Donnie only knew five people who proved they saw the book of druid spells. I still expected to see his face, with his half-mouthed smile to come to me and say, *there you go all-star—thinking me dead and doing it all on your own.* He'd be happy with me and it'd be like old times. Even though I buried him myself, something in the back of my mind said he could come back to me.

Chapter 2—Gargoyle Attack

The ruby on the torc glowed red and snapped me back to the present. The blue emerald occasionally glowed blue, but Old Donnie never got to that part of my training—before he passed. We always left if my torc glowed blue, not because it turned blue, but because he sensed an unnatural presence through owning the territory. But when the ruby glowed red, a gargoyle was near—within a few hundred yards.

Old Donnie believed only druids could wear this torc, even he couldn't wear it without being shocked. When I tried it on and it worked for me, he cried and explained how his grandfather's last wish, before a creature in the Appalachian caves killed him in eighteen-ninety-three, was to see a real druid wear it one day. I loved making Old Donnie happy, but it meant he had little information for me. The gems lit up as a warning, and it gave me vision that let me see at night and view magician magic—the magic the church used.

Focusing on the neck device, I turned off the ruby warning with a thought. The device became part of me when I wore it. The same thought to wiggle a finger or sniff let me use the torc. It was because of my attachment to the Fey Realm. I slipped the car into fourth gear even though it revved near four thousand rpm. Right now, I needed maximum control.

All my weapons remained in the trunk. I hadn't expected the church to release a gargoyle to chase me. They must have held one ready in case they came close to catching me. Gargoyles were a limited resource for the church, thanks to Old Donnie and I. Plus, gargoyles had a limited range, so this meant the church was certain they had my location to within ten miles. With I-285 being a circle and then heading Northeast, I was still within ten miles of Stone Mountain.

With my shoes off and my torc resting on my neck, I'd want to touch real ground to fight the thing. It was one thing to summon one into a circle and then bind it. It was another when the creature charged and attacked you. My connection to Earth was all I counted on when fighting the supernatural creature. This was only the second free gargoyle I fought without Old Donnie, and the other had run from me.

> *Gargoyles have as many types as there are types of rock. It's not they're made of that type of rock, it's they have the same silica content... dammit Corey, are you paying attention? Look, they're going to be hard like granite where you'll have to spike it for damage or soft like marble, which'll give you more options. Damnit, Corey. Once you fight, one without a circle, you'll learn this chemistry crap then.*

I wanted a do-over for an afternoon lesson on gargoyles three years ago. A mile from Suwannee, I prepared to follow I-85, where the split for I-985 happened when an eighteen-wheeler roared past me with its tires rumbling on the pavement. A blur jumped from the top of the trailer section towards me. I swerved two lanes to the right and slammed my clutch and brakes while I swerved through traffic into the breakdown lane. Antilock pumped my foot, but I came to a stop, popped my trunk, jumped out of my door, and ran to the back of my car. I scooped up the weapons on top of the pack before I ran to natural ground. One tonfa, the obsidian knife, a regular knife, a glass breaker, and one circle-creating-plate was what I grabbed to fight. The world became black and white, and sound became muffled. The gargoyle hid us from the real world. Old Donnie said this was halfway to the Realm of Darkness, like a place between the planes where the gargoyle became stronger.

Two steps backwards to step on the highway grass to feel the power from Earth gave me confidence. I frisbeed the circle-creating-plate back ten feet. My primary gift from the Earth was magical circles and my circles kicked ass. Circles, Earth Power, Plants, and Animals were the domains the Earth granted to me.

Right now, I needed Earth Power to get to where I could use a circle. Barefoot was the best way to connect to the power of the Earth, other than naked and lying on Earth. Man-made substances like pavement made me vulnerable.

When the world was black and white, most people in the world lost all contact with whatever went inside the realm. We could see them, just not interact with them. Gargoyles brought us into the realm of black and white to weaken my link to the Fey Realm. They didn't need the extra power to beat me, but they took every advantage.

There, a hundred yards from me, a gargoyle stopped rolling on the highway as cars passed through it. The only ones who could find me now were Miles—*or another gargoyle, or even a Snake-Hunter.* I hoped my friends tracked me to this black and white landscape.

I used the druidic vision of the torc's magic and saw no magician magic. At least it was only a gargoyle and nothing else—not that this was much better. I reached out to sense any animals and one deer ran near and I asked it to come to me with a quick spell. I communicated with animals, but if I used magic, it gave them a boost when they helped me.

The supernatural gargoyle charged towards me, using its four limbs. I had learned enough fighting to realize I didn't know enough. I was good, like beat ninety-nine percent of humans good, but that wasn't good enough.

WHEN I FIRST BELIEVED I'd become a druid, I thought I'd fling powerful magic like a wizard. While I cast powerful magic with a properly created circle and time, I only cast minor magic without a circle. Give me time to create a circle and start a binding, and I could fight anything from any realm. Without time, well, I was about to find out.

This gargoyle was what we called a granite type, and not one of the softer marble types. His flesh did not stay granite, the silica content of the supernatural beast measured closer to granite and his skin measured harder—according to a scientist that gave Old Donnie notes. When any gargoyle defended a part of its body, that part turned to stone.

My window breaker was foolproof to turn a limb to stone, but you needed to be close. It'd be nice to get the torso, but it was hard unless you had two competent people fighting it. Pepper gel was useless, that sat on my belt in the car. My stun gun was on the same belt, but would have been useless here, too.

The supernatural creature reared up on muscle bound legs, and its hundred-pound arm with razor claws ripped towards me just as I brought up the tonfa with a high block. The combination of the torc and standing on natural ground saved me and Earth Power gave me the strength to withstand the blow. I had seen what those swipes did to people, and it wasn't pretty. I had seen a claw strike like that rip through one of Old Donnie's pickup trucks. Earth Power was the only thing that had the power to keep me alive. Still with a perfect tonfa block, the Earth giving me strength, and years of bar fighting skills—my arm went numb.

Not having my weapons ready might cost me my life. But the cameras at Stone Mountain prevented me from having them out.

The bishop planned this ambush well. I jumped back further into the grass and down the incline, off the shoulder. *Square up Corey!*

Cars whizzed by in my black and white landscape and no one stopped to help a guy on the side of the road fending off a gargoyle. Old Donnie said so few people had visibility when the world turned black and white, even though the world was otherwise the same, that my helping him was the first help he received in over a century.

I pulled the regular knife out and the handle slid awkwardly in my numb arm—Earth Power didn't stop everything. Crap, this was the knife I was testing and not my normal combat knife. The gargoyle swung its other arm, and I slashed it with the knife. The supernatural creature shattered that blade, but I felt it break in time to fall back.

It was time to remember that I lived in the real world and not a tv series. While I healed fast, I needed standard medical care like everyone else. If I died on the side of the road, no one could stop the gargoyles from coming back and being controlled by those who'd taken over the church.

The deer showed up as I ran to the left of the gargoyle towards my circle-creating-plate. I asked the deer to jump in front of the gargoyle and then run far away for safety. Being able to talk to animals and ask them to do things was something I just did. With magic, I could give them extra power to do those things. I hated using magic, because it didn't protect them, it just made them more capable of carrying out my instructions. The spell from my Animal Domain I cast this time made the deer faster and more accurate.

While the animal got up to speed, the gargoyle turned towards it. I jumped on the five-foot plate and let the edges sink into the ground to create the inner and outer circle. Tossing the broken knife, I pulled out the glass breaker. This gargoyle was smart and was expecting the moves Old Donnie taught me. The church had fifteen decades of tracking Old Donnie and knew his moves. They knew he trained with a master from Okinawa in the sixties in Liverpool, England. Leave it to Old Donnie to study karate in Liverpool in the sixties, then come to the American south in the seventies before finding his favorite music.

Well, time to find out if the gargoyle understood dirty bar fighting. I took a natural stance and held the tonfa in my left arm at the ready and feinted an upward elbow strike. The deer jumped in its face, causing the gargoyle to make a blind mid-block. I rolled to the ground while spiking its leg with my glass breaker. The deer had put the supernatural beast off balance. I back-rolled out, landed behind it, and took a ready stance. I told the deer to run for its life. The gargoyle was mad, and the deer deserved a long life after that.

The gargoyle's left leg turned to granite after it hit. It wouldn't be able to move that leg for hours. It recognized it made a tactical mistake when it tried to lunge. The supernatural beast howled to the heavens. Even muffled, the howl was loud and menacing. My chance of survival had increased from next to nothing to possible.

I faked a swing with my glass breaker, dropped that weapon, and pulled the obsidian knife out of its sheath in my pants. I dove low again and wanted to drive the obsidian blade into an access point for its life force—where a human's femoral artery would be.

It expected the attack, and I realized my error when it struck my unexposed arm with its claws. When its gouge hit my bone, I screamed despite the comfort of Earth. The Earth buffered my strength and senses, but it didn't stop everything—not even close. This guy learned faster than most gargoyles.

Jerking my arm back as I rolled away, blood flung from the gash, and then poured from it. While a druid's connection to Earth healed me faster than normal, it didn't mean same day healing or even the same week healing. This is a wound that takes months to heal with only modern medical care and would kill me without care. With hospital care and my fast healing, I'd be okay in a couple of weeks. Without care, I'd either bleed out or an infection killed me.

I was out of options to fight it and needed to intimidate it or banish it. The creature jumped away with a sluggish move of one stone leg. I moved the plate off the circle, kicked it away, and exposed my circle to start the binding. I wished I'd had time to cut honeysuckle twigs with my sickle to power my circle up, but having an empty circle to bind would work—it needed to work. The gargoyle was smart. It recognized it had ten minutes before I bound it to my circle. Its choices were to flee beyond a mile, kill me, die, or watch me banish it to the Realm of Darkness. I was hoping it would run at this point. This arm wound was deadly.

Banishing a gargoyle was safer than killing one because the gargoyle had to be inside a circle and couldn't fight back. Killing a gargoyle meant it could never come back, unless another gargoyle ripped the name off of a druid's flesh. Plus, now it smelled blood. If a gargoyle drank the blood of a human, it broke its ten-mile shackle to its summoning point and could travel the world.

This large gargoyle, with a head devoid of horns, snarled, then flung out its arms and howled to the sky. Its eyes were typical large black orbs and jagged teeth without fangs filled the bottom of his mouth. Nothing but rock grew in the roof of its mouth. Dark gray stripes gave his torso a zebra appearance.

With one good leg, the thing leaned onto all fours and lunged for me. I ducked and rolled, but a large rock on the ground knocked the wind out of me and I failed the binding. Despite one leg made of granite, its speed was fast enough to catch me. I rolled and restarted the binding, and it prepared another lunge until a regular steel chain bound its good leg, and a magical green two-handed sword swung by a giant of a man connected and sliced into its torso. *Rachel and Miles*!

MY FRIEND MILES SWIPED it clean in the chest by surprise. Then, while it was off balance, Rachel kicked out its good leg and then back flipped into a defensive stance. The gargoyle's chest was gashed with the magical weapon before turning to that part to granite. The surprise and ferocity of the two-handed swing combined with Rachel's leg sweep knocked the one-legged gargoyle to the ground and made it scramble from the two-handed sword's follow-up.

My six-one height was not small, but next to Miles, Rachel at five-nine, and I looked tiny. Plus, once he accepted his fate as a hunter of the unnatural, his gym addiction had become fanatical. Well, until the past year. "Miles! Rachel!" I screamed in relief.

"Do your thing, druid boy," called back Miles. He kept the gargoyle off balance with careful two-handed swings of his Earth-summoned sword. This was so unlike his aggressive fighting posture.

Miles must have got leeway from Trish to help me today. His lack of availability had become a sore point between us. The biggest problem was he tried to leave Trish out of this part of his life and she made decisions without knowing the ramifications.

Her pregnancy sped up this talk of my becoming a loner. I didn't understand how a person wielded magic and hunted the supernatural, but did not tell his wife. Then again, in six years, I only dated three girlfriends and couldn't keep any of them. What did I know?

Miles and I had been best friends since high school and his parents treated me like family when I had no one else. That's why watching Rachel cover for his missteps was painful. Rachel was in her full focus and nothing broke her attention from the fight, but she was fighting for one and a half people with Miles out of practice. I had no worries for her. She'd been fighting gargoyles without powers longer than I had powers.

Contorting its arms wildly, the supernatural creature knocked it-self over and dragged its rock-hard leg towards me, howling with ha-tred. Miles was good against unnatural monsters, against the super-natural, well he had as much chance of survival alone as I did. Rachel had zero chance against a granite type gargoyle and could not hurt it at all. But we were together and wounded the creature. The odds had swung in our favor and the gargoyle was looking to escape.

I gritted my teeth and knew the pain in my arm dissipated in a minute—at least temporarily. Druid Magic took me somewhere else. The binding took five to ten minutes, depending on my circle and the strength of the creature I bound.

I faced in one direction and the wind blew my hair straight back like I was a fancy model—if fancy models had a nearly paralyzed arm dripping blood, and I began my binding. Once my binding on the small circle was ready, I followed our standard practice to contin-ue the binding with a loud voice to notify my friends. Earth Power flowed through me to the circle.

Bho àm immemorial, cumhachd an t-seanairginn a 'gairm thugad. A bhith ceangailte ris a 'phortal agam agus fo smachd mo thoil.

I felt a connection to power and became something more. I imagined myself floating above a beautiful green landscape brighter than here on Earth. My friends said I looked like a putz yelling Gaelic at scrapings on the ground. I preferred my imagination.

The numb and bleeding arm quit to be an issue with so much power in my body. It worked as well as my right arm, at least for now. The plate only created a three-foot circle, and it wasn't large enough to banish this large guy, and that meant I needed to kill it. One ben-efit of the binding was the supernatural creature could no longer run from the circle. The circle also made me the most powerful fighter in this battle.

To kill the thing, I'd need to jab my hand inside of its body and plant my other hand into the ground inside of the circle. The Earth would destroy it, using me as a conduit.

Miles retreated to me and the gargoyle picked me out as the threat and lunged towards me. Why did this gargoyle have to be one of the smart ones and one who resisted the draw to the circle? The circle drew most gargoyles into it. This supernatural creature must be one of the strongest the church had in the Southeast. The only way to guarantee a binding was to put the gargoyle's name in Gaelic or druidic magic inside the circle. Since this one was running free, I didn't have that information.

Rachel kicked at its head to turn it and I rolled on my back, blocked its wild swing with my good arm, as a bloodied Miles swung his giant sword and missed. The force of his swing made him off balance, and he fell. *Damn, he was out of practice.* The gargoyle sunk its claws into his gut before Rachel could get in the way.

Then, I rolled between its legs, thrust my obsidian knife straight upwards until ichor covered my hand and oozed down my wrist. The obsidian knife not only penetrated gargoyle flesh, it prevented the gargoyle from turning that part of its body to stone. Out of the corner of my eye, I saw Rachel bandaging our friend.

I jabbed my other hand into the ground inside of my circle and power from the Earth coursed through me. The paralyzed gargoyle howled and screamed. My frozen muscles prevented me from joining him in screaming, but after an eternity lasted only a few seconds, the gargoyle turned to dust around me.

I caught my breath and my upper right chest burned as the name of the gargoyle became tattooed on my chest. This would be my third Earth granted tattoo. Old Donnie had sported eighty tattoos. The two gargoyle names in inch half high letters from top to bottom on my chest, were *Qotsam* and *Brondreg*. I had a lost Gaelic word, *Sain-*

nithe in inch high letters around my biceps. I brought the word back to the world when I killed the Snake-Hunter.

The colors of the Earth came back, and we returned to normal from whatever weirdness the gargoyle did to keep hidden.

Chapter 3--Escape

Rachel grabbed the gear from the ground and brought it up to my car, while I dragged Miles up with my one good arm.

Rachel finished the equipment and put Miles into the passenger seat of his car, the one I drove here. She ran over to check my arm as I tried to tighten a t-shirt over it. "Corey, this ain't it. You'll need stitches."

"Is it bad enough to risk getting blood on your Charley Daniel's Band t-shirt?" She wasn't wearing it now, she had on a plain gray t-shirt. Her office must have a lax dress code.

Old Donnie had been a roadie for a band called Grinderswitch for a year and collected a bunch of concert shirts, and that was the only non-girlie shirt Rachel received. She treasured that shirt like we all treasured the gifts from Old Donnie.

"Let's not go overboard, now." She grabbed my other arm to help me stand and walk around the car. The second I stepped on the asphalt, pain roared back at once and overwhelmed me. I fell to the ground and fought to keep from passing out.

"Shoot fire Corey. How bad a shape are you in?" asked Miles from the car as he spasmed coughs. Miles dressed for work, but by the looks of him, he'd be going to an emergency care place first.

Rachel waved an ammonia capsule under my nose, then helped me stumble to the seat. I coughed my way over.

"The Earth Power dissipated and let all the pain through. I had the fight just where I wanted it," I joked. "Can you move my weapons and Old Donnie's duster to my trunk?" I hated asking her because she needed to care for Miles, but I needed a minute.

With ammonia fading from my nostrils, I stumbled to my car and sat in the driver's seat. Cars roared by us and the world was back to normal and no excuse explained this to ordinary folk. We needed to drive soon to avoid being noticed. One tweet or Instagram post of us and the church tracked us easier. The California AI guy told us pictures had meta-geo-tagging stuff. It meant if a picture of us was on the internet, another computer guy could tell where we were. Put our pictures at this scene, then compare us to Stone Mountain, cross reference school records, and computer guys identified us.

While failing to ignore the throbbing pain, I yelled as I grabbed emergency meds from my back seat. I threw ibuprofen in my mouth and swallowed them with water. Then, with the red t-shirt, I wrapped my arm tight.

"Hold up there, I can wrap that better," said Rachel. "But you better man up for the first time in your life." She winked when she said it. We had snuggled this morning since I'd be gone so long. I wanted to joke back, but I leaned back against the seat and held back tears. Rachel kneeled next to me as she worked on my arm. "Listen Corey, this is important and will take your mind off your arm. You know how I told you I get asked about you?"

I thought through the pain and tried to nod. I spoke with a gasp. "Yeh, like Mr. Wilbanks."

"Exactly. Well, those people also include relatives of Old Donnie."

This did not seem the time, but she had control. I yelled when she crimped the pressure banding on. "It makes sense, since you're related to him."

"Good. Remember, I'm your friend first, even though I've kept other people who care about you in the loop."

"Rachel, we are like white on rice."

She smiled and patted me on the shoulder.

She wrapped gauze around a t-shirt she compressed the wound with. "Lord willing and the creek don't rise, this'll hold. Time for us to jet."

She was right, so I switched the car keys with her. "You got a handle on Miles?"

"Yeh, he's bad, but not as bad as you." She slammed my trunk shut and shut my door. "Call me if you can't keep this going. Really."

The pain throbbed and burned, but it was 'suck it up or prepare to die,' time. "By the way, the cooler has a gift and the eight in my fridge are for you two."

Rachel shook her head, but smiled. Then she jogged to Miles' car, the one I had just been driving. She was right about us needed to vamoose and I caressed the silver knob on the five-speed shifter. My foot pushed the clutch in and I started it up. The engine roared to life with Rachel's improvements to give it a louder and throatier roar, plus the extra hundred horses. I popped the clutch and chirped my tires with power shifts into second and third gears, accelerating as fast as the increased compression from Rachel's upgrades would let me. I was relieved that the world was normal, with cars honking at full volume.

The convertible top was going to stay closed for the trip. The wind could damage my arm. I needed to hold the steering wheel with my bad arm to shift, clutch and sped up and the wound burned now, but I was in the light traffic and heading north. I kept the cruise off to help pay attention.

My arm burned worse than it bled with the pressure. An ache shot through my arm, to my shoulder and into my chest, but I had to drive. Two exits later, Rachel roared by me as I settled in to drive away long enough to be away from any more attacks from the church. I popped the med kit and grabbed bottles of ibuprofen and acetaminophen and swallowed a few more of each.

As many of these pills I swallowed, I bought everything generic and in bulk. Pain was common for us when fighting gargoyles. After the past two years, it became an old friend, telling me I survived another encounter.

I couldn't pass out nor stop for hours yet or risk being found. Depending on who found me, the church would either kill me immediately or identify me and kill me at their leisure. Those weren't good choices, especially if they exposed Miles. His wife, Trish, was pregnant, and that was an unsaid reason I needed to become a loner. Rachel had the protection of her family, what was left of her family, who'd been fighting gargoyles with Old Donnie for a while.

I focused on driving through the pain. Through tears, pain, swearing, and cursing gargoyles—I drove north. The green highway signs and exits blurred into my tear-filled eyes.

I KEPT MOVING TO WHERE I-40 and I-85 shared a highway until I found another truck stop and I pulled in. I perused the parking lot and pulled between a couple of RVs to perform more first aid. Rachel did a good job to get me through a couple of hours, but now I should spend time on my arm. The shadow of the two RVs and the muffled noise from the pumps gave me security.

Once the bloody t-shirt peeled off of my arm, it revealed the damage. I stared at the roof of my car with tears streaming and did my best not to scream. A few seconds later, I got control of myself and refocused. I set my arm on the steering wheel and balanced it so it wouldn't flex or bend along the wound.

The scrape stretched from an inch above my wrist to my elbow, with an eight-inch gash in the middle. Three inches of the gash penetrated to the bone. Grabbing my emergency medical kit from the back seat, and once I opened the door, I poured saline over the outside of my arm onto the ground and did my best not to scream with the burn. Deep breaths kept me focused on the task as I spread the antibiotic stuff on an absorbent compress and wrapped my arm with a few wraps of the four-inch gauze roll on top of the compress, using maximum pressure from my good arm. I'd used up my butterflies over Labor Day and used the replacements two weeks ago.

With a temporary bandage, and a quick change of clothes behind my car into spare shorts and shirt ensured blood and ichor did not give me away. I tossed the bloody mess onto my rear floor mat, swallowed my pain, put my shoes back on, and walked into the store. I put on the Georgia Thunderbolts t-shirt and it had survived the worst, and I was glad I had been shirtless during the fight.

The door dinged and the floor between the stand-up coolers was tight with display shelves. It had lots of coolers and, most importantly, public restrooms.

In a basket, I collected saline, ibuprofen, acetaminophen, two bottles of water, and another small first aid kit with gauze, compress, and butterfly bandages. Since I stopped and the compress hadn't bled through in the first five minutes, I also picked up lunch.

I purchased these and walked back out to the car. Customers crowded the store enough that people passed in and out constantly.

Once the burning mellowed out and my eyes stopped tearing, I removed the temporary bandage, dabbed my arm dry and put four of the butterfly band aids on the gash, pulling it tight. The sides of the gash were red, puffy, and jagged. Rachel had been right. I'd need a doctor for stitches, but for now I'd place butterflies on it.

I needed to sit and breathe in and exhale deeply, so I thought about happier times. Miles and I met in tenth grade. I had signed up for cross-country. One day, the coach had the cross-country team run a speed training exercise he called quarters. Part way through, I threw up on the side with a few others. A couple of football players came over to throw up as well from their drill on the field, and I caught the biggest guy who passed out and helped him to his knees to throw up. He called me his vomit buddy, and we became fast friends.

When my mother and sisters disappeared my senior year in high school—in that fire where the police couldn't help. Mr. Wilbanks and Miles' parents help me negotiate insurance companies, police stuff, and all kinds of legal crap that would have ruined my life had I not had their help. If Rachel kept people up to date with me, I was fine. So many people helped me then, I had a lot of 'good-people debt.' I knew little of her family. Nicole was her kid sister and Nathan her older brother. Their parents were dead, and they lost Old Donnie, who they called Grandpa Don.

Rachel had been an acquaintance but became our friend then because her parents died. We became close at mandatory therapist meetings. She and I became so close we forced the therapist to hold our sessions together. She was dating Logan then, and I dated Haley, and they were relieved they didn't need to console us on deaths. Not that they didn't want to, but because no high school kids had those skills. Haley was a champ, though. She and I would leave for school early to help Rachel and Nicole get ready for school, and Haley helped Nicole through eighth and ninth grade with things I couldn't help with.

We needed to be there for them. Rachel had the magic power of a specialist. She mastered a handful of skills better than humans should be able to. Shotokan, motorcycle racing, and fixing any engine were her big three. She sang like an angel. Other than that, she was essentially a fifth grader—unless she was around me. When we were together, somehow her mind became like a high school aged girl. A high schooler with experiences to draw on.

Since then, the three of us became inseparable. I couldn't imagine my life without Miles and Rachel. Except Miles was becoming further from us and the marriage to Trish had come to a head today. I don't know if we could bring him on any more trips in good conscious. Maybe this was good and helped me move towards being a loner.

I held a compress over the top of the mess of my arm, wrapped the gauze thickly over it tight, and walked back into the store since I hadn't grabbed everything or used the restroom because of the pain. A dozen people milled around, but everyone appeared to be a local. I ambled my way through the display shelves, past the coolers of cokes and beer.

"Hell of a bandage you got there." I turned to the man in jeans and a golf shirt. He carried two cases of beer and stared at my neck. *My torc! Old Donnie taught you better.*

"Yeah," I answered with a quick story. "My girlfriend popped a tire right before I had to go on a trip for work. Ripped the arm with a tire iron—hurts like the dickens."

"Ain't that like a woman?" he joked. "But we all need someone in our life."

I smiled and nodded. "Very few people can be loners in the world." I was one of them, but he didn't need to know that.

"Well, I will. She done left me."

It had only been a couple of months since Rebecca left me, and I knew his pain. I needed to keep names out of it, since the church tracked me. "I had a good friend, and he was good people. When my lady left me and I was all upset, he said I had it backwards."

"Backwards?"

"Yeh. He told me I only lost someone who didn't love me. She lost someone who loved her."

"Huh. That's good advice."

"It took me a while, and I still drank a case of long necks and went mudding with my buddies."

He laughed. "Thanks for making me laugh, man. You have a good one."

Old Donnie said I needed a healthier attitude towards women, but this man didn't need to hear that, and I couldn't explain what he meant. *Maybe you should focus on being happy as yourself without a woman before you add a woman to your life.* That made no sense. I was happy and when I said that, he said someone smarter would explain it to me one day.

After the man left to pay for his beer, I used the restroom, filled my tank, and hit the road again. After an hour, I ate the sandwich, without the bread, and relaxed as much as possible with the pain. I had a plan, escaped the church, and was alive. I powered on my alternate identity, Tyler Nash's, phone. On Tyler's phone, I pulled up urgent care centers near me and found one open until nine just before Durham, NC. Pain, cruise control driving, and monotony filled the next several hours. Convincing myself I didn't cry about Rebecca on the drive was easy. I cried with the pain in my arm. It was just a coincidence I was thinking about her.

Chapter 4—Rebecca's Decision

Rebecca sat on her bed and realized she had decided to break one rule of her grandmother's. She traced the blue flowered patterns on the fluffy down quilt her grandmother gave her. This normally calmed her, but today was not a normal day. This was a day she'd be breaking rules. Technically, she had broken the rules when she started obsessing. A young woman was not to obsess. She learned that was not a hard and fast rule. A proper woman could obsess about her wedding, a party, or a dress. What she couldn't get caught doing was obsessing about a boy. Especially a boy she had broken up with.

She looked around and her nightgown was on the floor, and her slippers were next to the bathroom. After moving the slippers to her shoe rack, she put her nightgown into the hamper, and it was full. The room was dangerously close to the type of chaos that could affect a young woman's life. She snatched up the laundry and carried it to her laundry closet and started the delicates first. The rest piled on the floor next to her apartment sized washer and dryer. These weren't appropriate for a young woman, but she did not have the means or space to have suitable sized units, so she made do. Unfortunately, traveling to neighborhoods which had laundromats was far less suitable for a young woman. Sometimes, choices needed to be made.

The living room, kitchen, and dining room were clean. She would skip vacuuming this weekend. Skipping a chore was a clear sign she was obsessing. The step she planned to take today pushed her over the edge toward becoming known as an obsessor. She dressed down today and wore an old jean skirt with tennis shoes in case she saw him and had to catch up to him. She wore a t-shirt with a jacket since it was getting chilly. It was better to sweat in a t-shirt in case she needed to run. Her face felt better without makeup and she removed her jewelry. The past two months, this had been her standard attire, where in the previous twenty-three years, she had made more appropriate choices.

She walked into the bathroom and put her hair into a ponytail. A young woman could let down her hair for an outdoor event, but there should not be hair lying loose. She had a matching blonde band to secure it and placed in three twists to ensure she got a tight hold for a long day. This plan was such a longshot, but she had to meet someone who could contact Corey—hopefully Rachel. Corey showing up worked as well, but this wasn't the ideal location for their next meeting. She touched her phone and saw it was six-thirty-three am. This was too early and this early of an arrival was not only obsessive, but the cemetery was closed.

Her body didn't want food, but she grabbed a hard-boiled egg she made last night and a small apple. She peeled the egg over the garbage and placed it on a plate and then cored and sectioned the apple. She placed the sections on her plate, grabbed a glass of ice water, and sat at the dining room table. One did not eat any meal in another room if she could help it. A proper young woman needed to run a household, and these habits aided her in the future—according to her grandmother. Just because she was breaking one rule, shattering it, didn't mean she should break others. In reality, she should follow other rules even more diligently. A young woman followed these rules to not only be prepared for a successful future, but to be safe. Young women who weren't safe often lost their viable future.

She pulled the laundry line from the laundry closet and hung it on the edge of her breakfast bar. Rebecca would invite no one over until this mess in her life had run its course.

Her phone had no more messages. The phone message from her mother got deleted. Her mother wanted Rebecca to convince grandmother to give them money. Grandmother gave her parents two million dollars when Rebecca was four and Rebecca received neglect as her share, as they spent it frivolously. When Rebecca was thirteen, her grandmother gave them another million dollars and said she would give them no more and they needed to learn to control their spending.

Her parents tried to cash in Rebecca's college fund behind her back when Rebecca was eighteen. Rebecca would not be calling. She had learned her life lessons from her grandmother to ensure she did not end up like her parents. Mother tried to explain the forgery of Rebecca's signature as fate that she had enough to cover their current bills and get them back to France to see their friends. They had not invited Rebecca.

Rebecca didn't believe in fate, but there were many coincidences that had brought her to this place in her life. She could pinpoint the day the coincidences started—at least when she noticed the coincidences starting. Corey measured her for a ring in August. Rebecca had already been told by her grandmother that Corey was fine for a young woman to have fun with but was not long term. Rebecca knew she wasn't strong enough to say no to Corey's proposal. She was barely strong enough to break up with him when she was upset. She asked him to remain friends and not only didn't contact her, he didn't return messages.

This behavior should have ended everything. But two weeks later, she saw him at the grocery store to ask why he was being such a jerk. After all, this was just a breakup and proper young couples were not dramatic.

She had eaten the whole egg, and she still had apple slices left. With another hard-boiled egg from the refrigerator, she peeled it over the trash and brought it to her plate. Today would be a long day, and she was only bringing one meal and two bottles of water.

That question spawned a fight a young woman should never be a part of. The fact it was in public was scandalous. That fight was when her life derailed. Surely, the breakup started the path, but discovering she picked a fight when Corey had lost Old Donnie devastated her. The next day, in the morning, she drove past the places she remembered Corey moved between. He had his main house, a storage locker by Oglethorpe University, and a place he stayed at where he called himself Tyler Nash.

That should have been her first clue Corey was more than he seemed. How many people have false identities that own property? She received that information a few months into the relationship, and he explained it away as family issues. She learned that he and his friend Rachel became close in high school when they both lost their parents. Their relationship was clearly inappropriate, unless you knew them and discovered how good friends they were. They were two very affectionate friends, and it didn't go beyond that.

She was driving while lost in thought near his house and a crazy ten-foot-tall beast ran in front of her. She used the term beast because she did not recognize what it was. A huge two-legged creature with nothing but muscles made from stone with claws, fangs, and it was huge. She'd seen a large black bear, and this thing dwarfed it. A quick jerk of her steering wheel brought her car into the parking lot, barely missing the curb. Her grandmother would have agreed screaming was appropriate.

The thing jumped up on the donut shop roof and it was being chased by a knife throwing maniac on a motorcycle with long hair. Then the color left the world, and it was like she put in hearing protection. Then this maniac threw green beams into a circle on the ground while the tall creature of stone muscles, claws, and fangs threw a black circle on the roof.

The circles were obviously magic, though magic did not exist. Green magic from the maniac and black magic from the beast met in air and it was no contest. The maniac and his green magic were winning.

Rebecca got out of her car and thought the maniac was Corey, but was this a hallucination? Corey had long dark hair, but he didn't ride motorcycles. He had well-used knife targets in his backyard. But guys enjoyed throwing knives at wood, right? He also had karate weapons next to his weights. That was normal guy stuff. He always cooked outside, but he had put in a beautiful patio. She loved putting on a bathrobe and eating breakfast outside with him. A local hawk called Tiberius flew in and ate sausage with them. *That should have been a clue.*

Soon the long-haired maniac's green circle reached out and turned the creature's circle green; and then the green glow encased the creature and dragged it towards the maniac's green circle. It howled and clawed until the maniac made everything go away. The maniac turned towards her—it was Corey. Her Corey!

He saw and recognized her. Panic hit his face. She screamed to get his attention. He scooped up his weapons and put them in sheathes on his body, ran to his motorcycle, and jumped on the bike's kick thingy, then took off with the front wheel in the air. This was not his first time with weapons or a bike—or creatures that looked like giant gargoyles.

Color returned to the world and so sounded. The motorcycle revved down Mabry Road. She drove to Corey's house and waited in his driveway for the rest of the day. He didn't return home. She unlocked his door before she left and pulled several of her hairs from her brush and placed them on the door's top. Then she locked it again. Corey used number pad locks and forgot how to change the code and used the same immature code from when he setup it up at eighteen. It made him seem more normal with the weird stuff she should not have ignored.

A few days later, her job required her to show up at the range. After verifying her hair on the door stayed put, she drove in and cleaned the range weapons. While getting dressed in the lady's dressing room to return to her office—over tired, frustrated and confused—she struggled to hold it together. Someone mentioned Old Donnie dying and Rebecca broke down crying. The other ladies came over and she opened up about how she regretted breaking up with Corey. She fought with him, not knowing his mentor had passed, and now she couldn't find him. It was unseemly, with a running nose and bubbles of snot, and her grandmother would not have approved, but she had lost control over her emotions.

The other ladies, though they barely knew her, turned into a private investigative service. It was the most remarkable thing she had ever seen. She discovered that the last will and testament left nothing to Corey but a lot to Tyler Nash—Corey's fake identity. So many things fell into place. Corey ordered a headstone and over a month later, they installed it in a graveyard as a remembrance. These ladies found everything for her.

Now she had found the gravestone and would park by it like she was a detective on a stake-out. She picked up her empty plate and rinsed it off in the sink and placed it in the dishwasher. After drinking the water, she put the glass in the dishwasher as well.

Her lunch sack, cleaned and ready, just fit the salad she bought for today along with a fork, a napkin, and frozen bottle of water. She got her large purse out and verified the Ruger LCP had a full clip, and the safeties engaged. Her charged stun gun and the pepper spray were ready. Then, she pulled her book reader off the charger and placed it in her purse and made sure it zipped up with nothing sticking out.

She pulled the delicates from the washer, as they had finished washing, and hung them on the drying line. She had no whites to wash, so everything else plopped into the washer on a normal setting.

Satisfied that her house was nearly proper for a young woman, she grabbed her phone, purse, and lunch bag, then locked her door on the way out. She got into her little reliable car. Proper young ladies should drive something better, but not at the expense of putting themselves in debt. Her parents were supposed to buy Rebecca a suitable car as one condition of receiving the million dollars from grandmother, but this did not happen. Rebecca purchased this car on her own, while she worked her way through college despite having a significant college fund from her grandmother. Excuses did not change the rules required of a young woman, and accruing debt was unseemly.

She placed her purse and bar on the passenger seat, locked the doors, and drove to the church parking lot.

There was little traffic on the road, and she pulled into the parking lot near the end within ten minutes of the parking lot opening. She made sure she had a direct line of sight on the gravestone and leaned back and began her long day with a ton of research material.

Dead end after dead end in researching told her she was on the right track. Important things got hidden. However, she may be fine with using searches and apps, she wasn't fine with trickier items. She also realized she couldn't post this online. If Corey kept this stuff hidden, including a second identity, Rebecca should not post these questions online. She didn't have close friends, and it stumped her until she heard that the computer people at her company's office were doing puzzles for fun. She didn't enjoy going to the fourth floor, because they always rolled their eyes when they saw her. But if they liked puzzles, she might find out information.

She usually walked to the fourth floor with CJ. He owned <u>CJ's Weapons Wholesale</u> and was a member of The Tribe. No one looked anything but professional around CJ, and CJ hired her from the range while she was still in college when he watched break down a Mauser M18 for a high school student who didn't know how to clean his rifle. They attached her to the special sales division and her job was to show, clean, and keep track of all demonstration gear. Sales was what Rebecca told her grandmother about the job. Sales was a much better description of a job for a proper young woman.

She monitored the grave and the parking lot. The parking lot had a dozen cars in it now, so she didn't stick out so badly, but no one had gone into the cemetery.

The day she walked into the fourth floor on a Friday scared her and all eight computer people's eyes rolled because they had been laughing and relaxing.

She got up her nerve. "Hi guys, I have a non-work-related question and was wondering if someone could get me pointed in the right direction?"

"Non work? Why heck, we can do this now," said one guy about her age. She thought and his name was Aaron.

"Yes. I have a puzzle without enough information to research it."

"To the conference room!" said another, and she walked with the eight of them into the conference room.

Aaron stood by a white board with markers out. "Okay. Don't give out all the information at once. What's the broad question?"

"Okay. A guy, mostly normal, fights a gargoyle with green flows. What's going on?"

"She came to the right spot," said the lone woman in the group. "Let's start with the guy. You said mostly normal."

"The normal parts are he's very sweet, has a house, and graduated high school but dropped out of college."

Aaron wrote these on the board, and Rebecca continued. "He always cooks outside, likes outdoor dates, camps too much, two weird tattoos, and his job involves the woods and mountains."

"Druid," said one guy.

"Hold on," said Aaron. "It's not a complete lock. What's his yard look like?"

"Oh, it's beautiful and wild."

"How often does he work in it?"

She had never seen Corey work in the yard, but then again, she didn't live there. "He cuts the grass, but few people have seen him work in the yard."

"What's the tattoos?" asked another guy who she didn't recognize.

She pulled a piece of paper out and handed it to Aaron. "It's weird lettering, but this is close."

Aaron wrote the words, Sainnithe—arm and Qotsam—chest, on the board.

Aaron looked at her strangely. "What about animals?"

"He didn't own any and gets upset at people who own pets, but animals loved him. A hawk in the neighborhood would fly down to eat breakfast with him. Every dog and cat loved him and would jump fences just to see him, and on dates, squirrels and raccoons would just come and hang out with him and his date."

"Raccoons? Were they friendly?" asked the lone woman from the group.

"Always," replied Rebecca.

"Friendly trash-pandas?" questioned another person she did not recognize.

"The word on his arm is 'trapped' but in Irish-Gaelic," said the guy, asking about the tattoo, putting his phone down. "No hit on Qotsam."

"Nailed it, Steven. The guy is definitely a druid. Probably a traditional British Isles druid."

Rebecca did not know what a druid was, but she noted it.

"Gargoyles and druids make little sense," said two guys.

"Not directly," said the woman. "But the catholic church has lots of gargoyles on its buildings and the catholic church wiped out the druids."

She hung out with them for another half hour, but she had enough to research and once she read about druids, she learned Corey was one. If one looked at facts and not history, it made so much sense. Her book reader had days of reading material because

she had taken two weeks of vacation from work to wait at this cemetery. She would study druids, how druids died out, the roman occupation, Hadrian's wall, medieval architecture, early catholic church
and Rome, and a few other items that were listed as references.

She had read about druids and contradicting lore when there was
a knock on her window. A man wearing a suit smiled and knocked
politely on her window. She was prepared for this. She rolled the
window partway because she was a single woman, and it was proper
for her to protect herself.

"Are you doing well today, young lady?" asked the man with an
Italian accent.

"Yes. I am reading about my genealogy, and I have family buried
in the cemetery. I wanted to be close to their spirits." She spoke with
as much air-headedness as she could help the general feeling that
men had toward blondes, and it worked. A scary man in a red shirt
stood a dozen feet away.

The man in the suit smiled and said, "good luck young lady."

"Ha una spiegazione ragionevole," said the man in the suit to the
one in the red shirt. "Potrebbe non essere lei."

Rebecca's major in college was appropriate for a proper young
woman. Her major was Classics. She didn't speak Italian, but she
had taken classes in it, and those two were looking for a woman. She
pulled a mirror from her purse to watch them walk away safely, and
the man in the suit's demeanor changed. Now he marched like a soldier.

Just in case she memorized the faces and gave them nicknames of
Red Shirt and Suit.

Despite being scared out of her wits, she stayed and the first day
passed without a single person viewing the stones, but she had two
weeks of vacation. She went by Corey's house and her hair on the
door had not moved. She went home to get a good night's sleep and
get up early to do it again.

Chapter 5—Appalachian's Hill Care

The pain raged through me during the drive until it slipped into the long-term pain someone like me accepted. It sucked because this burned and throbbed, but I'd had worse. I listened to Old Donnie's music to occupy my mind.

An hour before Durham, a beautiful FJ1200 like Old Donnie's bike blew by me on the highway. Rachel had his old bike now, but she was at her city job. The bikes were an old model, but Old Donnie loved the bike, but he thought the church had seen it near a gargoyle binding and he parked it at the same time I had to park my van from high school. We had an awful week and the church nearly got us and we both needed to lie low and change vehicles. I saved my van for some later date and hid it in the shed at Carol and Rachel's old property near Black Mountain. Miles, Rachel, and I told no one of this location and it was our go to hiding spot from the world.

That's when I bought this Mustang. *Son, get you the car you want and it'll be easier to hide. People will see you driving a car you love and you won't look suspicious.* Shifting between third and fourth gear with my good arm meant my wounded arm had to steer, and every move caused pain to shoot through the arm and into my chest.

Miles laughed at the thought of a druid driving a Mustang, but as my mentor explained to me, go back a thousand years and ask a busy druid if they wanted to travel somewhere in two hours or two weeks, they'd pick the two hours because they had things to do.

As I approached Durham, rush hour approached, I slowed to exit to the urgent care center. It took finagling with a wounded arm, a five speed, and a lot of traffic, but rush hour had passed, and I picked out the shopping center. I preferred my five-speed over Miles's six-speed, but Rachel had altered the gears for my taste.

The large parking lot had three shuttered stores and more trees around it than I expected, but the urgent care center was near the front, and easy to find. We were in the mountains aways and the leaves of the deciduous trees had turned yellow, while many brown leaves swirled around. The renewal cycle was switching from fall to winter here.

Near the lone building, the lot was empty except for two cars, and both parked near the door. A red cross and caduceus symbols stood out on the door over the name of the place, <u>Appalachian Hills Care</u>. A camera facing the road in the parking lot had fallen to the ground. That was lucky.

I unwrapped the wound, put the battery in my phone without the sim card, and took a picture. Then I re-wrapped my home-made compress, removed my easily identifiable torc, placing it under the seat, and walked in.

A DING SOUNDED WHEN I opened the door and the building was so quiet, I heard the heating duct blowing warm air. Two rows of cheap chairs lined up in the empty waiting room, and I walked up the empty room to the check in window.

"Insurance?"

"Self-pay," I replied to the bored nurse. I did not want to leave a paper trail. The nurse protected three-inch fingernails and stayed ensconced behind a clear plastic barrier. She gave me forms and a pen and typed into an old brown stained computer. I sat in a cheap, torn, beige chair, my arm throbbing relentlessly in the clean and empty room where everything was a different but boring shade of brown.

The clack of her fingernails on the keyboard mixed with the exhale of the heating duct, and the scratches of my pen on the forms.

When I brought up the filled in form, I smiled weakly and hoped she took pity on me. She painted her nails with vibrant red, white, and blue and came together to form an American flag. Her long black hair had inch wide loops six inches in diameter. The whole look must take her two hours to get ready in the morning.

I gave her one of the fake IDs Old Donnie created for me, Tyler Nash, from Suwanee, GA. She charged me $100, and I gave it to her in cash with the excuse I had cut myself doing day labor earlier.

I had my gig as I contracted through a company doing trail maintenance and search and rescue. So, I had basic work forms to hand her. These had nothing to track me and I would never tie Miles' store Miles Away from Town to gargoyles banishing.

While I waited, I read a book on the mythology of the Appalachians. Strange, this book was here, but I might as well occupy my mind. I read about special healing skills of the Moon-eyed people of Appalachia, Deer Women who stole the souls of men, links to the Fey courts in Appalachia, and Dark Fey creatures, who lost power under the brightness of the noon sun. The missing information on gargoyles convinced me to dismiss the book as harmless fun.

The doctor called me back. She appeared to be a short woman of middle eastern descent. She guided me into a sterile white room with three tables and medical equipment around the edges. Her eyes were bigger than normal, but I was woozy from being in pain for so long. I couldn't tell nationalities very well, but she smiled. She sat me up on a medical chair with the roll of paper on it and pointed to a metal tray to rest my arm upon. "My name is Dr. Kanoska, and it looks like a wicked injury. So, tell me about your arm here."

"I was camping—"

She interrupted me right away. "Sorry sweetie. You're still barefoot and I can sense the spark in the Realized."

I had forgotten to put on shoes but I did not understand her use of spark and Realized. "Um, pretend I am stupid."

She paused, working on my arm, and looked at me. "You are young. I guess it's possible you are untrained."

I was worried now this location exposed me as a druid. "Ma'am, this needs to be basic for me."

"The worry in your eyes tells me I should have brought this up slowly. I am half human and half Moon-eyed. Like you, I need to keep my identity secret. My people refer to those with preternatural powers as having the spark. If you are not latent, we say you are Realized. This means, not only do you have what normal humans call magical powers, you actively use them."

She was using big words and lying was not my strong suit, especially with someone as smart as a doctor. I took a chance, and it scared me to my core. "Do you know Donald Abernathy?"

She backed up and looked at me. "Are you Druid Don's young apprentice?"

I stabilized myself and started looking for a door, but my arm was on a table with medical things upon it.

"Please calm down. I am so sorry. Druid Don came to our village often for healing. Lately, he talked about this hotshot kid who saved his life. He said this kid was a true druid, the first in over a thousand years, and his potential was beyond anything he could have imagined."

I barely heard what she said when she mentioned my mentor. "Old Donnie passed in August." Damn tears filled my eyes.

The doctor hugged me. "I loved that man. He encouraged me and paid for me to go to medical school." She restarted the work on my arm. "Was this a gargoyle or Dark Fey?"

"Gargoyle." I winced as she put something deep into my arm. The local anesthetic she gave me only did so much.

"How did you find me? I am unlisted on the Internet."

"This came up first on my phone when I searched." I pulled out my phone with my other hand and she looked at it.

"You aren't good with phones and computers, are you?" She smiled as she handed it back to me.

"No ma'am. Old Donnie got me the phones I use."

"Treat these phones as part of your identity. And removing your torc does no good if the area underneath it is untanned."

An hour later, I had a few dozen stitches, wound adhesive, a couple of staples, a tetanus shot, a clean wrap, a pack of items for bandage changes, a prescription for an antibiotic, and two days of a real pain killer. I was another two-hundred dollars lighter, but it would be hard to track me with this visit. Once I paid the bill in cash, I was on my way.

I pulled into a drive through with the prescriptions, paid another seventy-eight dollars and was back on the road. With everything over, I relaxed into the leather of my Mustang's front seat. The black interior kept the car warm with the sun, whether the top was up or down. With my torc back on, I fired up the engine, and finished my drive to DC. I promised Dr. Kanoska I wouldn't drive on the prescription painkiller, so I took my dose of ibuprofen and acetaminophen and ignored the throbbing. The local painkiller she gave me helped but would wear off before I stopped again.

If the doctor was part moon-eyed, did that book contain more truth than I thought?

If I followed the doctor's orders and kept regular contact with Earth, the speed of my healing would make people's head spin. As much druidic magic as I planned to cast the next several days, it would be even faster. For now, I had to keep it clean, take the pills, suffer through pain, and keep anti-biotic ointment on the outside.

I put the top down on my car and turned on the heated driver's seat. Stitches and staples on my arm meant the wind wouldn't damage like earlier. The wind kept me going and gave me something else to occupy the monkey part of my brain. I drove and picked up I-95, more commonly known as Yankee highway, and was almost to my next gargoyle destination as my clock rolled past midnight.

I arrived near the beltway parkway just outside Washington DC, at two am, and despite exhaustion, I parked near a small playground called Trailside Park. With my shoes off, I slipped around the closed gate and walked near the edge. Touching the natural ground made me whole. The pain in my arm eased when my skin was in contact with the Earth.

The chain-link fence protected a playground and twenty feet of woods surrounded it.

Part of me wanted to rip off my clothes and lie naked on the ground to keep the pain away, but that wasn't the best idea to stay hidden. The only light was a hundred feet away, and the moon was a couple of days past last moon, so I had enough darkness to hide, but one police officer with a flashlight changed my life forever. There were four points I could pull in Earth power from to amplify direct touch. My feet were the easiest way for basic Earth Power. My hands couldn't help my feet, but if my shoes were on, they worked for the initial touch. To amplify the flow through the body, I needed to expose the temple, throat, solar plexus, and groin. Those coincidently were the combination of chakra points and key attack points in martial arts. When I told Old Donnie how it was an amazing coincidence, he looked at me like I had a screw loose.

If I wore a mask and had my shoes on, I might as well be a normal human. Take off my shoes and I was special. Keep my temple and throat free and I was a cut above that. My torc made the flow even stronger. If I combined all that exposed my solar plexus, sensitive people could see magic flowing around me. If I was nude with all four points exposed and if multiple points touched Earth, my power was addicting and was strong enough to double or triple my already fast healing rate. Then, the further I got from civilization; the more Earth Power became available.

I drew a five-foot circle and then a circle a few inches from it. This time I used my trek pole setup. One weighted trek pole, five feet of measured paracord, and a regular trek pole attached to the paracord with slip knots made drawing the perfect circle easy. This was my invention and one Old Donnie approved of. Since this was a small gargoyle coming, I did not bother with creating a honeysuckle bush and creating useful cuttings with my sickle and wicker basket. Instead, I only put the identifying symbol from the book in the circle three times. Then, I spent the ten minutes to create a circle and waited.

I separated gargoyles into two groups. The first group counted those on Earth and controlled by the church. They were the ones who could attack me. The second group were gargoyles in the Realm of Darkness. Druids had banished them there and recorded the information into the book of gargoyles I carried. The supernatural beasts were desperate to come back to Earth. They were easy to deal with since I bound them to my circle before they entered Earth.

My book contained nearly two thousand years of gargoyle banishing history. I also had a circle spell that looked into that realm thirty days forward and backward to verify the book or to gain information to update it, like when I banished a gargoyle. The book contained its name, magical symbol, last location, last banishing, next arrival, and other pertinent information gathered by the Abernathy line of Druids. The Abernathy line of druids were the only druids that survived the purge of the Romans and the church systematically hunted the family ever since. Now they hunted me.

Waiting for the gargoyle to answer the call was the worst part of a binding. Would the gargoyle find the conditions acceptable and come to Earth? Would it wait fifty years to try again, or would I fail and the church be able to collect it? From the notes in the book, this gargoyle preferred a large city. Even the outskirts of DC sufficed, since it had been bound in 1672 in Naples, and what qualified as a large city back then was barely a suburb in the modern US.

Gargoyles needed a portal between realms, and that's where my circle came in. If I drew it correctly with the correct symbols for its name, then I attracted the gargoyle, but if it was powerful, it avoided the call if I did not meet its conditions. If I failed, the church negotiated with it after the twenty-four-hour window expired. Old Donnie had told me our notes were so good with the symbols and conditions, they guaranteed a binding. I'd honor his memory by seeing the notes improved just as meticulously.

I kept repeating the binding to keep it active, and it warmed my torc. Old Donnie told me out of the people he trained, I was the first the Earth allowed to wear the torc. Though it made him proud, he didn't know why it worked for me. If Old Donnie didn't know something, neither did I. *God rest his soul.*

The circle glowed, my ruby glowed, my adrenaline surged, and I prepared to cast the banishment. The world turned black and white and the sounds muffled. Then the gargoyle showed. This was an ordinary gargoyle. I didn't know rocks. I knew granite looked like Stone Mountain and marble looked shiny, but those middle grades of rocks confused me.

As I began the banishment, it sneered at me in mid-spell. It was smart enough to leave our world before my spell fired. I'd have to research when he'd be able to return and update the notes with his intelligence and recovery date.

Good news and bad news. Good, that I had another successful binding and banishment, but I'd have to research this one in the next thirty days to find out how long his self-imposed banishment took. He had certainly saved himself hundreds of years. The adrenaline left my body and my arm throbbed and burned again.

At least this had been a normal binding. My wounds meant I couldn't handle another free gargoyle. The young oak tree held me up while I rested before leaving. I should move fast, but if the bishop guessed I was in Washington, DC, and could respond—this entire plan was a failure.

Two scrawny dogs walked up to me and whimpered. They must have sensed me. Since it was after midnight, animals recognizing me as a druid wouldn't give me away. I took the time to greet them.

Animals sensed the fact I was a druid. It wasn't the connection to the Fey Realm. It was something to do with how I communicated to them. Miles tried to call it Animal Radio, but that wasn't it. It was more like a calling tree—how dogs barked and passed a message over neighborhoods.

I'd call with my thoughts what type of animal I wanted to speak to—mammals, birds, fish, reptiles, amphibians, or salamanders—the closest ones answered and passed my message along. If no animals of the type were near, the message died.

Animals loved talking to me as much as I loved talking to them. In the south, Old Donnie and I healed so many, they'd help us. If they helped us, I had a magical spell that made them more effective at the task I needed.

These dogs were starving and were on a downward health cycle. I couldn't leave the poor dogs in this condition. In my Animal Domain, not only did animals recognize me, I had three minor spells. I sent messages to squirrels, animals could distract enemies for me, and I healed animals. When I healed them, regardless of the condition, except old age, I left them healthy with a full stomach. The circle I created gave off signature, but a fairly weak one and I remained confident that five more minutes for these poor dogs was in my safety margin.

My spell healed them and I spent a few minutes patting them and showing them some love. I wish I could rescue every animal, but it was impossible, and I needed to do what I could. It was rare animals came up to me at a location they wouldn't give me away. I've had to ignore animals before because I was on camera or being watched and it hurt.

I took the time to cast two squirrel messengers, my favorite spell from the Animal Domain, with the same message to let Miles and Rachel sleep better. *Stitched up, next gargoyle done. Plan back on track and, yeah, thank you, for the save today.* Squirrels only remembered twenty-four words, and the spell let them repeat in my voice. Rachel, Miles, and Trish would be asleep, but the squirrel entered their houses and left using the spell's magic.

I walked out of the park, started my car, and drove around the beltway, and looked for a rest area. Not finding one and slapping myself to stay awake, I got an energy drink, more gas, and drove until I found a truck stop.

The stop had an out of the way spot where I parked. I pulled down one rear seat, yanked the pads and sleeping bag up from the trunk to make my night's bed. Clicking the heavy clamps of the convertible tops was tough with one arm, but I got it done and drank a big gulp of water to swallow one of the real pain killers. Since I lost a lot of blood, I finished the second bottle of water.

Wishing I could risk sleeping on the ground outside, I instead crawled into the folded back seat, locked my doors, and kicked my feet catty-corner into the trunk. I shook and needed Rachel close. How could I be a loner if I had withdrawal from physical contact with Rachel? Pretending my pack was her, I hugged it, dropped my wounded arm into the area below the seat, and drifted off.

Chapter 6—Track Rebecca

Preacher Jon sat in his car and realized he was looking at his best chance for damage control. The young druid made decisions that may have seemed sensible to him, but since his knowledge was so light, he was unpredictable and scaring powerful people. If they could get him in the fold and teach him what he needed to know, everyone could be safer. He handed his binoculars to his grand-daughter, Rachel. She didn't have to look long.

"That is definitely her." She sighed and put the binoculars into the case. She had seen the woman who had dated her best friend, the druid Corey. Rachel liked Rebecca because Rebecca had made Corey happy. They were, as their former therapists said, co-dependent, but it wasn't as unhealthy as the therapist thought. They both lost too many people and locked themselves together to deal with their abandonment issues. With Corey living as a druid and Rachel as a Realized specialist, they needed each other for more than that and Preacher Jon was content to let them live like this. He wished they would make the leap and become lovers, but that was their choice, not his. Rachel didn't need to worry about birth control and he would ensure their child received the best, but that's as far as he pushed.

He was happy because he watched his seventeen-year-old grand-daughter constantly sad and contemplating dark thoughts become a smiling, carefree teenager who clung to a boy that everyone reported was an upstanding young man. When that boy turned into the druid who had the weight of the world on him, it hurt Preacher Jon.

"We will drive by. You get her attention and tell her to drive to Houck's Grill to meet us."

Preacher Jon pulled out his phone and clicked on the picture of the three wise monkeys. Nathan put this picture on the app to remind Preacher Jon to use encrypted messages. He used this application and typed *Houck's grill.*

The most common car in Georgia was the one he got for himself, because it fit him. He bought three of the most common colors and alternated them on trips. Today he drove the black model. He started the car and eased it across the road into traffic to ride a mile away before turning around. After today, he needed to sell this car because of this fifteen second conversation Rachel was about to have.

This girl they watched, Rebecca Adams, was not to blame for her choices. She had no way of knowing that her ex-boyfriend was being hunted. The boyfriend of hers, ex-boyfriend, he admonished himself, this generation made declaring a relationship important. Her ex-boyfriend, the druid Corey, was the biggest concern of the world and Preacher Jon wanted nothing more to get him protected, but with his mentor Old Donnie dead, he had no reliable way to get through to him.

Preacher Jon wanted Corey safe for so many reasons. His granddaughters, Rachel and Nicole, were alive and happy because of him. The second was because of the guilt he had become an accomplice in the coverup of hiding people the young man thought was his family. The third was he was the wartime druid and had the destiny of saving the world.

Corey was best friends with his granddaughter Rachel, but Preacher Jon understood her friendship with Corey meant more to her than anything else, and while it was an inconvenience, he could not take that away from either of them. Rachel helped today because saving Rebecca was in everyone's best interest. Preacher Jon neared sixty, if one counted years as normal humans, and sixty-year-olds could not convince the young lady of her peril. Rebecca knew and trusted Rachel. *Especially if she saw Corey fight the gargoyle, as Nathan thought.*

He turned right and immediately pulled into the turn lane at a traffic light. While he waited for his turn-arrow, he examined each passing car against his memory of the cars on the road when he pulled out. This is how he checked for a tail. If they followed him with multiple vehicles, this maneuver would not work, but a team of people was unlikely to be as careful as they'd been recently.

He made the U-turn, then turned left onto his original road. In the clear, he checked his granddaughter for her nerves. Rachel's hair was a mess, but that's because Corey wasn't here to braid it. Rachel had the spark, but did not have a class like Corey. She was a specialist and learned a handful of items extremely well—above human ability well. Her power had a cost, though, and she couldn't function much more than a young child. It was strange to have a karate expert that Grandpa Don said was a master who could train him, a mechanic who fixed any engine, and a motorcycle rider who could compete if he allowed her to, but barely be able to cook and clean for herself. She followed instructions, heated leftovers, and put on clothes laid out for her, but ask her to think of a meal and prepare it and she'd sit with frustrated tears.

Her calm demeanor showed her head was on right. Whenever she was near Corey or even kept him on her mind, her brain functioned better. There was no scientific explanation or even a magical explanation for the phenomenon unless you believed in love—in this case, the love between two friends. Preacher Jon believed and knew love was the most powerful force in the universe and accepted the relationship. It didn't hurt he loved his grandkids and would do anything for them to be happy.

Her sister Nicole, the youngest of his three grandkids, had picked up slack for her and promised to help Rachel if they could get an apartment on their own. But she had school projects that kept her busy, was the team's firearms expert, and disappeared at strange times. Recently, Corey had picked up more and more of the slack. He needed someone to work on his vehicles and needed someone to train him in fighting, but that's not why he helped Rachel. They were the best of friends who were more affectionate to each other than lovers.

No one had followed his car. He pulled into the church parking lot between an Alfa Romeo and a Maserati. Two Italian cars were out of place here, and that bothered Preacher Jon. It could be a coincidence. He parked next to Rebecca's car and rolled Rachel's window down.

"Rebecca!" called out Rachel.

When Rebecca rolled her window down, Preacher Jon felt the tension in his shoulders drop. Preacher Jon looked at the young woman up close for the first time. He had one love in his life and he believed he was in a year of ending his forty-year hiatus in their relationship, but he had to admit, Corey had good taste. For a young woman, she was beautiful. He only hoped she had her head on her shoulder.

"Rachel?" The shocked young woman had jumped when she heard Rachel. She pulled her long blonde hair from her face with two index fingers, using a practiced move.

Rachel smiled and waved, which seemed strange given the current danger they were in. "It's me. You are in danger. Meet us at Houck's Grille and we will get you information about Corey."

"Okay." The young lady rolled up her window and started her car. It appeared she had her head on her shoulders.

He pulled back onto the road and drove toward the restaurant. He hoped this meeting appeared to others as 'hey let's meet in the church parking lot and I'll show you how to get to the restaurant' kind of meeting. He hoped it didn't come to that.

"She's following us," said Rachel. She was alert and sharp and checking things out on her own.

He thought more about Corey and his place in his family's life. Rachel and Corey had been friends in high school, but the church had killed Rachel's parents in her junior year. Corey lost his family—at least the people he believed were his family, at the same time. Though they each dated someone else, they supported each other through the bad times. Corey and his then girlfriend, Haley, had picked up the slack when Preacher Jon, while depressed from his kids being murdered, had to rescue the Southeast again. To save the lives of his family, he had to separate from them at this crucial moment.

He pulled into the parking lot and waited to see if anyone followed. He saw one of his other cars and knew his grandson, his eldest, was already on the ball to sell the one he was in and would trade keys with him inside. The three grandkids were the only thing that kept him going after the murder of his children and wife.

"Walk with Rebecca into the restaurant and meet Nathan. I will join when it's safe. Rachel followed those orders and then would sit next to Nathan." Nathan also didn't have a class but had the spark and was sharp. He had one power where he could make any device work. If the machines needed electricity, he gave it to them. To complete his master's degree in cryptography, he needed one more semester. Preacher Jon wasn't so sure what it meant other than disguising computer and phone messages, but his grandson filled him with pride. His other granddaughter, Nicole, kept all A's in college but disappeared often. She was so responsible and took on whatever duties asked of her. He asked where she disappeared to a few times, and received satisfactory answers, but later realized he didn't have his questions answered. Could an empath like Nicole make things happen? It didn't seem likely.

This shouldn't happen to a man who made a living reading people in Las Vegas nor someone with his Realized power. Preacher Jon's power allowed him to circumvent any institution, legitimate or otherwise, establishing rules or laws. Circumventing the laws was how he built the southeast when it had nearly fallen forty years ago, when Grandpa Don came to get him, convinced him to leave his true love, and do his duty.

NO ONE CAME IN AND no one else watched, so he got out of his car and heard his left knee crack. It did not hurt this time. He walked into the restaurant and met the three young adults. He had a juggling act now. How much did he protect young minds and how much did he tell them?

He stepped up on the curve and realized time was running out.

Nathan closed his portfolio and stared at his glass of water. Preacher Jon sat next to him and Nathan whispered, "I apologize. I did not print a portfolio for this combination of facts. Rebecca comes from the Virginia Addkinson family and she viewed Corey at work." Nathan emphasized the words 'at work' to let Preacher Jon realize he meant banishing gargoyles.

If his grandson had not predicted the possibility of this woman, then the situation had grown in complexity. "Nathan, do you have that blocker device?" When Nathan nodded, he continued. "Please place it in the middle of this table and turn it on."

Nathan pulled out a small tan rectangular device longer than a set of Vegas playing cards. Nathan nodded when he viewed his laptop and closed it.

"This device will not allow others outside of a few feet to understand us. We may talk freely. Are you the granddaughter of Grace Addkinson who lives in the mansion just outside of Vienna in Virginia?"

Sitting this close to the young women, he no longer needed her to answer this question. The young blonde woman with regal bearing and smooth features was obviously a relative of Grace. This Rebecca had to be the granddaughter Grace spoke highly of, the one that came from her unlikeliest of daughters. This complicated matters beyond belief. The areas divided out to govern the Realized had access to the most powerful technology and the most powerful supernatural computing. They put it together into a predictive AI system, the Shared Supernatural System.

The system predicted Corey, the druid of phenomenal power, but not where he'd appear. They predicted at least one of Preacher Jon's grandchildren would shake the world. Now the only other predicted power of this new generation sat at his table and was heartbroken. The druid and this young lady were in his area and his responsibility. This would upset most of the world. Preacher Jon believed kids should be free to learn and love, despite their powers, and the other area leaders wanted to lock the kids down. Preacher Jon fought with every tool at his disposal to let the kids be free and learn who they were. It made him unpopular among his peers.

He reminisced of the one song forty years ago that decided if he came home to do his duty or stay with his true love. One song on a tv station, at that one time, may have decided the fate of these kids—and the world. He couldn't listen to that song by Crosby, Stills, and Nash without crying about leaving Mayven.

"Yes. Do you know her?" Rebecca's confusion showed on her face.

The waitress strolled over with a pad in her hand and interrupted. "Hi, will this be one check?"

Preacher Jon spoke first. "Yes. Please give me the check." He looked at the table and added, "please get whatever you would like. We have eaten out little together and we should enjoy this meal."

"Before he changes his mind, I want the full rack of ribs and the mixed vegetables," said Rachel.

"Do you really not mind?" asked Rebecca.

"Please," said Preacher Jon, and held out his hand. "I'll be getting the Maple Glazed Salmon as well."

"Well, that reduces the suspense, because that is what I would like."

Nathan chuckled. "Just because I don't want Rachel to feel bad about being unhealthy, I'll have the Hickory Burger, medium—fries cooked crispy—and tea."

"That'll be right up."

"Yes, I've been in meetings with your grandmother several times and I imagine you are the granddaughter that fills her with pride, the bloom from the unlikeliest of soil." Her grandmother would commonly represent the Virginian area. The leaders of the Realized divided the world up into areas and while witch covens ran many areas, they did not have exclusivity. For instance, the Southeast area Preacher Jon ran was druid based. The fact this young lady's grandmother ran in these circles and this woman interacted with Corey meant she was part of the upcoming struggle.

The Mid-Atlantic was where the Scion was supposed to arise from. If she was the scion, then this was the generation that decided if humanity survived. *Don't get ahead of yourself. A Scion of the True Church has been unfilled in three generations.* He smiled; these kids certainly needed nothing that heavy. The truth would be heavy enough.

"She has been a guide through a life that has had its difficulties," said the young lady diplomatically.

"Why were you at the grave marker for Don Abernathy?"

"We had a breakup." She looked at Rachel. "When I broke up with Corey, I asked him to be friends, but he ghosted me. We had a huge fight when I saw him in the store. The fight was so unlike him, and I responded poorly, unlike how a young woman should respond. His last sentence was he had to make arrangements for Old Donnie's funeral. The line haunts me because of how the meeting ended."

She took a sip of tea and Preacher Jon knew not to press. He wondered why the young lady broke up with Corey. She was obviously still in love.

"That wasn't your last meeting, was it?" asked Nathan. Nathan and Rebecca had not met, but Preacher Jon would bet Rebecca saw the similarities in features of the two siblings.

The young Miss Adams continued. "Well, a couple of weeks later, a giant beast cut in front of me and some psycho with no helmet was chasing it down with knives and wooden clubs."

"Tonfa," said Rachel. "Tonfa and knives are the only weapons he ever mastered."

Rebecca nodded. "The psycho was Corey, of all people. He made the monster disappear, and I called out to him and he panicked. The guy who never rode a motorcycle—I thought never rode a motorcycle—jumps on his motorcycle, kicks it to life, and takes off with his front wheel in the air. I visited his house and everything, every day, and searched all the local sources for a funeral for a Donald and found the gravestone. I wanted to apologize. Old Donnie was a mentor to him and we should not have fought then."

"Does he realize you still love him?" Asked Preacher Jon.

"What? I broke up with him." The panic on her face was the actual answer.

"Corey doesn't believe you do," said Rachel. "But I can see that you do too, and that means Corey might be the only person who doesn't see it. But he's clueless sometimes." Rachel tore through the tables bread, but her appetite would allow her to eat a full rack of ribs as well. Her muscles and shoulders were larger than most men's. When she traveled with Corey and Miles, she appeared normal, but at this table, she looked every bit like the bodybuilder and martial artist she was.

Preacher Jon nodded and wanted to help this young woman relax. "I left a woman too, and she never left my heart. The pain I feel, I see in your eyes."

The young lady peered at the table. "Please don't tell him. Grandmother believes he is not long term. He was going to propose to me, and I wasn't strong enough to say no. I had to break up with him."

Preacher Jon was old enough to hide the tears—the same tears when he thought of Mayven. "You did the right thing. Rachel should have told us Corey was falling so deeply, but ten minutes with you, and I can see why he did."

Rachel switched the topic. "I'm on your side. Because of, you know, he quit putting lotion on my feet when he did my toes or removed the workout tape. Now I get my feet rubbed with lotion again." Rachel's eyes danced and Preacher Jon would rather not know why.

"Corey, did uh, he say anything?" The young woman had her hand over her mouth.

Nathan pulled out his peacemaker voice. "Rachel and Corey are very close, but she doesn't break his trust and while she probably heard secrets of your relationship, she won't ever break Corey's trust. Even to us."

It was good for his grandson to learn to calm a table with an explosive topic out there, and this was a minor topic, and safe for him to work with his new skills. The mortified young woman may have just learned young men shared relationship information with their best friends.

"Our therapist says we're co-dependent," said Rachel with a huge smile, and took a swig of her tea. That saying had gotten old, and it bothered Preacher Jon because they used it as an excuse for so many things. While it was true, they used it to explain poor behavior.

The food came out, and the waitress distributed the plates of food. Preacher Jon wished he could still eat like his grandkids were eating, but if he ate as much meat as his granddaughter was about to put down... He shuddered just thinking about it.

A squirrel showed up between Rachel's right arm and the wooden wall and spoke in Corey's voice. *Things are crazy. I have a promise of safety. Gonna finish the plan and come back to you. I promise I considered your idea.*

With that, the squirrel was gone.

Nathan spoke first. "Using squirrels to communicate has its benefits but also its detractions."

"Rachel, thank you for trying. I know it was hard for you." Preacher Jon was proud of his granddaughter. She got Corey taken care of, Miles to an emergency room, and notified the druid of the attack. Then she even had time to make it to Durham and take out cameras—she even tried to convince Corey to stop leaving.

Rachel fought back tears and tried to hide them by drinking her tea.

"Rachel, you were a superstar the other day," said Nathan. "You saved Corey's life at least three times that day between the fight, the medical care, the cameras, and the warning."

"I always wondered why Corey and I had dates that looked like princess movies with all the animals." It was apparent Rebecca liked and trusted Rachel. He wondered what happened during the crazy test Corey underwent nearly a year ago to bring these young adults close to each other.

They ate in silence while Preacher Jon pondered his current problems.

"Rebecca, how strong are you emotionally?"

She shook her head. "I used to think I was a rock. I don't know what I am anymore."

He smiled. "The fact you answered it means you are a rock. The world exposed the truth of magic and you are holding it together."

"Barely."

"Here are a few facts. Corey is a druid and is exemplary, despite his age and lack of training. Corey now only trusts Rachel and we cannot risk their relationship." He looked at his granddaughter, who collected clean bones as she devoured the ribs. "If she even would help us with Corey."

"I'd do anything to help Corey," Rachel protested. Her mouth filled with rib meat and sauce covered her lips.

"Not if it caused him pain," said Nathan. "You're too close."

Preacher Jon continued before she protested again. "Corey thinks he knows more than he does and is bringing danger to himself. Will you help us with him?"

"To do what?"

"First to get him back from this trip and then show him all the things Old Donnie did not have time to teach him."

Nathan cleaned his mouth and added. "Corey was supposed to have five years of pre-training, which he completed in under two, partially thanks to you. Nathan unwrapped two wet napkins and gave them to his sister to clean up from the ribs.

"Things are so obvious now. You know how I taught him to shoot? I asked him about the targets he needed and recognized the Redneck Biathlon. I took him outside and told him to get comfortable. He took off his shoes and suddenly, he could learn."

"He's that way with everything," said Rachel. "He can't even read his spell books unless he is fully naked in nature."

The young woman looked lost in thought. "I should have figured it out. We'd make love outside, and it was so much better..." she covered her mouth and turned red. "I'm so sorry."

"Don't be sorry," answered Rachel. Her eyes danced, and she giggled. "I can tease him for using druid magic to be better at sex."

The poor woman didn't have anyone to talk to until now, and Preacher Jon would just pretend he never heard that last part. If truth be told, that might've been the first thing he did with powers at the young druid's age.

"I—I want a chance to apologize to him." The young woman looked at her plate and cut her salmon up into little pieces. She learned every bit of the society manners her grandmother believed in.

"He doesn't want an apology, he wants you to explain why you broke up with him," said Rachel. "He said if he hurt you, you could beat him, but he can't stand not knowing."

"Next time you see Corey, tell him it's part of growing up to understand other people can't always articulate their actions. Adults need to learn to move on," said Preacher Jon. He knew Rachel could never say that to Corey, but someone needed to and Preacher Jon had to treat the young druid with kid gloves if he opened up a line of communication.

"Yes. I will help you." Rebecca ate more of the salmon, which was quite good but rich for Preacher Jon's tastes.

"Good. Team, events are moving fast now and the luxury of me withholding bad news is gone. Here is the big reveal for all of you. The Vatican has plans to do something and Atlanta and Okinawa are two areas that will be affected. We have no other information and are running blind."

"That's not the devastating part. Chicago and Mexico City ran the AI calculations on the Shared Supernatural System. Our enemy is unknown. We don't know who, what, when, where, why, or how."

"Pinging Nicole," said Nathan. "Giving her a heads up."

Where was that girl?

"We can guess the when," said Nathan. "This year is the millennium anniversary of the druid fight that caused the fire in the Cathedral of Utrecht and the two-thousand-year anniversary when druids led a raid and killed Roman Emperor Tiberius's son."

"Tiberius is the name of Corey's hawk," said Rebecca.

Preacher Jon hated coincidences. There was no way Corey knew Roman history, and this was a coincidence, but not a good one.

"What the hell," said Nathan.

Nathan never swore, and he had Preacher Jon's attention.

"Nicole just said Sacred Heart just had a delivery with more guards than a brink's truck addressed to the head of the Curia in Atlanta. She thinks it's Bishop Pedrotti."

Preacher Jon nearly spat out his tea. "How does she know that?"

Nathan pointed to his phone, and the man known for laying down the truth in his youth put his reading glasses on. Nicole had typed out that one sentence. His baby granddaughter had more information than all the information put into the Supernatural Supercomputer System. "Could you ask her how she knows?" *Think Preacher, you're the one known for laying down the truth and your granddaughter just raised the turn on you.*

"She says she wants to tell me face to face."

There it was. She checked the river. Preacher Jon made a living of playing poker in his younger days and liked to think of things in terms of game theory and reading people. Nicole had been hiding a secret, possibly dangerous, mission from him and the team for years. He had to find out who else was involved. Rachel would give her away, and it was not Nathan. *It couldn't be Corey, could it?* He needed to soothe the young adults at this table. "I will follow up with Nicole, but now we have more information."

"While you're here, we need you to get approval for this purchase. Nicole found a line on a M240L and, wow, fourteen thousand rounds?" exclaimed Nathan.

"The weapon fires over seven hundred rounds per minute, so that's twenty minutes of live fire," said Rebecca.

Preacher Jon looked at the young lady with fresh eyes.

"I work for CJ's Weapons Wholesale. I'm a gun person," she explained.

"You know Combat Josh?" Preacher Jon gave up counting the coincidences.

"When he hired me, he said to always call him CJ. I loved working for him. Guns, Corey, and my job made life fun."

"He is a great guy." Preacher Jon now was worried. CJ was the leader of The Tribe. They were a group of Realized that did not answer to the authority of the area leaders. They had a foothold in the Southeast because Old Donnie was friends with them and Preacher Jon turned a blind eye. If The Tribe was involved, there were too many players for this pot. Unfortunately, Preacher Jon had become pot committed and could not fold.

Nathan woke Preacher Jon from his worry. "It's time for action. We need to set up Rebecca with an alternate identity and a safe house. With the Shared Supernatural System, I calculated a ninety percent probability the church identified her as connected to Corey."

"What give up my life? For text messages?" Rebecca was dangerously close to slipping out of reach, so Preacher Jon didn't press it. She had to come to her own conclusion.

"This is fair and we haven't gathered enough information yet," said Preacher Jon. He knew young adults needed autonomy.

"I appreciate this, but I have a life and I cannot throw everything away." Rebecca's eyes were wide open.

He was sure Rebecca believed most of the story and Preacher Jon wasn't sure what the holdup was. "Fair enough. Can we show you our command center, and what we have learned, and allow you to call you grandmother from there?"

"I guess so, but I'm driving my car."

"Of course you are," replied Preacher Jon. He wouldn't ever argue with a habit that kept a young lady safe and her insisting on driving her own car meant she had good habits.

Nathan switched keys with Preacher Jon. "Nathan, change of plans. We've been using older and cheaper vehicles for too long. Sell this car and we'll talk about new upgrades to confuse the people watching for us."

Money was meaningless when laws didn't apply, but it was the judicious use of money that was needed. Things were about to change in Atlanta and his team would change with it.

Chapter 7—New Hampshire

The past two days had gone better, but there were no gargoyles to banish. While I sat in a hotel room in a town called North Conway and tried to wind down before I slept, I powered up the phone I kept labeled as Tyler Phone, with the SIM card in to checking my messages, while I guzzled water. Miles sent me a one. He started a store, Miles Away from Town, and he thought the name was clever for a camping, hiking and fishing store.

He kept asking me to go into business with him and expand, but once we looked at logistics, it was impossible. I needed little money since my family's house had life insurance and mortgage insurance when it burned and it paid for my new house. I wanted to go into business with him, but I was the only one who banished gargoyles, and that made it unfeasible.

Hey Corey,

Rachel is looking for another girl for you. She thinks you'd take fewer risks if you had a girlfriend and she may be right.

Trish is super pissed I got messed up and I couldn't come up with a believable reason I spent the night in the hospital.

Brace Yourself now.

Rebecca came by looking for you with a dude named Preacher Jon. I told them you had gone to find yourself, but they didn't believe me and left a phone number.

By the way, she looks good. Just so you know how badly you messed up. Trish wants you two to get back together so badly she couldn't contain her excitement when she saw her.

Miles

The email had the man's phone number. *Why would Preacher Jon track me down?*

I heard of Preacher Jon and if Old Donnie trusted anyone; he trusted him. Rebecca, well crap.

I forced composure on myself, then replied and attached the picture of my stitches.

What's up Miles,

Stitches look good, and I'm going to be fine. Don't put any of the test knives out, they suck.

Dude, you need to tell Trish about this side of our lives. If you trust her enough to marry her, I trust her enough to know about me.

We need to find a boyfriend for Rachel.

Thanks for the other info,

Corey

I had three phones, all labeled. The <u>Corey Work Phone</u> was where I'd keep up with Rachel and take pictures for work. Old Donnie got some computer guy to set up my phones for me and now Dr.

Kanoska had me worried I didn't know enough. I kept it powered off with the sim card removed for this trip. The Tyler Phone was the phone I powered up when I left Metro Atlanta. The third phone was the Jim Byrd Phone. I used it for research and if I called someone on it; they knew I was in distress. I had done this on the Tyler phone, but to keep from being tracked while I drove, I left it off.

Instead of dealing with this, I ran through my plan. Old Donnie had never left the Southeast, and the church closed in on him and then on us. He never gave me a reason to not travel. I recognized the risk of starting the week off in Stone Mountain Park, but this was the crux of my plan. Make them think I was keeping things the way they had always been. The second gargoyle in DC must have thrown them for a loop, but Donnie traveled to Virginia once before and DC was just across the border. He told me the church had magical sensors over the Southeast to pinpoint magical signatures like the ones my circles made. Leaving the Southeast made so much sense.

I was chilly and walked around the queen-sized bed to the heater. I'd have to sleep diagonally on the bed tonight. The hotel had the heat set to sixty-five, and I needed more than that. I turned it up to sixty-nine and took a pain pill. Then, while my arm stuck outside of the curtain, I took a hot shower. Not a full one, just enough to feel normal. I pulled my hair back with a band to hold it loose to dry faster.

Now I wasn't driving anymore, I kicked my feet up on this bed and got over these darn emotions. Late August had been traumatic. Rebecca broke up with me, and then Old Donnie died while killing the Snake-Hunter.

"Run!" yelled Old Donnie. He ignored the gargoyle attacking him and stopped his binding. Instead, he cast one of the two spells I had not learned.

I didn't listen. I spiked the new gargoyle's arm with a glass breaker and helped turn him to stone. Then I ignored the distractions and completed Old Donnie's binding, which sent the original gargoyle back to the Realm of Darkness. Donnie had locked the Snake Hunter in an embrace and Old Donnie finished the second spell from the Protection Domain. The Snake Hunter screamed and quit moving as the gargoyle and circle disappeared.

"Old Donnie," I yelled and ran to him and kneeled between him and the emergency circle he created.

He coughed and black mucus dribbled onto his chin. "This thing still lives and will be up in a minute." He coughed up a handful of black mucous. "Put your hand on the tattoo on his chest and dig your other hand into the ground in a circle." Blackened blood ran out of his chest and onto the ground, where it hissed away.

Well, he was a dying man and today was the first day I defied him and his order to run. It would not happen again. The Snake Hunter, naked, devoid of hair, and genitalia, had Old Donnie's obsidian blade in its throat that slowly healed. It covered its body in tattoos. The too-smooth face had black orbs for eyes, round holes instead of a nose and a mouth filled with spike teeth, twice as wide as a normal mouth.

I dug my left arm into the ground inside of his circle and touched the chest of this thing on the tattoo of a Gaelic word. My right biceps stung and then the word disappeared from the thing's chest and it turned to dust.

"Good boy. You're it now. They gave me the blackness and we," he coughed more blackened blood, *"and we lost the ability to make the druid berries centuries ago. Put me in a hidden grave and defend it for seventy-two hours. Don't let humanity down."*

The world turned from black and white to color.

He had told me of what to do on his death before, but as I carted his body to the truck to drive him to a safer burial spot, I couldn't help but cry. Old Donnie died fighting—just how he lived, so the tears weren't for him. They weren't for me, because I hadn't earned tears. It was for humanity. I wasn't ready to be its soul defender.

I ran for supplies to watch Old Donnie's grave when I bumped into Rebecca and she said I was being a jerk for ignoring her. Still raw from Old Donnie's death, I reminded her she broke up with me. I still replayed the brief fight in my head.

"Just because you're not someone I want to date doesn't mean I don't want you in my life." Her beauty allowed her to get away with comments like this, but not anymore.

"Well, you didn't show up at trailhead or to go mudding. You didn't want me in your life that badly."

"We could still go out, just as friends." She swung her long blond hair around like she said the most obvious thing in the world.

"Ooh, we could still go on dates. You get to be with someone who likes you and will keep you safe, and I can just feel alone in your company?" Then I added a tad of sarcasm. *"Please*

kick me in the head on Sundays. Because when you find
someone to date and get rid of me, I'd miss the kicks more
than anything else."

"Look, you aren't reliable and you have this inner fighter in
you."

"Maybe you could have held on loosely."

"Leave your stupid jokes and stupid mix tape music out of
this. I'm the one who gets stuck if we had an accident or if we
went further into the relationship, and I didn't think it was
a good choice to take a chance of being stuck with you and a
baby."

That hurt, and I stepped back. "I have to plan for Old Don-
nie's funeral." Then I sprinted to my car to find a different
store.

So, the meeting didn't start well or end well. The middle part
wasn't good either.

Even though I had nothing to bury, I paid for Old Donnie to
have a grave marker.

Here lies my friend Donnie Abernathy
1955–2023
The people who owe him a debt of thanks
will never know his sacrifice.

I added one hundred years to his birth year to avoid unwanted
attention. After I left flowers there, I didn't make it back to my place
to be sure Rebecca got the message to forget what she saw.

Crawling under the covers caused me to quit thinking sad things.
I drop the sheet with my hands shaking. I wanted to hug Rachel

and even sit next to her. How could I be a loner if I couldn't stay three days away from Rachel without shaking? A girlfriend was what I needed to get my act together. The pain pill kicked in to put me to sleep while I hugged spare pillows, pretending it was Rachel.

SUNLIGHT SCREAMED THROUGH my room in the morning. I had originally intended to practice my stances, blocks, and strikes, but with my arm cut open, that plan was out. Unable to practice the dance moves for Rachel's contest, I rehearsed the moves in my mind and kept memorizing what parts of the song I sang.

I thought about contacting Preacher Jon. The two of us had never met, but it's no surprise he knew my name since he knew Old Donnie. What was a surprise was him knowing Rebecca. The two of them together had every bit of information on me. They had me over a barrel and I had to meet with them. On the way home, I would contact them. I got dressed, packed, and ate the free breakfast before loading my car.

Shopping for my friends was first on my list. I never traveled, and I wanted to find things they'd normally not see. Leaving the windbreak of the hotel, the wind hit me in the face with a frozen slap. The outside was freezing, so I walked back to my trunk and pulled out my Molly Hatchet hoodie. I didn't want to expose my duster to potential witnesses yet. The stores were less than a mile away.

The first few ginger steps got my balance with frost and patches of snow and ice. Leaves froze to the ground in a frost, but everyone walked around as if this was normal. If Rachel were here, we'd hold hands and help each other walk. She'd help me like I helped her in the singing contest. When I thought of Rachel and helping her for her contest, I stopped shaking and focused.

The first store I saw was a woman's clothing shop and, in the window, they had a pair of heels, like the kind Nicole wore. She called them kitten heels, and they had a curve in the heel. What caught my eye was the color. It was a green of the first bud of spring. I walked in and asked if they had that color in nine and a half.

"Do you have the size, right? How tall is the young lady?"

"She's about average. I put my hand up to my eyes. About five, ten, but I've bought shoes for her before."

"Then it sounds like you got the right size. Now which style of kitten heel?"

"The color is the most important, but she likes the round closed toe. Did I say that right?"

She brought out the heels in a box and showed them to me, and they were perfect.

I pointed at the wool section. "Is all this local?"

"Family farm," said the woman proudly.

I pointed to the women's pajamas. "I'm looking for another young lady. Do you have the wool bathrobes for a woman who is shorter than I am but with shoulders like mine?"

She looked at me as if I said something bizarre. "Could you explain?"

"This is the older sister of the first woman and we are good friends."

"We have plenty of sizes and if I may recommend you get the nine-piece sleeping set since it's a difficult size to buy for."

"Okay, I'm not sure of size. She is short, about five-eight, but her shoulders are as broad as mine, but her waist is smaller and she keeps her stomach ripped."

"What do you mean, ripped?"

I lifted my hoodie and shirt and showed her my abs. "Hers are even more defined."

"Wow, I see why you want this cut. For your friend." She said friend like it had another meaning. I couldn't give more information to defend myself since codependent people from Georgia who both lost their parents were rare. It would be too coincidental if it happened near the gargoyle banishing's.

Rachel regretted being such a tomboy for long and wanted to be more feminine and I was going to get these in pink.

"Put your arms on the hips of the mannequin like you'd hold your friend."

Again, with the emphasis on the word friend. It didn't matter. I wanted to get the right size and I wouldn't see this woman again. I walked to the mannequin and put my hands on its hips and rode them up like I would on Rachel. It didn't curve enough. "The hips are wider and the waste is smaller." I hugged the mannequin and cupped the right butt cheek. "She has about another finger of rear-end." I hugged the top half and followed that up with my hand on the shoulders. "The shoulders aren't even close and neither is the chest. Her cup size is a large-B if that helps."

"I need friends like you. Wow." The woman pulled two sets out and pulled long and short bottoms from one set and tops and the thick wool bathrobe from the other and asked me if they looked right.

Once she boxed that up in the box labeled sleepwear, I needed one more gift for Miles and Trish. "I have married friends who are expecting and am looking for a sheepskin blanket."

We picked out a nice thick blanket for a baby. I paid, left the store, and hoped the woman's stories wouldn't travel too far.

Strolling past a handful of small house sized store fronts with my bags, I found the store with copper tubes and glass bottles in the display. I entered with the pretense of buying a Christmas present for my real identity, Coire Norwood. The young woman in the front looked bored.

"Hi. My friend is a brewer, and he is having problems with consistent taste when he brews lagers."

The young lady at the counter held up one finger and called a man out from the back. "Lager brewer." While I waited, I noticed the glass and copper around the wall behind her. Books and yeast samples were on the far wall.

A man in an apron came out. After a half hour, he convinced me he knew more than I did and to try a liquid yeast, a more sensitive thermometer, and sold me two dozen new bottles with rubber swing stoppers for tops. I paid, and they shipped it to Miles' store.

A couple of steps out of the store and bitter cold slapped me in the face. The surrounding others ignored the temperature, so I toughed it up. It was time to focus on the real reason for my trip. I needed to banish three gargoyles today.

My arm had got to where the throbbing was constant, but the burning came and dissipated before spiking again. The wind picked up and cut through my hoodie and swirled leaves around me. Crows cawed at me. "You're right, it's too cold for me," I replied. I made the walk back to the hotel parking lot to get my car. The crunching under my feet was a pleasant part of this walk.

This vacation spot was primarily for hiking or skiing. November was a slow time before there was snow for skiing and cold enough to keep sane people away. I planned to finish the first two gargoyles by eleven and the last gargoyle by twelve or one. Timing was close with the time differential, but it still gave me two or three hours to spare. After today, I didn't need to worry about time for months, since the gargoyles came so infrequently. I got into my car and entered onto a mostly empty highway. It was safe to drive on the light gray pavement after the sun melted the ice.

A pool of water was the first location I needed. The second gargoyle had a requirement to be near fast running water, and I needed a mountaintop for the third. When Rebecca researched the vacation, she had found these three locations. She told me she felt these places were important to us. The irony that I came here with plans for a couple's vacation while alone did not humor me.

The Basin, a viewing location just off the highway, was a pool of clean water. There were a handful of empty parking spots leading to a small plateau on smooth rock, where a swirl of rushing water created a pool.

This was the crux of my plan. Get far away from home and go where no one in the church would suspect. Cast the bindings and banishments in proximity and vamoose to a different state. If everything followed the plan, I could bind three gargoyles, find the locations of any who left early, drive south, and be gone before anyone or any gargoyle from the church made it to me. Then, I'd trap a tiny gargoyle in Saratoga Springs, and finally drive to Mitchell, South Dakota, for the last two.

I planned to rest a day or two in Kansas City before heading home. Then the gargoyle's bindings slowed. I'd have three or four gargoyles a month until Spring. I guess three to five hundred years ago, winters were too harsh to hunt many gargoyles.

After I kicked off my shoes, strapped my knife sheath to my right thigh, and put on the day pack with my materials, I loaded my self-defense weapons. Grabbing my sickle, I slid it into its holder on my waist pack. I checked my prepared and wrapped magnolia seed pod, then pulled Old Donnie's brown leather duster over the top. With two steps, I crossed over the rock into the woods to the side of the stream. The wind whipped and blew my hair around. I didn't have a hair band with me to pull it back, but it was fine. Hair in my face would not get in my way.

Behind a handful of pine trees, over the wooden fence that had seen better days, I prepped a normal banishing circle. I created honeysuckle with a spell, cut four twigs with my sickle, and let them fall into a wicker basket. The Earth had granted me the Plant Domain and a minor power was that everything grew healthy around me. This meant I stayed nowhere for over three days a week, unless a vibrant yard gave away my presence. My three spells were maturing any plant, creating a coral honeysuckle plant, and I could ask a tree to give me a weapon. The honeysuckle creation was my most used of all my spells since I used honeysuckle twigs and trumpets as a focus, just like the stories said druids used holly.

I drew the circle with a honeysuckle twig and wrote the gargoyle's symbol with it, then alternated three honeysuckle twigs with three of the gargoyle's symbol between the two circles. The gargoyle showed up in my circle within a minute and I began the binding and banishment. The eight to ten feet tall gargoyle was normal sized. Typically, I banished with one binding, but sometimes they took two. My circle was strong enough. I wasn't worried.

The creature's face was typical of gargoyles, with a big mouth, jagged teeth, and horns. The gargoyle did not rage or struggle. He looked at me and spoke. "Mi capisci."

I ignored him since I didn't understand what he said.

"Me comprends-tu?"

I recognized French, but I kept my composure.

"Doth, thou understand me?"

I barely kept the binding going with my shock. My toes dug into the dirt.

"Fine, indeed, druid. Thy connection to the Fey Realm shall not help thou if thou keep playing with ours."

I kept the binding going, though I kept saying it louder. There was nothing special about this gargoyle. It was normal rock and not granite or marble. But it talked to me.

"Wot the temple shall find thou for us." Then he disappeared back into his Realm of Darkness of his own choice. I fell back into the fence and nearly tumbled over it. I grabbed onto a thin birch tree to stabilize myself. Old Donnie said nothing about them talking. Sure, they screamed and a few cast magic, but talk in my language?

No animals came to see me. What's going on?

I wanted to run, but my arm started throbbing again. If I hadn't slept well last night, I would have failed the binding when he spoke. I recognized Old English since I grew up attending a church that read the King James Bible. This week, two gargoyles left of their own accord, and one spoke to me. I wanted Old Donnie by my side.

Time to put away foolish thoughts because I had to put these two gargoyles into my next spell casting for banishing information. I needed someone to slap my hand and let it hurt since weakness endangered the sacrifice of Old Donnie. *No more failings.*

I took three deep breaths and touched my weapons and my gear. Words, even from a gargoyle, could not hurt me, and words weren't powerful enough to break one of my circles. I drank water and started up the car, and pulled back onto the nearly empty highway. There was no reason to be scared. My plan was on track, and I was proving I could be a loner.

I drove fifteen minutes to the next tourist trap, The Flume, which had closed for the season. I parked near the woods and popped my hood. This should allow me to fit in and give me cover. The parking lot was huge compared to the last place and had a row for tour buses. I cracked my neck and psyched myself up.

Chapter 8—The Best Laid Plans of Druids

The roar of a motorcycle echoed around me. I had no time to change tactics, and my torc lit up blue to make the situation worse. After I acknowledged it, it lit again. I was supposed to run from one creature which lit the torc blue and here there were two. A motorcycle roared into the parking lot toward the driver's side of my car. Why didn't I park far from the entrance? I collected myself. When the biker noticed weapons on me, he'd ride away. I had experience in bar fights with bikers and if I started nothing, there'd be nothing.

The chopper pulled into a location that blocked me from my car door. I opened Old Donnie's duster, so he saw my weapon load out.

The customized Harley rider killed his engine and rolled next to me. A large man wearing biker leathers but no helmet lifted a small girl in pink, who wore a Hello Kitty motorcycle helmet. Not exactly what I was expecting.

"Wait, please wait," cried out the girl in her tiny voice. She undid her helmet herself and carried it towards me as the large man walked over with a shrug, pointing to her.

"Sorry for my daughter, but she cannot sleep."

"I need to watch you banish the gargoyle! Please?" She showed me the pleading eyes of a small girl. She couldn't have been older than six or seven. *This was impossible!*

The man stopped and gave me space and took a non-threatening pose. "Cool Torc. Lights up blue for preternatural and red for the supernatural." The man pointed to my torc and acted comfortable with the rest of my weapons load out.

I smiled and pretended I wasn't completely in shock. Now, I learned more about my torc, but this new knowledge did not comfort me.

"I'm," I started.

The man held up his hands. "I promise we will keep your secret. My daughter. She has powers to see the future, and this week saw the end of the world. She says you are the key and if you can banish gargoyles, I'll have a daughter who won't wake up screaming in the night if she watches you banish one."

I nodded because what type of person would I be to argue? "Keep your eyes peeled and be prepared to run. More often than not, these bindings are safe, but if a free gargoyle comes, don't worry, I can handle both." I mean, I couldn't, but I didn't need them in my way.

The girl jumped and squealed... with delight? The biker—father took off his shades and looked at me again.

A gaggle of squirrels showed up them. They came to say hello, and I asked them to stand to the side, and warned them I was about to bring a gargoyle here. They chittered, then scattered up into the trees. I grabbed my hair and tucked it under my torc to keep a hold of it. The wind still whipped, but there were enough trees to slow it.

I stepped over the fence and created a honeysuckle plant and, with my sickle, cut off the four stiffest portions, and caught it them a wicker basket. If they wanted to watch me, I might as well make a good circle despite the strength of this gargoyle. With purposeful strokes, I took my time to create the circle for my unexpected audience. I kicked an inch of pine needles away from the area, so this girl could see the circle and began.

It took maybe two minutes longer than normal since I used the weighted trek pole and the sharpened trek pole with parachute cord. Clear strokes draw it deeper for the girl to see everything. I drew the inner portion with a five-foot diameter and the outer portion was four inches away. After I completed the two circles, I stepped back and verified the completeness, though I realized I had not messed up a circle in two years.

My bare feet dug into the hardened ground with effort, but I got set and placed three cuttings of honeysuckle in the circle, then looked up to the little girl. "If it was a bigger circle, I can use five, seven, eleven, or more clippings." I alternate focuses and the creature's symbol. I wrote the gargoyle's symbols using the honeysuckle twig between the two circles. Writing with the twig made binding the circle easier. If I had the name of the creature or its symbolic representation in the circle, it was more powerful for that creature. If I put focuses, honeysuckle in particular, in the circle, it increased the power dramatically as it gathered the power. Put both, and the specific creature had no chance to break free even from a novice druid—and I was no novice. "Now we wait."

Five minutes later, my torc lit up red, the world turned to black and white, and the small gargoyle granite appeared. It struggled and bashed against the magical circle. It was no matter. One day, this little guy might be powerful with his light gray granite build, but that day was not today. It stayed trapped in my binding, despite its howls and lunges toward me. After ten minutes of casting the binding, I banished the gargoyle and the little girl cheered. The world turned to color again.

However, I had created a second strong magical signature. If I was in the Southeast, the church pinpointed me easily and release a free gargoyle, but that's why I was up in Yankee territory.

The biker removed his glasses to peer at me, along with a seven-year-old girl. Things were as bad as they had ever been because I still had to get to the top of a mountain. With the time zone differences and the power of the next gargoyle, there was no time to change plans.

"Hooray, the world is going to be saved!" squealed the girl. "You and the blonde girl who didn't come with you will save us."

It made me happy that one of us believed. "I'm doing my best," I said to the girl. "Plus, I promise even though I'm alone now, I'll keep the gargoyles at bay."

"Do you know Druid Don?" asked the biker.

The comment caught me off guard, and thoughts of Old Donnie flooded into my mind, but I held back tears. I choked out the answer. "He trained me the past couple of years until, you know, his demise."

He gave me a sad look, then got on his bike. The girl jumped on behind him with her Hello Kitty helmet snug on her head and held onto hand holds built on the back of his black leather jacket. They were gone before I had packed up.

Two magical signatures were up and I was about to create the largest signature I ever had made by myself. But if the priests of the church were in the White Mountains of New Hampshire, I wasn't smart enough to save humanity. Accepting these circumstances, I drove twenty minutes along a lonesome highway to Loon Mountain. This was Franconia Notch near the top of the Appalachian trail. If my stints as a trail angel carried any luck, I needed it now.

If the church had a priest who could sense magical signatures, they'd be at the first and second by now if I were in the Southeast and they could bring manpower to bear to track me. My hope rested on the church, having no one near me.

Overhead, a plane flew and reminded me that Miles had asked if I'd fly up and rent a car, but despite the privacy issues, there is no way I'd pack myself into a metal contraption and fly that far above the Earth. If man-made materials surrounded me, it'd cut me off from Earth Power. Also, If I was that high in the air, I had no access to my powers. Together, they sounded terrifying.

Pulling into the Loon Mountain parking lot shocked me since cars packed in, even though it was too early for ski season. The hotel on the far side had a handful of cars, but these vehicles near me were for the gondola. The icy wind had picked up and bit into me, so I threw on my hoodie and duster, then grabbed my pack and combat belt, knowing other options were gone. I buttoned my duster and strode across the parking lot to the bottom of the gondola with my hair in front of my face and strode to the ticket booth. They cleared the parking lot of leaves and the deciduous trees were bare. The evergreens stood out at the bottom of Loon Mountain.

Up the stairs, I took two red painted stairs at a time to get to the ticket booth and hoped they had heat there. They didn't, but tickets were free even though they gave me a day pass. Fresh blue paint adorned the right wall and it appeared as if they were in the midst of getting ready for ski season. Some gondolas sported fresh paint as well.

Rebecca had chosen this mountain to ride a gondola instead of hiking up the taller of the mountains we wanted to see. I kept the choice since time prevented a six to eight-hour hike each way. I banged my arm into a moving piece of gondola and I grabbed it with tears filling my eyes.

"Your arm okay, friend?" The warmly dressed man who talked, smiled and carried a bible. He traveled with his wife and kids.

I gave the same story I had in South Carolina. "My girlfriend blew a tire just before my business trip. I gashed myself with the tire iron." Fear crept up on me and kept me from acknowledging the pain anymore.

"Been there," said the man in motorcycle leathers traveling with a young girl who wore a pink leather jacket, carried a Hello Kitty helmet and a bible. My heart raced. The first man rode with his family up in the gondola. *There was the source of my fear.*

I turned off the two blue warnings for them. The next gondola arrived, and the girl ran inside. The biker held out his hand to have me enter.

When he sat opposite me with his daughter on his lap he said, "we've cleared the way for you here and your next destination, which is my territory past Chicago. Please get with the man you call Preacher Jon as soon as you're done and certainly before you travel again," he whispered to me. He nodded to his daughter. "Your secret is still safe—outside of the two covens who just approved your emergency passage." He nodded to his daughter. "She viewed your whole path outside of your territory."

"I can't wait until you buy me ice cream with the other girls," said the little girl.

"Yes, sir." There was no way to understand what either of them talked about, but I had acknowledged a third blue light here, and I learned why Old Donnie never left the south. Plus, this man's instructions were simple. I didn't dare sense for magic around these two.

My stint as a bar fighter taught me a few lessons that were in play here. First, a person who has nothing to fear will be pleasant and nonthreatening and carry no weapons. I was the one with weapons here and this biker was all smiles and helpful. Every sense told me I could not fight him and he probably chuckled at my sentence about how I would protect him and his daughter.

Right before the gondola door closed, a woman wearing a dark blue velvet dress and a long, purple coat joined us. She made a large show of pulling three feet of black hair out and letting it drape over her coat. She sat next to me and turned to face me directly. Her timeless face was pleasant, but I recognized the look of a predator and though she was not hunting, she was no stranger to fighting. Her hands did not rest on her lap. She put her right arm on the seat behind me and winked.

The small plastic seats had our knees touching and when I moved back an inch, she patted my leg and winked. Then she slid closer to me, so our whole legs touched.

The gondola lurched forward, and we started the slow descent up the mountain. My confidence was back in my car. I wondered how trying to be a loner had me trapped in a gondola for the next ten minutes, with two people I was afraid of.

My bar fighting skill was in play again, and this woman had a fear of nothing. Even the man monitored her, and his demeanor had changed, but not because of me. I knew my look scared people. I was a six-one, one eighty muscular fighter, who wore scars from fighting and carried myself ready to fight. Women avoided me. The only people who confronted me were other fighters. If she came closer and flirted, it meant she had zero fear of me, and that terrified me. *What type of woman could scare me and the biker?*

The woman's playful smile stressed her flirty nature. "Did you come to church or did you forget it was Sunday and just get directed here by fate?" She winked at me when she said fate.

I swallowed my terror like Old Donnie taught me. I acted like them and talked to them politely as equals. "You're right. I got surprised, almost like fate guided me here today." When I made the plan, I must have known it was Sunday, but who looks for churches on the top of mountains?

"You made it here fast," said the biker to the woman.

"Your message was the most interesting message I've received in three hundred years," she replied and laughed. Then she put on glasses and looked me up and down again.

The little girl climbed up on her father's lap and gave him a hug while she watched me. He hugged her back and told me, "You'll like this church service. It's laid back and welcoming. Everyone knows people stop by accidentally and have no cash on them. Please enjoy the safety of the mountain service."

The woman hadn't stopped staring at me. "How old are you, sweetie? Thirty? Forty?"

"Twenty-four ma'am." Being scared out of my mind, I did my best to look relaxed.

"Ma'am? Oh my. But if you're twenty-four, I guess I am a ma'am. If I was six-hundred years younger, you would be mine," she teased. *I hope she was kidding.*

The man took his glasses off and stared at me, grabbing my attention. "You are twenty-four years old, lost your mentor, and keeping true to Druid Don's legacy?"

Apparently, this biker thought this woman should have my identity. I would not have picked to talk to either of these people on my own, but everyone acted pleasantly, though they weren't harmless. "Yes sir. Druid Don's memory needs to be kept, and I am the only one."

"Are you that strong—inside?"

"No sir. I am scared every time I come across a gargoyle or the church, and today is the most terrified I've ever been."

"Don't you flirt with me, young man," said the woman with the long velvet coat. "The last druid who spoke like that broke my heart." She laughed at my confusion and the man leaned back and kept watching me. *I wasn't flirting! How did she know I was a druid?*

"Has a gargoyle ever broken your circle?" Asked the man.

My identity was out with these two and my fear told me to be honest with them for my safety. "No sir. The second day, Old Donnie trained me to take over circles. I could take over his whenever I wanted to. He never took one of mine over and said nothing that touches Earth will ever touch my circles. Once he told me to let a gargoyle thrash for six hours inside my circle before I banished it so I'd believe him."

"Oh my. Unless you're trying to give me a green gown, you to need to stop talking."

Leander laughed and put his hand to his forehead. I became completely lost and tried to smile when the woman joined him in laughter. I pretended I didn't know what it meant, but Rebecca had a degree in the Classics and took a lot of languages and literature. After we made love outside the first time, she showed me a book from the time around the Canterbury Tales about giving a maiden a green gown. It was like a thousand-year-old way of saying 'roll in the hay.' I focused on not peeing my pants from fear.

"You know, now I see how the blue emerald matches your eyes—I'm glad I donated my necklace to create the Torc of Awareness. We were in my castle in Avalon... what was it, eleven-twenty, eleven-twenty-five? It doesn't matter. Well, he had to have an emerald, but since he was a druid, it couldn't be green and I had a necklace with a blue emerald in it. It's the old story of a witch in love with a druid, and the witch bends over backwards for him. Do you know the story?"

"Not with a witch," I answered.

"Which way do you bend your girls?" She laughed as my face became bright red.

"The ruby and blue emerald make it beautiful," said Leander. He gazed at the ceiling of the gondola.

"The blonde girl likes to rest her fingers on it when she kisses him," teased the little girl with an impish grin.

"You are right, young lady. I see her in his mind. I won't get anywhere with this druid until the passion for the blonde girl simmers," said the woman. She pulled her long hair to her right shoulder and looked at the ceiling.

I peeked at her eyes and they changed colors from blue to purple to green until I looked away. I didn't know whether to be mortified or afraid.

We finished the long ride with the little girl shouting with glee when she saw a deer run underneath us. At the top, the three of them left first, and I hung back and drifted along the path with a couple of dozen other people. The wind was stronger up here and the torc no longer contained my hair. It whipped around and covered my face and slipped into my mouth. I ignored the hair and the freezing temperature. I had bigger issues.

Chapter 9—Animals Just don't Understand

A couple of hundred yards from the gondola was a cleared-out area just above what would become a tree slope. The three of them strolled from the gondola along a path worn to tan packed dirt to the front row to talk, and I didn't need to be smart to realize the topic was me.

The chapel area had three columns of wooden benches, ten rows in each column, with a platform that overlooked the mountain. Evergreens and a few barren deciduous trees surrounded the chapel. We were nearly at the tree line and behind us, most trees were barely as tall as me. Bushes claimed most of the background to the top of the mountain. The chapel could seat a hundred people, and I sat in the back row. I couldn't leave here without looking suspicious and did not know what to do.

Thinking through Old Donnie's teaching, I concluded that although they had identified me, I could still complete this mission. When he had a few beers in him he'd say, *as long as you can move, you don't even need to stand, you can make things happen if you keep your cool. If you need to, schedule your showdown at high noon.* My new plan would be to wait until after the service, then go to the mountaintop as the gargoyle required. I'd banish it and try to get to my car alive. I didn't think I needed a showdown, but the time came close to high noon.

"You can see Canada today," said a new lady with a pink dress under a heavy coat with a broad smile. Her height only came up to my chest, maybe like five foot four, and she wore a thick blue coat un-buttoned to her knees. "Oh honey, your torc is lighting up blue."

"Oh, thank you." *Number four.* If I ran, they'd get me, whoever they were. This woman did not frighten me even though she lit up my torc blue. Her white hair had a slightly curly nature, but her eye-brows were as dark as mine. Her hands had no wrinkles, and neither did her face. I wondered what caused the illusion of age upon her. Her short, curly white hair made her appear older and motherly, but I felt it was an intentional choice. Her smiles and doting eyes on me helped calm my nerves.

"The view is beautiful," I answered. I pulled my duster bottom out and sat on a bench in the back. The extra pressure on my arm got it to throbbing, so I grabbed my regular pain dose and drank them with water.

I took a peek at the three from the gondola.

"Don't worry about them, sweetie. They're trying to figure out if you're just young or you're new."

I smiled and said, "thank you." I did not know what she meant.

"If you were back home, how would you wear your hair?" She brushed some hair from my face.

I braided Rachel's hair so often I lost count and Rebecca had liked the upper half of my hair braided with the lower half hanging free. When we knew we would fight, Rachel and I would have matching top and bottom braids, though Nicole or Trish braided my hair. "With winds like we have here, I double braid with a top and bottom braid." I scooped the top of my hair and held it. "I'd braid this and then braid the bottom. But I brought nothing for my hair."

"Please. It's been so long since I braided my children's hair. May I braid yours?"

I needed to do something about the window and the large gar-goyle. Terrified or not, getting my hair braided was necessary at this point. "I'd like it, if it's not a problem."

She kneeled behind me and braided the top part of my hair, and she got the braids tight. Trish would pull them tight like this and her braids lasted on me for a couple of days. This woman, who gave a blue warning—but didn't scare me—stroked and braided my hair with her hands. It relaxed me.

Some squirrels chittered around, but it wasn't too obvious they were here for me and a couple of them ran off. Squirrels would come in ones or twos around humans to look for food.

Then, my powers gave me away. A white-tailed deer stood next to me to hang out, and a red-tailed hawk landed next to me as well. "No hunting, creatures visiting," I sent out a warning to all animals. The warning was necessary because a fisher cat came close, and squirrels, raccoons, and possums. I tried to pretend like nothing was going on, but it was obvious.

There were so many animals close by that my message went out to nearly a dozen animals and a dozen birds at once and they spread it further. Soon the trees filled with birds and small animals and larger animals gathered around the edge of this outdoor chapel.

A bird called for help and struggled toward me. Its left wing barely moved and still had blood from a vicious bite. A house cat had leaped for it and the poor bird barely got away. It landed in my hands. I saw its red breast and knew I held a nuthatch. I cupped it to disguise my heal. How could I resist healing a bird that flew to me as its only hope? It flew away, and I noticed at least a dozen people stared at me.

Animals did not come around humans, unless domesticated, and did not curl up and relax. They certainly did not fly in injured and fly away singing the praises of a druid.

"The animals up here have never seen a druid," said the woman, who finished the top braid and began the second. "The Abernathy's spent all their time in the south, so you're a curiosity."

"Do I stick out that badly?" I had screwed up and I may have lost my identity.

She whispered to me. "No dear. You got unlucky. The daughter of the Witch's Coven in Chicago viewed you in a dream. To help protect you, he notified the coven up here. I give you my word you are safe."

She finished with the braid. She pulled a mirror and showed me. "How does it look?"

I looked and touched the tight braids. "These are great. This is exactly how'd I'd be wearing my hair if I had known about the wind."

She beamed and said, "thank you for letting me do that."

Things were settling down and people looked at the creatures and the kids smiled and laughed while their parents said to be careful of the wild animals. Then a coyote showed up. He was about to hunt the creatures next to me, and I turned around in my stern voice and said, "No. No hunting near me."

The coyote slunk its head and sat down behind the chapel. I turned around and realized what I had said. Leander was laughing and telling the lady with the long black hair to sit down, and everyone stared at me, mouth agape. "Sorry," I muttered.

I turned to avoid the stares and checked out the view. "The animals listen to him," whispered one small child.

"He healed that bird. I know he did," said another kid.

Ugh. Focus on something else.

Though past peak leaf viewing season, yellows and oranges still lit up parts of the mountains that announced the seasonal change in the renewal cycle.

"The others tell me your name is Tyler Nash. My name is Samantha, by the way. Samantha Norwood."

I almost fell off the bench. This woman shared my real last name! She smiled at me.

Two new arrivals, dressed like they stepped out of 1970, sat at the pulpit. The woman played bongos, and the man played an acoustic guitar and sang a religious song.

More new arrivals came and Samantha stood up and introduced me as Tyler Nash to each new couple and person arriving, and beamed as they remarked about the two dozen animals around the outdoor chapel behaving well. This was not staying low key!

To help calm myself, when the parade of new people ended, I focused on the pulpit. It was a glorified hunting stand, overhanging the slope at the beginning of the ski slope. On the pulpit, the musical accompaniment continued with the bongos and guitar played by the hippie couple. This definitely was not a Catholic Church. That was one thing in my favor.

The minister who showed up was a ski bum. He wore ski clothes and a broad smile. He started the service a little differently than any service I remember.

"What up? For those of you visiting, welcome. We don't pass collection plates up here, but we are building a house for a couple who lost their house in a fire. So, if you want to donate, help them. See Kita and Bjorn for details." He pointed to the two hippies off to the side with the acoustic guitar and bongos.

They both smiled and waved to the crowd of nearly one hundred people, and at least that many birds and animals.

The ski bum continued. "Also, during snow season, the gondola is free Sunday mornings, and you can ski all day for the cost of listening to me ramble about God. I guess it even counts for animals, since they seem excited today."

Good natured laughter answered him, but a lot of eyes looked at me and the animals that shared the bench with Samantha and I.

The biker and the two women who lit my torc up blue sat together and talked. I pretended to be clueless about their glances towards me. My plan to leave the Southeast looked really stupid now.

The only positive takeaway was I learned why Old Donnie never left the Southeast. I may not be a novice with banishing gargoyles and magic, but I was in over my head here.

I forced my shoulders to relax because there weren't any more warnings from my torc and I seemed in no immediate danger. There were plenty of good-natured chuckles for the minister and another person read through announcements and relayed where people met for events.

The ski bum minister stood up, and the regulars got quiet and he began talking like a normal service.

"I'm glad to see so many people here, because this week I've been thinking a lot of how companionship helps us in the world and with our faith. I'd like to start with a reading from Ecclesiastes chapter four, versus nine through twelve."

My panic from Sundays came back when I realized I was in church without my bible, then I remembered I was an adult. Samantha slid closer and pulled a bible from an inside pocket of her blue wool coat and shared it with me.

> *Two are better than one, because they have a good return for their labor: If either of them falls down, one can help the other up. But pity anyone who falls and has no one to help them up. Also, if two lie down together, they will keep warm. But how can one keep warm alone? Though one may be overpowered, two can defend themselves. A cord of three strands is not quickly broken.*

I internalized how many times Rachel and I, Miles and I, or Rachel, Miles, and I slept together on the ground to keep warm and how we fought together. My mind shifted from thinking this was a waste of time to realizing I had to step in and help Miles.

The sermon kept going, and I followed along with Samantha. When he asked for examples of a time when two people together were overpowered, I couldn't help but think of my helplessness in saving Old Donnie and teared up.

He died trying to protect humanity, while the priests who had taken over the church wanted to capture the gargoyles and all the magic for themselves, and their power. Though I learned plenty of magic, I hadn't been able to learn any that would have saved his life.

Samantha put her arm around me, and tears ran down my cheeks. "I'm sorry," I whispered. I wiped my eyes and stopped thinking of Old Donnie. This was not the place to appear weak.

The church service ended, and most left to go to lunch. Samantha placed her hand on my shoulder. "May I give you one piece of advice? It will be some time before I see you again."

"I could use all the advice I could get."

"In a time of peace, when no one is a warrior, gentle souls are common. In a time of war, when we all are warriors, the gentle soul is a blessing to everyone. Remain a gentle soul despite what you encounter."

I nodded and understood nothing. She kissed me on my cheek and left with the others for lunch.

There was an opening, and I took a path to climb higher up the mountain. The animals followed me and I let them. Any pretense that I had kept a low profile was gone, and it was time to do what only I could do.

THE TOP HAD A BRUTAL wind that whipped my braid, but it stayed intact. It blew my leather duster like it was cloth. The clear blue sky let me see the whole of the range, all the way to Canada, and it looked like I could see into Maine. *Focus!*

This circle needed to be huge and powerful. I kicked off my shoes, let the animals know that a large gargoyle was coming, and soon walked alone on the cold rock on the mountain top. I drew the circle with a six-feet radius, and I used seven clippings of honeysuckle in it. The question of why did the number of gargoyle symbols and clippings need to be prime got me a scowl from Old Donnie.

"You'll regret dropping math and college. Prime numbers build all numbers and numbers build all magic. For instance, if you learned more about things like the Fibonacci sequence, you could break a circle with any natural item that follows that pattern instead of only using the magnolia seed pods."

It hurt to admit my intelligence. "I didn't drop out because it was easy. The classes confused me and I just couldn't do it."

"That's crap. I hired the best firearms instructors for you, but you couldn't hit nothing until that pretty blonde girl taught you. Three weeks later, you only needed ten bullets for eight difficult shots."

There was no argument because I don't know why Rebecca could teach me to shoot and others failed.

I felt eyes upon me. The others had followed me and watched. It was too late to stop now, so I pretended I was alone. Everything about my trip had become a grand failure, and Old Donnie should never have trusted me. But now, the world had no other choice. I had drawn the circle barefoot with a direct connection to the Earth, and I placed the last honeysuckle on the top of the circle. This was the largest circle I ever created for the largest gargoyle listed in the book for five years. With confidence from the promises of the biker and Samantha, I started the binding, knowing this signal I'd make would light up like no other spell I cast.

Thirty minutes later, my torc glowed red, and the largest gargoyle I've seen appeared. The world turned black and white. The beast stood twelve feet tall and had a wingspan of ten feet. Its skin glistened like obsidian except for his face. His claws and teeth were at least six inches long, his face had stripes of gray granite in it, and when it smiled at me, sounds of rocks cracking echoed over the mountain top. "Do not start the binding, thy skill is known and I shall take my own leave. I do lack to talk to the new druid." His voice echoed and sounded immune to the muffling that affected the wind.

There was no reason to stop, but something caught me in the patient tone of this gargoyle. Maybe it was the crazy day or the overconfidence of facing a bound gargoyle, but I stopped the cast before it got underway.

"Sure." I kept my hands ready and the binding start at the forefront of my mind. I wished I didn't have to look up to it, but a six-foot-one druid had to crane his neck to talk to a twelve-foot-tall gargoyle. I steeled myself, acted like an equal, and prepared to talk to him politely.

He was a combination of granite and obsidian patches, and I'd never heard or seen of obsidian in a gargoyle. Obsidian is something I used to attack gargoyles.

He collapsed his wings, and his arms hung at his sides. "Being the last druid might not but be hard. The temple hath killed they kind and they shall eventually release the Snake Hunters to dispatch thou like they killed thy ancestors."

A Snake Hunter got Old Donnie. He said they were from the time of Rome's occupation of England, and they murdered their way across Ireland, and eradicated the complete history of the lands. But I needed to focus on this gargoyle. "I'm just a man doing what he can. You are correct, the church will do their best to stop me."

The gargoyle laughed joyously and the strangeness of a laughing gargoyle threw me. This was certainly a week for first time experiences. "The last binder was a hybrid of temple teachings and druidic magics. Yet thou, thou only use the magic of time ere. That I but depart with one word. There are factions of gargoyles and not all of us work with the temple, and some of us shall willingly live with humanity."

"That would be good news, but what is actionable for me?"

"Thou art wise for thy years and this is causeth for celebration. However, the magicians of the church planeth to open three portals to the Realm of Darkness and one is in thy normal territory. This shall beest at the minute of dark during winter solstice. You may call me Strumath."

Old Donnie never mentioned factions, but he never mentioned talking gargoyles or bikers and women who discussed being centuries old, either.

Then the gargoyle smiled with jagged teeth and waved, disappearing back to his plane voluntarily. The circle I made snapped and disappeared with him. Nothing surprised me anymore. Now a gargoyle talked about aligning with me and I believed him.

I fell back to my known procedures and verified my symbols and honeysuckle disappeared with it. With my faith in the promises, I cast the spell to get the information on the last and the next thirty days of gargoyles. With the sound of twigs breaking behind me as the watchers left, the spell fired and let me know the gargoyles would return in five hundred years, three hundred years, two hundred years, three hundred years, and fifty years, respectively. The information of the spell looked like a scroll that appeared in front of me. A scroll of light green with forest green writing appeared in front of me. This is how it worked for me, and no one else could see the scroll. I memorized the information to record in the <u>Abernathy Book of Gargoyles</u>.

Gratefully alone, I took the lurching gondola back to the bottom, and jogged to my car, and updated the notes. I should rush, but my car was the only one around. I put in each gargoyle's location notes, description, and expected date of return. The dates were in the Julian calendar and, in Old Donnie's notes, Gregorian. Before leaving, I sent Rachel a squirrel about my thoughts on ending this plan. I hoped she was somewhere private.

My Mustang rolled onto the road, and made a beeline to get out of New Hampshire, and on my way as fast as I could, without breaking a single law.

I waited on contacting Preacher Jon. Despite Old Donnie's warning to never let being scared change a plan, today's experience shook me to the core. The talking gargoyles, the church, blue gem warnings, the biker, the girl, the flirty woman, and the woman who calmed me, combined with the distance from home. I so desperately wanted to talk to Old Donnie one last time, but I was alone. Needing, Rachel ate at me.

There were no more musings. I put in my music player and listened to music that Old Donnie and I both enjoyed and tried to shake the day's events from my mind. With a bit of effort, I put a positive spin on the day's events. All this happened alone and exposed no one else. Heck, fearing the flirty woman could mean I was developing a healthy attitude towards women.

Except I knew that was false. Old Donnie was very specific when he said I had an unhealthy attitude towards women. *If you don't have a girlfriend, you're looking for one. You don't even date a girl a few times, it's always serious. You need a girl to fill in something in your life and that ain't healthy. Before you add a life partner, you need to fill the hole yourself.*

Chapter 10—Deer Woman and a Cardinal

The trip to South Dakota started off fine. I drove up north to Saratoga Springs for a gargoyle that wanted to be near a place where men gambled. Just before the large college town was the parking lot for the racetrack.

At four am, I removed the chain blocking the parking lot and pulled into the lot. I drove over to the edge, kicked off my shoes, and created a small circle. My initialization and binding of the circle went smoothly and soon my torc glowed red, and I was in the world of black and white. I banished the little mixed rock guy, despite its feeble struggles, and everything returned to normal.

I returned to my car and left Saratoga Springs and drove west, thankful for an uneventful binding and banishment. It meant I banished six gargoyles and defeated a seventh. There were only two more gargoyles left in my plan. My dismay of the previous day dissipated, and I drove towards South Dakota with more confidence.

Last year, after a bad day, Miles, Rachel, and I got on our motorcycles and go mudding with a case of beer. Not being able to do that was the lame part of adulting. I thought a case of beer and mudding with my friends sounded awesome. If it wasn't for my healing arm, I'd even go for a good old bar brawl. I wanted to stand up on the bar one time, wavering for being drunk and saying, 'is there anyone who wants to take me down?' And get into an old-fashioned throw down. But those days were in the past.

The reason I hated to think about was another reason I needed to become a loner. On days like I've had recently, dark thoughts can enter my mind. It's easy to get rid of them, though. If I die, the church will target Rachel, Nicole, and Nathan. Killing the four of us ended druids forever. I would fight a demon from hell to protect them from having to face what I do.

I took the time to switch out the bandages in a rest area and the pain was under control now, with only ibuprofen. Three days and the healing seemed fast, even for me, but the nineteen stitches stayed in place and I still had two more doses from the Z-pack. The braids from the woman in New Hampshire stayed tight, so I took a sink bath and left them in.

Today was supposed to be the day I practiced my dance moves for Rachel, but the whole arm thing threw that away. On the way back to my car, with a bag holding my bandages, I saw a couple meet-up, and they kissed before they got back into their car.

Rachel once asked me to ask out her younger sister. Nicole just turned twenty-one, but I still thought of her as my kid sister. I also knew she developed a middle school crush on me and I became protective of her. Strangely, I caught her this past week lying to me. I'd written a couple of her answers down from the past month to check on her. Realizing I still protected her by checking up like this meant I would not ask her out.

Feeling better, and after a day out of New Hampshire, I relaxed and got back to my plan. The next two gargoyles desired a location where the people visited temporarily. I had to drive through Buffalo on my route and if the church was trying to catch me; I bet they'd wait at Niagara Falls. They'd never suspect a place called the Corn Palace.

I saved the last three prescription drugs, and the throbbing became bearable. I finished the antibiotic and was only alternating ibuprofen and acetaminophen for the pain. The arm was almost usable now, and the wraps were clear of puss and blood. To help pass the time, I thought through strategies to fight a Snake Hunter without the Protection Domain Old Donnie used.

I checked my Tyler Phone and there was a *911 Call me* text from Rachel. I could count on one hand how many of these I'd gotten from her—in my life.

"Hey sorry about making you turn Tyler's phone on, but this is big."

"No worries, I miss you something fierce."

"Preacher Jon called me late last night, and said you bumped into a Leander, and it is critical he talks to you."

"Okay."

"Corey, I had a nightmare about you, and Rebecca saved your life." She sounded scared.

Nightmares were usually just nightmares, but with a druid involved, we didn't take them lightly. "Gotcha. I promise to contact him immediately. And, yeah, if Leander was the biker, then he has a right to be scared. I'll fill you in face to face, but I am safe."

"Corey, I can't lose you. Please be careful. How's your arm?"

"Just a thin bandage and pain controlled with over-the-counter stuff." The other end got quiet. "Yeh, this was fast even for me. But how is Miles? He said he was at the hospital."

"Trish is upset. They held him overnight in the hospital, but he's back at work."

That was a relief. "We can't bring him anymore."

"Please Corey, you need to get in contact with Preacher Jon."

"Okay. I'll contact him now."

I ran to the restroom and tried to think of what to say. Back in my car, I settled into the leather seat that seemed to have grown as part of me and texted Preacher Jon on the Jim Byrd phone before I chickened out.

Preacher Jon, this is a burner phone. Congratulations on tracking me.

Preacher Jon replied quickly. *You had a hornet's nest before you pulled off your plan, but you've scared the church, and I've had a call with two covens.*

I texted back. *I know you have too much information about me now. What are you looking for? You might be the only person who knows my mentor told me I had to stay a loner.*

Thank you for Don's grave marker. What do you mean by too much information?

I ignored the part about Old Donnie. *You tracked me with another person.*

Rebecca? I caught her up to date, so she won't give you away. But the three of us need to meet.

Preacher Jon didn't follow best practices with text messages and it was causing my anxiety to rise. *Again, you might be the only other person alive who knows why I need to be a loner.*

No. I'm the only other person alive who knows *all* about you and one of five who knows you cannot do this alone. Your meetings with two witches' covens should have convinced you of that.

This was as bad as I feared. Old Donnie kept everyone at bay because every time he brought someone in, they died. They also were a liability for the information they had about you, and the church was the most despicable organization in aggressive interrogation techniques.

However, he had me on the witches. I didn't know witches existed before New Hampshire and while they treated me kindly, something told me they did because they felt sorry for me.

He didn't wait for my response. *Look. Let's at least talk.*

He had me over a barrel and had information I needed. I calculated my trip and if I stayed in KC tonight, left at seven in the morning, I'd be in Chattanooga for an early dinner tomorrow.

Okay. Mellow Mushroom in Chattanooga across from the aquarium at five pm tomorrow.

Excellent!

I didn't think any of this was excellent, but what's done was done, and Old Donnie said I could trust Preacher Jon a little. Hopefully, he sent Rebecca back to her life and if he took care of that loose end for me, then I owed him. Plus, if he gave me information, so this whole witch fiasco never happened again, I'd be stupid to ignore him.

I took a few minutes to go through my packs. Items like the sickle, wicker basket, and weapons were difficult to replace. I needed to keep track of the magnolia seed. If I was losing a battle, it was a get of jail free card for me. It was also a get out of jail free for an enemy against me. I have a regular touch-inventory that included the seed pod.

THE DRIVE WAS A BOTHER. My legs hurt and I couldn't find a comfortable position for my back. These were minor compared to the meeting with Preacher Jon. Worse, I needed to ignore that to banish two consecutive gargoyles.

It was difficult to put into words why I didn't want to meet Preacher Jon. First, when I fought the church, meeting a preacher didn't seem wise. Second, Old Donnie warned me that while I should trust Preacher Jon, the man was so smart he could out-think all of us and get us to act like his puppets. This sounded like an emergency-only kind of thing, and no one had told me of any emergency.

I pulled into Mitchell, South Dakota, and looked at the Corn Palace, and hoped the gargoyles wouldn't see what this place looked like before they decided whether to arrive. Across the street was a pleasant restaurant that served burgers, which had a train track running through it. The parking lot had a direct line of sight to the corn palace. When parked, I thought through the next events. I waved at a small gaggle of squirrels who came off the electrical wires and a couple of dogs came by. They were without collars and hungry. When no one was near, I cast a spell to heal them.

It was time to eat, and I needed to take my time. I had driven for so long I needed to make sure my head was on straight. Next to the restaurant were a handful of retired trains that blocked sightlines. It looked perfect if the gargoyles came quick.

The hamburger was remarkably excellent. After eating and between the trains, I created a honeysuckle plant, and sliced a good sturdy twig from it with my sickle into my collapsible wicker basket. After creating both circles, I started them one at a time. I bound and banished the first gargoyle and then the second. I was back in my car in under an hour.

It felt good that the part of my plan to throw off the bishop worked. I took a careful saunter back to my car to avoid attention and pulled back onto the highway. I saw no signs of the church.

The drive south from Sioux Falls gave me time to think, and I booked a hotel room in Kansas City for the night. *Eight gargoyles bound and banished with a ninth killed in under a week, without being caught by the church.*

Driving the rest of the day, I relaxed and remembered that I promised I would do the karaoke duet contest with Rachel on Friday. She had drilled me and given me lessons to practice. She could sing, and well... I was willing to put forth the effort for her. I practiced singing the entire afternoon. It kept my mind off my legs and my back. It also stopped the shaking of my hands.

After the drive, I was exhausted and lucky to find the hotel I booked. The place was one of those hotels with rooms as suites. I hid my weapons and Old Donnie's duster in my trunk. With my torc under my seat for a quick retrieval in the morning, I carried my day pack and my messenger bag into the hotel. Checking in by an amiable lady was uneventful. I jogged back to my car and brought the presents in. Back inside, I pulled out the bathrobe for Rachel and put pillows inside of it. It stopped my shaking and let me sleep. My messenger bag contained my druid and gargoyle book and stayed on the table in the room. It was late, and I went right to bed.

One of the best things about sleeping alone was when I had a sex dream because I could just let myself enjoy it. If I snuggled with Rachel or camped with Miles, I'd need to end it. This dream started on my patio with Rebecca, and a woman tried to get between us. I ignored the woman despite her beauty and sex appeal. I wanted the dream with Rebecca.

Rebecca wore the white baby doll lingerie I bought her. Her blonde hair billowed in the wind and intermingled with mine. I picked her up and spun her around and she slipped her right breast out of her see through lace on top of the satin. She giggled and leaned in for a kiss.

The woman was back, and Rebecca was gone. "I'm more fun and more permanent," she said. Her light deer-brown hair cascaded down her back. Then the wind caught her hair and intermingled with mine. She purred and traced her finger down my bare chest. Who describes hair as deer brown?

I pushed the woman away to hold Rebecca's hand again, but she disappeared, and the woman returned.

I screamed, "No, I want Rebecca!"

The outside remained dark, but that meant nothing in November. Time was anywhere from six at night to six in the morning. The woman from my dream clung to my arm and had one arm on my crotch, while we walked by the parking lot towards the woods. "Let's duck into the bushes for a little fun."

Everything appeared in black and white, and the area muffled her voice. The hotel on my left was dark and my car had a light glowing inside of it.

My feet stood on a manicured lawn about one hundred feet from some woods. I pushed the woman with all my might, kicked off my shoes, and ran to a tree. My bare feet kicked up dew on the ground as I ran. The book from Dr. Kanoska's office ran into my mind. It said Deer Women stole the souls of men!

She teleported back out of my reach and screamed, "Bishop Pedrotti granted your soul to me!"

Who? Is that the bishop causing me issues?

I had my minor magics, my connection to Earth, and fighting skills. The woman charged me fast, faster than I could run, and as I barely tucked and rolled her headbutt glanced off my hip. Earth Power surged to the area, but that hurt. If she had hit me square at that speed, that'd seriously hurt, if not kill me.

I jumped around a tree and found a pine to ask for a weapon.

The woman reached around the tree and punched me in the gut as I asked. Rachel punched me harder than that in practice. The tree responded, and I pulled two tonfa from it. *Without her speed, her hits were feeble!*

I cross blocked a two-fisted slam and then walked towards her as she gauged the change in odds. She jumped eight feet high to escape me, and I hooked her right ankle, yanking her to the ground with the tonfa. Evil spirit creatures would not exist on my lands!

I slammed the other tonfa handle into her jaw to knock her teeth together with enough force to knock her out. She turned into a deer unconscious on the ground.

I used a tonfa standing and turning in one spot to make each circle. Then, despite the embarrassment that I still stuck out of my shorts because of the Deer Woman's dream, I began casting the binding with a connection to the Earth.

The binding was done and I couldn't banish the unconscious deer yet, so I continued. I repeated it two more minutes before checking again, and the binding still did not have enough strength to banish. I wished I had a focus, but if I didn't cut the honeysuckle twigs with my sickle and catch them in a wicker basket, they wouldn't work. Sometimes magic was weird.

The deer stood on wobbly legs, and I continued the binding. It tried to walk over the circle but did not have the strength to cross the barrier. Three more repetitions had the most powerful unfocused circle I'd ever made.

The deer panicked, but the improved barrier held against its rage. At the tenth recasting, my binding was at my full strength without focuses. I began the banishment.

Tha Rìoghachd dorchadas a 'gairm agus le mo chumhachd rìoghachdan ceangailte tha mi a' cuir casg ort gu dorchadas!

When I prepared to cast it again, the deer turned back into a pleading woman. Within a minute, she pulled a blade and plunged it into her own heart. One more repetition and I'd have banished her, but she preferred to die.

The circle exploded and threw me back ten feet as the world became color again. The woman's corpse turned into a green light, which flew over and entered my chest. Old Donnie never prepared me for any of this.

I stood up, checked around, and I was alone. With a thank you and a hug of the pine tree, it reabsorbed the two tonfa, and I felt its gratitude of removing the Dark Fey Deer Woman from this area.

Ten bindings were the maximum any circle could take, and I had spent twenty minutes getting this binding to the full strength, without focuses or the creature's name. I had just laid the most powerful magical tie to the Fey Realm with my signature since New Hampshire. The church would recognize my signature and realize it wasn't a gargoyle. If she told the truth about Bishop Pedrotti, they were already on their way—whoever Bishop Pedrotti was.

If I left, they'd have my car's description and my Tyler identity. *Crap.* This was time to hide in plain sight. I stood up, checked around, and I was alone. The world changed back into color and the blue light in my car faded. *Stupid! I could never leave the torc uncovered in my car at night.*

I put my shoes on, gave the tonfa back to the tree with a thank you, and watched the tree reabsorb them. Then, with a bit of acting and genuine shock, I meandered to the front of the hotel and knocked on the door. Luckily, the women who checked me in saw me and pushed the buzzer to talk. "Sir?"

"I'm sorry. I was sleepwalking and locked myself out."

"Sir, are you okay?"

I appeared sheepish and came up with a story. "I'm a frequent sleepwalker when I get overtired. So, some of these scrapes aren't new."

She let me in and escorted me to my room and looked around. The clock read five, and I had no interest in trying to get two hours of sleep. After thanking her, I closed the door. For a good hour, I lay on the bed and thought about how my world had changed. Witches, Preacher Jon, Rachel, and Nicole. There was a lot going on, but I was navigating this life fine. I plucked grass from my hair that fell into my face.

Once showered and packed, I made sure I presented clean, and wore a long-sleeved shirt to cover the scar on my arm. To make my day bag look like a regular bag, I changed the configuration of the day pack handles. Then I walked out for the free breakfast.

Three priests sat in the free breakfast area as I walked downstairs. *You got this, son.* I steeled myself, drooped my eyes, walked in, and put my stuff on a table next to them.

My default thought that these were evil priests. They'd be investigating the magical signature I left last night, but it was possible they were innocent. I walked in and scoped them out with sideway glances.

The cardinal and one priest needed practice hiding weapons. The stocks of the weapons pushed out the vestments and gave the weapons away. Clergy didn't carry concealed weapons as a general rule. Time for a show.

On the bar with the breakfast items, I toasted an English muffin, then prepared a plate with eggs and sausage. With two milks, I sat, and a cardinal, or at least a man dressed in red vestments, joined me at my table. "Good morning, father."

"Good morning, son. Were you awakened by the ruckus last night?"

Luckily, the confusion on my face was real. No one would have heard anything. Then my brain caught up to the fact that he was looking for someone to slip up. "I slept like the dead."

"You sound originally from the south as well." The cardinal was looking past me for someone else.

"You got me. Georgia Native." I scooped up eggs and ate them with sausage.

"Heading home then?" One priest talked to a young couple who walked in for breakfast, while the third kept his eyes peeled for those leaving the hotel without stopping to eat. It was time to ask a question, so I seemed interested.

"Yep, will be back at work tomorrow. Also, I have a friend who attends the big Parish downtown, and he said they are getting ready for something big. He's been helping a lot. Are you involved with that?" Nicole had a friend Wesley who crushed on Rachel in high school who was a devout Catholic, but I hadn't seen him in years.

The Cardinal turned back to me. "Your friend must be talking about the upcoming monsignor visit in December. Is he a deacon in the church?"

"No. Wesley has taken the classes to sponsor confirmation, but wants to finish his master's degree before moving forward with that."

"Let's hope you are one of his first."

I almost spit out my milk. "Caught me, but I have attended."

"Keep attending and spending time with your friend. Drive safely, son."

He marched to another solo person eating breakfast. "Thank you, father." I finished eating at a normal pace, and I walked out to my car. I pulled out the back entrance, then drove to a gas station to top off. Hopefully, my path drew no suspicion because my car stayed far enough away.

An hour after I left the hotel, I allowed myself to relax and put my torc back on.

WITH REGRET FOR MY legs and back, I got back in the car and tried to think about anything else on the drive to Chattanooga. Old Donnie's teachings were a nice way to distract myself.

> *You have a few sources of power. The first is your connection to the Earth. You will develop a personal relationship with it, and over time, you will develop powers. It's good you can use the torc. It will give you warning and druidic vision. Over time, your relationship with the Earth will incorporate the torc.*

Old Donnie didn't know why the torc worked with me and not him. But he beamed with pride when it worked with me. The magical abilities were secondary to remembering the look in Old Donnie's eyes when I first wore it.

> *Now, they say druids wrote nothing down. That wasn't exactly true. The books were invisible to everyone else. These have the most powerful spells in them. We have one book between us with ten spells. Don't fret about learning them all, they don't all match your domain. They say the books exist in the Fey Realm, which keeps them invisible.*

So, there were five spells in that book I hadn't learned in two years. The explanation made sense. I had different domains that Old Donnie had. Each druid had four domains, and I had Circles, Earth Power, Plants, and Animals. Old Donnie said the church spells came from his Protection Domain. He had weather too, and that made his life pretty sweet.

The other difference was in reading our spell book. Each page had notes in Latin, and Old Donnie used Latin words to make spells work. If I didn't use Old Gaelic entirely, nothing worked. Church magicians used Latin for their spells. Old Donnie was a hybrid druid because his spells had both Gaelic and Latin. Magicians, like those in the church, used Latin. Druids used one of the Gaelic forms. There were other languages with magical ties. Old Donnie said that Shinto Kannushi speak Ryukyuan from the Yayoi period. If you think I learned that in Georgia Public schools, you ain't from around here.

I skipped lunch because of construction and besides that one stretch of construction. A half hour out of Chattanooga, an FJ1200 roared up next to me and pointed to an exit. I did a double take and saw it was Rachel. I pulled off the exit and went into a gas station. She followed and pulled in behind me.

She took off her helmet as she jogged to me. I got out of the car and stretched my legs and back. Her hair was a mess.

"We need to make this quick," she said with a nervous look on her face.

Despite that, we hugged. I can't believe we were apart for so long. Her hug was so tight I lost my breath. "What's going on? Do you need help?"

"Remember when I said I kept Old Donnie's family up to date with you?"

"Yeh, what's living rent free in you?" We still held hands, and I wasn't letting go soon.

"Preacher Jon is my grandfather and Old Donnie's great grandson."

This was a little surprising, but not Earth shattering. "Okay, that explains a few things." Mainly how Preacher Jon and Rebecca traveled together.

"Your world will turn upside down and I need you to know that I am, was, and always will be your friend. I was never a spy, but I couldn't tell you everything."

"Rachel, you're freaking me out... wait a second, was it you who passed me in Durham?"

"Yes, I took out the cameras for you."

"How? What? How?" My confusion had gone off the charts,

"My brother is like a computer whiz and saw where you looked up for medical care on your phone. He located the cameras and let me know."

The message from Dr. Kanoska came to me. "Whoa, what's going on? Did your brother program the phone, so it helped me?"

"We are running out of time and there is a lot Old Donnie didn't tell you, but I want you to know I am your friend."

"Old Donnie said Preacher Jon was smarter than all of us combined, and I should be careful."

"True. Look, I have to beat you there, but please be nice to him. Did Old Donnie tell you of the other people he trained who died?"

"Yes."

"Preacher Jon is my Grandpa Jon. Both of his parents, his wife, and his two kids with their husbands were in that group. My mother being one of his kids.

Preacher Jon was the grandfather I never met??!!

We had a lot of therapy and talked about this, but sadness still covered her. Rachel and her mother were very close. "Wow. This is..."

"Please. Remember, I am your friend."

"Rachel, no matter what, I trust you. We're fam."

"Go with Grandpa Jon when he asks you."

"Whoa." I held up both hands. That seemed like a big issue for being a loner.

Her shoulders slumped and let go of my hands. "Please, at least hear him out." She ran to her bike, put her helmet on, and took off. Back in my car, I did not know what was going on. My best skill wasn't thinking about stuff. It caused me to feel stupid. I probably should write things down like I did with gargoyles and Nicole, because I was missing important stuff or forgetting it.

I arrived in Chattanooga on time, nearly but still confused. However, I was back in my home territory and it felt good. The center lot was almost full, but I parked in front of the aquarium in one of the last places and walked over to the restaurant. I walked right past Rachel's FJ1200.

However, fifty degrees never felt so good, and I basked in the warmth of the normal November temperature. Hundreds of people milled around between the plaza in front of the aquarium, to the theater on my left, and the restaurants and shops on my right. Past the entrance, I looked inside and recognized Rachel walking to a table with Nicole. Rachel's hair was in a tight braid now. But I needed to focus. My hair whipped about wildly, so I grabbed a band and pulled it back tight.

Chapter 11—Chattanooga Kiss

I walked in through the double doors covered with local band advertisements and into the restaurant with nearly two dozen customers. To my right, next to the cash register, a splash of red caught my eye. A waitress with strawberry blond hair in disarray that looked bored made eye contact with me. Her smile caught my eyes like a net and went right to her. "Hi, I'm Tyler and looking" then I saw the Appalachian Trail pin on her uniform next to her name tag that had 'Stormy' written on it. "Oh, you've hiked the Appalachian trail?"

She touched her pin and smiled. "I want to hike it."

"My friend and I did a couple of stints as Trail Angels over the past two years." Old Donnie and I renewed our connection with Earth often, and helping the teams seemed a good way to accomplish something worthwhile.

"That's so awesome. Have you hiked it?" Her smile lit up her face and red hair splashed across her fair and she didn't wear makeup and her freckles highlighted her smile.

"A couple of times."

"Your party is waving for you and I don't want to get in trouble."

Turning, my bar fighting skills came into play. I put on my game face. Old Donnie prepared me for Preacher Jon and needed to be serious. I took a defensive stance and a stalking gait over to the table with Rebecca and the person who must be Preacher Jon. He would not punch me, but I needed to think quickly. I understood fights, and that's how I treated confrontations. Theory was theory in my book.

After removing the emotion from my face, I prepared myself to listen and respond like Old Donnie wanted. They sat on opposite sides of a four-seat table. I took the chair from next to Rebecca and sat at the edge of the table. The seats were flimsy, and the table had a piece of cardboard on a leg to keep it from wobbling.

She was stunning and didn't need makeup. She had gorgeous blonde hair just a little shorter than mine and wore a baby blue blouse. I'm sure she had a tan or jean skirt on underneath the table. But if Preacher Jon assumed my ex would soften me, I steeled myself.

Rachel and Nicole walked over to join us. The pushed another table and brought two chairs. This was a planned manuever.

Nice move, old man. He didn't show the strength of his force until I chose my chair. Classic fighting technique. I had an out and needed to undo this advantage and put myself back on top. I'd clear up the Nicole situation first. "Nicole, I didn't know you and Rachel would be here. Would you walk out to my car and help me carry the gifts?"

"I will," piped up Rachel.

"You sit. I haven't wrapped your gift." I winked at her and smiled.

She made a playful, pouty face. I offered Nicole my hand, and she took it and walked with me to the door. She stood as tall as Rachel at five-nine, but wore two-inch kitten heels everywhere.

We walked outside. The confrontation was unnecessary. She looked as if I had caught her instigating a fight. "You're lying to me. Should I prove it to you, or are you ready to 'fess up?'"

She looked at me wide-eyed. "I never thought you'd be the one to catch me. What do you know?"

"I know you're lying and have been lying for years." I realized she had to be using a power no one recognized, and I knew it had been going on for years. If I took the information from the team, sat naked in the woods, I could put the entire story together. But I wouldn't let that out yet.

"Yes. My Realized empath power has grown and I can now predict what the correct thing to say to get the reaction I want. I can also read a thought in your mind instead of emotion, so when you thought you wouldn't let it out that you put the entire story together, you already have. That's how I was hiding my actions from everyone."

I didn't understand what that meant, except she could hide information from people, and it didn't matter right now. This was no longer the little girl I held after her mother died and made her breakfast before middle school.

We crossed the street into the big square parking lot, where I popped the trunk. "Please, stay by my side. First. No more using that power on me. If I am going to help you and keep your secret, I have to trust you. Second, you don't have to tell me today. I will let you figure out how you want to tell me the secret."

"I'll tell you more because it's getting dangerous and I need help. Since you first came into our lives, after the church murdered my parents, I've been searching for my parent's killers."

Eight years? She was a kid. "You were in middle school!"

"That's why it's taken eight years."

"Okay. I am keeping your secret, but if you need any help, call me immediately. You need to promise that if you feel in danger, you will contact me." I took stalk of Nicole and she wasn't little Nicky anymore. She had become a woman. I made a mental note to stop treating her like a kid.

"I promise."

"Yes, but let's save that for the table." She pulled me in deep into her conspiracy right away, which was good. This is not something one person should do, despite her ability. "I promise. Now hold up this sheepskin rug."

"Hold on Corey. We need a cover for how long we've been out here. But you're right, this rug is beautiful."

"That's the present for Miles and Trish. When we walk in with one bag, we'll say we merged bags, and I didn't need help afterwards."

"That's a start, but we need to pretend that excuse is a cover for something else. Kiss me."

"What?!" Kiss her? "Why?"

"I've kept under cover for eight years. Please treat me like an adult and trust me."

She had me, and I just promised I'd treat her like an adult. "What kind of kiss? A peck?"

"No, make it real. Kiss me like you're judging whether I'm a kid sister or a woman."

How much harm could one kiss do? I stepped forward, pulled her into my arms. My left hand slipped up her neck to the back of her head while my fingers sifted through her hair. She leaned in and I tilted to suck her bottom lip with a gentle caress of my lips. She ran her tongue around my lips and I slid up for the full kiss.

Heat rose to my face, and I pulled her close with my right arm and I imagined us together sitting on the swing of the front porch of the cabin, locked in an embrace. When her tongue circled mine and she pulled it back, I pulled away from the kiss.

I looked at her with fresh eyes. She wore a pink dress with a high collar. Her long brunette hair had nice light spots that shone in the sun. The makeup was just enough to catch my attention and draw me into the mist of her gray eyes. She wore small diamond earrings as her only jewelry. With her heals she stood only a couple of inches shorter than I and I wanted to wrap my hands around her shoulder and pull her close. I held the gift bag with two hands to act normal.

She folded the blanket and put it back in its bag. "We were supposed to hold this in front of us. I got too excited to kiss you." She blushed.

That was not an innocent kiss. How was I going to stop thinking about her after that?

"Remember, I'm an empath and I can perceive exactly what you're thinking. That was a kiss of lovers." She smiled.

My mind jumbled, and I struggled for a coherent thought. I grabbed the other bag and shut the trunk. I took her hand, and we walked back in and sat at the table. There was a time and a place for those thoughts, and they weren't now. I need to make sure everyone could stay safe with my plan to stay a loner.

"That was a beautiful rug," said Rebecca.

"I thought so too. We merged bags, so he didn't have to carry it all in."

Rachel grinned at the two of us.

"I got the sheepskin rug for Trish and Miles for the baby," I explained.

I picked up Nicole's chair with her in it.

"Ooh." She squeaked as I moved her and her chair a foot to her right.

With my chair, I sat between Nicole and Rachel and pulled Rachel's chair close to me so we could touch, and I felt whole. I pulled out the first box and handed it to Rachel, knowing I neutralized Preacher Jon's coordination of the seating.

"Pajamas!" she exclaimed. "Ooh, this bathrobe is nice."

"You wanted less tomboy stuff, so I got a nine-piece sleepwear gift with the wool bathrobe."

She held up the halter top over her chest. "Hot pink."

She leaned over and hugged me. "You are so awesome. How did you get the size?"

"I spent an uncomfortable ten minutes with a saleswoman hugging a mannequin while she kept saying, '*your friend*' when referencing you."

The entire table, including Preacher Jon, laughed.

Stormy walked over and had tried to put her hair into a bun, but it fell out chaotically and framed her freckled face. "Hi, I'm Stormy and I'll be serving you today. Oh, hi again, are all of you hikers like Tyler?"

Preacher Jon chuckled. "No, Tyler here is enough outdoorsman for all of us."

When Stormy left with our orders, I pulled out the shoes and handed them to Nicole.

"Nicole, I remembered you like rounded, closed toed kitten heels. But this color is the first bud of spring and I wanted to get these for you."

She pulled them out, and a tear left her eye. "They're beautiful. You know my favorite shoe?"

"You bought those shoes days ago," said Preacher Jon. I had him on his heels and backing up. I had confused him, but this was accidental.

"Yep." To Nicole, I answered. "Of course. I don't know if you have anything to match the color, but it felt like the gift I should get you."

She wrapped her arms around me. "Oh, I will find something to wear with these." She pulled them out and put them on and stood up. "You even remembered my size."

"Nicole, we've known each other for over eight years and you love shoes. I think everyone knows your size and your favorite shoe style."

Nicole turned to the table. "Rebecca gets a pass, but Grandpa, Rachel, do you know what size shoes I wear?"

Preacher Jon shook his head.

Rachel laughed. "I don't even know what size shoes I wear."

"Nine," I answered.

I SAT FACING FRONT. I got into my stance for combat. This would not be physical, but the mindset should keep me straight. "I'm sorry for delaying the meeting, but I haven't seen Rachel and Nicole in a long time."

"What happened to your arm?" asked Rebecca.

"Nineteen stitches a week ago." Ten of the stitches had dissolved, and the rest were almost gone. "It's healing up nicely." I took out the phone without the sim card in it and showed them the original picture.

I'm not sure why she asked about my arm if she didn't want to see the original wound. She recoiled from the picture. Preacher Jon looked and nodded. No doubt he had seen worse on Old Donnie. But now, a week later, the wound looked fine, and I had taken nothing for pain in a day. Of course, thinking about it made it burn.

Preacher Jon spoke first. "Don probably never told you, but he and I are family. That's why he tolerated me from his loner life."

"He told me out of all the people in the world, I could trust you a little. But don't hold Old Donnie's solitude on him. He dealt with a lot of loss and learned what it took to save the world." Then I wanted to swallow those words after remembering what Rachel said. *Why did she dump this on me?*

A tear ran down Preacher Jon's cheek. "Thank you and thank you for honoring his memory, and everything you say and remember of Grandpa Don is mostly true."

I nodded, and my eyes watered as well. Old Donnie deserved so much more. Instead, he had an unmarked grave to keep it hidden from the church and a token grave marker from me.

Preacher Jon had seen me counter his setup and felt obligated to make the first move. "Let me say something first, so we don't talk around each other. I agreed with Old Donnie's plan for his five-year training plan for you. We would not introduce you to the rest of the organization until year three. Unfortunately, because of the church, you are missing important information he intended you to have."

I peeked over at Rachel, who had pulled my arm around her and snuggled in. If she wanted me to be kind, I would be. "This trip has taught me that there are some things he did not teach me and I am more receptive than last week." Then I remembered the advice of Old Donnie about Preacher Jon. Preacher Jon is smarter than both of us and he'll get you to do what he wants.

Preacher Jon became serious. "Don would have never tried to get all eight in one week. That's why we need to talk. The church expected to pick up at least three new gargoyles. Some in the church assumed they'd get five since you were new. Instead, they lost one."

This was his attack. He didn't like my judgment. "He would be proud of me for getting all eight, plus killing off one already here."

"Yes, he would. He'd also figure how the church would react to being down a handful of gargoyles in their plans now. However, he would be all over you for meeting with two covens."

Stormy brought our salads, so we stopped talking for a while. I had eaten little this past week, and the magic and wound had sapped me, so I tore into it. I had two cherry tomatoes, a cucumber, and lettuce in my mouth before I even noticed the blue cheese.

"Hungry?" asked Rebecca.

"This week was crazy, and I left signatures everywhere. Stopping for food isn't a safe choice," I whispered. I didn't have a good argument for Preacher Jon. "The first coven was out of my control. A seven-year-old girl couldn't sleep and begged to watch me. She and her father knew about Old Donnie and me. What type of person would I be if I ignored her request?"

Preacher Jon ate his salad much slower than I. "The other coven?"

"Who puts an outdoor church on top of a mountain? And what type of covens meet at a church?" I finished my salad and realized I never stopped to put dressing on it.

We talked lightly until Stormy brought the meal. "You chunked that salad down. I bet you're going to sop up this pile of meat and cheese, too." Her accent was slipping, interesting. I smiled and said, "the food is nearly as tremendous as the service."

When Stormy left, Rebecca shook her head. "You were always charming."

I ignored the comment. I could be over her but not respond properly. Assess the situation. In a fight, this was a feint. *Don't respond if you're not comfortable.* Sitting, I tore into the calzone. I didn't miss pouring the sauce over it. I held back at the mounds of bread at either end. This was my one slip up, while cutting for Rachel's contest.

Back to the conversation, Preacher Jon was right. Old Donnie would have been all over me for this plan. No time to exercise, terrible food, and poor sleep were nonstarters for most plans. Now that I said the part about the witches out loud, he would have accepted my answers.

"The covens declared no more traveling into their declared lands for now. However, they'll talk with you about trading travel rights, so this worked out."

"Well, the rest of the plan was sound."

"Really? What if that cut was a little worse and required hospitalization? Hold on, I am being short sighted. I apologize." He took a deep breath. "I ran away from home at fourteen and it worked out for me. I recognize you made a plan with the best information you had, and made it work. For that I congratulate you."

This felt suspicious. He acted as if he was a friend of mine.

"He is a friend of yours, Corey," said Nicole. "Look at his face when you make his granddaughters smile."

We ate uncomfortably for a little. Rachel took a pepperoni off of her pizza and put it on my tongue. I smiled and swallowed it. "Oh, I left that for Nicole." She started giggling.

"You keep teasing and I'll kiss you."

She made a pretend kissing face, and I looked foolish. I was off my game, and I had done it to myself.

"Pardon me," said Rebecca. "Nicole, could you come to the ladies' room with me?" Rebecca looked at me and rubbed her lips. *Crap.* The two young women left the table.

I wiped my lips and saw pink lipstick on the napkin. I realized everyone saw, but I played it off like it was normal eating.

Nicole and Rebecca rejoined us at the table and pulled up their chairs without a word.

Preacher Jon ignored the joking and continued. "I need to tell you something." Preacher Jon pulled a rectangle out and placed it onto the table. "With this, we can talk with details. What do you know about the church's latest activity?"

To get back my dignity and establish I did not want to fight, I gave him info. "First, to show you I am not an enemy, I need to tell you something sensitive."

"Okay."

This wasn't just good faith, everyone needed to hear this. "There are two factions of Gargoyles, and Strumath said one will work with humanity and they dislike the church."

"That makes sense."

"But that's not all. He said during the minute of dark at the Winter Solstice, the church will open three portals to the Realm of Darkness and one is in my normal territory."

"That's incredible. Do you have any more bombs of information that could point us to saving the world?" Preacher Jon was genuinely shocked. Whether it was I pulled the information or the information itself was unknown.

I dropped the most recent news. "Bishop Pedrotti tried to kill me with a Deer Woman last night. Does that count?"

"The head of the Curia in Atlanta?" asked Nicole. She took a large bite of pizza and guessed she was hiding her expression.

"How did you learn that?" asked Preacher Jon. His head was on a swivel between us.

She finished chewing and answered slowly. "Wesley brought me to his parish some months back, and they had a big promotion for him. Nathan can look it up."

Preacher Jon looked like he didn't recognize any of us.

I jumped in to help Nicole's source of info. "Nicole, I needed to drop Wesley's name with some priests this morning. Please keep an eye on him."

Preacher Jon smiled like when a person in a fight discovered the opponent outnumbered him. I pressed the advantage to get him to look for a draw. But I did it by giving him the last piece of information. "Yep, they mentioned a monsignor is coming to Atlanta from the Vatican for the month of December."

I looked at Preacher Jon. "That's the third thing. Sorry, I'm scatterbrained with all the information I found out on my trip. It worked out to go to all the places Rebecca picked out for us." That was my big swing. I dismantled his argument with the information he needed that I gained on my trip.

"Holy crap. I'm getting Nathan up to date on everything," said Nicole. "I'm setting up dinner with Wesley to let him in on Corey's talk. Rachel, will you come with me? He is still crushing on you."

"Slow down," ordered Preacher Jon. He looked cornered and was ready to deal. "I see it in your eyes Corey, you realize you got me to fold top pair and you're right. Let's take these things one at a time. Deer woman first." Those were poker terms, and I didn't get the reference, but I understood the implication, so I waited to hear his deal.

First, I'd give him the basic information. "I was in the hotel and had the dream where a Deer Woman attacks unfortunate men. I broke out of the dream, fought her and when she couldn't break my circle, she killed herself."

"How did you break out of the dream?" asked Nicole.

Heat rose to my face, and I would not admit it in front of Rebecca.

"Not as important. She killed herself and you were in self-defense?" He asked.

"One hundred percent."

"That is important. I need to report this since the areas are up in arms." He picked up his phone. "Nathan, call an emergency meeting about the power surge last night. Tell them it's solved and good news." He hung up the phone and looked at me again. "Talking to priests?"

"I stayed in the hotel to follow my training for hiding in plain sight. They were scoping out the breakfast bar."

"Good. What happened?"

"They were looking for someone to slip up, so I had breakfast with the cardinal who had a rifle stock sticking through his cassock."

"You talked to priests when they were looking for you?" Rebecca wasn't up to date on what I did... well, Nicole and I did.

"How else do I gather information?"

"Don said you had nerves of steel. Excellent job." Preacher Jon's praise seemed honest. "Look, we need you in Grandpa Don's role."

"Bishop Pedrotti is attacking me and can track me somehow. I'm worthless until I take him out."

Preacher Jon shook his head. "No, the threat to Atlanta and the world is the most important item."

I fought the anger welling up inside me. "When I look around the table, I am the primary target. Nicole and Rachel are next, and finally Nathan. Without the four of us, nothing else matters. I am the front-line defender of the last of the druids."

He leaned in and smiled. "We learned Bishop Pedrotti is the current enemy, and the future threat is a monsignor coming to cast a spell during Winter Solstice, which will destroy Atlanta and eventually the world. We need to focus on the entire story."

"I'd like to point out that Bishop Pedrotti sent a free gargoyle after me," I turned to Rachel, "that would have killed me without this wonderful woman arriving. Then he directed a Deer Woman right to me. They could never target me before. I will not be alive for Winter Solstice if I don't take him out. If I die, Rachel and Nicole are fighting him off without help, and you'll have to kill me to allow that. No one is going after these two while I live."

"The Deer Woman. That's the danger I dreamed of where Rebecca saved you." Exclaimed Rachel. "You must have broken out of her sex trap by desiring Rebecca."

Heat filled my face, and I looked at my plate.

"Which is why you didn't want to answer the question earlier. Everyone, pretend my autistic mouth stayed shut." Rachel tucked her head into my chest. I rubbed her back. She wasn't trying to hurt me. I was just embarrassed.

It would only make things worse by staying. "Preacher Jon, we can talk again after I take out Bishop Pedrotti."

"Please take over the territory pole, Corey. It's causing issues that Don's signal is fading."

I gave him the thumbs up.

Stormy walked over with our bill and Preacher Jon took it. I said goodbye to Preacher Jon and Rebecca. I hugged Nicole and whispered; 'he suspects you.' Rachel jumped up and hugged me till I nearly lost my breath. Once I breathed, I asked, "Will you be at the cabin tonight?"

Rachel released her grip. "Go to your house for two days. We'll have a lot of cabin time coming up."

Made sense. I altered my mind to drive to my house. I had three properties: my house, the one I bought with the insurance money in high school, then the Trailer in Buford, and the cabin in the mountains. The trailer was the only one I didn't like, and I used it for hiding and emergencies.

Nicole pushed her chair out. "Rebecca, drive my car back, please." Keys hit the table behind me and as I walked out the door, Nicole ran forward and grabbed my hand. "I'm coming with you."

Unsure what her goal was, I held the passenger door open. She sat in the seat with the shoe box and her purse in her lap.

I got back in the car and put my seatbelt on and started the car up and pulled out. "Okay, why are we riding out together?"

"A lot of reasons. Grandpa didn't know what was going on with you and I. This keeps him guessing and can't focus on wearing me down with questions. Second, you and I are doing the same thing. We are loners and are going after the same person. Bishop Pedrotti used to be Priest Pedrotti. Priest Pedrotti is the priest who killed my parents."

Wow. That was a revelation. I pulled onto the highway towards Georgia, and I barely hung on to the steering wheel. That was big. "So, we are loners working together?"

"Not together. I don't fight and you don't spy. When you need info, you come to me. When I need protection, I come to you."

"Okay. We are going after Pedrotti and share skills."

"How do you feel if we pretended to date as a cover?"

That was a scary question. Thirty minutes ago, I would have jumped at this, but now I was confused. I couldn't pretend now because I needed to deal with this.

"Me too."

"I said nothing."

"I can't turn off being an empath. But I am with you. I did not realize that kiss was going to be like that. Wait." She took a deep breath.

"You know my friend Wesley has crushed on Rachel. Well, he started crushing on her in middle school, when I started crushing on you. We both still are. Every pore of my being wanted that kiss to go like that."

That was a lot to deal with it. "Okay, I'm throwing stuff out now because my brain cannot organize my thoughts. Miles almost died because he cannot keep up with the training. It makes me sick to risk Rachel with me, but we can't function without each other. Plus, she's a better fighter than I am. Even so, only I can banish gargoyles, only I should be at risk. I can hide in the woods and go deep. That's why I'm a loner."

"What do you think about dating me?" She turned and looked right at me.

"I wish I knew, but I'm confused now, and I can't think about complex things without a connection to Earth."

"That's fair. I'll tell people we're confused and don't know what to do."

"Wait, that's the truth," I joked.

We joked about light topics for the ride home.

Once home, I got out bear pelt and a couple of deer pelts and put them on my patio. Animals died all the time, and it was a remembrance to them when I used their pelts instead of letting them rot.

I would set up a bunch of pelts to sleep on next to my fire pit. I quickly threw them back in the waterproof container in the morning and pulled them out when I slept outside.

"You can set up in any bedroom. I have to sleep out here." She nodded and went into a spare bedroom. I threw my clothes off and slept outside. I was tired, my muscles cramped, and confusion ripped through my head. But a night connecting with Earth would do wonders.

Chapter 12—Fighting Practice

In the middle of the night, Rachel pulled shorts onto my legs. I helped pull them up, because this is how she joined me to snuggle unannounced. She'd put shorts on me and then snuggle with me. Her body curled up to mine, and I fell back asleep, complete with Rachel. We didn't do nudity around each other. If I'd have known she was coming, I'd have left them on.

Light pierced through my eyelids.

"Should I feel jealous?" asked Nicole.

Rachel's arm rolled over me as I rolled over. The sun was out. My body rejoiced at the night's connection to Earth, and snuggling with Rachel certainly helped. "What time is it?"

"Almost eight," said Nicole.

"I'm surprised it wasn't three of us snuggling after yesterday," said Rachel with a yawn.

"Rachel, you know better than that," I said.

"I saw the kiss," she replied.

"That's the problem," said Nicole. "It caught us both off guard."

"Well, if you two wanted to give Grandpa and Nathan a ton of work, and confuse the hell out of them, good job."

After a night outside, my arm had healed considerably from the first day, and the stitches were gone. "I'm going to shower and then I'll cook for us. The plan to be a loner did pretty well for its first week, being the busiest week in years for gargoyles."

"I don't believe anyone has stood up to him before," said Nicole as she plopped into one of the heavy Adirondack chairs.

"Not even Old Donnie?" Old Donnie would stand up to a rock if he felt justified.

"No one under one hundred years old and Grandpa Don never showed up to a meeting with his combat face." Nicole tried to stare me down.

I rolled my eyes and strolled back to shower. After patting my wound dry from my shower, I put antibiotic cream on it just in case. I stripped my bed, the guest room bed and my laundry and threw it in the laundry room and started a load. Then I grabbed eggs and sausage and rejoined the sisters.

My patio was large, and Rachel helped me install a large wood-fire grill and a few hand-carved wooden Adirondacks with chairs around the edges. I also kept a work desk next to my favorite chair. The stones were flat, and I had a ten-by-ten section to work out and practice karate. If I wasn't in the woods or the cabin, this was my favorite place to be. It was unfortunate that my presence turned an acre or two around me into a beautiful landscape, which gave me away.

I kept my dumbbells, throwing knives, and spare weapons out here in a covered but open storage. I rarely got lazy, but the reminders of weights and weapons reminded me I'd fight gargoyles and that spurred me to action.

Tiberius joined us and hung out, eating a piece of sausage with us. He perched on his favorite part of the railing next to the grill.

"I'm pulling out food for the afternoon. You're going to host a cookout," said Nicole.

"Anyone I know?" I joked.

"Nathan, Rebecca, Wesley, and the three of us." She gave me a wicked wink and said, "You looked trapped. Can you turn a trap around on someone?"

What a weird thing to say. "If I wanted to, I have no problem walking into a trap."

We ate and Rachel and I moved into weapons practice. We put a sheath on my arm for a bit of protection. "You work out to get a good lather and put your shoes on. Nicole, please tape me up while you ogle him."

I ignored the teasing between the two sisters and grabbed my dumbbells. Rachel liked me to exhaust my muscles when she trained me so she could keep watch on my form.

I had nearly an acre in my backyard and only about a third of it was grass. I had a pleasant wave shape around my patio before the rest of the backyard had bushes, flowers, and trees. Next to the trees near the right side of my property, I had a pull-up bar and wooden braces. I carried the padded bench, water bottle, and my dumbbells and worked out over there.

Rachel joined me and got in her work out as well. She had so little competition in her that she never tried to one up me or compete with how much she could lift. She strived for her best. I helped her get her best, and she helped me to get my best. With Miles, it was different. We'd yell at each other, compete for pullups, pushups, or repetitions. We tried to get each other to our best, but it was vastly different. I liked both methods with the correct person.

Once we were sore, Nicole brought us more water and workout shakes. Rachel made me put on shoes after we put away the workout gear. Today was more important for my fighting practice. I missed working the previous week because of my arm and the crazy schedule, but it was time. The form of karate Old Donnie taught me had twenty-five stances, forty blocks, and one hundred and nine strikes between arms and legs.

I received a hard lesson one day from The Tribe. Old Donnie said, *you can take a punch and you're tough. Yeah, you exercise and aren't afraid to mix it up. Yeah, you have good instincts. But, if you come up with a similar opponent, it's training that will win. Today we'll see how many people there are like that.*

The beatings I took that day in the ring set the lesson hard in my head. Besides learning, I'd never want to make The Tribe mad—back then I learned I wasn't the toughest guy. I realized I'd finish the gauntlet now, but it's only because of the last three years of training.

I grabbed my tonfa and sauntered to the other side of the patio, near the spare bedroom window, and took my first stance. "Okay, set," I called out.

Rachel grabbed her staff first to give her the most options to attack me. I kept on with tonfa because I couldn't learn anymore weapons. It was like my brain was full.

After twenty minutes, we took a break and ripped off my shirt and revealed my sweaty torso.

"Look at those muscles pop," teased Rachel.

"I've been cutting for your contest. Hope you appreciate the effort." I winked.

"Hey guys, I just watched how much better Rachel is than Corey with his shoes on. Can I check out how Earth Power affects him? I rarely get to see that."

I kicked off my shoes and wiped my arms and tonfa. As Earth Power surged through me, I felt my arms recover enough to fight again. Rachel put down her staff and picked up lighter weapons. Her arms and shoulders were popping, and her staff swings were too slow to challenge me with Earth Power.

She engaged me with her training kama first. She loved the sickle-like weapon and when she wasn't tired, the weapons moved so fast in her hands it was difficult to follow.

As we danced around the yard, my brain considered dating Nicole. It wasn't the kiss that had me shook up, well it was, but it was the kiss that revealed I thought of her as a woman after finding out how competent and driven she was. Within a few minutes, she changed from little Nicole, who attended college, to Nicole, the woman who was intelligent, driven, competent, and fighting for the same cause as I am.

Wood clacked, and our feet danced over the grass. What bothered me is now I didn't think about dating. My mental images were about marriage and kids. What if this was a rebound from Rebecca? If my being messed up over Rebecca caused me to lose Nicole; I doubt I'd forgive myself. I peeked a glance at her, and the sun hit her hair and it lightened the area in the back and it looked nice. There was a bronze color, the sun reflected. The further she looked from Rachel was good, but the sun making her hair light up looked nice.

Rachel kicked my legs out from under me. "Dreaming about my sister?" Sweat had soaked her shirt and shorts. Drops landed on me as she stood over me, grinning.

That was stupid. I needed to engage her in conversation if my mind wandered through the stances, strikes, and blocks. "I was wondering why you haven't dated recently. It helps both of us when you're in a happy relationship."

I recovered as she backed up and picked up her tonfa. "How does it help you other than distracting me?" Tonfa wood clacked on tonfa wood as she pressed and tried to get me off balance, but I was more aware now.

"I swear that when you dated Steven, and I dated Tiffany, when we'd snuggle, it was like we could even heal each other."

Her attacks became fast and furious. She had a pleasant relationship with Steven and still talked to him sometimes and didn't understand why it was a sore spot, but I figured she'd given me a lot of grief, so I pressed.

"I want you to be happy and satisfied and if you dated again, it would help." Earth Power was all that kept me blocking her rapid attacks. She didn't have Earth Power and got tired.

She moved her feet too slowly, and I did a sweep and took her to the ground and pinned her before she recovered. "Why is giving

Wesley a chance such a big deal? Is it him and you'd rather date some-one else?"

She let go of her tonfa. "Wesley is great. I wouldn't make the best of girlfriends."

"You better have a real good explanation if you think you're get-ting off the ground today."

"I shouldn't have fought you when I was tired, and you had Earth Power." She struggled, but she taught me pins too well.

"Maybe it was fate because you just said the dumbest thing either of us has ever said."

"Corey, I need help navigating life. You pick up so much. It's not bad with you since you need help with engines and fighting. No one else needs that."

"That has little or nothing to do with being a girlfriend. Treating him nice and being happy to see him are the most important items. Plus, you'll always have me to help. My week away from you gave me the shakes, and I made mistakes everywhere without you."

"You got shakes too?" Sweat poured off her forehead into her hair.

"Yes. In fact, I had to put stuff in the bathrobe I bought you and hug it to go to sleep." We were both too tired to lie, and these mo-ments got raw honesty.

"I came to your house and slept in your bed to smell you."

I knew she knew better, but she may have convinced herself when I wasn't around. "Wesley has known you and Nicole since high school. He must have learned part of this. If your relationship gets serious, explain it to him. If it's a deal breaker, we'll find someone else for you, but dammit Rachel, you need to be happy."

She smiled and tears rolled out of her eyes.

I rolled onto the grass and hugged her. She pushed me over and got on top of me. "Turnabout. Why aren't you dating Nicole?

"I can answer that," said Nicole. "You two finish with the strangest practice moves."

"How can you answer that?" asked Rachel.

She pointed to herself. "Empath. He's not thinking about dating me. He's scared since he is imagining us married, and is worried I'd be a rebound from Rebecca, and doesn't want to lose the chance to marry me."

Rachel's eyes got wide when she stared at me, and I deflated. My secrets and fears were out. "Wow. My little Corey is growing up. I guess if you're considering Nicole for marriage, I can give dating Wesley a shot."

"Do you two have breakthroughs like this when you practice?"

"Sometimes," said Rachel. She grinned and helped me stand. "Since you're on a roll with friendship, why don't you address the Miles situation? It hurts."

She was right, and this was my responsibility as a friend. "Okay. It's my job."

"Well, I'll cut the tape off Rachel because Corey has a haircut in an hour and needs to shower and change. Rebecca is bringing over your new clothes, Corey. I picked them out. Your ratty jeans need to go unless you're in the woods."

"Hair cut?" I grabbed my hair. "I like my hair."

"Don't worry, it'll stay long. Plus, I'm getting more of the bronze highlights you ogled."

I showered, dressed, did a bit more laundry, took out the trash, and walked outside with Nicole and met Rebecca, who drove in with Nicole's car.

Rachel came out and said, "Toss me your keys. I'm changing out your car and we finally found another Mustang convertible with a shaker hood scoop. We also need to ride our new bikes together. You've not ridden yours yet."

"The 'stang is a manual transmission, right?"

"Of course. Convertible, GT, light bar, and competition orange. I can't wait to get my hands on the engine."

"No more sub ten second cars." I held up my hands and remembered the three oh two from college she put over a thousand horsepower in. I never got the car out of third gear before I totaled it.

"Wimp. You roll one car and put the three of us in the hospital a few days and you lose your nerve."

I laughed. "That wreck scared me straight."

"I'll ride with Rachel," said Rebecca. "I'd like a last ride in Corey's convertible."

That was a weird comment, but I got into Nicole's car, and we drove to the hair stylist to make sure we'd return for the cookout I was going to host. Sitting in the passenger seat, I turned to talk to Nicole, but it gave me a chance to scope her out while she drove.

She drove confidently and with no aggression. Others cut in front of her without getting mad and drove pretty close to the speed limit the whole way. We talked comfortably when the car slowed enough to talk, but never turned around and kept both hands on the steering wheel. We couldn't be more opposite as drivers except for our confidence. She looked up and her blue eyes scanned the road and mirrors with confidence and her dark brown hair showed off those bronze highlights I enjoyed noticing earlier.

Her red cotton dress had a flowered pattern with buttons that spiraled around, that stopped just below her knees. Her white heals didn't hinder her driving or walking at all. Somehow, as long as I knew her, all of her dresses, skirts, and shoes were pretty.

She wore a little makeup around her eyes and a few earrings. I'd seen her with a few styles of makeup and whatever she decided always was a good choice. Her lips and nails were bright red now and for the first time, I imagined us standing side by side and realized she was pretty.

"You need to think of something else. No one has ever scoped me out as thoroughly as you've done the past ten minutes."

How did I forget she was an empath? I looked up at the sky and thought through strategies to fight a snake-hunter. First was the strategy to create a circle, but if I didn't have one up, I was going to take a beating. Gashes, broken ribs and a broken arm all could be acceptable. A combat knife in my right hand and a tonfa in my left could keep close defense.

"Oh my god, that's your backup? I'd rather you ogle me."

"Miles and Rachel are half joking when we say I either love or fight."

"Let me ask you a question, then. Your reason for not dating is as sweet of a reason I could have heard and I'm willing to wait you out. However, I need to tell people I have a boyfriend. Is that okay?"

"That may be a good way to test it out. For instance, if we double date to make sure Wesley and Rachel are comfortable—I'm fine. If you or I need a date for an event, we can consider each default dates. If you need to tell someone you have a boyfriend, I am there. How does that sound to you?"

"You realize who in particular I'm talking about?"

I thought for a bit. "Preacher Jon?"

"Yes. You heard the issue, but not what goes on behind the scenes. He specifically told Rachel not to worry about birth control, if she spent time with you."

"But we weren't sleeping together."

"He doesn't grasp how you haven't made the jump yet. But I'm considered the best chance to produce new druid babies."

"You're going to find it in my thoughts eventually, but I have a couple of fantasies that you ended up fitting into without a change."

"Ooh, salacious?" She grinned like her sister.

"Not those fantasies. Like I have one where I'd have a wife, and we'd sit on the front porch of the cabin and talk. I never had an image of her or what we'd talk about, but now when I picture the swing, I see you and I swinging on with glasses of tea."

"Oh my, I see it in your mind. That is nice."

"The big one, though, is I'm always going to need to shift between houses and I imagined I'd be married and separately Rachel would be married. Sometimes the four of us would site together so Rachel and I would be together."

"Oh my god, that's a sweet image too. Wait, there are kids in the room too." She smiled and tilted her head as she drove.

"Yeh, Old Donnie prepared me how I'd be raising the next generation of druids if something happened to him. But the kids just showed up in the image when you showed up."

She pulled into the shopping center and we got out and grabbed my hand while we walked into the hair place.

Chapter 13—Dance Practice

W e sat on my deck and I fired up my wood-burning grill. With my new haircut and shave, I was wearing new clothes like I was civilized. Black jeans, boat shoes, and a shirt that had buttons that lined up all the way down the front.

I'd need to bring wood from the cabin soon, but I no longer had a truck. Old Donnie and I drove a cord of wood here and it was over half gone.

I couldn't wear my thigh sheaf on the inside of pants anymore because the pockets didn't have a big hole to grab the knife. I'd keep my old clothes for camping and gargoyle banishings. Rebecca, Nicole, and Rachel kept doing double takes on me and turning away like they couldn't believe what a dork I looked like.

Nathan had gone to pick up Wesley at his place and we would be back soon.

All of my muscles were sore. Rachel and I slumped as if we melted in the Adirondack chairs. Rebecca and Nicole sat in the dining room chairs they had me carry outside. The ones I bought were metal and weighed nearly fifty pounds each.

"Have you gotten over the 'I'm a loner thing'?" asked Rebecca.

"Why would I get over it? It's the right choice."

"I'm not fighting, but you are keeping Rachel around you and you're dating or about to date Nicole. You use Nathan's phone and let the team buy your new car and motorcycle. It doesn't seem like you're a loner."

"I kicked off my boat shoes and put my feet on the patio so I could think."

"Shoes off time," declared Rachel. She kicked hers off, too.

"Put yours on sis, Wesley is coming over and you said you'd give it your best," said Nicole.

Rachel stuck her tongue out but slipped on her flats.

"This is difficult to explain, but as a loner, I decide for myself. I will help the team as much as I can and accept help. For instance, I go alone to banish gargoyles unless I ask for help. I decided with Rachel to stop Miles from going out with us and accepted the responsibility of addressing the situation with him."

"What if everyone did this? Like if Nicole was a loner, Rachel was a loner, Miles was a loner, Nathen was a loner, and everyone supported each other but did their own thing. It'd be chaos."

"Not if we communicated with each other."

"Your splitting hairs. Why are you going after the guy going after you instead of following Preacher Jon's plans?" she asked.

"This may be uncomfortable for you," I said.

"Until yesterday, I've been under house arrest for my protection. Make me uncomfortable."

"Okay. There are four people Bishop Pedrotti wants dead. I am primary. If he gets me, Old Donnie's legacy comes next. Rachel, Nicole, and Nathan."

"Preacher Jon will protect us to the point he is doing his job. He only needs one of us to produce the next generation of druids."

"He told me to not take birth control and if Corey and I became lovers, he'd be happy," said Rachel.

"Do you know Nicole's powers?" I pointed to Nicole to make sure I had Nicole's attention.

"Empathy?" She looked at Nicole.

"She can tell you if I'm lying. Nicole, please Tell Rebecca if what I am saying is the truth."

Nicole gave me a thumbs up and sat next to Rebecca, and the two of them stared at me.

"While I was in New Hampshire, a little girl who sees the future wanted to watch me banish a gargoyle. Well, she told me three things."

"The first is the world would be saved if you could banish gargoyles," said Rebecca. "Preacher Jon told me."

"The second thing she told me was the blonde girl who didn't come with me was needed to save the world." I waited for that to sink in.

"He's telling the truth," said Nicole. "He remembers it clearly and I see it playing out in his head."

"Now, I kept that secret from Preacher Jon, because the second I said that, you become a piece on his playing board. Now, knowing you have to be there to defeat the church, how do you feel about me making it a priority to be there with you?"

Her face turned pale.

"Nicole, catch her." When I saw her wavering, I jumped to catch her.

"I'm okay. I'm okay. Could I get cold water?" Color returned to her face, but that was scary.

Guilt hit me because I laid it on heavy. I ran into the house and got water with ice and brought it out. When I came out and handed it to her, she was leaning back. "Sorry, I guess I should have been more diplomatic."

"No. It isn't you. You brought up memories and I don't need Nicole to tell me you are telling the truth. Thank you for keeping it between us. I don't know if I can do anything when the time comes."

"The third thing isn't about me, is it?" asked Rachel.

"It might be. The third thing is, she said, I and other girls would buy her ice cream."

"I have to save the world and Rachel gets to go out for ice cream?" exclaimed Rebecca. She smiled and recovered, and it was a relief to see her joke.

"Hey, I have to do both and who knows if I'll keep my 'V' if I eat ice cream!" I joked.

Rachel stood. "That's the threat. You and I are destined to lose our 'V's. She put her hands just under her abs where the V-shaped muscles went downward.

We all sat and laughed as Wesley and Nathan walked into the house. I watched them walk past the kitchen window as they headed to the sliding glass door that led to my patio.

"It's good to hear laughter. I thought we'd walk into a big melodramatic snooze fest," joked Nathan. He carried out the meat on a platter someone else had prepared. "I'll grill today. From what I hear, you cook every day, Corey."

"By all means. Today's workout turned me to spaghetti." I stood up and shook Wesley's hand. His big smile, soft body, and attempt at a firm handshake reminded me of him in high school. I was there to meet Haley when the school bus rolled into the school from a contest the Matheletes had that was the same weekend as my track regionals. He had the same smile, and I shook his hand then after he had his picture taken with a trophy. He had changed little except for the confidence in his eyes.

"The fire needs more wood, but we have good coals," said Nathan.

I pulled out wood and walked over to my weapons to get a knife for shaving.

"Man, this is a manly man's house," said Wesley. "Do you use those boards for target practice?"

I felt happy and picked up six knives. I turned, made sure no one was in the way, planted my forward foot towards the first target, and threw the knife. *Thunk!* With the same method, I hit four more targets. "I'm going to need new targets soon," I said and carried the last knife to the grill to shave thin starter onto the wood to get it started. I didn't need to look to know I hit the center of each target.

Rachel collected the thrown knives and put them back. "Don't be too impressed with him. He only is good with tonfa and knives."

Once the fire started, I turned around and saw Wesley, with his jaw dropped, staring at my backyard. "Are you okay Wesley?"

Tiberius flew in and landed on his favorite perch on the porch.

I walked the wood and the shavings over for the grill. "Could you cut a piece of meat for Tiberius? Set it on the railing and don't feed him."

"This isn't normal. No one can grow a back yard like this and tame a hawk. No one keeps those kinds of weapons and can throw like that. You're..." He stared at me like he was looking at a monster.

"Sit down Wesley. We'll be getting you up to speed, but you don't want to alarm Corey with mad deduction skills." Nicole grabbed his arm and pulled him back.

"He'll slobber over your lips like he did with Nicole," teased Rachel.

"With that out of the way," said Nathan while his voice cracked. "Let's talk about more important items. Wesley, we're bringing you in house about a supernatural threat we're fighting inside the church."

"We need to back up," said Wesley. "I'm lost."

I chimed in and planted my feet to connect with the Earth. "Wesley, I know you are a devout Catholic. When we say church, we aren't talking about people you interact with. We are talking about the Curia based in the Vatican. They have a contingent in Atlanta, and they are the ones directing everything we talk about."

"Good. A definition. That helps."

"I'm not up on a lot of this stuff either, so I bet my simple definitions may help. People who can use some type of magic or power have a designation called having the spark. Everyone with the spark either has a significant power or a power and a class. Class just means a magical job with more powers, like druid for me or hunter for Miles." I didn't mention I just learned all this from Dr. Kanoska a few days ago.

"Following so far."

"Okay. People with the spark have either a moderate amount of magic or a class with a lot."

"It's not that easy," said Nathan. "Grandpa Jon, the man you know as Preacher Jon, is just as strong as Corey, even though he only has a single power."

"The single powers are strong, but the key to remember is latent and Realized. The four of us are called Realized, because we use our powers."

"Yours is latent," added Nathan. "Hanging around Corey will probably bring out your power." Nathan rolled his eyes. "But you're here because Nicole and Corey dropped your name. We want to protect you, as you've been a family friend since you've been in diapers."

"So, you guys are Realized people with magic and are fighting the church?" asked Wesley.

"Exactly. Preacher Jon leads a Southeast area. I understand little here, but apparently the most powerful split the world into territories, and they each have different leaders, and most of them act like immature children."

"Not everything," said Nathan, flipping over the meat. "Wesley, this is obviously on the down low. But Corey is a druid and Nicole is an Empath. I need to know if Nicole and Corey are faking a relationship, and I want the advice of someone who knows them."

"Nicole, would you like to prove it?" asked Nathan.

"Here?" Exclaimed Rebecca.

I glared at Rebecca.

"Not like that," said Nicole. "I mean, I hope." She winked.

I sped up the Wesley and Rachel connection. "Wesley, will you go with Rachel on a double date with Nicole and I?"

"I uh, well does, uh Rachel want to?"

"Ask her."

I saw him steal himself and he looked at Rachel. "Rachel, would you go on a double date with me, Corey, and Nicole?"

Rachel was a trooper, and she said, "Wesley, I'd love to go on a date with you and if we need to drag those two along on the first date, we can do that." She gave him a smile, and I stepped towards Nicole.

"May I kiss you and you tell Nathan the image that comes to my mind when we kiss?"

She smiled, so I stood up. I cupped her head with both of my hands. I leaned forward and felt her warm breath hit my lips. We pressed together and her togue intertwined with mine. I pulled away reluctantly as I looked into her eyes.

She sat and had a tear in her eyes. "It's a new vision. We sat on the swing on the cabin's porch. I was pregnant, and we each held a toddler in our arms."

I sat down and I needed to slow with the kisses because my brain was moving too fast.

Wesley let out a whistle. "She's crushed on him since eighth grade, but yeah, that was like a movie kiss."

"Crap. That means Grandpa will set me up with an arranged marriage," said Nathan and he started handing out plates of food.

"See Rebecca, as a loner I have marching orders. I will practice for the karaoke contest tomorrow at Nicole and Rachel's house, then I'll go do my freelance work, I'll confront Miles, perform with Rachel in the Karaoke show, banish the next gargoyle, help Nathan find a girlfriend so he doesn't have an arranged marriage, and move forward on my main goal. No committee decisions are needed.

She shook her head at me. My stomach did a turn. Finding a new girl was supposed to help you forget about an old love. I hurt seeing Rebecca sad.

We had a fun cookout and kept everything light after that. Once everyone left, I pulled all the animal skins out of the locker and beat them with my wicker rug beater. Old Donnie gave this to me as a gift and it was an intertwined ratan Celtic circle and it was great for cleaning the skins.

Once I laid them out, I got to sleep on the patio fully engaged with Earth since Rachel and Nicole left for their place.

IN THE MIDDLE OF THE night, I woke in a sweat and had a panic attack about my packs. With no explanation, I couldn't go back to sleep, so I checked out the equipment load in my trunk. My eighty-pound pack was in the back, my large pack was in great shape, as was my day pack. The problem was my waist pack. My magnolia pod was missing. For me, this was the only thing that could erase a circle. Erasing a circle was fatal for the one who initialized the circle. Only I could create a magnolia seed pod strong enough to erase my circle, which is why I only ever had one.

This was an emergency.

I grabbed my sickle and folding wicker basket. At the magnolia tree in my front yard, the silver sickle cut the first pod, and I caught it in the basket. Then I cut seven healthy magnolia leaves the same way. I walked back to my trunk and pulled out twine I made from vine and without touching the pod, wrapped the pod in magnolia leaves completely and secured them. Everything got placed back into my waist pack.

Rachel never opened my packs, so someone stole the only method to break one of my circles from me. I searched through everything else item by item, and that was the only thing missing. I put everything back to the way it should be, closed the trunk, and looked in my new car. There was a rose on the armrest with a tiny card. It had a heart and Nicole's signature. That was sweet.

Some restless hours later, I showered, changed, grabbed a bite, and got into my car. I didn't get to enjoy my new car and drove there with my mind clouded. I knocked on the door and focused only on the practice. We all kept keys to each other's places, but I knocked at Miles' house when Miles moved in with Trish because, well, it was polite. I didn't barge in on Rachel, because while it was cool for her to walk in on me, walking in on two single women didn't seem appropriate.

Nicole opened the door, and I heard the shower in the back. "Oh Corey, come in. I took too long in the shower and Rachel is still finishing getting ready." Her hair was damp and styled and had not put on makeup. She had on pink shorts and a halter top and was barefoot.

"Hi Nicole, it's good to see you. I'll just pop into the practice area and stretch while you she gets ready." At that moment, I remembered the kisses. I needed to avoid kisses like that if I was to become a loner.

The door opened into a main room and a tv took up one wall across from a leather couch and two chairs. They bought four tables for the living room. Why four tables? I couldn't figure it out and I didn't want to ask. I walked into what most people would use as a dining room. This room's setup was a mini recording studio and a hard platform on top of the carpet for dance practice. The walls and ceilings had those foam pieces with triangles at distinct edges around to help mute the sound in and out.

"I'll give you even more details later, I promise." Nicole looked around and pulled a notebook out. "I was told not to track down my parent's killers, so I've been doing this on my own for eight years and one person I know is at the scene was Priest Pedrotti. When I heard Bishop Pedrotti was in charge, I tracked him and have a lot of information. When Nathan pinged me, that name being key to us, things came to a head. I promise I won't use my powers on you and will keep you in the loop."

I kneeled at a table and thumbed through the pages. They were a combination of notes, printouts, pictures, clippings from magazines, and newspapers. This was a tremendous revelation and all I could do was to protect Nicole, but part of that was emotional protection, too. "Okay, Nicole, you've done a lot here."

"I have ten of those notebooks. I keep them off the computer to hide this from Nathan."

"Ten?!" This impressed me. I'd need to spend a lot of time just trying to comprehend what she collected. "Holy crap. Nicole, you've done so much better than I could do, so let me help you. When you need support or backup, I promise to help you and keep this on the down-low."

Nicole beamed. *That's right, she's an empath.* "I will... and Corey, Thank you. Please treat me the same, so Rachel doesn't guess. I'm going to act like ditzy Nicole again."

"Oh, thank you for the rose."

She smiled and kissed me on the cheek and skipped to the back of the apartment.

"Corey," called Nicole. "We have an issue."

I jogged to the back and into Rachel's bedroom. She had little furniture. She had a king-sized bed we had snuggled in before and an armoire. The closet is where she kept her motorcycle gear and weapons. Her bathroom was plain as well.

"Our pants are so low for the contest, and the shirts are sleeveless. Nicole just waxed me, and now you need one."

"Nope."

"Why?" asked Rachel. "It's for the contest and you two are dating."

"I'll tell you, but it's salacious." They'd hear this story and it should end this silly talk.

"Back in May, Old Donnie and I had a week off. Rebecca and I were going to take a romantic trip, but before that, we waxed each other... everywhere."

"Corey!" exclaimed Rachel. "But your chest hair was gone until like October."

"Well, we liked it. You better tell no one that I enjoy the feeling. Rebecca and I waxed each other every five or six weeks when we could take four or five hours to... well, you know."

"Corey, I picked out pants to show off both of your muscular ab-domens. You don't want hair sticking out. Especially after we do your chest. Come on, strip," said Nicole.

"Please Corey?" asked Rachel. "I'll be in the shower."

Nicole and I were kind of dating. When Rachel left, I pulled my clothes off and lay on her bed. I tried to think of anything else except the other waxings. It didn't work. Nicole was beautiful and uncov-ered me as soon as I pulled the sheet over me.

"I need to see to wax it, silly." She pulled the sheet over me and sat on it. Nicole grabbed me and started slow strokes.

"What are you doing?" I whispered.

"Oh, it looks so lonely. I'm just playing with it." Nicole used her other hand and pulled the hair like she was judging the direction. Then she needed both hands to apply the wax.

Phew. That was over. I tried to think of anything except how good it felt. It was time to focus on the wax and forget about it—*right?*

I grabbed the headboard slats behind me for the first pull, and Nicole knew enough to get the hair with one tug. By now, my hair was used to waxing, and it wasn't nearly as long as the first time. When they finished, my armpits and moved to the hair on my stom-ach.

"Let me give you a gift," said Nicole.

I was about to say 'what' when I felt her tongue. I grasped the headboard with my other hand and there was no stopping.

A few minutes later, three things happened at once. I moaned, snapped the wooden slat of the headboard, and Rachel opened the bathroom door.

"Nicole!" exclaimed Rachel.

I bent my neck up to peer around, and Nicole held up an index finger.

"Corey?" Rachel exclaimed again. She had changed in the bathroom.

I put the slat down and pulled a pillow over my face.

"There," said Nicole. "Feel better?" She covered me with the sheets.

I lay there while Nicole patted my stomach.

"Corey, go rinse off," said Rachel.

I stood up. "Sorry about the slat." I pulled up my shorts under the sheets and ran to the bathroom to shower.

"Shower," said Rachel, pointing at the bathroom.

I showered, dried, and got dressed. I was more relaxed, but man, I was confused. With a bit of mortification, I walked into the dining room, and I wondered where I stood. I kicked off my shoes and stretched.

"Put these on and make sure I got the right size." Rachel's hair was still wet too, and she wore her workout clothes with cowboy boots. She handed me a matching black pair of boots.

I put the boots on, and they fit. "What's with the boots?" Luckily, we were ignoring what just happened because I had no explanation.

"I knew your shoe size too, sweetie," said Nicole.

I slipped them on. "They fit."

"Okay," said Nicole. She giggled and Rachel rolled her eyes. "Corey, you practice shirtless, so I pick out the right costume style."

"My lovely sister is helping us with costumes for the contest." Rachel wore a sleeveless woman's shirt from Old Donnie. A Rossington-Collins band shirt. I pulled my hair back into a ponytail to keep it from swinging.

"Nope, leave your hair down," said Nicole.

I removed the band and let my hair fall. Then I focused on Rachel's instructions.

We practiced singing, dance moves, and the choreography, which was a basic two-step and putting the flips and karate moves I was comfortable with. Not only could I not sing, but I couldn't dance either. Doing it in boots changed things slightly, but I managed the limited moves Rachel taught me fine once I learned to be more forceful with bending my feet.

"I'm going to be in the back doing work," said Nicole after a half hour. Both of them worked some city job inside the city. I knew little about jobs and city jobs, but they did what they called working from home a few days a week. Rachel had taken today off to practice with me.

The three of us ate a salad for lunch and practiced until dinner time, where Nicole baked dinner for us, while we practiced. When we finished, Rachel walked me out to my car. "Thank you so much for doing this contest with me, and you know—everything."

"No worries. We can keep earlier quiet," I asked.

Rachel blushed. "If you two weren't dating, I'd have words for you, but please be more discreet. Now go charge up in the woods before you confront Miles."

I was about to shut the car door when she yelled back, "no more sex with my sister in my bed!"

Chapter 14—Fey with your Friends

I drove to the cabin, and before doing anything else, my first task was to keep a promise to Preacher Jon. Replaying the discussion in my head, he was reasonable. First, it'd be a quick jaunt to the pole to take over the circle. I didn't have access to the spell to control the territory, but I could take over the pole and Old Donnie's spell.

Holding the rose from Nicole, I headed down the dirt road. The ground packed in over years of weather and not heavy use, and it felt good on my bare feet. White pines behind Virginia pines created a stadium seating pattern and told me I was close. The pole was off the roadway and hidden in thick brush at the bottom of mounds, all of which were hidden between trees. To take it over, I created a small circle around the pole.

I initialized the circle and saw it was empty. Old Donnie was gone, but something told me the Earth hadn't given up on him. There was just no proof.

I took ownership of the pole using my circle. Soon, my senses changed and I could experience everything supernatural and unnatural in my lands. The input overwhelmed me. I knew everything that walked in my lands, where and what was the intent. Well, not everything, just the unnatural and natural. I knew where every animal was, and if it was in distress or not, and whether the distress was natural. Blessedly, I could shut it off.

Then, I prepared a large circle around it. Around Atlanta, I kept about a dozen unused circles. I had one at the cabin, one at each house, one on our test area at the store. There was one on the nature trail, two in Stone Mountain Park, two on the silver comet trail, one in Piedmont Park, one on the Georgia Tech Campus, and one in Centennial Park. I added this new circle to my repertoire for emergency circles.

That done, I grabbed my waist pack and eighty-pound pack and sniffed the rose. This all started when I caught Nicole lying to me. I was barefoot and thinking clearly. Nicole was the only one who had access to my car, other than Rachel, when the Magnolia seed pod went missing. It couldn't be her... with her ability to detect emotions, thoughts, and lie. Oh no.

But why would she have done the gift earlier today? Even connected to Earth, nothing made sense. This is a time I wish I was smarter.

I got into my car and drove a few hours east into the mountains and found a good place to park. I planned to spend two nights in the mountains, so time was on my side. A tree fell and blocked a path and stream, which was ruining protected wildlife. I plugged the coordinates into my handheld gps and it said I had twelve hours of hiking and recommended two days. Because of my Earth Domain, if I was barefoot, my speed in the woods was incredible. Still, this was a way, and I had three to four hours in front of me.

Old Donnie gave my freelance setup gear to me. I had a box called a hotspot. It did some type of satellite thing, and my other stuff would work. My Tyler phone and freelance work pad were both connected to it. The work pad had a work button that would show a screen of work in my area if I had marked myself available. I liked to stay available because that's how search and rescue got a hold of me. The best part of search and rescue jobs was how The Tribe had many people in it I missed. The park service referred to them as VASAR. I got to work with Old Donnie's friends during those tasks like we were still close.

The hike was pleasant, and I barely broke a sweat since it was cool out. My pack weight was just north of eighty pounds with the axes, saw, and other equipment I carried. Animals ran alongside me for a few miles, but many didn't want to keep that pace up. This was power granted to me because of my Earth Domain, like talking to animals from the Animal Domain, or growing any plant to maturity from my Plant Domain.

One test I had before I was allowed to solo gargoyles was the Redneck Biathlon. They clocked me running up and down the mountainous forest at four-minute miles for ten hours. The hardest part was the eight targets I needed to shoot. Guns and I didn't get along until Rebecca helped me.

The trees were changing up here, and I loved the view. There wasn't much of a path most of the way, but using my Earth Domain, I didn't leave a trace and only a hunter or supernatural creature could track me. Clive told me he could track me by the scent of my blood, but he'd have to be within a mile or two of me, and not in the realm of black and white where it muted his vampire senses.

I found the fallen tree, and it was doozy. It's a shame the old tree fell. With the amount of work in front of me, it made sense for me to set up my campsite first, so I found a good place away from the path and set up a safe campsite.

The day was mostly over, so I removed everything man-made on me and fully connected with Earth, and pulled out my druid book to study. After a few hours of refreshing everything, I turned in and prepared to get up and start work at first light.

After a quick breakfast, I got to work on the tree. Since I was alone, I had to take smaller chunks off the tree, and while Earth Power would give me more endurance, I'd be getting a good workout today since I only used axes and saws.

I worked until lunch and cleared the stream first. Clouds overhead and the thickness of the canopy made the day darker than it should be. After putting up a couple of lanterns and splitting wood for my fire tonight, I kept working and finished clearing the path in time for dinner.

When I did jobs like this, people would ask me why I didn't bring a chainsaw up and do this quicker, but it just seemed wrong, and unless Rachel was with me, I couldn't always get those things to work. She made any engine work.

The system needed pictures of the unblocked stream and the hiking patch. The angles I took showed the foot clearance on each side of the path using the lantern light. I saved them for when I had cell service to post them.

With a small fire, I made one of those cruddy freeze-dried dinners. As hungry as I was, I polished off a dinner for two. Once my fire was embers, I climbed into my camping quilt and went out quickly.

I jolted up. My brain was fully engaged with Earth and a thought came through. Only Nicole could have taken my magnolia seed pod. My last thought was that it was strange no animals hung out with me while I worked.

It was pitch dark, yet I could see colors. I walked out of my shelter and saw a short person sitting on a rock. Peace coursed through me and I shook it off, while looking for a place for a circle.

"Whoa, calm down. You are strong. My name in Verenuala and I am from the Spring Fey Court and I come in peace."

I looked at this person as I walked over to a log he pointed to. He was about four feet tall, had a tall, pointed ears, and I couldn't tell if this was a man or a woman.

He kicked himself into a squat position onto the rock and peered around. "Please don't call me an elf. I should get over it, but I find the term offensive. It's like if I called your mentor a 'Yankee.'"

I sat on the log and noticed he had cleared it of debris. "I get it. How should I reference you?"

"Daione works."

"Deeneh?"

"Not too bad of a pronunciation. So, yes."

"Verenuala," I pronounced it slowly to say it correctly. "What do I do the honor of this visit?"

"I'm scoping you out for the Spring Court." He turned to me and watched me. "You've taken down a major Dark Fey and we are determining your worth."

"I'm glad you got me in full contact with the Earth. When I have my facilities and I study the books, I think of myself as the first bud of Spring with druids. We've had a thousand years of winter with hybrid druids keeping the promise of spring alive after the fall, where druids died and fell like leaves."

The Daoine slapped his knee, and grinned, and light came from his torso, and lit up a face that looked like a freshman guy in high school. "I like you. Tell me, if the court accepts you, do you have a choice for a bard?"

I thought and remembered bards were performers and singers. "Rachel. If you can, find us at a Cleave's Bar and Wings tomorrow night. We'll be singing together and you can check out how well she performs and how she even got me, hopefully, to be competent."

"It's a date, true druid. I will let you finish your night. Oh wait, two questions. What's your favorite tree where you live?"

"That's easy. I have a red maple at my house and a red maple behind my cabin. Woodrow likes the maple at the house and he stained the bark black. The one at the cabin is nearly one hundred feet tall and growing."

"The second, who was the lady you were with next to your normal friend?"

This was a tricky question, but I answered without a lot of details. "That's Nicole. Rachel's sister."

"Have a pleasant night." He stepped into a tree and disappeared.

I walked back into my shelter and slept until the light woke me. A quick breakfast let me consider the brief encounter last night. The Spring Fey court, from what I read, seemed a lot of fun and I hoped to see them again.

After strolling leisurely to my car, I drove home. The situation with Nicole weighed on me, but I promised Rachel I'd deal with the Miles situation. I showered, thinking through how I'd get through to Miles and decided the only method to get through two stubborn people was direct and, in their face, and deal with the consequences. This would lean on my friendship with Miles. I got into my new orange Mustang and drove to <u>Miles Away from Town.</u>

CAROL RAN OUT TO MEET me. Her mom Members Only jacket flew back as her white mom-tennis-shoes hit the pavement.

My mother, before she disappeared, worked afternoon and evening shifts and I needed to catch my breath before I walked home to cook dinner for Traci and Tracy, my younger brother and sister. Miles introduced me to his mother, and she instantly adopted me and would not let me walk home. She drove me home and began hugging me along with Miles.

Her minivan was the vehicle I went on my first date in. Miles, Trish, Haley, and I double dated and Carol drove us. She gave me advice about keeping my first girlfriend, Haley. When my house burned to the ground, and I had the death certificates of the others, she and Richard took me in. They just did, though I never asked.

Her husband Richard was a gadget guy. He was so happy to see me and show me gadgets. Half of them would fail with me, but he was always so happy whether they worked. *Hey Corey, check out new gear!* He fired up his barbeque sometimes and he, Miles, and I would sit and talk. I learned most of my grilling recipes from him.

Carol hugged me regardless of the situation, so I ran up and hugged her. I had never hugged much before meeting her and she refused to let me shy away from a hug. As much as my life turned out well because of her and Richard, if Carol wanted a hug, she was getting one.

"That is a sweet looking car."

"Rachel picked it out, but you know she was going to nail the choice."

"You're famished, young man. Come with me to my favorite new lunch place to talk."

I was hungry, but it wasn't weird, she knew. I think she'd known me for so long, she could read my face.

We walked into JennyF's Burgers, and I held the door open for Carol. They had a large rectangle counter with a grill behind it and a few stools. There were five tables and twenty chairs. I kept the door open as a delivery driver walked out with four large bags of food.

"I love this place. They don't use buns, they make a grilled cheese and then put the burger on that."

The smell of the fries mixed with the grill and I realized this would be a treat—not a healthy one, but a tasty one. Everything was red and white and the speakers played soft rock.

"Carol!" exclaimed a smiling woman behind the counter wearing an apron and her blonde hair in a net. "You didn't trade in Richard, did you?"

Both women laughed. "This is Corey, the young man I told you all about."

"Mary, come on out here. Carol brought in Corey."

"Another woman walked out with a pink dress and an apron with her brunette hair in a net."

"Wow Carol, they didn't make them like this when we were their age."

"Ladies, I'm going to get the usual, but what will you have, Corey?" asked Carol.

"I'm still cutting for the contest tomorrow, so I have to go easy."

"What's cutting?" asked the woman behind the counter.

"Reduced carbs to expose muscles." I lifted my shirt to show my abs. "It's for showing off where bulking is for putting on size."

"Let the man cut, Jen," said Mary. She playfully backhanded her friend on the arm.

We ordered and sat and Carol started off. "I'm glad you're confronting Miles. This has gone on too long and he shouldn't have gotten married without telling her."

So much going on behind my back recently shocked me. I half figured this was coming. "Okay. I'm not too bright and didn't even realize you knew about Miles. What do you know?"

She laughed. "Realized classes are hereditary and hunters, like Miles, skip a generation. I understood my kids would become hunters before I met Richard because my mother was one."

"Even little Ava?"

She chuckled. "*Little* Ava graduates high school this year. She is still latent, but that is normal. You and Miles becoming Realized at such a young age is unheard of."

So, she knew about me. "When did you learn about me?"

"When you and Miles became inseparable. We've learned those with the spark attract you. I hear has caused you some heartache recently."

"Rebecca doesn't have pow..." I didn't finish that sentence. "I'm pretty dumb."

"No. You are thoughtful, generous, and loving. None of that is dumb. Who else who couldn't sing would join a singing contest for a friend?"

"A dumb one?"

She punched me on the shoulder playfully.

Jen brought the food. "You come back after the contest. Mary, and I want to bet on how much you can eat."

I laughed, and Carol continued. "You need a trip to Alpharetta, but you need a good reason to attend and go with someone who thinks they're there for a good reason."

"Why?"

"The podcasters don't have enough visibility, but try to forget I asked you to go." She stirred her tea with the lemon in it.

"This is actually the least weird thing anyone said to me this month." I chuckled. "Let me ask you a question. Is there a way to protect me from empathy, strong ones?"

"There is a rumor the church is using them. One second." She typed something into her phone. "Do you have an immediate need?"

"I needed one yesterday, but I think I escaped."

She laughed. "So, how are you going to talk to Miles?" She began eating her sandwich.

"Confrontational. Trish and I are friends and I'm going to tell her about me. Then I will put Miles in a spot to blame me."

Her eyes became wide, and she swallowed her food with a drink. "Well, we have not tried that."

"Miles and I have a history that will let us overcome a fight that may happen. We actually rehearsed these scenarios in anger management classes."

"I hope it works. You can't take a beating with everything going on."

I looked at Carol and shook my head. "You didn't see the gargoyle fight. I don't need to stand on Earth to take Miles. That's how far he has fallen. Rachel and I agreed we aren't taking him out anymore until he can fight. I'd like to stay on Earth, because I can stop him without hurting him."

"Is it that bad?" She frowned.

I nodded and felt her sorrow with mine. "Remember, he can be in civilian shape and not in supernatural fighting shape."

"Let's go then."

We tossed our trash and walked across the parking lot. There was no one here in the middle of the afternoon on a workday. Cars passed on the road, but they'd need to slow down to see us. This was good, because I planned on a demonstration. I pulled the bag with the blanket out of the car.

Trish and Miles stood in the parking lot in front of the store. They had an area with dirt and grass for testing camping gear, and I psyched myself up. I jogged over and called out to them, "Miles, Trish."

"Hey, you two, talk," said Trish. "I need to go in."

"Please stay Trish," I said.

"Maybe later."

I put a commanding tone in my voice. "Trish, I have known you for eight years and I never once got in the middle of you and Miles. I never asked you for anything until now, and you need to stay and listen." This was strong, but I wanted zero chance they thought it was fake.

Trish turned around with her jaw dropped. Even Miles didn't talk to her like. I wanted to see Miles' face, but I stared at Trish.

I talked to the animals and called the birds in the area to me.

"Dude, what's going on?" Miles took a step towards me but stopped when I glared at him.

"I have something to say." I spat it out, but not in anger, in command. The difference the court ordered classes taught us. "Trish, I am a person who has what people call the spark, and I am Realized. I am a druid and can cast magic and use it to banish gargoyles in order to save the world."

Without looking at her face, I raised my hand to the sky in an unnecessary show. Pigeons and crows landed all around us and I called all the mammals to listen to me in peace. Dogs, cats, squirrels, raccoons all came and surrounded us.

"Miles, why aren't you freaking out?" asked Trish. She was freaking out. "You knew."

"Trish." I raised my voice to get her attention. "This looks like a suitable area for a brand-new honeysuckle bush." I cast a minor spell from my Plant Domain and created one next to the large rock.

"What the hell! Corey? Miles? Carol? Why am I the only one surprised?"

"Trish, this is obviously a secret." I paused to let it sink in and then protected Miles. "If someone kept my secret to help me, I want to free them." I released all the animals and left them with the message. *Thank you. Evil comes soon, and I may need help.*

Thirty birds and an equal number of animals ran back to what they were doing.

"Dude," said Miles. He hugged his shaking wife. "You could have done that with a bit more subtlety." He took a step towards me, stopped, and took ten deep breaths.

Thank goodness for the anger management classes. I kept my mouth shut and waited.

When he finished and had control of himself, he asked, "Why now?"

"Rachel and I decided that until you get in better shape, we aren't bringing you for your protection, but even though we have an emergency over the next two months, I will go in shorthanded rather than throw your life away."

"Can I sit?" Trish was shaking and staring at me and her husband.

Carol put her arms around Trish. "Corey, if you're through, I'm going to help Trish sit back and get her some water. Miles, you and Corey should talk."

"Thank you, Carol. Trish, I wish I was smart enough to convince you without showing you a couple of my minor powers." I emphasized minor, so she'd understand what she was dealing with.

"Dude. I said I would not tell Trish about me."

This was time to give him an out of the confrontation. Though I was splitting hairs, I didn't want to show Miles how far his fighting skills have fallen. "I respect that. I told her about me—not you."

His face squirreled up, and I had him thinking instead of arguing. My bar fighting skills told me to avoid a fight I needed to keep him thinking. "Look, I failed at being a loner. Completely and utterly failed. Things attack me in my dreams. A Bishop is trying to steal my soul, and witches across the country are talking about me."

"Was that you the other night? The power that shook the Southeast?"

"Yes. A deer woman attacked me."

"The mountain succubus? Shoot fire, Corey."

"Dude, you joke about how I only understand how to do two things: love and fight. Well, you're right and it ain't enough. I need help and you've always been there. I need you back."

He looked down and shook his head. "How far off am I?"

"I checked with Rachel and she agrees. I don't even need my shoes off to kick your ass now."

"Crap." He shook his head while looking down. No demonstration was necessary and my hopes lifted.

"Look. You can blame keeping the secret on me. I set the excuse up. Your marriage needs to stay sound. I will do anything you want to help her get past this shock."

"Man... Corey, if you treated girls you date like you treated Rachel, you'd know I couldn't do that. Look, I've got some work to do with Trish and I guess I should thank you, since I don't have to worry about how to broach the subject."

"Wait, do you know what my problem with women is?"

"The world knows. You treat girlfriends as a critical piece of your life and not as a partner. Your women get put on a pedestal so they won't break and... well, hell, after what you just did, I can be brutal. You are still shocked at being abandoned by your family. You're scared to be abandoned again."

I had nothing to say and tried to understand what he said.

"Well, the look on your face means I at least got you back a little for this. Tell you what, let me handle Trish now and I'll talk to you after Rachel's contest. Because even if I decide to kill you, I ain't ruining Rachel's night." He laughed, and I ran and hugged him.

"Oh, here. It's not the best time, but I bought you a sheepskin blanket for the baby while I was in New Hampshire."

"Dude. You are all over the place."

"You have no idea. I'm going to see Rachel now," I said, and I said one more thing. "By the way, if you see a four-foot-tall young dude with pointed ears, do not use the e-word. They're called Daoine."

"Deeneh? Does the e-word rhyme with 'shelf'?"

I gave him two thumbs up.

"It sure does," said Richard. "They're good people." He ran to us. "Hey Corey, check this out." His big grin when he had new gadgets spread over his face and instantly made me think of good times. I almost expected to be sitting there with one of his gadgets.

He pulled out a hole pounce looking device and *kerchunked* my ear lobe. He twisted a piece of metal in there. It hurt, but I stood and took it.

He looked at it and nodded. "When you focus on the earring, think of topics you want blocked. Things like attack moves or sneaking."

I could sense the earring like I sensed my torc. "Wow, thanks Richard. I don't know how I can pay you back for this."

"Pay me back? My best tester? I had access to a druid to test magical items. Every time you held one that didn't work, you saved me a week of testing. Every item you held that worked, you saved me a month. You saved me at least ten years towards life's work."

I looked at Richard and did not know what to say. "Did I walk through life this clueless?"

"Clueless? Corey, you are like your friend Rachel, only to a lesser extent. If it's important to a druid, you're smart. If it's not, your brain moves on to the next thing. Don't beat yourself up for focusing on what's important."

"Dude, beat yourself up. Someone needs to," joked Miles. "Seriously though, you're fighting church empaths?" asked Miles.

I focused on the earrings and blocked my suspicions of Nicole. "Unfortunately, yes." I thought a little more and blocked all thoughts of magnolia trees and seed pods, theft, the earring, and empaths.

Richard put his arm around me. "Corey, I'm realized and I discover and identify lost magic items. I don't have a lot for a druid, but when you come back, check with me about your torc."

"I will, and thank you." The list of people I needed in my life kept growing.

As I got in my car, Miles yelled back, "by the way, next time ask all the birds to use the bathroom elsewhere."

Chapter 15—The Karaoke Show

While driving, I thought about how Miles told me my problem with women was obvious. I should have been elated he would talk to Trish, and he and I did not fight. A bishop who wants me dead should scare me more, but all I could think about was how I treated women like objects on pedestals, and I barely knew what that meant.

The front of the cabin had room for three cars. An SUV was already up there. I pulled to the left of the SUV, since Rachel was on her way.

We stained the deck two years ago and replaced a few bad boards, but the color seemed dark now. I used to like to sit out front here, but the more my powers had grown, the more I liked to be in the back of the cabin and saunter into the woods.

My messenger bag got tossed on the couch and I walked back to the front porch and sat on the swinging seat for two. I used to imagine I'd have a girl, and we'd sit on the porch like this. We'd drink tea and I couldn't for this life of me imagine what we would have talked about. Did I just imagine some placeholder out here as part of my life without thinking I'd change my life for her?

I focused on the earring and added the magnolia pod, searching my car, anything with a fight, and sudden movements to the earring. I can't believe I had to worry about this. Was I suspecting Nicole because I was pushing her away? Was this all overkill?

This was depressing. To stop myself from thinking, I jogged around the back and chopped wood. I ripped my shirt off when I began to sweat and let the cold air chill me so I'd work harder and faster. My brain needed to be occupied.

When my muscles nearly gave out, I started the fire for the outdoor bed and chipped the small ice on top of the water in the trough. I chopped until my arms ached and even Earth Power would not let me continue. I moved coals around the trough and under the bed and built up the fire again.

Before I got the oven fire going, I cleaned the stove and started the dinner that I promised Rachel. Rachel wasn't here yet, and I didn't have the strength to do any more. I used my fire starter and ignited the fire. While I watched the flames, the comment about being abandoned by my family came to me, and I remembered the aftermath of the house fire.

> *Miles helped me when I said I didn't believe everyone died in the fire and he drove me to the backside of my old house. The police said no one could go in because my mother, Traci, and Tracy burned inside.*
>
> *I snuck inside after midnight, and every room except my bedroom was empty. Not only no bodies, but no furniture remnants, nothing. The house was dangerous and falling down, but I saw enough. No one died in that fire and my mother, along with my brother and sister, faked their deaths, but left me to fend for myself.*
>
> *The police made me give it up and told me bad people were watching.*

Yeah. The therapist was correct when he said I had abandonment issues, but dammit, it sure seemed I had a reason. Why would my family fake their deaths and leave me? Tracy and Traci would start high school next year.

To make sure the bed stayed warm enough for Rachel and me, I added wood to the fire and pushed most of the coals under the bed. After putting a few more coals around the trough, I threw my clothes in and plunged in. After washing the laundry, I hung them on the wood next to the fire to dry, then scrubbed my body with the soap while sitting in the cold water. I took the worst of the chill off but left it cold so I'd stop thinking.

I left the clothes drying but wore spare shorts and a shirt, for Rachel's sake.

A new motorcycle rode up, so I finished cooking dinner for her. I walked outside, and the rain sprinkled on a blue and white GSXR.

"Sweet ride."

"I know, right? You have a F800GT in your carport for you.

I should have been excited and want to go ride it, but I was still thinking about Miles' comment.

"What's wrong?"

I put a smile on my face and put a plate on the table. There was no sense in burdening her the night before a big day. "I confronted Miles and Trish."

Her hair was a mess, and streaks of oil covered her face and hands. "Oh wow, spill it."

I led her to the sink and washed her hands. "It went okay. Trish needed Carol and Miles to support her and I wasn't asked to help."

"Oh Corey. You did what you needed to." She dried her hands while I washed the streaks off her face.

"Miles said, if he was going to confront me, it would be after tomorrow night, because he would not let this ruin your big day."

She smiled. "Well, I can help you two. Could you warm up water in the trough so I can get a quick wash before we sleep?"

After dumping the old water and refilling the trough, I put more wood on the fire and prepared the bed after moving coals over to the trough to heat it.

"Wait inside and I'll call you when I'm done."

I cooked her dinner while she washed and tried to get my head clear. I focused on Rachel's contest, but luckily her bath was quick in the chilled water.

"One second. I've been waiting for so long to wear the new pajamas." She ran into the bedroom to change. "We needed to hand wash these in cold. I prefer the shorter ones that the long pants and long sleeve shirt for comfort."

She walked out and wore the jacket open and, as I hoped, it was like a sports bra and shorts. "That looks great on you," I said.

"It's almost sexy, but it is comfy. Why did you choose hot pink?"

"You said you wanted to be less tomboy, and I promised to help."

She wrapped herself around me, and life felt better. We climbed into the heated bed and fell asleep in each other's arms.

"AREN'T YOU TWO COZY?" said Nicole.

"I rolled over from a deep sleep and realized Rachel and I had been so tired, we stayed entangled in each other's arms and legs."

"Hi Nicole, what time is it?" asked Rachel.

"Almost eight."

"We were tired," said Rachel and she rolled out of bed first to beat me to the bathroom.

"Just throw on something quick. You need to try on your outfit so I can tailor it," continued Rachel's younger sister. "Wait, a second. Do you have an earring?"

"Do you like it?"

"You have a big gold heart on your ear."

"Let me see," said Rachel.

"Is it big? I was too scared to check it out when I got it."

Nicole rummaged in her purse and when I peeked, I saw the unmistakable color of a magnolia leaf. "Here, look."

"It's not bad," said Rachel. "It's the heart that threw me."

"I want to be more of a lover than a fighter." The earring was a golden heart, it covered most of my earlobe.

Rachel ran to the bathroom now. "Hold the thought." She pointed a finger at her sister. "Don't do anything."

I swung out of bed and sat while I waited on the bathroom. I lowered my voice and because I hadn't gotten Miles' comment out of my mind. "Nicole, you're an empath and this concerns you. Do I put women on pedestals because I'm scared they'll leave me, which causes them to leave me?"

She sat on the bed next to me. "Here's some alcohol to help your ear from becoming infected. It's not as bad as all that, but yes. You were afraid of losing Tiffany and then you wanted to keep Rebecca so badly that you hid most of your personality." She rubbed my back with her fingernails and it felt good.

I felt my shoulders slump. She lifted my chin with her fingers and her eyes danced playfully. "Questions of an empath aren't free. Tell me, do you use magic to make sex better?"

"Uh, what? Who said, I mean, it's just Earth Power to strengthen me... and uh..." I couldn't believe that came out of nowhere. My face was burning and my flight or fight response triggered. I sprinted to the bathroom.

"What's going on?" asked Rachel as she passed. She was laughing.

"Nothing," I said in passing.

"You're welcome. I got rid of melodramatic Corey so you can rehearse today," disagreed Nicole before I was out of earshot. They were giggling when I shut the door.

I stayed in the bathroom extra time and washed up to get my mind on anything else. Who would've told them? I kept that secret from Rachel. The only one who knew was Rebecca, but young

women wouldn't talk about that... would they? At least the only secret I had was the one about Nicole.

I threw water on my hair to get everything wet. After washing
up, I threw on a pair of shorts and joined them in the kitchen.

"Is this how he normally dresses?" asked Nicole.

"He makes me breakfast too," teased Rachel.

I stumbled into the kitchen, drying my hair.

"I should go for a run today and work out," I said as we sat down
and ate.

"Don't worry about running. Practicing the dance before
tonight will get that energy." Rachel winked at me. "I'm the only one
left who can actually get you to do an aerobic exercise."

I picked up the plates and washed them and said, "let's get
dressed and practice."

Nicole helped me with the dishes. "Let's measure the clothing
first." She handed me the boots, pants, and a vest.

I put on the pants but called out, "where's the shirt?"

"Just the vest for you," said Nicole.

I came out wearing black leather pants and a black vest on top of
the black cowboy boots I danced with last time. "I'm glad I've been
cutting. Holy crap, could you dress me any less?" I definitely needed the wax. These were low cut pants, and I couldn't understand how
they stayed on.

"Not within the rules," said Nicole. She grinned mischievously.

"These nights have a big contingent of older business people of
mainly ladies getting drunk," explained Rachel.

"You don't think my voice will win them over?" I joked.

"You've worked very hard and I'm proud of your improvement."
Came a too-diplomatic response from Rachel.

"Wow," I said. "That was a backhanded compliment."

"Take these off and I'll have them ready. You two practice."

"Wait," I saw Rachel had a vest shirt that tucked in. "With Rachel's shoulders, she needs to show abs. It doesn't have to be a lot."

"I told you," said Nicole, who stuck her tongue out at her older sister.

"Fine," said Rachel with a sigh. "But not too much."

"Oh, Corey, I'm moving your messenger bag to the bedroom." She tried to lift it, and it didn't budge.

"It's weighs one hundred pounds now." When I moved it to the bedroom, I saw that Nicole had put one of her notebooks inside. I focused on the earring and added my books to my forbidden thoughts. My books hadn't been touched.

Nicole took the costumes, and we put on regular clothes to practice. I worked out while Rachel re-iterated all the moves with the timing and then we practiced. We practiced all day with a brief break for lunch and rest.

When we got close to time, I washed in the trough and set it up for Rachel to bathe. I sauntered into the bedroom and dressed in the newly fitted outfit.

When I walked back in, friends packed the cabin. Trish was there with Miles. They were all smiles, but Trish looked around like she was seeing things for the first time.

"Coach White is watching the store with Diego and Juan," said Trish.

Miles still favored his abdomen. Still, he found the strength to tease me. "Dude, you can't sing. You're eye candy for older women."

Nicole walked over and put her hand on my chest. "He's right. I watched you practice, and this accentuates the parts that will get the ladies on your side." Her hand on me roiled my guts. She placed a hat just like Donnie Van Zant's on my head. *Why did I kiss her?*

"Can I say, hand to God, I love this hat?"

THE FIVE OF US RODE in Trish's SUV to the bar with the live band karaoke. Rachel sat between me and Nicole and kept me focused on the competition. Rachel hated competing in female or solo competitions because drunk men voted for the winners, while thinking with the wrong head. She would not act like a hussy to win. She hoped a duet would be a fairer way to compete.

The problem was, I was the only one who volunteered. She tested me on a dozen songs, before narrowing to one song she could teach me. She drilled me as hard as she did with karate.

There was nothing I could do tonight except give it my best and totally sell out. I had hoped for a southern rock or country song to sing, but there wasn't one duet that didn't cause Rachel to cringe at my voice. She searched through my favorite songs on my music player from Old Donnie until we found one, she thought worked. It was two males singing the duet. However, Rachel had range and could sing. This song was smack dab in my range. I sang the Donnie Van Zant pieces—well, most of them. She handled Don Barnes' parts and the parts I couldn't manage.

Trish parked in the lot, and we walked into the bar. Past the hostess, we walked to the right side of the bar and signed in for our registration. The band loved the song choice and their normal singer pointed us to the back. "I got a couple of forty-pound dumbbells back there if you want to give it a quick pop." He winked at my outfit, and I was sure he figured out Rachel's strategy.

Miles came back with me to give me extra resistance on the dumbbells and helped me pop my pectorals and biceps. I wanted to talk to Miles, but I needed to focus on the performance now. This was for Rachel.

Trish and Miles must have an incredible ability to put things behind them. Or maybe they were like me and would do anything for Rachel. Trish did my hair, and I put on the tight leather pants with butt padding, and the leather vest with the black boots. The hat as the only thing that fit comfortably.

I looked like a half-dressed mortician. Rachel came out in matching leather pants and a shirt that was little more than a vest. It was the first time she displayed cleavage in all the years I've known her, which told me how seriously she took this. "Say nothing."

There was no way I was going to let this go. "You can give me pants with butt padding, but I can't say you glow up, right?" I didn't mention her abs made the whole look work.

She blushed. "Exactly."

"I picked these outfits out for the two of you, and both of you have this sexy old south vibe going on, and it works on you two."

Stay focused for Rachel. "Okay, should we practice the dance moves since these pants are skintight?"

"Give it a couple of tries. It's not leather under the crotch, so you should be good."

I did a front flip, then a back flip, then a front flip before landing in a split and flexing. I knew I was there to show off, but truth be told, my body didn't take to muscles like Miles, and I worked hard for these. Also, I had no problem with women telling me I was sexy. It's not like it was a common occurrence.

The real reason I was doing this was for Rachel, but I'd flex, show off muscles and flexibility, and otherwise try to get votes for Rachel to win.

"Damn, you two came to compete," said the guitarist and another man with him. The man who wasn't in the band had a clipboard and a pen.

"Yeah, we did," I said.

"Where do you want lights and guitarists to highlight?" He flipped a couple of pages and I saw he had marks on the page for our song.

They asked me, which was good since I would not let Rachel hide in her big moment. "There is a first small guitar solo right after the first chorus. We need the light on Rachel from there all the way to the 'the fight for the lady in black' line. The long guitar solo should be on me. I've got a forty-second routine Rachel planned for me. We merge for the two lines of wild-eyed boys. Then when we sing the words 'honkeytonk angel', could we get a light on just Rachel and nothing else?"

"Would you like a slight delay for the hoots?" Asked the guitarist.

Rachel gave the thumbs up, but her eyes were wide.

The man who was writing the notes said, "Yep. We got you. Also, leave your vest on for half the song, but if it gets too sweaty," he winked at me, "you can take it off at the end."

When they walked out, I told Rachel, "When you're behind me and I'm on the ground in a split, it's past the halfway point. Take my vest off."

"Me? How?"

I got into a split and had her walk behind me and pulled off my vest.

"Miles is selling you two," said Trish, walking back. "Rachel, that's not how you undress a man. Let me help you."

I put the vest back on and Trish said, "peel it off like this."

Rachel practiced a couple of times and Trish asked, "is this for a joint sexy move or are you doing a muscle pose?"

I didn't need Rachel running her fingers over my chest. "Yeah, I can give a good chest flex with my arms behind me." I wanted to lighten the mood and turned my head up to Rachel and said, "unless you want to rub my chest on stage." I couldn't hold my laughter though and ruined the joke. It was too bad. I owed her for the pepperoni joke.

Rachel rolled her eyes and walked out with Trish to check the competition, while I played the song and my moves in my head.

The contest announcer came back and gave me the set list. The scheduled us last, and I read the songs in front of us: <u>Time of my Life</u>, <u>Don't go Breaking my Heart</u>, <u>Barbie Girl</u>, <u>Islands in the Stream</u>, and an <u>Up Where We Belong</u>.

I sat and closed my eyes in a meditation, reviewing the complete song. After a few songs from the other competitors, I heard Rachel walk back.

"Okay," said Rachel, walking back to me while they announced us. She rubbed something on my bicep tattoo and my gargoyle name tattoos and I saw the tattoos shine. "There are two tables of older women to the right, ten pitchers of margaritas deep. That's your target. You are on full reverb and I have none, so you can go for it."

Well, fish or cut bait. I heard them announce us and the women screaming was unexpected. "Oh," said Rachel. "Miles and Trish sold your body to the drunk women." She grinned and walked out. The drums, bassist, and two guitarists were back out of the lights and two microphones were near the spots marked with blue tape.

I followed her into the lights, looked for my mark, took a wide stance and lifted my extended arms over my head and gave the crowd a flex like I was stretching. When the women catcalled me, I winked towards the noise. I couldn't see anything with these lights. The heat started me sweating immediately.

When the band signaled they were ready—I grabbed the mike and said, "Wild Eyed Southern Boys." The band kicked in and I shouted an Old Donnie line to the crowd while I flexed. "The temperature is warm tonight 'cause of all the hot women."

That got the cheers, which accomplished my goal. Screams covered my first line, and I belted out the first two lines of the song before the screaming stopped in time for me to sing 'rhythm and blues.' Then Rachel belted out the next lines and the entire bar cheered for her. She was a regular competitor and the only reason we got an invitation to this contest. She came to win and her voice was on point.

I did a back flip right before the first chorus and we belted it out together. Rachel's plan had worked, and we had the entire bar involved. Then it was Rachel's turn in the spotlight. The guitarists flanked her, and she got the whole spotlight. She sang and did her flip and split and got up in time for the chorus.

The pressure was on me, so, to psych myself up, I danced around and gave the women's table a good booty shake during the chorus. Then came my forty seconds. Rachel had choreographed this for me since I couldn't dance. There were a few flips and a bunch of karate moves mixed into a basic two-step. It ended with me in a split and flexing my arms and chest.

Rachel remembered to peel off my vest, and I flexed my chest inwards while she removed it. The crowd's response was what we wanted. I hated to say it. It felt good with a bunch of women screaming I was sexy. It's not something a guy hears when he removes his shirt on a normal day.

We finished out the song and it was only another minute since the solos at the end were out by the band. I survived the three minutes, waved to the crowd and walked backstage with Rachel to our designated area.

We waited backstage, and each grabbed a bottle of water. They walked us to the wings, where the announcer brought each duet out for the round of applause for judging. I was still pouring sweat to want to put the leather vest on, and Rachel said it was fine to leave it off.

Cheers for all the duets were crazy, and the bar never got quiet. When we walked out for judging, the announcer screamed over the crowd, "You all know Rachel, but tonight is the first night we learned she was part honkytonk angel—and tonight she brought along her own wild eyed southern boy. Let's give it up if you like them!"

Rachel and I kept with our plan and flipped into a split together and bowed. Then we both flat kicked to the right to stand and stood in line with the other groups.

I got my first look at the competition and the ladies wore a collection of slutty dresses and hung with wimpy guys. On costumes alone, Rachel should have won. Well, Nicole picked out the costumes, and it appeared she did well. On voice alone, Rachel should win most competitions she entered.

There were enough people who liked Rachel's singing to go with the women's night out tables for us to win, and Rachel was ecstatic. "As often as sexism cost me in one of these contests, I'm going to take it." She hugged the other female contestants, and I shook hands with the guys and two of them tried to give me their number.

A couple of "No thank you's" later, we were back and Trish and Miles joined us and gave us our regular clothes.

I stepped behind a curtain and changed into jeans and one of Old Donnie's Molly Hatchet shirts he gave me. I gave the pants, vest, and boots to Rachel. "You knocked it out of the park."

"Thank you so much for doing this with me. I know you hated it."

"It wasn't my first choice, but I didn't hate it. It ended up being a lot of fun. I wish I actually could sing to help you out."

Miles clasped my shoulder. "Dude, you pulled it off. We all knew Rachel could do it, but you weren't horrible."

"Thanks Miles."

"Plus, the ladies loved your show," said Trish with a giggle.

"Speaking of that, can we leave out the back? I'm a little afraid of drunk ladies." There woman in the gondola flashed into my mind. "The flexing and butt wiggles may have gone too far."

Rachel put her hand on my back. "That's supposed to be my line."

Verenuala was there with another Daoine.

Trish noticed the same time as me and said, "are those..."

"They're deeneh," said Miles quickly.

Verenuala jumped up and hugged me. "You spread the word for me."

The one with him walked over to Rachel, walked around her and said, "it's all real. Let's report."

He hugged Nicole, who was surprised. "Nicole." He smiled and nodded, then winked at me.

"I walked over to Rachel. By the way, I invited the Spring Fey Court to watch us tonight."

The look on her face told me I got her back for the pepperoni joke.

Nicole looked at me curiously. "Since it's over, we're double dating tomorrow night and it's your first date with Wesley."

I hugged Rachel. "It'll be fun and I'll be right there."

I held hands with Rachel and Nicole and we walked out the back and walked back to the SUV. On the way to the cabin, Trish sent me a clip where I did not appear like I was there for eye candy and it was mostly the chorus where Rachel and I were both singing.

Rachel and I stayed at the cabin and there wasn't time to set up the outdoor bed, so I put wood in the cast-iron stove and pointed the induction fan into the bedroom and Rachel and I got into that bed and snuggled and went to sleep.

Chapter 16—Trish and Date

We woke Sunday morning and had nothing on the schedule. Rachel wrapped her leg around me as I rolled into her arms. I could stand to sleep in a bit more, and I wasn't even sure what woke me up.

"Holy crap," said Trish. "Close the door, Miles."

"They're not having sex, they're just snuggling," said Miles. "Guys, this is why people think you're dating."

"Man, do we sleep in a lot recently?" I brushed Rachel's hair from her face. "Wake up, time." Trish and Miles didn't seem mad, which was good, since we weren't ready for a confrontation.

"Guys, Nicole woke us up early yesterday," said Rachel. "Let me use the restroom. Corey apparently had another dream with a deer woman and needs a moment before he walks around. Wait, are you dreaming about Nicole?" She pushed my shoulder and grinned as she teased me.

"TMI!" said Trish.

I needed a minute, but Rachel could have let that be a secret. "Miles, I chopped a lot of wood. Could you start the stove?"

"Good idea. Crap, dude. You two snuggle closer than Trish and I."

"We were apart for a week and it was hard." I got up and followed Rachel after she finished in the bathroom and we both brushed our teeth when I finished.

We sat on the couch, and she handed me the brush and bands to do her hair.

Trish spoke first, and I noticed Miles had made two cups of coffee for them. He handed Rachel and me mugs of white tea.

"Thank you," I said.

Trish sat in a kitchen chair Miles pulled over before he sat in the recliner. She spoke first. "First, Corey, that rug is beautiful and for you to think of a present for the baby is sweet. Thank you. The gift is perfect."

"Yeah dude, you rocked it."

Trish continued. "We came over to say thank you for being brave, Corey. Wait. You snuggled all night long after dancing on stage, and now he's braiding your hair?"

Rachel sipped her tea. "He has on shorts and I'm wearing the pajamas he bought me."

"You two are more intimate than Miles and I, and I'm pregnant."

"It's just hair," I said. "Besides, we're double dating tonight. I'm dating Nicole and Rachel is dating Wesley."

Miles chuckled at his wife. "You didn't believe me when I said he did her feet and they were close."

She shook her head. "No. I watched him tape up your feet and hands for fights too, but you never snuggled. Wait, you guys are dating other people and you do this?"

"He has too," said Rachel with a finger towards Miles. "The three of us shared a sleeping bag when it got freezing a few times. I caught those two snuggling before, too."

"Not since we married," argued Miles.

Trish looked at her husband with some shock. "Never mind. Miles, take notes on how Corey acts with Rachel because I'm jealous."

I laughed as Miles rolled his eyes. "Yes. Nicole and I are dating, and Wesley and Rachel are going on a first date."

"Dude, congratulations. Don't screw this one up. Rachel doesn't need luck like you do."

Trish held up her hands. "Let's hold off normal topics so I can get this out. What I want to say, Corey, is thank you for being brave. Putting everything on the line to the point of ordering me around showed how serious you were and that's a risk real friends take."

"Thank you, Trish. I was so scared to lose you guys, but I couldn't keep going."

"Really man," added Miles. "I saw exactly what Clive said when you scared him straight. I was reeling and not thinking well. Old thoughts came to me and when I went to square up, there was a guy standing up who was going to stop me to make sure I hurt no one else. There was no doubt in my mind that you could pull it off. Once I realized you were making sure I couldn't hurt Trish and the baby, everything came back into focus."

I finished braiding Rachel's hair, stood, and leaned to hug Miles.

"Put a shirt on first."

I grabbed a shirt and threw it on while Rachel giggled. Then I hugged each of them.

When I hugged Miles I whispered, "keep the purpose of the earring on the down low. Other people will think about it and give it away."

He whispered back, "my dad told me that. It's cool, but the heart is funny on you."

"So, Corey," continued Trish. "To make sure Miles can train, we want to ask you two for help."

This was great news, and I was willing to help. "What do you need?"

"Could you use the gym around the store more often to work out with Miles? Plus, when you brew beer, please setup a Sunday night with us to come by and drink beer together."

"Dude, also could you come by and do more camping stuff in the store? We also talked to a Preacher Jon, through Mom, and he says Rachel and Nicole can help there too, so we can keep me in the loop."

"It'll take some logistics. But yes. I'll start off with this dark Friday thing." I loved the way this turned out.

"Black Friday. Right now, we're heading into the store. What do you have planned?" Miles grabbed his keys.

"I need to change out more vehicles today," said Rachel.

"Whose sweet Mustang is in the front?" asked Trish.

"Mine," I said. "Rachel picked it out as my new car since they've compromised my old one. I'm going to study, enjoy the date, and I leave at three am for a gargoyle."

Miles escorted his pregnant wife to their car. "Really. Good luck."

Trish came back and whispered something to Rachel and then skipped back out to the car.

When they pulled out, Rachel said, "Keep it quiet from Miles, but she is going to get him a dirt bike for Christmas and wants me to help pick it out."

"That'd be nice," I said. "Did we do good?"

"I think we did." Rachel hugged me. "Will you cook me some breakfast before I go?"

"Yep. Get dressed and I'll cook."

"Oh Rachel. If you see the Daoine from last night who looks like they should be in high school, do not use the e-word. Call them Daoine."

"Deeneh?"

"Excellent pronunciation," said a voice, walking in through the back door.

"I can tell they talked to you first," said a second voice.

"Rachel, I'd like to introduce Verenuala and guest."

"Fionnestra," said the newcomer. "I am what your kind would consider female and you would consider Verenuala male, but these are not terms we are comfortable with. I say this for your comfort."

"Should I sit?" asked Rachel.

I sat on the couch and pulled her onto my lap.

Verenuala sat on the couch and Fionnestra looked at Rachel and took a similar position on the lap of Verenuala. "Yes. This is a splendid position," said Fionnestra.

"So, Rachel," Verenuala stumbled over her name. "We watched your performance last night at the request of the druid to consider you for a bard position."

"We watched you two and your affection and find you are normal and average for Spring Court members in your affection for each other, which played into the decision. Humans have lost much of the power of affection." Fionnestra changed her position to wrap her leg around Verenuala, much like Rachel had done with me, and nodded approvingly.

"Bard?" asked Rachel. "What does this mean?"

I kept quiet, since this was Rachel's choice.

"The Fey Spring Court is ecstatic to offer you the position of Bard of the Spring Court. Not only will you resurrect the class to humans, much like your partner has with his druid skills, it would task you with staying with the druid and recording the deeds of the two of you."

"Would I change?"

"You would have a class and the power of song. You would be members of the Fey Spring Court. Nothing else about you would change other than the bardic class choices," said Fionnestra.

"We are to work with the covenant of the area owners and will register your choices with one Preacher Jon and his second, Nathan Abernathy."

"Would my powers let me hit Dark Fey and hurt them, not just hinder them for someone else to hurt?"

The two Daoine look at each other. "Possibly. It depends on the choice of your powers," they said together.

"Then yes. I am excited to become a bard in the Fey Spring Court."

Verenuala spoke. "Coire Norwood, do you accept the position of Druid of the Spring Court?"

"I do."

"Excellent. We will follow the protocol and you shall find information as the slowness of old humans allows."

Rachel and I both laughed and the two Daoine joined in the mirth. They departed just as quickly, and Rachel and I ate breakfast.

MY STUDYING WENT WELL, and I put my clothes back on and started a fire near the bed to make coals near the trough. I chopped the ice off the top and poured the water out. I cleaned the inside of the trough and pumped it full of water. All the coals and burning wood got placed around the trough as I refilled it and when it was full and not too chilled. I got in and cleaned in and soaked. The air was chilly, but the sun was out, and Earth Power kept me protected. With the coals and my body heat, the water didn't stay too cold, and I took the time to relax.

I didn't know enough about the seed pod situation and needed to reserve judgment and enjoy my time with Nicole. I was protected, knew the situation to make changes on the fly, and I would watch to see what happened.

"Look at you getting all relaxed," called Nicole from the door. "When you finish, come join me on the porch."

When she walked back in, I got out, emptied the water, dried off, and threw on a pair of shorts and a shirt. I threw some wood in the wood fire stove, and started a fire, and joined Nicole on the swing on the porch.

"Sitting on the swing with you is nice. I see why this keeps coming up in your vision."

We sat next to each other and held hands. Rachel had delivered Nicole a new car. "You have a hot girl car." She wore a thick cotton black dress with paisley patterns and had on black pumps. I'd never seen her wear such large heels.

"I wanted to be your height when we danced tonight. What makes a hot girl car?"

"One that you drive."

She laughed and slapped my knee playfully. "It's a four-door and not a convertible. I couldn't get the stuff I wanted in a convertible. Rebecca got a convertible, though."

I laughed. "It's a smooth-looking sports car and not an old woman SUV, plus it's a beautiful red."

"It is a beautiful red, but it looks sedate next to your orange car."

"I still get to act immature," I teased.

"Speaking of immature, I hear it's immature to walk into a trap laid for you if you think you can turn it around."

This was the second time she mentioned this. "Springing traps are not immature, it's calculated. It depends how much you know of the plan and how prepared you are. The strategy is effective."

"By the way, we convinced Nathan we are dating. He said the kiss embarrassed him."

"When we kiss—I feel such passion... oh no."

"Oh, no?"

"Rachel and I joined the Fey Spring Court. They're the court of fertility, rebirth, renewals..."

"Passion and youthfulness," she finished.

"We are going to have to be super careful because I don't know what it means yet and we could accidentally push our relationship too fast."

"We'll find out more, I'm sure, but let's work through it and discuss it like we've been doing."

I placed my head on her shoulder. "It's very hard to go slow with you."

She patted my head. "Yep, but I've been waiting a while for you to come around. This area is pretty and I see why you wanted to sit out here and talk. Let's do this more often."

I looked up and smiled at her. "Yes. Let's."

"Now you need to get dressed so we can be on time for the date."

"I probably should be more on top of that."

"Wesley was so excited he jumped the gun. I helped him coordinate the date so all his nervous energy didn't freak you and Rachel out. Get dressed. I laid your clothes out in the bedroom."

While dressing, I dove into my seed packets and grabbed a seed. When I brushed my teeth, I found a couple of safety pins, and now I would look competent for a date. I looked at myself and my hair still touched my shoulder, and I had what the stylist had five day's growth.

I had on regular person black shoes, dark blue slacks and a light blue button-down shirt. A gunmetal necklace that covered the untanned area where my torc normally sat. There was a tan jacket, so I put my pepper spray, keychain, and stun gun in a coat pocket. I also put my mouthpiece in my pants pocket with my Coire Norwood wallet.

I walked back outside and offered my hand to Nicole.

"Hold on, we're getting a picture." Nicole set her phone up in her car and it snapped a few pictures. We posed through a few pictures.

She cycled through two. "Which one do you like?"

They looked the same to me, so I picked one. "This one. Can you snap it to Trish and Miles as well?"

"You mean can I tag them so they see it as," she teased.

"I don't do social media. Whatever gets it to them."

"Done." She put her phone in her purse.

"Do you want me to drive?"

She held open her passenger door. "Your backseat won't work for Rachel and Wesley. Get in, immature boyfriend."

"I think I'm supposed to do this for you."

She got in and we drove and picked up Wesley and Rachel at Nicole and Rachel's apartment.

I turned to the left to talk with them while we drove to the club.

"You better not scope me out like you did earlier."

I turned towards her. *Man, she is sexy. I hope I can keep my hands off of her.*

"Ah!" She laughed. "Stop that."

I turned to the confused couple in the back seat. "What is this place we're going?"

"Frenco Tavern and Dance," said Wesley. "They have a nice dinner menu, and it's trivia night. After every trivia round, they have a DJ for a half hour of dancing."

"Sounds like a great idea." Poor Rachel did not look comfortable in a skirt and a blouse, so I ignored it completely to take her mind off of it. "Rachel, the new Mustang is kicking." I set her up to think about something else. "The power band is missing where I like it, though. It just doesn't have the pop from thirty-five to sixty that I enjoyed in my old car."

"Oh, don't worry. First thing is, since you've become a sissy, I'm going to put new brake rotors and steel braided brake cables. Then, I'm going to beef up your suspension, so the new horses will sit lower and safer for you. Then we'll start with a cold air intake, better exhaust and a tuner and see if you're ready for a supercharger like we have on your old car."

She had stopped pulling her skirt down and acted animated.

"Wesley, besides your time at the church, what do you have going on?"

"I've converted from my master's program to a PhD program." He shrugged.

I had next to nothing here. "What's your thesis?"

"It still needs to be narrowed down, but I'm looking at Diophantine equations and the difficulty in solving them in security applications in quantum computing."

Holy mother of God, I didn't even recognize all those words.

Nicole started laughing. She took her hand off the wheel and patted my knee. "It's okay sweetie, you recognize most of those words."

I laughed. "I chopped up a tree to save an endangered plant two days ago. That's almost the same."

Everyone in the car chuckled, and I tried my hardest to think of a topic of conversation to get Wesley and Rachel talking.

Nicole jumped in. "Did you guys here that Trish and Miles are hosting a New Year's Eve party at the store this year?"

"Yes," said Wesley. "Nathan invited all the Matheletes."

"The band from Cleave's is going to play the party too," said Rachel.

Well, Nicole did better than I did, but the two were talking in the back seat.

WE GOT OUT OF THE CAR and while Nicole helped Rachel adjust her skirt, I put the seed in the ground and grew a pink calla lily next to the car. It had two bulbs, and I took the two off and I gave one to Wesley with a safety pin.

"Boys?" Said Rachel.

I walked over to Nicole and put the flower against her dresses lapel and then secured it with the safety pin.

"Look at you being all prepared and stuff," said Nicole. "What's the excuse to have a spring flower in late November?"

"I have a small greenhouse as an amateur botanist." I needed to use that lie quite a bit as a druid.

She giggled. "Ok, it's beautiful."

I didn't turn. "Have they figured it out yet?"

"Almost. Keep looking at me. You're more comfortable around a woman's breast on a first date. What kind of rogue are you?" She grinned.

"I didn't even think about that, only for the flower to be straight."

"Yeh, you are good at controlling your eyes and thoughts. Every other guy would be all about checking my cleavage."

I couldn't resist, and I checked out the smooth skin of her cleavage and how her bra pushed her breasts together.

"There you go. I didn't choose this bra and dress for you to ignore them."

I chuckled. "It's good you gave me something to do. I doubt I'll be any good at trivia."

"It'll be fine. We're here for fun." She hugged me and whispered, "they're done."

The four of us walked inside and the waiter escorted us to the high-topped table, gave us an electronic pad, and handed out menus.

Nicole listened to music playing in the background and nodded approvingly.

"I'm not a very good dancer," I said.

"Oh no," said Nicole. "You just spent a month dancing with my sister. We are dancing tonight."

"Ok then," let me use the restroom. I focused on my earring and put fighting, scoping out the bar, and a handoff of the magnolia seed on the forbidden list. Then I scoped out the bar.

So far, Rachel and I were the only two fighters in the place. Near the restroom was a second door with a bouncer to the parking lot and very little else. Tables were filling up, and it appeared trivia was popular here. I didn't need to use the restroom, so I washed my hands and got a good look at the earring. It was hardly noticeable since it didn't extend past my earlobe. If you looked directly at it, it was unmistakably a large heart.

I got back to the table and menus were there for ordering and I asked the waiter for water. "Please put it in a glass. I'm cutting, not cheap." I wasn't still cutting, but I didn't need to drink before a gargoyle banishing in ten hours.

The waiter took a step back. He smiled friendly and joked. "My name is Derek, and I'm here to help, but I don't know. You may have to take off the jacket so I can see."

I played along, and Derek helped me remove my jacket. I noticed he brushed my earring, but it felt like an accident. When the coat was off, I pulled my arms in and pumped out my chest.

"Got you. Trivia begins in fifteen." He tapped Nicole's shoulder. "I hope you're appreciating that man's effort. It is going to be a pleasure serving you tonight." He drifted off.

"He didn't ask me to flex," joked Wesley.

"If you flexed your brain on him, Rachel might have to fight him to keep you as a date."

Trivia started, and Nicole was the superstar. Questions about pop music and current movies and tv shows were hers. Rachel got excited to answer a car question and Wesley not only helped with the pop culture, but hit the science questions too.

The food arrived. "You all are doing so well, how is muscles doing?" Derek put my salad down.

"Muscles can't keep up with the rest of the table geniuses," I joked back.

"Don't worry honey, what do you need to get a question in?"

"I work for Park Services, so unless you have questions on invasive plant species, I think I'm done." I didn't have a better answer for him.

He handed Nicole her salad. "He's saving the planet and becoming sexy. Is it just for you?"

Nicole winked. "I hope so, but he also rescued a puppy right when I picked him up."

She and Derek giggled.

He moved over to the other side. "I remember you. You join the Math team that comes in here a couple times a month," he said to Wesley.

"That's me."

"And you have a beautiful date for tonight?" He turned to Rachel. "Honey, we all love that team when they come in. You caught a good one. Don't be afraid to reel him in."

Wesley and Rachel both blushed.

"Did I say something wrong?" Derek look taken aback.

"It's a first date," admitted Wesley.

"Now that's sweet. You two get desert on me. I'd give the entire table but the grilled chicken on regular salad with no dressing couple who are cutting would waste it."

Rachel laughed. "Nicole might take a bite of mine."

I looked and Rachel had ordered a steak, baked potato, and two vegetables.

The first round of trivia ended and Nicole grabbed my hand. "Our salads won't get cold. Come dance."

"I haven't danced since high school prom," I said. I stood, but I wasn't leaping at the opportunity.

"Start off with left foot cat stance and drift," said Rachel.

We got out to the dance floor and there was no way I'd recognize any song unless it was something old Donnie listened to, and it didn't sound like this was that kind of place. I got out and looked at some other guy out there, took the stance and tried to emulate his moves.

"That's not bad," said Nicole. "Now lift your arms and keep them moving with the beat."

Derek came up behind me. "Bend your knees just a little more and mix in some front and back steps, too."

I followed both pieces of advice.

"There you go. Once you're comfortable, just try to move with the music."

"You can relax now. You are nicely dressed and muscle bound. Take advantage of people being acclimated by society to think you're sexy."

"Paranoia is more of my natural state."

Nicole laughed, and I tried to copy her carefree flow. We stayed up a few songs when they got a slow song. Nicole pulled me close. "Place your arms around me and just sway with me."

"The last slow dance I had was five years ago at prom with Haley, and this felt good. Someone holding you felt good. Since she wore larger heels, she was only a couple of inches shorter than me. Close for a kiss, but we shouldn't kiss again. Those kisses kept rocking me and I wanted to move slow."

"We can do a quick peck instead of a full kiss. That shouldn't rock you."

This song finished, and we did a quick kiss, and she was right. It was just a kiss. She grabbed my hand and led me to the table, and I felt her hand tense, and two men walked into the bar. I focused on my earring and put thoughts about those two on the forbidden list. Those two were fighters. The one in the red golf shirt with bulked out muscles like Miles carried a gun, probably in one of the large pockets in his pants. He favored his left leg. The other wore a suit, walked on the balls of his feet and peered around the room, looking for his opponent.

Our eyes met, and I nodded to ensure he understood I was down to fight. He turned away when he scoped me out. That was unusual. These two were looking for a fight. Nicole recognized them, and the guy backed down from me without a good reason.

We sat at the table and Rachel looked at me and knew something was up. I gave an eye pass to the two guys as they passed to her by nature. I should have ignored her, but there was no way I could ignore Rachel.

"Oh my god Rachel, calm down. Even Corey didn't jump."

"I saw them, but I did my best to hide those thoughts and emotions. I focused on you so you wouldn't get upset with me."

Nicole smiled, and I focused on eating my salad, but monitored the two. They ordered drinks at a table for two near the bar. The man in the suit kept his eye on our table, while the other scanned the room.

We played the second round of trivia and the music played again.

"It's our turn to dance," said Rachel. "Hold my purse." She slapped her purse into my chest playfully.

"I'll use the girl's room," said Nicole. She placed her purse on the edge of the table and I slipped it next to Rachel's purse.

When Nicole was gone, using the cover of Rachel's larger purse, I reached into Nicole's and underneath the magnolia leaf; I popped a seed off the pod she took from me. I closed the purse quickly and slid it back. There, that was corrupted and unusable.

Red shirt and Suit were walking over to the table. I reached into my coat pocket, got my mouth guard out, made sure they saw it, and popped it into my mouth. I stared Suit in the eyes and smiled.

He arm-barred his friend, and they stopped and walked back to their table. I sat back down and soon Nicole joined me.

"A mouth guard, you were going to fight."

"Rachel was right. They were coming over. I wanted to make sure they knew I was ready and felt confident I could take both of them."

"You can take both of them?"

"Suit is the professional, and he's the hard one. Red shirt is a hired muscle guy, so I could use him as a diversion. If Suit was better than I, he'd have one shot before Rachel came in and they'd both be heading to the hospital. Even without Rachel, I'd win, but I'd be hurt."

"You're imagining things."

"You weren't around much in Rachel, Miles', and my angry years. Bar fights are a primary skill of mine."

"Well, I'm going to put an end to this. You'll see my primary power in play. Stay here." She grabbed her purse and walked over. I knew to watch for the magnolia seed pod and magnolia leaves, but I kept my mind alternating between her ass and her safety. I needed to give her something in my mind. Sure enough, she tried to hide it, but she handed the seed pod to suit, and then convinced them to leave. She walked back over and said, "there. Do you feel better?"

Trivia was about to restart, and Wesley and Rachel came back. Rachel looked at me and she wanted to talk. I nodded we needed to, but I started focusing on tonight's gargoyle.

"By the way, where are Nathan and Rebecca?" asked Wesley.

"She's packing, and wanted privacy, and he had work," answered Nicole.

I took part the rest of the night and when I was dropped off at my car, I got in and headed out. I'm sure Nicole realized something happened during our date, but the gargoyle was my concern right now.

Chapter 17—Rebecca's kidnapping

Rebecca sat on her bed and traced the flowered patterns on her comforter with her finger. The act calmed her brain and let her think. She needed to take stock of her position and decide like a proper young lady. The recent days had her making quick decisions, and these were the decisions that got a young woman into uncomfortable positions. Slow, methodical decisioning helped a young lady remember her training and navigate this world safely. Only now, the world changed and the old decisions had gotten her into uncomfortable situations.

The last two weeks were crazy with new experiences and little time to reflect. Now she didn't know what to think. She followed her grandmother's advice religiously her whole life and things paid off until this year. This year is when the advice dried up, not that her grandmother wasn't willing to help. She had run out of advice to give, and Rebecca's life stalled.

Now she broke up with Corey, fought with him, tracked him, got picked up by a secret magic organization who knew her grandmother, and then met Corey at Mellow Mushroom with Preacher Jon. She agreed to the meeting to help convince her ex-boyfriend to come to the command center. It had failed spectacularly. She thought she could be hard, but Corey showed there was a different league she did not qualify for.

He flirted with the redheaded waitress in front of her. All of his softness was gone, and he was hard—scary hard. This was the side the people who feared him saw. She always wondered why the men at the gun range didn't mess with him. Not that Corey gave them a reason to. He was polite, gracious, and treated everyone with respect. But the veterans and longtime hunters gave grief to everyone, but not Corey. Everyone at the range stopped hitting on her when he said the two of them were dating, but one day, she gave him a kiss after they began dating. It was an innocent, *I'm glad you joined me today* kind of kiss. After the others viewed that kiss, some men even quit checking her out. Now she understood. There was danger in Corey's eyes, and he walked like a cat about to strike. Rachel had a similar demeanor, but he showed an extra level.

How could she have never seen that side of him? *Because he loved you and only showed you what you would love.* Her inner voice needed to shut the hell up. There was work to do.

The first step given to her by Preacher Jon moved her into a protected building with luxury condominiums. She did not know how Preacher Jon's team afforded everything, when he certainly did not have access to generational wealth. Her grandmother said to trust this Preacher Jon. She liked Rachel and had since Rachel was the one who convinced her to ask Corey out. She had more in common with Nicole, but there was a sizeable gap in liking people and uprooting your life for them.

Step one would be to bring a weekend bag. Nathan would pick up the rest of her bags and then deliver them at two different times to avoid the appearance of moving until she moved in. There were three different luggage sets that she needed to pack. She needed a weekend bag, a necessities bag, and an 'everything else' bag. They had some plan to move her to safety without drawing attention. They did not want her to be alone, but it had been two weeks and she put her foot down. She needed to be alone to process everything.

The first item was she would reject the stupid fake identity. Nancy Wheeler was a horrible alternative identity, and she wanted no part of it. The name reeked of a fantasy name of Nathan—a role he wished for Rebecca in his life. That had zero chance of happening. Besides, she enjoyed being Rebecca Adams. Just because her life was in danger, was no time to change who you were.

She missed her job at <u>CJ's Weapons Wholesale</u> more than anything—well, anything except Corey. CJ knew Preacher Jon and wished her luck. He also said The Tribe would have her back. She shed some tears when she lost that job as much as she loved it.

Besides, the whole reason for a new identity was the people who wanted Corey dead kept getting their butt kicked by him. Those enemies had identified her. All she needed was to hide from them until Corey finished his butt kicking. Corey would certainly win. She never saw someone like him before.

Those enemies were also nebulous. They were called the church, but not the proper church. This sounded convoluted until Nicole explained there was one bad guy with a few lieutenants in charge and they had taken over the church's resources. Gargoyles were where Corey came in. He banished gargoyles to keep them from the church, and he was good at it.

The same Corey who liked to start off his kisses with a gentle sucking of her lower lip before kissing her entire mouth. The guy who brought her on dates that included him barbequing and serving the beer he brewed. He always remembered to bring a bottle of wine for her. That was the other half of him—the half she fell in love with. Everything about him was perfect, except he did not meet with her grandmother's approval.

Rebecca learned the hard way that it was hard to have the looks and elegance of wealth, but to be poor. Men, even ones only partially worthy of dating you, viewed you as an object to possess and parade around. Corey saw her as an individual even before they dated. His first words included, 'I promise I'm not trying to hit on you,' and he wasn't. He respected her shooting skills and wanted help.

Reminiscing wasn't getting her bags packed. She stood up and walked to the spare bedroom. Her weekend bag included the Italian Brič, which her grandmother gifted her. The sealed section had room for daytime make-up and basic toiletries. She would not be going out in the evening, at least until she got more luggage back. After placing two hundred rounds of three eighty and two hundred rounds of nine-millimeter in the case, she moved her bedside Glock to the bag. Then three days of necessities, a set of tennis shoes, one nightgown, a pair of jeans, and two polo shirts. If she wore a neutral set of flats, a khaki skirt, and a flowered blouse with a jacket, she would be set up for days. The jewelry she currently wore was fine as well. The Ruger LCP stayed in her purse, with the pepper spray and a stun gun.

She pulled the box from under her gun. Corey had bought Rachel sleepwear, and they were normal. She pulled out the baby doll lingerie Corey brought her. White satin, spaghetti straps, see through lace up top. It was beautiful, and he ogled her even before she put it on. These purchases told her everything about the relationship. He didn't see Rachel as a lover relationship, but he viewed Rebecca as a lover.

She placed it back in the box and took a break. It hurt when Corey flirted with the waitress and then kissed Nicole. Now the two of them were dating, and it hurt. It shouldn't, but it did. She broke up with Corey, and this might be a rebound relationship to get over her. It had been over two months and she had no reason to be upset. *Why are you then?*

What she needed to be upset about was this was ten days since she had been home and it was only for one day to pack. She'd no reason to believe she was being watched or was in danger, but her grandmother verified she should trust this Preacher Jon. She needed to stop thinking about Corey—easy.

To get back to packing to protect her from the nebulous threat she'd never seen, she could focus on the only gift her parents gave her—the freedom to choose her own pastime. Her parents squandered the wealth grandmother granted them because of their birth. Now they had nothing to show for it except a neglected daughter. The sole benefit was proper parents would not have let her join the marksmanship team in high school. It was the one genuine joy she had in her life until Corey.

She trusted Rachel. Nathan was harmless—physically harmless. He gave her gaga eyes but didn't understand how to talk to her other than strictly business. Rachel had no problem talking to Rebecca. Rachel convinced her to ask out Corey that one day in the mountains. Not that it took much.

> *Her job paid her double time to volunteer for this event in the mountains. She was to clean and service weapons up on the Appalachian trail. She went to get her hands on weapons she could never afford. Plus, the extra money paid for ammo and range fees for a month.*

> *A strange man sat next to her called her 'baby' and asked if she needed help with the weapons. Another man from the range ran over and pulled him away and warned him she was Corey's girl. That's when she met Old Donnie and Rachel.*

> *Rachel, who she recognized from Corey's description, grabbed Old Donnie and told him something, and apparently, she knew of the agreement between Rebecca and Corey. The agreement with Corey had been simple. He would not hit on her and would tell others he dated her. This allowed Rebecca to shoot at the range in peace.*

> *Old Donnie stood taller than Corey, and thicker. Hard life thick, like he may be as strong as Corey, though the younger*

man, had muscles popping out everywhere. He had long gray hair and a gray beard, but his bright blue eyes constantly glanced around and caught everything. He walked over to her. "So, you're the one training Corey and occupying his thoughts. Tell me, can he shoot now?"

Rebecca heard Corey say that Old Donnie acted tough but was a softie, so Rebecca acted on that and smiled at the old man. "Not really, but with a couple of tricks, he can hit the eight targets in one try on a good day." Rebecca realized it might be a slight exaggeration, Corey would never be a good shooter, something with his eyes and focus, but he was competent enough.

"Would you trust him with this?"

He handed her a Winchester twenty-one from the first run during the great depression. She saw the custom build, and they marked the trigger plate Deluxe. "Wow. I wouldn't trust anyone with this weapon. This should be in a museum. It's a sixteen-gauge made for heavy firing instead of a twelve gauge and, wow, they have replaced the bore at the factory, but it still has heavy use." She handed him the gun back in awe. That rifle was a beauty.

"Huh," said the old man, and he looked her up and down, and let her get back to cleaning lesser weapons.

The next set of bags fit half of her wardrobe, the rest of her toiletries, and almost everything she needed. The Mossberg slipped into its case, and the three-oh-eight Lady Hunter snapped into its case, and she placed those on top of the next set of bags. All the ammo filled its own small pink hard container bag. She latched it, locked it, and sat down and remembered the day she asked Corey out. The next day at what they called the Redneck Biathlon.

"Don, your boy here, we can't post this. Others would die."

This event was called the Redneck Biathlon, where people would need to be in the woods for up to a week, track and shoot eight targets, and return with all the equipment. It was a contest for men who thought with the hair on their chest.

Why Corey competed was beyond her, as he never mentioned it, and everyone who elected to take part in it, older men who called themselves The Tribe, talked about nothing else.

Old Donnie slurred some syllables together that Rebecca interpreted as, "gon need the tape."

Rebecca was lucky enough to sit next to a monitor someone else was to use. She wasn't supposed to use it, but even if men didn't hit on her, they liked to be near her. The man who watched the monitor and setup next to her, stood next to Old Donnie with shock on his face. Rebecca flipped a knob to power it on, and she watched the replay as they showed Old Donnie. Corey, with the scope she grease-marked for him and his yellow tinted glasses, hit a target from two hundred yards out. That made her proud. He had taken all of her advice and made it work.

After locking everything up tight and instead of the day hike around Coward's Pass, he got a running jump and jumped off of Idiot's Cliff. Two feet landed on a tree branch, which allowed him to jump down and grab it with his arms. Then he bounded down a few branches, jumped towards the cliff, and hit a tree on a lower level. Without regaining his bear-

ings, he jumped to the ground. It had to be trick photography, or he was some type of specialist gymnast—no, definitely trick photography. Only now she knew it wasn't.

Then he verified his rifle case stayed sealed and jumped down a fifty-foot waterfall into a pool and swam to the opposite edge. Then he stopped and freed a raccoon from a bear trap. The raccoon didn't attack him and didn't limp away, even though it had a mangled leg before Corey arrived. Afterwards, Corey sprinted off as if it was nothing.

Rachel walked up behind her and whispered, "you can't tell anyone. The Tribe don't care, but you never know who else is here."

Rebecca turned off the monitor with a little embarrassment.

Rachel smiled and said, "he'll never break his promise to you, so if you want to go out with him, you'll need to ask him out. I know he'll say yes."

"He's gonna shatter your record, Don," said a man she'd never seen before to the one called Old Donnie.

She didn't believe they talked about Corey; he had been too far away. Then Corey sprinted up a hill wearing just a pair of shorts and carrying the rifle case. He looked every bit like a movie star. Shirtless, gleaming with sweat, and wearing a smile of accomplishment. He hugged Rachel, handed Old Donnie a handful of something, and laid down on the ground and grinned, trying to catch his breath.

The new man laughed. "Beat your beat time by six hours." He paused and checked his notes. "Wait one day and six hours. Is that right?"

"He could've done better, but yeah, it's right." He looked down at Corey. "Friday at noon. Be ready. You earned your first solo."

Rebecca saw her chance and strolled over and put her knee next to his chest. "Don't hug me, you're sweaty and you stink. If you start work again on Friday at noon, you can take me out on Thursday night."

Instead of answering, he looked up at Old Donnie with pleading in his eyes.

"Please Old Donnie," said Rachel. "He's been so lonely." Rachel wanted Rebecca to date him.

The old man looked at Rebecca and sighed. "As long as he's back and in good shape at the cabin noon Friday."

Corey grinned like a goofy kid and said to Rebecca, "I'd love to."

Stupid reminiscing about Corey. What she wouldn't give for something to take her mind off of him. The last set was a cheap set of luggage and it fit everything else. She only packed a couple of large towels and didn't bother with sheets. The comforter from her grandmother with the matching duvet got rolled into its clear container and put with the third group.

She dragged two bags at a time and lined them up in a row just how Nathan asked her to. She wouldn't miss this cheap apartment. It had done its job and showed she could manage bills and get away from her parents leaching off her, but it held no pleasant memories that didn't involve Corey.

After the luggage lined up in the living room. She wondered what she should do with the last hour. Wooden splinters flew by her, landing on the ugly beige carpet with a boom. Her door flew to the ground and four men charged in. She pulled her stun gun, but it dropped when they stunned her. She tried to roll out and regretted not listening to Corey's description of escaping holds when they wrestled. However, whenever he showed her holds and escapes, they were unclothed during the play times. He had occupied her mind with more pleasant topics. Her thigh felt the sharp jab of a needle and her eyes closed.

Chapter 18—Rescue Rebecca

The drive down I-20 was mind numbing in the dark. Sleep called to me, but I had a couple of hours to stay awake. If nothing happened, I may even get a hotel room for a nap. Back when we were stupid, Miles and I would race this long stretch of road. It's one of those stupid things where we were glad nothing happened.

The night's date needed to happen, but I needed a connection to Earth to figure out how I got played so badly. Luckily, nothing bad came about from this. There was no fight. I corrupted the seed pod, and I didn't fight. Barring extreme tiredness, I intended to turn off right before the Birmingham Airport exit, find a quiet hotel, and create a circle near it, bind the gargoyle, be back home before rush hour, and take a nap.

Turning off before the airport exit, I found an old hotel with some woods, while it was still dark. I kicked off my shoes near some of the eastern honeysuckle and converted it to coral honeysuckle. The Earth Domain was my fourth domain and besides giving me power, it gave the most beneficial of all the minor powers, even though I hardly used it. I could travel at breakneck speeds if I was away from civilization in the woods. I timed myself at four-minute miles for hours. Besides powering up, I had two other magics. Earth absorbed a creature's life force from it through my circles, and I could take ownership of a section of land about the size of an acre to thwart unnatural powers.

I let the local animals know I was about to banish a gargoyle here. Then, between four ugly pruned pine trees, I cut a twig with my sickle and caught it in my wicker basket. I created the circle, created it with three sets of three of them for focus, wrote the symbol with the twig three times, tossed the twig in the circle, and waited for the gargoyle. After fifteen minutes, my torc lit up red, a beautiful red marble gargoyle showed up, and began casting a spell. It was maybe six feet tall, granite composition, and did not struggle.

Old Donnie had mentioned that old large gargoyles could do this, but not a young one. The key to keep the binding was to get the banishment done fast. Old Donnie had told me he had never seen one complete a spell. But gargoyles talked to me, so I focused on the banishing.

I cast the binding and focused on making it perfect. Halfway through the gargoyle disappeared, my circle and honeysuckle disappeared with a loud pop, and there was a red spell book in place of the circle. It looked just like my current spell book. I used the druidic vision in the torc and saw fading red and fading green lines where my circle used to be.

Lights came on in the hotel, so I grabbed the new book and walked to my car nonchalantly. I placed the new book in the messenger bag with the other two. It was identical in size to my other spell book, and the books nearly didn't fit.

Starting up my new car quietly, I pulled back out and drove towards home. When my Mustang crossed over the Alabama-Georgia border, a phone rang in my car. *I didn't even bring my phone, so the sim card wouldn't give my location away.*

After a quick search, I opened my console and the Jim Byrd phone I gave to Preacher Jon was in there. He had even programmed his name into the phone.

"How did you get the phone into my car?"

"We can talk later. They took her." Preacher Jon sounded stressed.

"Who took who?"

I didn't know Preacher Jon well, but he had the voice of someone scared. "Someone, probably with the church, took Rebecca."

"How—Why—What?" Then I started putting things together. "Do you have empath protection?"

"Richard came over and gave me a few, said you were worried about the church. It isn't the church, is it?" Preacher Jon's voice sounded sadder than confused.

"No, but I don't know enough. Use it, but keep it a secret. Let's focus on saving Rebecca, since this could be an inside job." I had to ignore the Nicole part for now.

"She called an emergency phone of Don that I kept."

"What do they want—and—where is she?" I needed facts.

"First, she called twice and the second time said they changed the story, and believe you have something of theirs. They want both it and the book. Nathan tracked her to a building on Northside Drive."

"Text me the address and tell them it will take me time to return. Try to stall them as long as possible."

"Hey, thank you. I'm sending Rachel to help, and Nathan and I will protect ourselves. Corey, please keep this down low. We need to handle this in house without interference."

I agreed but, this is precisely why people shouldn't get involved. Crap, I was wrong about thinking that. She didn't get involved. She wanted to talk to me and now was in danger. Ex-girlfriend or not, she was my responsibility, and I'd do what I could. Leaving someone with the most despicable organization in humanity's history wasn't the type of thing I did. I pulled the sim card and battery out of the phone and put them in my pocket.

I HAD A LONG DRIVE down I-20 and concluded that if they learned I had a new book from the gargoyle, then they knew where I was coming from. The west side of Atlanta made it tricky to get anywhere easily, but I had contingency plans. I had to be patient and realize I needed to make safe choices to stay off the security cameras.

First, I needed to park and get on the train, but of course I couldn't take GA-400 north to park at the station. I had to go up another exit, turn around and then park—all this at the beginning of rush hour. However, rush hour was a benefit for hiding, if not for speed. Mustangs also blended in the Atlanta traffic.

After parking at Marta, I took the train to my storage. While riding the train, I stood with my back to the wall and memorized the path from the storage to the location on Northside drive. The duster and being still dressed from my date helped me fit in as a businessperson. The location of Rebecca appeared to be across the street from the Waffle House near I-75.

After I got off at Oglethorpe station, I walked to the storage facility and kept myself nonchalant. I did not jump the fence into the storage area, but timed my walk and tailgated behind a person while showing him my Tyler Nash badge. This way, it was off the computer log.

Inside the storage locker, I had little to choose from. Rachel had done maintenance here yesterday, and it was a mess. I'd need to straighten it another time. I found a face mask and two helmets. There was not much in the way of weapons. I geared up with the duster, tonfa, a waist pack, and my combat and obsidian knives strapped to my thigh.

I rehearsed the blocking and striking lessons to calm myself. Rachel told me I had improved this past year, but I could feel it now. I'd never be near as good as Rachel or Old Donnie, but I could hold my own with another human. More than one human or a master—well, I'd bring out bar-fighting Corey.

After attaching the spare helmet to the bike's rear seat, sliding the tonfa into my jacket, pulling the cold-weather mask over my head, I zipped the burner phone, sim card, and battery into my jacket. I buttoned the bottom button on the duster to keep the weapons hidden, made sure I tucked my hair in, and put on the helmet.

The bike roared to life fully clean with plenty of gas and rode through rush hour traffic on back roads near Georgia Tech, until I pulled onto Northside Drive.

A mile north and at the bottom of the hill was where I parked at the Waffle House. I secured both helmets to the bike, tucked my tennis shoes into the helmet, but left my cold weather mask on. The rain had been light and consistent for a couple of days now, and everything was soaked.

A GSXR pulled up next to me. Rachel removed her helmet and her hair was a disaster zone. We didn't have time for that, though.

"How's Wesley?"

"Nicole and he are eating breakfast. I know nothing, and Grandpa said to follow your lead. But what's the plan?"

Crap. I hope we didn't need to rescue him next. "Let's go across the street from the house and hide in the woods. We need an exit plan. Come check it out with me."

"Got it. Besides the possibility of a gargoyle, there is a Dark Fey nearby, too. I'm ready for it, though."

I stared at her. Where did she get that information? Nathan? It didn't matter, one thing at a time. "I'm hoping for a burst entry and escape. It will be hard to protect a civilian in a protracted battle. I'm sore from last night and I haven't slept."

She gave me the thumbs up and pulled her surujin with its long chain and weight ends. This was her favorite weapon.

A quick jog across the street led me into the woods across from the house. I had no plans and hoped these guys were only priests and not security. Ducking behind bushes, I hid and picked out three people passing past the windows on the lower floor.

However, I knew my limitations. If they had spells or weapons, then Rachel's limitations around magic prevented her help, and I'd need to take a tremendous risk. I was cranky and tired and this was a terrible mix and I felt anger rise in me at this situation.

Rachel put her hand on mine and whispered. "Count to ten."

I took in two second breaths, held it for four seconds, and exhaled for four seconds through my mouth. One. I did this ten times and regained control of myself.

Squirrels and raccoons were nearby, and I asked them to standby because I needed help. They sent a call out and the trees came alive with movement. You never realize how many small animals live with us until you call them to help.

Eventually, two people in civilian clothes stepped out of the house. It was Suit and Red Shirt from trivia night. I can't say I was shocked. Rachel grabbed my arm. The priest in black vestments stayed in the house and yelled to them, "Oh, pick up extra cream and sugars."

"Looks like we're up," whispered Rachel.

When the car crested the small hill down the road, I popped in my mouth guard, counted to ten, sprinted across the side road, and yanked the storm door open as I pulled a tonfa and pepper gel out of my duster.

The priest stood, raised his hand to cast a spell. When they did this, a bolt of blue would come out and strike me like lightning. My muscles would convulse and pain ripped through me until I could stop them physically. I steeled myself and got mad, but nothing happened. *Bad time for a power outage.*

The priest stood there wide eyed and slack jawed but didn't get to finish looking stupid before I sprayed his face with pepper gel. He howled and clawed at his eyes and I followed up with an uppercut to his jaw with the handle of the tonfa with all my strength, and he crumpled to the floor. *That's why you wear a mouth guard in fights.*

They tied Rebecca up and gagged her. She looked worried. A second priest came out from the back room, and I maneuvered around a recliner. I picked up his short ass and threw him against the wall.

"Cut Rebecca loose. I'll handle short guy," yelled Rachel.

I pulled my knife, slashed her ropes and then pulled down her gag.

"Briefcase, a trap," she expelled. "Papers in desk."

My torc glowed red. The world turned black and white.

I threw an end table out the window to my right. The gargoyle howled, picked up the struggling body of the first priest, yanked his head off, and poured his blood down its throat. Crap, it had powered up with life force and its range had become unlimited. We had to kill it.

"We have to kill it. It's unfettered to its summoning location!" I yelled.

"I got the papers," yelled Rachel.

The other priest was down and out, and a bone extended from his leg.

"Fight it outside," I shouted. Grabbing Rebecca by the belt and shirt collar, I jumped out the broken first-floor window as the gargoyle lunged toward us. *This is a kind of exit plan.* The supernatural creature crashed into the wall and bricks from the side of the house fell off next to the window. I took the brunt of the fall and let her land on me. Earth Power coursed through me, through my bare feet, and I barely felt the fall.

With my toes dug under the grass into the dirt, I whipped my glass breaker at it like a thrown knife and nailed a gargoyle leg through the window. The creature tripped as it took out the window frame and the leg that turned a shiny beige marble caught in the bricks. It howled and thrashed to free itself. I called the animals and asked them to delay the gargoyle as much as they could without risking themselves. Thank goodness this was a marble type and Rachel was more effective.

Rachel's surujin wrapped around its neck, and she rode the supernatural creature to the ground and jumped off into her stance before it could retaliate.

Squirrels showed up first and jumped into the face of the gargoyle, and I jabbed my combat knife into its left arm.

I drew a circle on the ground.

It swung its right arm at my chest as two raccoons leaped onto it. They slowed the punch, but even with Earth Power, it knocked me back five feet.

Rachel had picked up my glass breaker and jabbed it into the creature's back. These soft marble gargoyles were almost a gift compared to the granite type.

It howled as it turned to stone and I leaped as I stood, and jabbed my obsidian knife into its pelvis, and pushed my hand into the gory internals of the howling creature. I placed my other hand in the circle.

Soon my chest burned, and the gargoyle turned to dust.

I thanked the animals, especially the raccoons, and told them to hide because the battle wasn't over. Rachel tucked my glass breaker into my belt and I offered Rebecca my hand. "This isn't over yet," I said.

With Rebecca's hand, I yanked her around the brick, broken siding, and broken glass, and the three of us sprinted across Northside Drive. The cars could not see us, but I swear one changed lanes through me.

I guided her to my bike, put away my mouth guard, and said, "phone," and held out my hand.

"Corey?" Rebecca's voice was weak.

"Not now. Rachel, stay away from Nicole. I'm taking Rebecca to emergency location black." Emergency location black was a place we came up with when we used to run from the police back in our bar fighting days. Miles, Rachel, and I made a promise long ago not to share the location. It's where I parked my old high school van in a shed. We called it black because it was in one of Carol's and Richard's properties next to Black Mountain.

Rebecaa handed me the phone and fumbled with the chin strap on the helmet. "I've never been on a motorcycle before."

Rachel said, "this will hurt." And yanked a piece of glass from Rebecca's shoulder.

I cast squirrel messenger and described Miles. *Emergency, I'm going to take your car and going to black.*

Rachel ran around the bike to bend my license plate in half, while I put my shoes on.

We were in a hurry, and I couldn't be compassionate. I grabbed the sim card and battery out of Rebecca's phone, pushed her hands away from her helmet, and fastened her chin strap before securing mine. "When I come back, put your feet on the pedals and don't take them off until I turn the motorcycle off. Hold on to me for dear life and keep your chest planted in my back. Do that and we live." I put all three pieces of her phone into my motorcycle jacket with my burner phone pieces, then zipped up that pocket.

The world was still black and white. Rachel pulled a grenade out of her pocket.

Where did Rachel get a grenade? Three running steps got me to my motorcycle and Rebecca's sat on the back of the bike wide eyed and her jaw slack.

Rachel took a stack of papers and tucked them into my jacket before zipping it up. "I'll go after your pod."

"Don't worry. I corrupted it when you were dancing. Before the date, I figured Nicole out."

"Stay with me honey... I mean, Rebecca. We're almost free." There went my tough-guy image. I slipped and called her honey like we still dated.

I started the bike, rode down the dirt embankment, and jumped the curb onto Northside drive. My torc lit up blue. The GSXR started, and it had a louder, slower thump today. Rachel tuned it for speed. Rebecca gripped me tighter. I heard a police siren. *The policeman couldn't be real if it chased us in the realm of black and white.*

The cop in the rear-view mirror had mandibles for a face. Rachel's GSXR roared up to the cop car. She bashed the passenger window with a glass breaker glove and threw a grenade inside of it. I knew Rachel was good, but with her helmet and leathers on, it was as if my rearview mirror became a movie screen.

Rachel's engine roared to life and drowned out my bike. We were doing ninety in a thirty-five, near the top end of my bike with two riders. We rode on Northside Drive and stayed left away from the highway cameras, then weaved around traffic. There was no telling when I'd pop back into the real world.

The new bike of Rachel roared by me with its front wheel in the air like we were standing still, and I heard an explosion behind me. The shockwave wobbled us and if it wasn't for my speed, I bet we'd have wiped out.

I'd have to rely upon my knowledge of Atlanta's back streets. I raced north on Northside Drive and avoided the highway. Then I turned right at the shopping center that took me to Buckhead.

Rebecca's shoulder planted into my back, and her grip was almost too tight. *Perfect.*

I cut over the streets until I came to Peachtree, one of the many streets named Peachtree, and picked up I-85 north and pulled onto the highway. Then the word came back into view and color and I eased up on the accelerator. Rachel was nowhere to be seen.

I thought about other things to get my mind focused on the escape. Rachel wouldn't have left me if there was still immediate danger. She bragged when she tuned for racing, she could pop the front wheel at eighty and ride it to one-twenty and top out at one hundred and eighty-six miles an hour. Now I knew it wasn't bragging.

There was no telling if anyone followed me in the heavy traffic, but when I pulled off on the exit, it became easier to verify we had made it away. Soon, I was in Suwannee and pulled into Miles' driveway and pulled the bike into the back of the stairs and covered it.

Miles met us in the garage. "I have food, med kit, and supplies in the trunk. How bad is it?"

"They kidnapped Rebecca, and it was an inside job. Nicole is an empath. Stay as far from her as you can."

"My dad gave Trish and I earrings too after he did yours." He helped Rebecca into the passenger seat and gave her a towel to hold. "It's an hour and a half from here, so keep pressure." He leaned her seat back.

I backed out and drove to the safe house.

Chapter 19—Black Mountain

"Are we just going to drive in silence and you tell me things when we get there?" asked Rebecca.

"I'm sorry. Your world is even more upside down than mine and I lost myself. My brain that was too stupid to see I was being setup." I put the cruise control on and sifted into the middle right lane. "You are about to see my biggest secret. This is where Miles, Rachel, and I would hide out from the police until whoever was mad at us dropped charges. We kept it secret from everyone else."

"Back way the hell up. Ugh..." The pain from her shoulder must get to her.

"One second." I reached into the back and got out the ibuprofen and a bottled water and handed it to her. "Sorry, we can take care of the wound soon enough."

"Thank you."

"Okay, before I left on my week trip, I caught Nicole lying to me. In retrospect, she probably set me up. I'm too stupid to have caught her."

"Just give me the facts because you make so few mistakes that you beat yourself up when you make one."

"Okay, in Chattanooga, you saw me confront her. I told her not to use her major power on me. She can predict what to say to a person to get her desired outcome. It's probably actions too, because I guess she used it on the kisses to make me fall for her."

"No extrapolation. She wasn't faking that kiss."

My heart lunged at that hope and I beat that dumb shit down. No way I would believe Nicole again. "Anyway, she's been disobeying her family, and tracking down the killers of her parents, and has been since middle school. She has notebooks full of top-notch stuff I could have never done."

"That's what attracted you. I was wondering." She chuckled.

"What?"

"You're attracted to competent and strong women who can hold their own with you. As long as it was the Nicole who wanted a man, you had zero interest. As soon as she became super spy Nicole, who could thwart allies and enemies, you got a raging boner."

"I never had sex with her, thankfully." Wait. I kinda did. Ugh.

"You know what I mean. Go on."

"Well, I agreed to keep her secret and protect her. We pretended to date so Preacher Jon wouldn't put her in an arranged marriage." I tried to get just the facts out.

"It didn't look fake, and you had a light in your eyes." She sounded a little sad.

"Yeah, fooled with magic. I told it could turn into more, but we'd go super slow but we'd tell others."

"Interesting." Rebecca recovered her composure.

"Well, when I got my new car, I inventoried my stuff. My magnolia seed pod was missing, and she was the only one besides Rachel who had access to it."

"What does that do?"

"It's the only thing that can break one of my circles."

Rebecca sat up and grunted, "What?" She exclaimed.

"Yeh. I keep one for emergencies. I created a new one and then, on the double date, I saw it in Nicole's purse. Long story short, Suit and Red shirt, the ones who left for coffee, made a deal with Nicole and she gave it to them."

"The two professionals had your magnolia and were bragging about it. Corey, they guaranteed your death."

"Luckily, I corrupted it first."

Rebecca lay back down. "You live a crazy life. But thank you for explaining everything. And all your actions make sense for what you've described, and I believe you. However, I think there could be more than one explanation. How did you circumvent her power?"

"My new earring blocks empath powers." I pointed to my ear.

"Nice. Let's go hide and after we both sleep and eat, let's work together to come up with a next step."

"Okay." It was nice talking to Rebecca, but I was falling into the same trap of believing someone who didn't have my best interests at heart. She dumped me and I needed to remember I was a loner.

We pulled into the small town, then down an old road that needed to be replaced before I was born, and then to the third farm down a dirt road. I parked Miles' car behind the shed and grabbed the key from the fake rock by the shed. We walked up the stairs, and I held her hand past the hole in the wooden porch, and we ambled into the old house.

Step one was medical. We sat in the kitchen and she removed her jacket. "Let's get this taken care of so it doesn't get infected. It's not terrible."

"Just in case you're wondering, it's one of the worst wounds I've ever had."

"Sorry, my life is kind of violent."

"You know, I hardly believe Preacher Jon when he talked about you." She removed her sweater and wore one of the fancy-cut t-shirts she liked. It had been white, but blood had soaked a third of it. *Not too bad.* She had pulled the sleeve and exposed her shoulder and the glass embedded cut.

Her cut was slight and had almost stopped bleeding. Grabbing a large band aid and extra gauze. I held a towel under the cut, and she grabbed it from me, and held it. "This may sting a little." I poured saline over the cut and, as she dabbed it dry, I put antibiotic cream on the gauze and then patched it.

"Not much for furniture?" Her hands shook, and she made a joke to calm herself. Being kidnapped, facing a gargoyle, being rescued by an ex, and riding on a motorcycle for the first time while escaping captors, apparently raised her adrenaline a little.

"Normally we sit on the floor of the living room and ask each other what the hell we were doing with our lives." Those were good times.

She laughed. "How'd you stop? Being as stupid?"

"Miles got back together with Trish and I saved Old Donnie's life. When he found out I was Rachel's Corey he laughed so hard he nearly wet himself. He gave me a purpose. In turn, Rachel got a purpose and eventually Miles—until recently."

It was time to check out my wound. I eased my shirt off and touched my chest. Nothing broke, but I took a wicked shot. The red was already spreading with the broken capillaries.

"That looks like actual damage, like internal bleeding."

"Probably. This is a gargoyle punch."

"You have a third tattoo up there. Why's that?"

"The biceps tattoo is from when I killed the snake hunter and reclaimed the word. Each of these on my chest are the names of gargoyles I killed. I've killed three of them."

"Don't you do that all the time?"

"I banish them all the time. When I banish them to the Realm of Darkness, they can come back eventually. They aren't dead. The one I killed is dead unless the gargoyle can take my flesh."

"Take your flesh? Jesus. You don't make being a druid sound fun."

"Sometimes it is, but yeah, I hear you. My retirement plan is to find someone to guard my grave for three days so the Earth will reclaim the names on my skin."

"So, what's the plan? Do you go to the ER?"

"For this? No. I heal fast. That's the fortunate part of being a druid. Get hurt a lot, but heal fast to get hurt again."

She giggled like nothing bad happened today and that made me feel better. She kicked off her flats on the floor and her jean skirt, contrast with the rope burns from the tight ropes. "Why are you dressed up?"

I sat down and pulled out the picture of Nicole and me from last night.

"You knew at this point. The light had left your eye."

"You are right. I'd already protected myself from the magic." Now I felt sad.

"What now?" There was a weird tone in her voice.

"I'm back to being dumb, Corey. But at least it proved my point of being solo was right. I had no one to talk to switch everything up."

"Corey, she was soloing too. If neither of you soloed, this wouldn't have happened."

"You hoped it wouldn't happen. Traitors happen regardless."

"Don't assign malice where stupidity is possible." She used a fancy sentence on me.

"Whatever that means."

"Corey, it means she may not be out to get you. People do stupid things—like all the time. Assume stupidity causes actions before you think people are out to get you."

"You know, if I was just here to save the world, I'd run away and live in the woods. But I know I can't do that until Bishop Pedrotti is dead, since he can track me down. That and I'd never leave Rachel."

"A heart break and you're ready to give up on the world?"

"Heartbreak? I've done everything right. I take on beasts, fight bad guys, and hide from the law to protect people. The world takes Old Donnie away. You break my heart, but I persevere and keep doing the right thing. I work with people, and I think I can have a relationship in the future, and it turns out I was a gullible fool that almost got you and I killed. If that's just heartbreak, I'd hate to see what's next."

"I'm sorry, you've had about the worst three months possible." She sounded genuinely remorseful.

"I'm cranky and going to take a nap. Miles packed food and medical, so grab whatever you want. We'll figure things out later."

PREACHER JON FELT OLD. He had everything under control and Corey was coming around. Now Preacher Jon had been required to contact The Tribe for help. Grandpa Don was friendly with them and the Southeast was the only region that didn't prosecute them. They were a group of Realized that didn't recognize the authority of the area owners. They liked the woods and trails, and hung out at the shooting range, and ran crazy survivalist contests like the Redneck Biathlon. When Preacher Jon asked for help, they said no. When he told them it was Grandpa Don's boy that needed help, they agreed.

CJ himself put on his tactical gear when he learned it was Nicole and Corey. The man had become close with Grandpa Don and would often train together. The leader of The Tribe was taller than Miles, but as thick as Old Donnie. He was full of weathered muscles, gray hair and beard, and wore camouflage everywhere.

When Preacher Jon explained the situation—not one of them blinked. He did not know what was going on with Nicole, but he had to be ready for anything. The coffee shop was a little crowded, but he made out the small round table for two with Nicole and her friend from first grade, Wesley. He strolled over there next to CJ.

"Grandpa," exclaimed Nicole.

"CJ from The Tribe is with me. He is immune to all Realized powers."

"What?"

"Are you coming in handcuffs, or would you like to ride in the car like my granddaughter?"

Nicole started crying and stood up.

Preacher Jon refrained from hugging his youngest granddaughter, but it hurt.

Nathan came up behind him and placed her coat over her shoulders. "Wesley, you can ride with us without cuffs as a friend of mine."

"What's going on?" said Wesley.

Preacher Jon put on a show because he was sure at least one church agent was here. He kept it low, knowing they'd be bugging Nicole's table. "Nicole Hendrix, we hereby charge you with the theft of a circle breaker from Coire Norwood and delivering it to the church. Wesley, you are a person of interest. Please join us."

Preacher Jon and Nathan escorted the two to the new SUV. Once everyone was seated, Nicole burst out of her tears and said, "it was just a plant he never used."

Nathan turned and said, "It's the only thing that can break Corey's circle from any realm and the only guaranteed way to kill him."

Nicole burst out crying and couldn't answer.

Preacher Jon looked at the faces of Nathan and Wesley, and they had tears as well. This was going to be a devastating day. CJ sat next to Nicole and his face stayed hard as well. Preacher Jon did his best to emulate the look.

They rode without talking and let Nicole cry herself out. The four of them, joined by CJ, Combat Josh from The Tribe, walked into the control room, and back to the anti-magic room. Preacher Jon sat Nicole down and called Rachel in.

Rachel burst in with new tears and puffy eyes. "Nicole, tell me you didn't kidnap Rebecca and plan to kill Corey."

"I didn't. I'm so close to finding the location of the man who killed mom and dad. It was a trade."

The explanation may be the truth, but it would take a long time to get to the end.

Preacher Jon had learned a lot about empaths the past couple of days and when Richard explained Corey asked for protection from an empath, he realized he was a day late and a dollar short. The only thing that confused him now was how the hell Corey put it all together but couldn't graduate from college. But now was not the time for this. "Please sit Rachel."

He walked over to the switch and changed the lighting. "The room's truth detection system is in place. The room will light up red for a lie and purple for a half truth or missing information. Rachel, did you know of the plan to kill Coire Norwood, the druid?"

"No." Rachel started crying.

"Nathan, did you?"

"No, sir."

"What is going on?" asked Wesley. "We double dated last night, and no one planned to kill anyone. Corey and Nicole danced all night and were riding together when they dropped us off."

Preacher Jon nodded. The lights never once changed. "During the date, our enemy received Corey's stolen magnolia seed pod from Nicole Hendrix. CJ, could you explain what your agents saw?"

The gruff old man in combat gear stood up. "We try to monitor Don's kin. He was good to us. We had been watching the boy, but we discovered Nicole traveled in dangerous crowds and moved resources to watch her. That night, our first agent in disguise as a waiter, touched a new piece of jewelry on Corey. He discovered the young man protected himself from empaths. He immediately called in reserves."

"How?" asked Nicole. But Preacher Jon cut her off.

"Don's boy, Corey, is sharp but overconfident. He identified the team assigned for transfer, and prevented their plan, and challenged two professional killers to brawl. The one in charge measured Corey and backed down."

CJ Shook his head. "That boy has been overboard with training. However, we have an eyewitness that saw him do something to the item and place it in his pocket. Nicole took the seed and made the transfer herself."

"He never used it. It was a seed he carried," Nicole admitted the truth, and the room kept its blue tint.

CJ sat and remained stoic.

Preacher Jon explained. "It was his emergency seed. It's the only thing that can break his circle. If they break his circle while he is in a banishing, he takes the full impact from the release of the magic. This will kill him. Even if he discovers some new form of magic to protect him, he'd still have to fight the creature without a circle."

Nathan added, "snapping a circle during a binding is one hundred percent lethal in all recorded instances."

Nicole looked up to see the room stay with its blue tint. "Is the lying turned on?"

"I'm sure Corey is taking this in stride," said Rachel.

The room turned red and Nicole burst into tears again.

"I'm not close with Corey, but I've known him for a decade. He's always a borderline emotional wreck. Can we help him?" asked Wesley. "He was so happy just yesterday."

"I know a way to help," said Rachel, "but I need some help from CJ to do it safely."

Combat Josh looked at Rachel. He growled, "help from me? Do you remember me?"

"Yep, and I rode on your shoulders to keep up with Grandpa Don. If I can access the shed, I can get Corey out of the dumps and thinking clearer."

Combat Josh grumbled and tossed her the keys with a scowl.

"Send us information so we can get a good idea of what is happening." Preacher Jon didn't realize how close Rachel was with CJ or he'd have made contact earlier.

Nathan shouted, "grab the box on my desk and hand it to Rebecca."

Rachel jumped forward and kissed the gruff man on the cheek, and ran out of the room.

Preacher Jon steeled himself. This was going to be a long day, and he'd have to get into too many details, but he had to. He had three hopes. The first was that Nicole was guilty of being naïve. Second was that Corey corrupted the seed pod as reported. The third was that he could keep this all from getting out to the other areas. "Nicole, when did you first notice you were an empath?"

Nicole sniffled. She had tested this procedure and Preacher Jon doubted she'd ever be on this side of the questions. "The day the police told Corey to stop investigating his parents' death. His emotions overwhelmed me."

Chapter 20—The Blues always makes me sad

I sat in bed and wondered if anything was worth it. Nicole played me so thoroughly I couldn't trust myself anymore. Old Donnie's voice came back to despite me, not wanting to hear the advice.

> *There are going to be days where you question everything. Why save people? Why fight bad people? Let me tell you, the lesson of letting bad things happen and seeing the results hurts. Knowing you could have stopped it will break you. When these questions come—and they will—fight your way through, because this will be the hardest part of your life.*

I didn't believe it back then with my dreams of being a hero and helping the weak. Now the only reason I wanted to help was because Rachel wanted to. I rolled over in the bed and it was still dark out. I finally let my emotions out and cried into my pillow. No one needed to see me. I cried like when Rebecca left me and I knew I would eventually fall back asleep, but until then, this damn pillow could soak up my tears.

Tears fell from my failure to go solo. I cried for not having Miles anymore and Rachel not being nearby. Rebecca's breakup came back and, of course, the betrayal of Nicole. Dropping out of college proving I was stupid got its time, but most everything was for Old Donnie. He could have made everything better.

The bed depressed, and I jumped.

"Just me. Put your shorts on," said Rachel.

I slipped them on. "Sorry, I'm a failure."

"Shut up and cry out all the sadness. I'm going to cry too." She climbed under the covers. "I just watch the first part of Nicole's questioning."

"If we're crying about our lot in life, can I join you?" Rebecca called from the door.

If she needed to cry, we might as all be pathetic together.

"Come on in," said Rachel. "Ripped from your life, kidnapped, and shown a world that sucks—you better join us. Come cry it out with us."

"Why would have Nicole done that, if she was going to do this?" I asked the pillow.

Both women put their arms on my back. There were no answers.

I slid over to make sure there was room and soon the three of us cried like we were little kids away from home for the first time.

I DON'T KNOW WHO FELL asleep first, but when it was light, I lifted my face off the soggy pillow and sat up and looked around.

Rebecca and Rachel were under the blanket and beginning to stir. I opened the closet and saw we had left a bunch of old clothes here.

"I put away the groceries," mumbled Rachel. "Make breakfast, I got a surprise."

I grabbed an old set of jeans and an old Allman Brothers Band shirt. The shirt was tight, and the pants were loose. I thought I used to be in good shape, but the large waist and small chest and arms of my old clothes told a different story.

I'd be using a stove today, and I had to remind myself how to use it. Rachel had bought a bunch of eggs, bacon, butter, and bread.

She even got frozen pizzas. This was one of her best jobs going to the store alone.

Rachel sat in the living room, looking at the papers from the priests. I grabbed my messenger bag and pulled out the notebook from Nicole. "I don't know if this is any good, but this is what Nicole gave me about her research."

Rachel wore leggings and showed a honeysuckle tattoo on her right ankle.

"Ah! What's that?" I pointed right at the tattoo.

"I got this after I killed the crab like Dark Fey in the cop car."

"You can't have that!"

"Why I killed the Dark Fey?" She picked it up and showed it off.

"Corey finds ankle bracelets and ankle tattoos sexy." Rebecca giggled. "He bought me like three ankle bracelets."

She lifted her foot up and wiggled her toes. "I like it."

I returned to the kitchen and eventually came out with plates for everyone, along with glasses of water. We didn't get drinks, but it still rocked given what we sometimes ate up here.

"I need to tell you guys something." Rebecca helped distribute the food. "Nicole got things from my place. Others didn't need to see to protect me. She also used woman privilege to be the one to screen my pictures, so no men saw them."

"Go on," I said.

"Remember the slinky lingerie you got me? She protected it from anyone else seeing it. There were pictures of you and I on my phone of an intimate nature, and no one else saw them but her. I don't think Nicole is a bad person."

Rachel hugged Rebecca. "Thank you, I agree. Corey is going to have more problems though, since Nicole gave him oral when she waxed him and, you know Corey."

"Oh Corey, I'm sorry. By the way, can you do a wax without sex because..." She tailed off when she saw my face. "I guess not."

"Corey, try to let that go and think with just one head, okay?" said Rachel.

"So, Corey, what's the deal with the magnolia pod?" asked Rebecca.

Why were things confusing me? "It's the only way to erase part of my circle. If you do that, it breaks the circle instead of dispelling it, using it, or defeating it. If it breaks, all the energy released would backlash onto me. This would be fatal to me, but with the strength of my circle, it would be deadly for a pretty big radius around me."

"Holy crap. Why don't you tell people?"

"Because I believe telling people the easiest way to kill me is shortsighted."

Rachel laughed.

Passion and intimacy subjects got mocked for whatever reason and to get past this Nicole issue, I needed to bring them up. "Help me out. Could it be I'm a good kisser and that's why the kisses with Nicole rocked?"

"Stay focused Corey. They have one and are going to trap you with it, and I think I know where."

This was hard to explain the importance of for me. "I corrupted the seed pod they have. But this is important. Maybe Nicole is innocent of using her powers to get me to like her. It could be I'm just a good kisser."

Rebecca turned around and rolled her eyes. "Geez Corey. Yes. You are an exceptional kisser. I still dream about you gently sucking my bottom lip before moving in for one of your passionate kisses. You are a passionate lover and your tender touch still causes longing in me. Is that what you want to hear?"

"Um, no, but it's nice. I'm wondering if Nicole wasn't using her powers on me and I was a good kisser and she responded to that and that's why the kisses had power."

Rebecca turned bright red. "Oh. That makes sense. Forget about the other stuff. Yes, you're a good kisser. Now, what do you mean you corrupted the pod?"

"Could you teach Wesley about kissing, because he needs help," interjected Rachel.

"I'll tell you how to guide him to make it better." I walked to the new pants I no longer intended to wear and grabbed the seed from Nicole's pod. Which a quick throw, the seed landed in front of Rebecca.

She wore camouflage leggings and a tank top with an American Eagle on it. That wasn't her usual choice. She must have raided our closet of white trash fashion. "Nicole left me alone with her purse long enough to pull the seed out. However, even me touching it should have corrupted it, but breaking the fibbo-something or other sequence definitely broke it."

"Fibonacci sequence?" asked Rebecca.

"That's it. They have a worthless seed pod, not one untouched by flesh. A working pod needs to be cut by a druid between midnight and dawn using a silver sickle, caught in a wicker basket, wrapped in magnolia leaves, and secured with plant twine. Once it's touched, it has minutes before it loses potency."

"You can remember all that, but you can't remember the name of a famous mathematician?" asked Rebecca.

Rachel chuckled. "In fairness to him, only one of those pieces of information keeps him alive."

Last night's emotional drain helped the spirits in the room and despite not being manly, I was glad we all did it and did it together. It hit me; I wasn't mad at Rebecca anymore. "If you want to know more. Old Donnie couldn't erase part of my circle with his seed pod. Only I can make a seed pod strong enough to break my circle. That's why I only keep one on me and I check for it regularly."

"Corey. I know how you can beat the bishop, but you're going to need a team of people," said Rebecca. "Plus, I know you're willing to walk into a trap."

Where did I hear trap referenced before? Wait a second. I was talking to Rebecca, and it was normal. "Oh, my god."

"What?" exclaimed both women.

"Rebecca, I no longer have animosity towards you. It finally sunk in you did nothing to me in malice, that you made the choice to break up with me for a reason you thought would help me. I apologize for the way I acted the past few months."

Rebecca's jaw dropped. "I can't process this now. Could we go back to defeating the bad guy with a team of people?"

I felt better and leaned back against the old chair. "I can put together a few people, but I don't know where he is or where he is going to be."

"Nicole does, and the papers from the priests confirm a lot. Oh crap. I forgot about the box."

A thought meandered through my brain. Nicole kept talking about walking into a trap. "Wait, you said trap. Nicole has been telling me I'd willingly walk into a trap."

"That's the crux of her plan. She must have been secretly running it by you." Rebecca stood up and opened a box and plugged it in.

"Living room plugs don't work. Come into the kitchen. We have one working plug in there." I looked at her. "You know, the way you fill out those camouflage leggings—would've turned my life around back in the day."

"Yeh, I never filled them out like that," added Rachel.

"There wasn't a lot to choose from up here." Rebecca blushed.

We waited while she put it together and I reminisced about how people would joke Rachel wasn't allowed to pick her own clothes, but I could never tell, and the same people would tell me the same thing.

"Okay Corey. Preacher Jon needs some questions to ask Nicole." Said Rebecca once she had the box with lights working and a pad in her hands.

"Corey, be careful," said Rachel. "We've detained her in the interrogation room, where there is no magic. The room detects what she says is the truth or partial truth, or a lie."

"So, no asking her if she loved me or if I was just a good kisser? What else is there?"

"Geez Corey, kiss me," said Rebecca. "Test it out and get it out of your system."

"What?" That was a weird statement.

"Kiss me, dammit. I don't want to hear this anymore." Rebecca sauntered towards me aggressively wearing the camo leggings and her breasts swayed without a bra in the tank top with the eagle on it. Flashbacks of her dating came to me, when she took that stance and would push me on the bed. She put her arms on my shoulder and rested her fingers on my torc like she used to when we dated.

This was the easiest way to answer my question. I lifted her chin with my finger and I started the kiss off like I started all my kisses with her. My hands rested on her temples, and I gently sucked her bottom lip and lingered for the full kiss. When I felt her tongue caress mine, I ran my tongue around hers. The emotions of our summer love rushed to me. We'd meet at parks and date on the grass. She'd dress me up and go to fancy places where she'd smile and make feel like I belonged, and we'd make love on the patio for hours. I stepped back and caught my breath.

"Shit, that was a mistake," said Rebecca. "I forgot what that felt like."

"Holy crap, Corey," said Rachel. "That was a cut above the one with Nicole."

Sitting in the kitchen chair, without my anger at her, all the emotions of not being over her flooded back in. "I'm sorry for making you do that." No covering up these feelings.

"I, um, I think I made you. But are you satisfied that it's not Nicole's special magic, and it's you and kissing?"

"Yes."

"Can you two kiss again so I can get a video of it?" Asked Rachel, holding her phone. "It's to show Wesley."

If I kissed Rebecca again, I'd need to go somewhere and collect my emotions. Even the question brought tears to my eyes. "I think that's my last kiss until I figure out what's wrong with me, and why I need that so badly." In no way could I kiss Rebecca again without looking the fool.

Rachel pouted and put the phone away.

"Look, let's get past this," said Rebecca. "Ask the questions." Her voice cracked, but I didn't dare look at her.

"Good idea." I thought for a second. "How did she trick me into thinking I caught her?"

"She didn't Corey. You're not dumb," said Rebecca.

"Then we'll know that for sure," I replied. "Here's another. How truthful is the book she gave me of the information about Pedrotti?"

She typed into the pad that came with the box she opened. "That's a good question. I'm going to add where is the most likely ambush spot and date?"

I needed a question to figure out the setup. She was shocked I could take out the people who were picking up the seed pod. Did she think I could not fight from all the training earlier? "The morning of our date, she asked me to train with Rachel using Earth Power. Was that to wear Rachel and I out in case there was a fight? Oh and, what information was worth the seed pod?"

"Okay, it's ten am and we can start drinking," said Rachel. "Come out and see my surprise. Corey, grab the ice from the freezer."

Rebecca did something and put the pad down, satisfied.

We followed Rachel out, and there was a trailer with dirt bikes on it and coolers. I put ice in the cooler and the beer was already cold from outside. She bought a couple of cases.

Rachel picked up two bottles of wine. Large bottles. "I got a bottle of red and white that the woman at the counter said would go good with mudding."

"Well, I'm dressed for it," said Rebecca. She grabbed a coat and Rachel and I grabbed the dirt bike gear off the trailer and put it on, then rolled the dirt bikes onto the ground and got them started. Rachel secured the coolers on the back of my bike and she rode Rebecca to Keyton's Swamp.

WE STOPPED TO UNLOAD the beer and a second pair of hands helped me grab the cooler. Verenuala smiled and helped me move the cooler next to the sitting rocks. He and Fionnestra smiled and sat on the rocks, while they watched me make a fire to warm the resting area. We had a pit and wood ready since, even in summer, the swamp mud stayed chilly. The temperature was near freezing today.

"Rebecca, let me introduce you to the two Daoine, who have guided Rachel and I to the Spring Court."

Fionnestra skipped to me when I finished. "That kiss was something else. It's hard to keep track of all your passionate kisses, but this one had the court talking." The Daoine hugged me and Verenuala hugged Rebecca, who was not as uncomfortable. "We love people who can be passionate with members of the Spring Court."

"Do you all watch us at all times?"

"Of course not silly," said Fionnestra, who held my hand and stood like I'd seen Rebecca stand. "When a Spring Court member experiences passion, it opens a portal to the Fey Realm to share it."

"He holds you in his heart and that kiss was so wonderful," said Verenuala.

Rebecca hadn't picked up the wine yet, but that was enough for her to open the bottle of red and pour some into a plastic cup. "Wine?"

Rachel had just chugged the first beer. She grabbed a second and tossed me one.

"You should hang around and you can see what youth do after a bad day," I said.

"We'll watch for a bit, but looking at all the intoxicants, we'll give you the powers and have young Nathan tell you about them tomorrow," said Verenuala.

"Sorry, our bodies cannot handle Earth intoxicants," added Fionnestra.

I felt a burn below my underwear line. I pulled my pants and underwear and to the right of the little druid, I had a tattoo of the sun. Rachel was looking at her tattoo, too.

"Congratulations Druid and Bard of the Spring Court. Now we can watch your plan to be happier." The two Daoine took a seat on the sitting rocks, on either side of Rebecca.

The dirt bike was alive after I gave it some gas. I put my goggles over my dirt bike helmet and yelled watch out for Rooster tails. Tires ripped into the mud but too much front brake flew me over the handlebars. Everyone joined my laughter and applauded.

After standing, I moved the kick starter out and kicked the flooded engine to life. While standing on the pegs, I took a large circular path on the drier but rougher parts of the old pond to get used to the to the different terrain. Braver, once I built up confidence, I took a jump to the edge of the puddle and splashed mud all around. With all the back brake, I slowed, planted my left foot, turned the handlebars, and popped the clutch. Mud splattered my back and from the mirror the mud up fell from twenty feet up. The front wheel came up, causing me to lose control and wipe out into a puddle.

I got the bike up and needed to get it to the side to clean off the chain and let it unfold itself again. On the edge, with my helmet off, I cleaned the packed-in mud until I heard Rachel start her motorcycle. "You coming in?"

"Drinking a second beer first. I never got to go mudding, so you'll have to show me," she shouted.

I rode over to talk without shouting. "Here are tips. Keep your feet on the pegs and be prepared to stand a lot and keep your butt back on the seat. Brake evenly and you can use your clutch to do a lot of your breaking. Street bikes are mostly front brake but do not do that here. That's how I did the header."

She laughed and guzzled down her beer.

"Keep momentum and most importantly, do rooster tails ever couple of jumps."

"What's a rooster tail?"

I drank down my beer and put my helmet on. "Watch how the mud looks."

I kicked the bike to life, planted my left foot, popped the clutch with the wheel pointed left, and kicked the rear end around with a spinning back tire, and then took off in a wheelie.

The mud must have coated her and still might be raining down. Her bike roared to life behind me.

We rode around and she got me back with a rear tire kick in loose mud. She coated me with mud as I tried to stand up my bike after wiping out in a puddle.

We stopped to drink a beer and the two Daoine wished us luck and took off laughing and shaking off mud.

"They are nice," said Rebecca. "You two made a good choice in joining the Spring Court. You fit in perfectly."

"Do you want a turn, I asked Rebecca." She sat with a full plastic cup of red wine next to the fire in her coat.

"I've never ridden."

"I'll show you."

"That's a bit much, but can you ride me around a little?"

Rachel put a helmet and goggles on her and made her wear boots while I drank another beer. She got on the back of my bike and held on. I started off in a circle and then took off with a wheelie. We moved forward and took off with the front wheel in the air. I power turned with foot planted rooster tail, and took off again to hit the jump, and felt her barely stay on after the second bounce. Then we raced Rachel around the track.

Her grip around me was reminiscent of the kiss this morning. She held me like she never wanted to let me go. Then I realized this wasn't me making it up. She still loved me, too. We were a mess.

Rebecca hit my side and pointed to the coolers. I headed over there and dropped her off. "Mother of God. I see why you do this. That was all adrenaline all the time. How do you keep your heart from bursting?"

"It's like an addiction," I replied. "Fight gargoyles and your fun needs to be a bit more than a game of checkers."

We alternated drinking and resting with beer and chatting with Rebecca. Mud covered all of us and the sun was about to go down. We were all exhausted. "Two beers left," she said.

"I got an idea," said Rachel. "Let's give proof to everyone that Rachel has good ideas."

She put the saddlebags back on and took off and I followed her, glad we were on private property. We pulled up to the back of the cabin and parked. Rachel pulled her phone out.

"Okay, first one, helmets on. Now helmets off."

"Mud is covering you two," said Rebecca.

I looked, and mud covered her face, too. I laughed, and I took the picture with us both laughing. "Last one drinking beers."

I turned the camera to the video. "Video us racing." I started guzzling. She keyholed her beer, popped the top and shotgunned it, while Rebecca turned up the bottle of red wine.

Rachel finished and belched. Rebecca turned the bottle of red wine upside down and watched one drop fall out as she peered into the bottle, looking for more. By the time I finished mine. I could barely contain my laughter as I belched as well and lost my balance and tipped over and fell on the ground.

"You aren't really going to send that, are you?" Asked Rebecca.

"Of course I am," said Rachel. "I snapped the pictures and video while I tagged Corey, you, Nathan, Nicole, Trish, CJ, and Miles with the caption. *Rachel has good ideas!*"

She showed me and replies popped up immediately. *Jealous,* replied Miles.

"Nathan just replied, saying I am a bad influence on you!" I exclaimed.

"He's jealous," added Rachel, who started laughing.

I put out the fire and covered it with mud and Rachel packed up the back of my bike with the coolers. We rode back to the house, and I pulled out the hose to get the bulk of the mud off of us before we walked in the house. Each of us kept falling over and we had to focus on getting things clean. The sun had gone down, and it was getting dark.

"I'm running to get the first shower," yelled Rachel. Lights popped on in the house.

"Take too long and I'm joining you in there!" I joked. While I shivered, it was probably a half-joke.

I turned the hose on Rebecca, who squealed. She jumped up and down and yelled, "that's cold!"

"Has anyone has ever hosed you off in the yard before?" I asked.

She ran into the house with most of the mud off of her. "No! I'm freezing."

I cleaned our chest protectors, gloves, boots, and helmets. Water ran brown with mud in the yard, but the gear was clean.

Inside the house, I peeled off the jeans and shirt and ran into the kitchen in my underwear and popped two pizzas into the oven. Then I stood outside the bathroom and shouted, "Pizzas in the oven. Hurry or I'm coming in!"

"Come in if you're brave enough. We're not getting out," shouted Rachel.

Eventually, we all showered, and the ladies were changing in the other room.

When I pulled the pizzas out, I called out. "Pizzas are ready." I cut slices in the pizza and pulled them out into the living room.

Rachel got up and stumbled into the wall and then into the bedroom and got a pair of pink shorts that said *hot* on the back. She tossed them to me. "These were too big for me. I bet they fit you."

Holding onto the recliner, I stood, then slipped them on in the kitchen. I walked back into the living room. "They fit."

We all laughed when I showed them. "I'm going to bed because I doubt I'll stand again if I sit down." I barely made the bed and was asleep before I found all the covers.

Chapter 21—The Tribe

I woke and my head didn't quite feel as it should. *What happened?* I cracked my eyes and went to rub my eyes, but heads pinned my arms down. While I blinked my eyes rapidly to get some moisture, I heard '*mmmmm*' next to me and someone moved. It was Rachel. That was good.

When my eyes stayed open, Rebecca was on my right arm. They both wore muscle halter tops, and I felt their legs and torses on me and everything felt right. To enjoy the moment, I thought through my brain fog to yesterday.

> *We went mudding. I put out the fire, and we cleaned up our trash. Did we send out a video? Back at the cabin, we washed off with the hose and I cleaned the gear too. I cooked the pizzas, and we showered and changed. Nothing bad there. We ate pizza and I could barely stay away, and then everything was blank.*

"Holy crap, Corey. Explain this!" exclaimed Miles from the other room. "That's not snuggling. Two women and half naked!" I saw Nathan and a guy in camo turning. He was taller than Miles and looked like he was laughing.

"Keep it down, Miles," said Rachel. "This is as happy as I've felt in a long time."

"Miles. Rachel is right. I am surrounded by happiness and peace for the first time I remember." Everything was peaceful and happy. I wish I could live like this. "Plus, we are all three dressed."

"Get dressed and come out, but you ain't living this one down." Miles sounded exasperated.

I paid attention to the room and came back to reality from my moments of bliss. "Miles, have we given up the location of emergency location black to everyone?" My head was foggy, but there seemed to be too many people for a secret location.

"Dude, everyone knew already."

"What's going on?" asked Rebecca in a sleepy voice.

"Miles doesn't understand bonding anymore," said Rachel. She stood up, and I pulled the pillow over my face.

"Are you two decent?" Clothes landed on me, and I sat up and got dressed under the covers as fast as I could and walked out with the two into the living room.

Nathan and Miles had cleaned up the pizza and the towels in the living room. I sat next to the picture window and leaned my face against the cold glass. Rachel sat next to me.

"CJ?" asked Rebecca. "How did you find out about this?"

"Don said I'd be bumping into you for a long time," said the old man. "I'm glad the changes agree with you." He changed his demeanor. "Corey, it looks like you took training seriously."

"Your lessons stayed with me." I rubbed my chin where I hit the ground from his punch during the gauntlet.

"Good. I wondered if Don made the right choice for you. I don't know if I could have put you through the gauntlet or been as straightlaced as the Preacher was yesterday. You guys have a toughness we never thought."

Nathan handed us all large bottles of water and vitamins. Rebecca sat on the other side of me and scooched next to me. She confused me about where we stood.

"Man, Corey, how can I explain this to Trish?"

Rebecca answered. "Tell Trish that we've had as bad a few days as anyone could have. We needed an emotional reset and we've been bonding to give each other strength."

I put my arm around Rachel and brought her in close. "Rachel, your idea worked. I was ready to quit yesterday and today I feel normal. I mean, other than the hangover." It's amazing what a good cry, shared sorrow, friends, being stupid and bonding with friends could do.

Rachel leaned into me and smiled.

Nathan stood while everyone else sat. "Good, let me give you news to absorb. Nicole wasn't malicious. Her biggest crime is stupidity and a single-minded drive to do everything on her own. Corey, to answer your question, you detected her lies before anyone else, and you caught her, and protected yourself before anyone else. Everyone wants to know how you could fail out of college, but out think everyone else."

Rebecca elbowed me. "Told you. Told you both things."

"I wrote her answers down when I got confused. One day they didn't match," I replied. "But that doesn't matter. I asked her to not use her power on me and I needed to trust her. She didn't go three days before breaking my trust."

"We validated she didn't use her powers on you," replied Nathan. "Given that and the output of the questions, Preacher Jon has asked that we pretend Nicole was setting up the church and working with you."

I thought for a minute and couldn't figure out why. "My mind doesn't work well," could you explain it to the dumb druid?

"It's for your protection, Corey. The other areas want to shut you down but can't. The story will keep their noses out of our business."

"How's Wesley?" interjected Rachel.

"Shaken," replied Nathan. "He's coming around, but he's helping Nicole deal with everything. Honestly, we're lucky he wants to and can support her."

"I'm down with that plan, Nathan. We take care of this in house." It hit me that I said 'we,' and 'in house.'

"Me too," said Rachel.

"This makes sense," added Rebecca.

"I guess my whole, being a loner, ended in a dismal failure," I added.

Rachel and Rebecca both leaned over and hugged me.

"Dude, I'm eating part of the blame, too. I'm going to pick it back up. It was half my dumb idea." Miles stared down at me and shook his head.

"You should have been here and showered and snuggled with me too," I teased, to lift his spirits. "I could have washed your hair like the old days in the gym shower."

Nathan interrupted with a broken voice. "All of Nicole's information is solid, and she thinks Sunday at Lookout Field's parking lot in Chattanooga is the likely trap."

He looked uncomfortable. "Now, your last question has an embarrassing answer. She did not ask you to do extra training to wear you out, so you could not fight. She wanted to judge how much better sex with you would be when you used Earth Power to enhance sex with her."

CJ laughed out loud. "I told Don you'd be using powers like that."

Miles stood up and paced. "Dude? Really. You have lots of beautiful women and you use magic to make them... you know what? Good for you. I would too." He sat back down. I wondered what was going on in his mind.

"It's not the case..." I tried to explain.

"Just own it, Corey," said Rebecca. "I'll vouch for you. It's worth it."

Nathan interrupted everyone again. This time, I was thankful. "The reason for the trade of the magnolia seed pod to the two hired guns was Nicole gained the last pieces to put the location and time to attack the bishop. Her plan was that Corey would kill him and she could explain everything away."

"Rebecca figured out the plan to make it work," said Rachel.

"Let's compare," said Nathan. "Nicole has a good plan as well."

"You guys don't have enough information. I need to go to Alpharetta to get one piece of information," I added.

"What information?" asked Miles.

"If I knew, I wouldn't have to go. I figure a date would be a suitable cover."

"Then I'll be your date," said CJ. "Your faces are being distributed and traveling together will increase the odds of being detected. Corey, you're known for traveling with women. Your singing video and drunken motorcycle video specifically have gone viral among the Realized and area owners. The church has probably picked you and Rachel out. I doubt anyone will recognize Rebecca from yesterday's video, hell I didn't, and I've known her for years."

"It's not a gauntlet run in Alpharetta, is it?" I joked.

"We'll have enough of The Tribe covering us and we could put one together if you want another go." He stared at me. "Given that you squared up to a professional from out of the country with zero knowledge of his training, I was wondering if you had gotten too big for your britches again."

"My confidence has grown, but I had backup close or I would've thought twice." I nodded to Rachel.

"I'm going to tell you something everyone one should tell you. Stop fighting. You are the only one who can do the magic stuff, and one miscalculation in a fight puts you out of commission. Find others to fight and act like a druid."

I couldn't argue with CJ. In principle, he was correct. The problems come down in the details. So, not knowing what to say, I nodded.

Nathan continued like he was checking items off of an agenda. "In case anyone doesn't know, consulting no one, Corey and Rachel have joined the Spring Fey Court. They are the official Druid and Bard of the Spring Court."

Shouldn't there have been applause?

"I met the Daoine yesterday. It's a good choice," said Rebecca.

"Come on, the Daoine worked with you and Preacher Jon," I protested. "It wasn't on our own."

He replied while looking at the ceiling. "There is a thought that a young man who has a passion addiction and wakes up in bed with multiple women may not be a good fit for the temptations of the Spring Court."

"We weren't having sex," I protested. "We snuggled and bonded. The Spring Court is right that humanity has lost too much of its passion. If I didn't have that kind of support from Rachel and Rebecca, it would be hard to function. I think it's the perfect choice and I am happy to spread the message of more passion."

Rebecca patted me on the leg. "You've got the passion down, honey." She caught herself. "I mean Corey."

I let it pass since I had slipped the other day, too.

"All good," said Nathan, "except remember the two trees you told the court were your favorite?"

"Yes, there are two beautiful red maples. The big one behind the cabin and Woodrow's tree at my house."

"Precisely. Both trees are now portals for Spring Court members. You can travel to and from the Tree Foyer next to the Fertile Fields in the Spring Court using them."

"Sounds like a plus. We may even move between the two places easily." I knew Nathan was getting to something, but I wasn't sure what.

"Well, nymphs, dryads, sithe, and other faeries can too, and they can move up to five hundred feet from the trees safely. They increase the desire for passion and love by their very presence."

"Okay, important safety tip. Everyone, be careful at my house and the cabin. Or don't, I'm not your father." I chuckled at my joke.

"I'm going to convince Trish to spend Sunday night there," said Miles.

"Cool. Go wild, the faeries will be happy." I winked at Miles. Trish was already pregnant... Whoa. *Are those two having intimacy problems, and that's why he's called me out recently?*

"You aren't taking this seriously, Corey. Wesley joked the cabin was going to become a love shack and Preacher Jon made it the official name in the system. Plus, your libido is barely in control now."

"Hold on," said Rebecca. "His libido is in full control. He avoided anything but kisses with Nicole and has had no one else, other than me, since he broke up with Tiffany years ago. He is not driven by sex, even though when he is in a relationship, his passion is... well, you get the idea."

"Mostly in control," mumbled Rachel.

"We have a different definition of sex. We consider showering with two women and snuggling with them to be sexual activities. Miles, would Trish let you do that?"

"Leave me out. I'm wondering if we can fund an extension on the love shack."

"You can't turn Don's rustic hunting cabin into a love shack," said CJ. "That's like sacrilege.

This was too far. "It's not a love shack. The cabin is my favorite building in civilization. I am in control of myself. Rachel is in control of herself. This is not a problem. The only thing the Spring Court will be is an enhancement to couples." I was louder than I needed to be, but this was silly and it needed to end. "How does this change anything?"

"Let's table that discussion. Moving on. What's your status with Nicole?" asked Nathan.

"Do I need to tell her it's over or has she figured it out?"

"Tell her Corey," said Rachel.

I wasn't sure why she'd need to be told. If you're stealing behind my back and pretending, we're on a date to make a transfer of something you stole from me to my enemy pretty much seals the deal. "I will tell her."

"Okay, it's getting close to lunchtime and lover boy hasn't eaten and is getting grumpy. I'll take him for lunch in Alpharetta, and you all put together the plan for when he gets back." CJ stood up and pointed at me.

CJ looked at Rebecca. "I knew you were something else the day I hired you. Never sell yourself short."

I stood up and grabbed my shoes, torc, jacket, and messenger bag. I left the notebook of Nicole with them and walked out with CJ.

CJ'S PICKUP TRUCK WAS old and smelled of stale cigarettes. Age ripped the cloth seats, and he replaced the radio with something he called a CB. It had a walkie-talkie on it. Still, it was nice to get something done I've been meaning to do. I pulled the jacket up to cover my torc and let my hair go over the back of the jacket.

CJ had a gruff voice, but he was caring. "Is the life Don promised you?"

I chuckled and did my best Old Donnie impression. "This life doesn't promise you nothing but work. It's up to us to make more out of it."

CJ laughed. "Miss that old man. So, you know what you're going to do with all the women you're juggling?"

"I'm not juggling any woman now." Leaning in my seat, I said, "I am as single as the day I was born."

He snapped his head around. "Do you really think that?"

"I shouldn't have to break up with Nicole, but I'll do that so she has closure that backstabbing and breaking the one promise I asked for is the same thing as breaking up. Rebecca broke up with me and last night I finally realized I was no longer mad at her and I apologized."

"Rachel?"

"Rachel and I have always been friends. Sure, we are intimate for prudish tastes, but we need each other as friends more than anything else."

"I saw Rebecca sit next to you and call you, honey." He backed the truck out and pulled us onto the road.

"We dated a while. I slipped the other day and called her honey. It's no big deal."

"If I'm right, let me know."

"Right about what?" Everything confused me recently.

"She has designs on rekindling the relationship." He smiled like he knew something I didn't.

I thought about the kiss. "We were goofing, and we kissed in the kitchen and, well, we're both lonely and it caught us off guard. That's probably what you're detecting."

"Huh. Maybe. What about Nicole?"

"Nicole is easy. We were going on dates, not dating, and the trivia night was our first date. I am sure if I said I had to trust her and she breaks my trust on a first date, she knows it's over."

His old truck needed attention from him, but he continued. "Well, I'd not think that. You're good with treating woman like they're normal, but you also need to remember that women are also very different creatures with a different way of thinking. Figure that out and you'll be just as happy with women when your looks and body get old."

"It may be too late, but I'll be following Old Donnie's advice for a while and figure out why I need a woman in my life before I add one." That was the truth.

He laughed then. "That was Old Donnie's advice. You didn't know Young Donnie, and he thought no such thing. He was quite the womanizer."

That blew me away.

The truck pulled off of GA400 and onto Old Milton Parkway towards downtown Alpharetta and they set it up as a winter wonderland, without the snow. I looked out the window and turned on my druidic vision. There was a large building with a Christmas tree out front. "Holy crap, that's where we're going." There was enough church magician magic emanating from it where I could feel it vibrate without my druidic vision.

"I was afraid of that. Let's get lunch at this brew pub."

"I won't be drinking anything but water today." Too many beers in one day did me in.

"Were all those dead soldiers in the trash bag from yesterday?"

I shuddered remembering how much we drank. "Yes, but we started at ten in the morning and drank until like eight."

"This past year I've been wishing I was young again, but seeing you these past few days has me kind of glad I made it through those years."

"I've had a bad few months," I admitted.

We walked into the brew pub and I ordered a triple burger called the Frankenstein and probably drank sixty-four ounces of water to get the food down. We sat at the bar and sat on old-fashioned stools that swiveled. The lunch crowd was thin, but this was like a four-day holiday for normal people or something around Thanksgiving. That was the problem with bad guys. They didn't respect time off.

We finished eating and stayed parked at the restaurant. The two of us sauntered across the street. Then we meandered through the crowd to the Christmas tree.

"You act like you're going in." CJ sounded like that was a bad idea.

A sign said, Alpharetta Administration building. "I sense a circle in there if you'd rather I do something blind." He shrugged behind me as I walked. I walked in and stabilized myself. I saw property records were on floor two zero two. Property records. I would work with that.

Two effects were going on. I needed to be careful of all the church magician magic, and I needed to hide in plain sight for the normal world.

There was enough church magician magic inside that I couldn't distinguish the lines without taking forever. I turned off five red alerts and walked to the regular guards.

"Hi, my grandfather is looking for the property records of a trailer in Sandy Springs," I said to the guard.

"Room two oh two," he replied and shrugged to the stairs to my right.

We walked up the wide half semi-circle stairs to a tiled hallway with half dark paneled walls. Behind an unlabeled door, lines of church magician magic spilled out from the space between the door and the floor.

CJ Whispered. "Your *grandfather* spotted ARX200s on the two guards to the left and they made you as a fighter. You need to learn how to walk like a normal person."

I walked into the room where a dozen people waited in line. To the right, a table with stacks of forms scattered. We walked over there and pretended to fill out a form. I whispered back. "There are five gargoyles at the bottom, and that unmarked door leads to them."

"No. I'll get more recon from people who are good at it," he whispered. "We've got two minutes before they send someone up to track the trained fighter."

"Okay, you hold these forms and if you see someone close, pretend you don't have one of these items." I pointed to the list of required documentation. CJ was good and now I would listen to his advice until we were clear.

We strolled to the stairs and took them down. A guard met us halfway down the stairs. "Good afternoon, gentlemen. Can I help you find something?"

He had one of them fancy guns like the other guys, and was my height, and had seen combat, but his stance was a little off. I could take him, so I acted polite, like Old Donnie taught me. "Thank you, sir. We came in for records." I referenced the paper CJ held and continued. "My grandfather normally doesn't bring a lot of identification with him, and we are going home to make sure we have everything before we come back."

"Well, I can help you. Why don't you come with me?" He pointed his gun at me like I couldn't take the butt of the weapon and break his nose with it.

I chuckled. "No, thank you." I walked around him and headed down the stairs.

CJ caught up with me, and I held the front door open for him. "Straight to the truck. We need to move."

I wasn't sure why, but I listened, picked up the pace and crossed the street before the restaurant and headed for the truck. We made it without incident. He pulled out. "Duck low."

I got below the window level until he said, "clear." I sat back up, and he was terse. "What the hell was that?"

"Was what?" I didn't do anything.

"You scoped out the professional, saw you could take him, and talked to him as an equal." CJ was lecturing me.

"That's what Old Donnie taught me. Fit in and hide in plain sight. Talk to everyone as an equal and don't get identified."

He turned right and looked in the rearview mirror. He picked up the walkie-talkie. "This is boss. I have a 10-33." He put the microphone in its clip and talked to me. "Is that how far your training got?"

"If there is stuff to know about fitting in after that, yes." I was doing exactly as my mentor taught me.

"Corey, they were former Italian Special Forces. They're not used to someone checking them for a fighting stance and concluding they're not a threat."

"*Boss, Rabbit. 10-23.*" Came over the CB thing.

"We're going to be fine, but you are done in Alpharetta for the immediate future."

"Unless Bishop Pedrotti is here."

"Then you come with a team and I'm inserting myself into your command structure. Don would have wanted to complete your training, since you've excelled in what he taught you. Once this emergency is over, we are going to get you back into training. You've done so well with Rachel and Miles that I thought you were training everything. You've only learned to be a killer."

"Given I fight gargoyles and Dark Fey primarily, it makes sense."

He nodded. "It ain't your fault, son. The Tribe should have stepped up for the man who stepped up for us and taken better care of you. Frankly, I'm amazed at how far you've come and Old Donnie would be proud. It's up to me to make sure you can do everything Old Donnie thought you could."

"I'm not trying to sound like I know more, but while I would benefit a lot. Rebecca, Wesley, Nathan, and even Nicole needs the goodwill of Old Donnie more than I."

"Yeah. You are right, but you'll make the best use of it, though. I'll talk to The Tribe and then to Preacher Jon. It's past time we formalized the agreement we had with Old Donnie and we can help pay our way. Watching over Old Donnie's kin and the pretty girl who was a natural with guns will be an easy sell. Where am I bringing you?"

"Bring me to my house. I'll pick up my motorcycle since I haven't ridden it yet. I'll send out some squirrels to give out my location and study my new druid book in the woods."

Chapter 22—The Campsite to Study

I rode my new motorcycle to the cabin. It definitely wasn't called the love shack. I grabbed my waist pack and headed toward the woods. I picked up my pace and turned toward my close campsite. The cabin did not have enough nature to make up for all the driving I did recently.

The first stop was comfort rock. This morning's issue was almost painful, and Rachel was right. I couldn't get caught by Nicole like I had the other day. Comfort rock was a smooth curved light gray rock I could lean on and rest. It was almost a perfect curve for a body and in summer I'd sometimes come here for a nap. Today, it was for a release, so I didn't have an accidental one while snuggling. It didn't take long. After I cleaned up, I continued to my campsite with one task off my list.

For personal use, I made two remote campsites. I wasn't sure if the first one was on private property or part of the national forest. It would take me an hour to arrive if I didn't wear my shoes, and I took advantage of Earth Power. If I brought someone, which I never did to my personal sites—not even Rachel—it'd take all day.

None of the hike was on man-made trails and parts even skipped over game trails. Earth Power kept me from trampling vegetation and made it nice to get away. The close campsite was the one I told everyone about, and it was something where I needed to be in the woods but would come back quickly. The further campsite was in North Carolina, in the Cowee Mountains, and good luck finding me there. Your best bet would be to wait in Asheville and convince me to join you. But since I didn't tell anyone where this was, this is where I got away from everyone.

I'd like to spend more time out here, but not only did I get lonely, it cut me off from all the information. When people actively hunted me, information was key. Today, I just wanted to get back in touch with nature, without the man-made stuff in my way. I brought a pack, but it was for the basics. It had water, a water filter, food, and my basic tool set. I made my site, and it needed cleanup since I had not been here in weeks.

My site was a primitive dugout shelter and not a place to set up a tent. I surrounded it with possomhaw, snowbell, and needle palm, so no one would find it. With a lot of manual digging, I dugout a seven-by-seven pit almost three feet deep. With extra dirt, I made a four-inch lip around it to keep rain inside and used the excess dirt to slope the area around. A channel around the site let the water flow in heavy rain. A mixture of buckthorn and holly, which I grew to build out the walls, joined with winged sumacs to stabilize the ground around. Fallen trees and branches made a lean to around the walls for a roof. Bark covered those whenever I pulled large enough pieces from fallen trees. I cheated a bit and brought a bearskin, and a couple of deerskins up here for more comfortable sleeping, but in reality, a small fire to heat some rocks was all I needed except on the coldest of winter nights.

I left most of the fallen stuff that didn't threaten the integrity of the shelter to keep everything as close to natural as possible. This was a nice place to commune with the Earth and study the druid books. If I didn't have open wounds and was just battered, it was also a great place to heal. Old Donnie made shelters and protected them from the weather with that domain, and used protection spells. Wanting some comfort, I tucked the bearskin over my sitting rock and rested. I'd need to use the entrenching tool for some facilities and to fix the drainage, plus I'd need to chop up some downed wood for a fire, but I was in good shape.

Old Donnie checked it out and was shocked how I could grow plants where I wanted to without extra sprouts. He told me a lot of my powers were minor, except they worked great for comfort. This location was better for relaxing in the woods than a midway point to anything. It was my favorite campsite shelter.

Old Donnie's Grandfather made the southern Appalachians safe in the nineteenth century. As long as you stayed away from the cave network. This was far enough from the cave network that I was safe from the creatures driven into the deep caves.

I opened to the first spell in the first book and practiced over the five I learned, the two I didn't, but Old Donnie knew, and the last three. I'd never learned the protection domain spells, but I could learn something to help me with other spells. With the book still open to *Create Circle*, I opened the new book. They were both twelve inches by eight inches and two inches thick, red bordered books with a red symbol on the front. The book I used up to now had a red Celtic Knot on it. This new book had the Tree of Life in red. The area between the borders felt like a rough leather of a green, so dark it became black. The inside had a rough paper that never turned brittle and hadn't yellowed. It was light beige now, as I imagine it always had been.

The first book had word replacements in Latin. Old Donnie used them, but I could not. That's one reason it took me so long to learn spells, because they lost some of these words in Ancient Gaelic.

The second book was not only spells. The first twenty pages were two sections of text I'd need to translate. A page of word translations for Latin to Ancient Gaelic followed.

Last, there were four minor spells. These looked easier to master than any spell I'd already mastered, and I did not see a single word in Latin. The spells were relatively simple and I bet I could cast them within a week—if I got the time.

Curiously, this book looked prepared for me. All druids, according to Old Donnie, had four spheres for magic. Everyone had access to circle magic and Earth magic. The other two were different for people. My two unique domains were animals and plants. The four spells in this book had one Animal Domain, one Earth Power, one Plant Domain, and one circle spell. If the gargoyle qualified as a benefactor, I'd have four new minor spells.

I read the spells and got them slowly. Before it got too dark, where a fire didn't allow me to read, a squirrel came to me and spoke in Miles' voice. *Don't forget you're at the store tomorrow.*

A night in the woods and I'd be right as rain. I'd go to the store tomorrow and hear the plan. Then I'd kill Bishop Pedrotti.

MORNING CAME, AND I walked back to the cabin. I washed up and changed into my comfortable clothes. Then, after packing up, I got back in my car and rode to the store. I stopped by a Waffle House for a big breakfast since I hadn't been bad about eating in a while. An hour later, I parked in front of the store and it was already open and a madhouse.

"Corey," called Trish. She worked the cash register and reached below where she sat. "Catch. Could you answer questions in the camping section?" She tossed me a vest, and I put it on and walked to my right to where lots of customers milled around.

"What are we looking at?"

One guy in a suit said, "We're looking at fire starters and good knives for camping."

Another woman said, "What's a sleeping quilt?"

"Good, let's all walk out front to the demo area. I grabbed one of the five good fire starters, two quilts, and two sleeping bags and carried it all out to the test area."

We stood out on the dirt in the parking lot and I fought the urge to remove my shoes. "Knives are something that Miles and Trish get mad at me about. I only recommend this knife."

A quick flick of my wrist, and I pulled the knife from my thigh sheath to hand it to the man. "I don't remember what they're called or cost, but if you tell anyone you want to get the Corey knife, they'll understand exactly what you mean. Between my packs, I own a dozen of these for all my load outs. Four-inch blade keeps you legal in Georgia."

When I pulled my backup knife from around my calf, I heard a couple of snickers.

"Watch how easily I make kindling." I made some, then opened up the five starts and showed each one.

"You made a fire with one try each time. Suit handed me my first knife back. Is it this easy for anyone?"

"Try these two. The pocket sized is the most convenient, but the rod is the easiest to use."

I rolled out the camping quilts and the sleeping bag. "I'm a quilt guy."

"Why's that?"

"Because he tosses and turns and likes to push me onto the ground," said Rachel. I turned and Rachel had joined us.

I gave her a smile and continued. "In cold weather, if you toss and turn, the compressed part of the sleeping bag will expose you to the temperatures unless you're small enough to turn inside the bag. When Rachel and I camp together, our shoulders always grab and pull the bag with us. Try both out, but consider how you sleep and how often you turn."

"Where do we pick up the Corey knives?"

"I'll bring you," said Rachel. "Corey, Nicole will be here in the afternoon and has no idea you're breaking up with her. Try not to make a scene."

The guy in the suit and his friend chuckled and followed Rachel to the knives.

"Which of the camping quilts do you recommend?" asked the woman, getting out of the quilt. I picked up all the gear and walked inside.

"What time of year and what location are you camping in? Temperature and weight will tell us the most of what would suit you."

The rest of the morning went well, and I took a long lunch with Trish in the office. She had ordered pizza. I got to say hello to Coach White, the werewolf. I stopped Miles from hunting him when I discovered Coach was a volunteer football coach. Later in the morning, I met Candy, the new RV person, and Diego and Juan. The two new contractors that Miles and Trish extended for a year.

Carol came in and gave me a hug. "I'm so sorry to hear about what happened with Nicole."

I shrugged. "Things happen."

"Well, see Richard before you go. He has information on your torc."

I popped next door to Clive's gun store and said hello to him. Clive was the vampire who was the last straw for Rebecca when I squared up with him. Luckily, we worked together and his life was on track now.

I walked back to the store and underneath the <u>Miles Away from Town</u> sign, Nicole jogged up to me. I focused on my earring and turned off all topics and emotions.

"How are your emotions a blank slate?"

"Really Nicole? If I told you that, would you sell that to the church, too?"

"Corey, I'm so sorry." She moved in to hug me and I stepped to the side. "What's wrong?"

This was incredible. "What's wrong? I said I needed to trust you and our first date was just a cover for you to set me up as a victim to have the one guaranteed way to kill me taken from your purse. You didn't realize I could take those two guys, so it may even to have me beaten down."

"Corey! They weren't going to fight you." She was loud now and our emotions were high. "I didn't know why they wanted it, but they wouldn't have had time to use it."

"Christ Nicole, you realize you can't steal from me and make me look like a patsy and think we're good, can you?"

"No, because we worked for the same goal. You would have killed him and then everything would be fine. I'm sorry I didn't know what the seed did."

"Nicole, it isn't cool. You don't treat people like that."

"I've copied everything about you since I started. Are only you allowed to work to one goal and leave everyone behind?" She was getting loud, and this was a scene. "Rachel begged you to rethink your trip north, and you blew her off like she was a stranger, and did what you thought was best for your goal. You blew off Preacher Jon. Nathan has spent years protecting your life behind the scenes and he's not even worthy of a thank you. I made no progress on finding my parent's killer until I started acting like you. Acting like you gets things done. I thought you, of all people, would recognize it."

I took a step back and some ugly realizations hit me.

"Yeh. You see. Well, kiss my ass, Corey. I waited for you and tried to be just like you and it turns out you don't like yourself very much."

My ass hit the sidewalk after I backed into the wall. Why was I such a jerk? "I—I didn't..."

She started crying, and I didn't hear what she said as she ran away. I put my head on my knees and cried as well. She was right. I didn't like myself very much. I hid myself from other people and was only a killer. That's why I drove everyone away from me. This is what Old Donnie was trying to tell me.

MILES FOUND ME SOME time later, and picked me up, and brought me inside the store, and sat me in the office. "Dammit, Corey, when did you become such a mess?"

"The last time I remember everything being perfect was February. Everything since then has either been a lie or a disaster."

He led me to a couch in the back of his office and sat next to me on the brown leather. "Before my marriage."

"Before I met Rebecca, before Old Donnie died, before this bishop started tracking Old Donnie and I, I don't even remember what else now."

"It's been a tough year."

"Yeah, well, Nicole just pointed out how much of it was my fault. It sucks to realize what an asshole I am."

Carol walked in and hugged me on the couch. "Miles, go help Trish. I'll help Corey."

"Hi Carol, it's hard to help when Nicole laid me out with the harsh truth."

"You want to know what's harsh? I was twenty-three when the song <u>What's my age again</u> came out by an oldies band. It had the line no one likes you when you're twenty-three. Now I have a twenty-four-year-old son and I'm about to be a grandmother."

"If it's any consolation, you do not look like a grandmother."

"Thank you, Corey. But, yes, you're self-centered. You focus on what you think is right and you have strong opinions despite not knowing everything. But that's what you're supposed to be now. Focus on your other qualities. You care about others. You are trying to get better, and you risk your life to save people who'll never learn about you."

"Rebecca is consoling Nicole and they're going to come in here. Are you ready?"

"I looked at Carol. Is it possible to be ready?"

"Just be yourself Corey."

Carol stood, and Rebecca held Nicole's hand. Carol brought Mile's chair over, so the two women could sit across from me, then left while closing the door.

Rebecca stood up first. "This is getting fixed here." She pointed at me. "Corey, this will hurt and be emotional, but you have to do this."

I'm not sure why Rebecca was doing this, but she had the look that meant I might as well listen to her because she was getting her way. "I'll start then. You're right. I don't like myself very much. That's why I hide things about myself from other people. It's important to find a person in my life to be around, so I don't have to be with myself. Today, I figured out what Old Donnie was trying to tell me."

"Corey, don't," said Nicole.

"It's okay. Everyone sees it. CJ pointed out that I'm a killer. I've figured out why the team wants me around so bad. I bet that's your plan—find the bad guy and Corey kills them. It's a good plan, it's what I do. What I hate about me is how I drive everyone away. Miles left the team, Rebecca left, and I just devastated you. Throughout this, I didn't realize what I did until you cleared it up for me. Which is another thing I hate—I'm stupid."

"No Corey, I lashed out. I need to apologize to you."

"You can apologize for lashing out, but you spoke the truth. I'm so sorry I had to hurt you to hear it. Miles told me I was afraid of being abandoned. Preacher Jon says I'm afraid to give up control, and you told me I hid parts of myself from people. Everyone is correct and those are the things a person who doesn't like themselves would do."

"Well, shut up and let me talk now."

I nodded.

"You are there for everyone. When my parents died, you made sure I had breakfast and lunch money. You made sure I dressed and washed. Haley and Tiffany showed me girl stuff, because you brought them to me. You even introduced me to Carol and Richard, who could help me more. I idolized you. I was a thirteen-year-old girl in braces, who lost her parents and this sweet boy came in and said, don't worry, I'll help you."

That was ordinary stuff that cost me nothing, but I would not interrupt her after she told me to listen.

"Well, imagine my surprise when you're the person my mother predicted would come to save the world. My mother was a druid like Grandpa Don. Nothing like you. She had peace, light, and compassion for domains to go with her circles. Grandpa Don said she was a peacetime druid, but we were going to war. We needed a wartime druid to show up. It's all my family ever talked about."

She wiped a tear from her eye. "I'm in high school with my life back on track and one day Grandpa Jon gets excited. It turns out, the young man who saved Grandpa Don's life was the guy I already idolized. You are the wartime druid who will fix everything. I couldn't believe the sweetest guy I ever met was destined to save the world."

Tears flowed from her eyes and her voice cracked. "Then you started doing it. The church became scared—scared of the guy who held my sister and I when we cried over our mother."

I did not comprehend where she was going with this.

She wiped tears from her eyes. "Well, you were this larger-than-life image in my mind, and then I found out you were a person like me. I made it my goal to become just like you. Only I couldn't fight like Rachel or do magic like you. So, I weaponized empathy and went out to prove I could be like you. All this to say is, I copied the wartime druid version of you."

"Nicole, I believe all that is true, but it doesn't change the fact that I hurt you by not paying attention to you."

"No, but it means we share blame." Nicole took a deep breath and held Rebecca's hand. She put her head onto Rebecca's shoulder and started balling. Rebecca held her and rubbed her back.

"There, you two have a much better foundation to discuss what happened and what's next," said Rebecca.

"Rebecca, why are you helping so much? You're doing great, but I want to understand how you're such a good person." This was crazy she was an ex helping Nicole and I.

Rebecca kept supporting Nicole and turned to me. "Corey, you finally decided to be a team member. When I see you with the team and realize what it can accomplish, I have hope to have the future my grandmother promised. This team is my life. It's easy because I've lost everything I had, but I need this. A misunderstanding between lovers cannot derail us."

I was an immature jerk and the girlfriend who dumped me just saved me from one of the biggest mistakes. "Thank you. I'm not smart enough to figure out what to do. Right now, the people I trust without questioning—I can count on one hand—you, Rachel, and Carol. There's a bunch of others I listen... look, I'm not good at talking, but I need help right now. Rebecca, we've got two days and I don't have time to figure things out. What do I do?"

She frowned. "I can help a little, but there's a big reason I can't help much."

"Help what you can?" I didn't understand what reason she had, but I needed something to grasp on to.

"Corey, use Nicole's term. In two days, we need the wartime druid."

"Corey the killer?"

"Wartime Druid. Stop using killer, you're not a killer. But stuff is going to go down you've and you have to walk out alive or when the monsignor arrives, he gets a free pass."

I nodded.

"Okay. After that, you need to figure out what you're doing with your love life. You are all over the place and those of us who are considering you—Rachel, Nicole, myself, and probably other women we haven't met yet, need to understand what you want because until you know what you want, no one knows who fits with you. You pull us all in and then change who you are."

I wished I'd shut up. "Let me focus on killer Corey. I'm going to study. Please ask Rachel if she can find me, and if she can join me."

"Call yourself Wartime Corey, and I will."

A voice echoed from nowhere in the office. I recognized the voice; it was Samantha from New Hampshire and it was her advice. *In a time of peace, when no one is a warrior, gentle souls are common. In a time of war, when we all are warriors, the gentle soul is a blessing to everyone. Remain a gentle soul despite what you encounter.*

I stood to leave. "Well, on Samantha's advice, Wartime Corey is heading out."

Rebecca and Nicole looked at me as if I did something, but there was little point in talking about something I didn't understand. "I like the advice," said Rebecca. "Please take it to heart."

"Slow down, Wartime Corey," said Richard when he opened the door. "Show me your torc."

I pulled it off and showed it to him.

"You have a historical torc here."

"It's not called the Torc of Awareness, is it?"

"How did you learn that?" He took the torc and fiddled with it.

"I rode up with a witch in New Hampshire who said she donated the blue emerald while her lover created this in the twelfth century. I thought she was making it up, but..."

"Corey, be careful around her. She is the most powerful witch to ever exist. If legends are true, Merlin created this torc while he and Morgan le Fey were lovers. Here."

He showed me the torc. "Push both gems in and push with your thumb here." A slot opened in the torc. "It used to be holly berries would go in here for a focus, but you would put a honeysuckle trumpet in here, and it will amplify Earth Power by adding a focus for a small period of time."

I couldn't figure which comment scared me more. I took the torc back and held it.

"Oh Corey," cried Nicole. "Go back to confident and arrogant, Corey. Don't let me be the one to shake you. I still love you."

Rebecca held me as well. "Check it out. I'm wearing the necklace of the tree you got me." It was bittersweet seeing her wear it again. I bought that when I thought we'd be together forever.

After closing the torc, I put it on. "You know what? There are enough problems today. The other stuff is on the tomorrow problems list." I kissed Nicole on the cheek, and Rebecca on the cheek, and shook Richard's hand.

"I'm glad you took my advice on grilling and not women," he joked.

"Early breakfast at the love shack Sunday morning," said Nicole. Her puffy eyes still had tears.

"Early breakfast at the rustic hunting cabin, Sunday morning," I corrected, but I smiled.

Chapter 23—Fertile Fields

I stood in front of the giant maple tree behind the cabin. My bare feet stood in the cold and my messenger bag slung over my bare chest. My dark blue gym shorts did nothing for the cold. I shivered from the cold and checked to make sure I had both druid books, the gargoyle book, and the folder from Nathan. Taking a breath before I walked smack dab into a tree, I took two steps and walked into the tree and kept walking.

Warmth caressed my skin, and I stood in a grove of trees. I recognized Woodrow's tree next to the giant maple I walked out of. The green of the lush ground caressed my feet and calmed me. Large and small trees of every shape and size dotted this area and did not appear natural. It was like this was an entrance area or foyer.

Small faeries about the size of butterflies twittered around, and larger faeries about the size of a parakeet flew around me, and took turns landing on my shoulder, and head while they checked me out.

The first item on my personal to-do list was to find a place to set up a campsite for quiet study. With that thought in my mind, the landscape rushed around me. Trees zoomed past me, and I passed over rolling hills and fields of flowers. Soon, woods surrounded me again, but actual woods. It was like Earth, but greens were more vibrant and colors chaotic, but the scene made sense. Vibrant yellows, bright greens, deep browns, blues, and reds surrounded me. Lighting came from multiple angles instead of one overhead position and gave me a better view.

Sitting on comfortable moss, I reached out to the plants like I used my Plants Domain and created an eight-by-eight shelter with natural plant growth and walls like I created for my primary woods shelter on Earth.

I created a soft spot of thick moss on the floor large enough to sleep both Rachel and I. A sitting area large enough for the two of us, should she arrive, came next. Branches grew from the plants in the wall to form a table, and I placed the books and folder on top of it. I sat back and adjusted the position of the plants to get the proper light for reading near me.

I removed my shorts and opened the fourth point of power on my body. The four points were: temple, throat, solar plexus, and groin. When I removed my shorts and opened all four points of power to Earth Power, I could channel power quickly and restore my connection with the Earth. Doing this in the Fey Realm was nothing short of euphoric.

I enjoyed it for a few minutes, then I pulled the folder off the table and read the notes Nathan made for me. How to use the trees, how to travel, and how to create a shelter were all covered. I probably should have read it first. There were a lot of political items, but Nathan underlined an item that they considered it good form to sacrifice an enemy to Queen Niamh in the Halls of Youth.

There wasn't much else. The court altered many druid spells, but there was not a definitive list, so I'd get to experiment. The two trees were the responsibility of Rachel and me, and last, the first decade of service was for the court to view us and how we fit. We, of course, were stewards of youth, passion, and love on Earth. I wasn't sure what Nathan was worried about. These requirements seemed easy to meet.

I put the folder back and pulled open the second spell book, and studied with the power for the Fey World powering me. Slowly, the butterfly-like pixies joined me and looked over my shoulders. They became bored quickly, and I focused on the four spells.

Rachel brought in lunch and joined me. She exposed her solar plexus and wore a sports bra, and a skirt instead of shorts when she sat. She pulled out her songbook and folder from Nathan. We both covered ourselves with towels for modesty while leaving ourselves open to the power from the magic ground.

"I can track you here," she said. "It's crazy. I knew the second you went into the Fey world."

She put the songbook on her lap. "This is crazy—the increase in my brain. Have you been getting this boost all the time? Is this why you're almost a nudist?"

"Yeah, the Fey world combines with the connection to Earth and I can learn easily now. I don't know things I never learned, but my thinking and learning grows. Unless I have full Earth Power, I can't read the druid spells. I can study things I've already learned just by being barefoot, but that's it. Here, it's like the magic of the druids is my normal language."

"Now I regret all the times I teased you for being a secret nudist."

I chuckled. "Is Nicole better?"

"Yes. Rebecca, Nicole, Trish, and I had a long talk about things." She sat across from me and moved her left leg between mine so we could touch while we studied.

"I screwed that up, and Carol and Rebecca rode to the rescue."

She sat next to me. "It's not riding to the rescue, it's part of being a team. Someone falls down and there's someone to pick them back up."

"Speaking of that, I've treated you poorly."

Rachel laughed out loud. "Poorly?"

"Yeh. Nicole pointed out..."

"Shut up Corey. Remember when we used to tease each other? I'd say all boys are jerks, and you'd say..."

"All girls are mean, but you're the nicest mean girl I know."

"And I'd say you have enough niceness to overcome being a jerk."

I chuckled. "Yep." Those were good times.

"I knew you were a jerk, but not nearly as much as other guys. Plus, you have so many other qualities. I accepted your occasional jerk behavior long ago. When it bothers me, I tell you, and you fix it."

"That's right, you tell me when I'm being a jerk." What a relief that Rachel didn't hate me for being a jerk. We both read and studied until it became too dark to read without lighting a fire, and we both put our books away.

"Now, for something more important. Corey, you and I need to make an agreement."

"Of course. What should we agree to?"

"You know better than I that we will spend time around these faeries and other influences. We need to minimize our time together here."

"Our sun tattoos protect us from the faeries and they have a rule to only affect couples, so they don't cause chaos on Earth."

Her grin grew wide. "Cool. Nothing new between us."

"Definitely," I answered.

She grinned. "You get this ability to think here. This is nice."

We studied until it was late and went to sleep and avoided the attraction of the faeries.

THE NEXT MORNING, SHE stood and got dressed as I turned away. "Oh, cut Nathan some slack about how he gave us the rundown of the Spring Court."

"I'd already forgotten it. What did he do?"

"A couple of snide comments. But he had to calculate probabilities of how much physical intimacy you'd have with his little sister right before he came over."

"Poor dude. Consider him completely forgiven and forgotten, and I won't mention it unless he brings it up." That must have been rough for him.

"Thank you, and he will appreciate it."

A Daoine resembling Fionnestra walked into the shelter. "Please eat breakfast before you leave." She placed a platter on top of my folder on the table. I recognized nothing, but grabbed a light green piece of fruit and took a bite. Sweet juices flowed down my parched throat.

Rachel grabbed one as well. "Tomorrow morning, eat breakfast at the cabin."

The Daoine left the shelter without even giving us her name. Rachel left, and I was soon alone to pull out my book to study.

I finished the platter while I studied, and soon I had four new spells. The circle spell was crazy. I needed to bind myself to the circle and then I could take the form of the dangerous beasts in my area. They called that Primal Savagery. However, I read something about that spell being changed by the Spring Court, but the folder had no details.

My Earth spell allowed me to own the area. Instead of just taking over Old Donnie's spell, I could create my signature for my area with the Earth Domain spell. This too was altered by the Spring Court.

The Animal Domain spell, Animal Warrior, allowed me to take a local animal and let him fight using my knowledge alongside me. That was changed by the Spring Court as well. I pulled the folder out and saw I could summon a creature from the Fey Realm as a partner for the day, whether to fight or travel with. One of them had gotten documented.

My excitement at magic dissipated because the last spell made any mature plant give *Berries of Druidic Magic*. One line. The berries that would have saved Old Donnie's life was one lost sentence in Old Gaelic. The fun of learning new spells had worn off. I appreciated the gargoyles granted me the spell and returned it to druids, but I was sad for Old Donnie.

Being sad, I no longer wanted to spend the night in the Fey lands. I grabbed my belongings, put on my shorts, and thought of the large red maple tree. The landscape whooshed around me and I was at the tree. Stepping through the tree brought me to the tree by the cabin. I stepped inside to get dressed, grabbed my waist pack, and then took it off. Feeling paranoid, I inventoried it again—silver sickle, wicker basket, magnolia seed pod wrapped as I left it. Stun gun, pepper gel, fire starter, satellite items for freelancing, first aid kit, and two emergency blankets. Perfect.

Feeling better, I sauntered to the territory pole to cast the spell.

The ground was cold, but I left my shoes off to stay in contact with Earth Power. Earth was a pale imitation of the Fey Realm, but it was familiar. The walk to the stadium seating trees and created a honeysuckle bush was chilly, but pleasant. I cut five flowered twigs with trumpets from it and placed them in the circle. After I cut a trumpet, I placed it into my torc, the way Richard showed me.

When I focused on the territory pole, I emulated the old spell and changed it for my preferences. Specifically, I wanted more location sensors, alerts, and strength. For the first time, I had a measure of my mentor's strength and mine in an apples-to-apples comparison. Absorbing the power of the Deer Woman had increased my power, and I was stronger than him before it. Maybe this is why Preacher Jon said all the old people didn't like me.

Once the spell completed, my senses changed, and while I could sense everything supernatural and unnatural in my lands, I narrowed it down. My spell turned down the senses to new unnatural in my lands. I didn't need to track the handful of vampires and werewolves in the Southeast. When new ones appeared, I wanted to know. I played with sensing magician magic from the church until I only sensed magic in Sacred Heart and the Alpharetta Administration

Building. I didn't care about all the minor spells. The result was I'd always know of supernatural creatures in my lands, strong magician magic, new unnatural creatures, and if I wanted something else, I could focus on it.

I stepped back from my pole and could sense the difference in my territory now. When I walked barefoot, my feet tingled with Fey power. The Spring Court must have boosted the spell. It felt like every step was like the first gulp of cold water when you were thirsty. It may not do too much, but it was an experience that made life worth living.

Back at the cabin, I prepared my outdoor bed, cleaned up the cabin and went to sleep when the sun sank.

"GOOD MORNING. WE'RE getting up early," said a sleepy voice.

I rolled over, and it was still fully dark. "Rachel?" She stood over my bed.

"Yep. Did you add the Fey touch to the Southeast last night?"

My mind was clouded, and I wanted to sleep. "Oh, yeah. I made the territory pole my own with my new Earth Domain Spell."

"Hold on, I'm going to try something." She kicked off her shoes, her face scrunched up, and after a couple of seconds, she smiled.

My circle behind the cabin was in use, but I hadn't initialized it. "What? What is going on?"

"The water in the trough is warm. I can use or enhance any circle created by a member of the Spring Court."

Steam rose from the trough. "Blah blah blah, warm water?" Three quick steps and I tested the trough's water, and it was steamy. "Turn around." Before she told me not to, I got in. I sunk in and let out a sigh. "Holy crap Rachel. You are officially more powerful than I." I enjoyed the steaming water, even though the outside was below freezing.

"It's just a minor power."

I did my best Old Donnie impression. "There's no such thing as a minor power. Those are just powers you don't know how to use."

I heard more laughter along with Rachel's behind her.

"You drew him a bath?" exclaimed Nicole. She laughed, and I was glad at least some of the drama had passed.

"She made this luxurious," I answered.

Rachel had a huge grin. "I tested my Circle Appropriation Domain. I can make any area suitable for a bard to entertain with a circle someone from the Fey court created."

"Should I plan to make two circles today?" My mind was already shifting to the battle.

"No, I won't use a circle in battle. I'll strengthen yours. Where your dominant power is in the Circle Domain, mine is in the Song Domain. History and Courage are my last two domains."

"Who is bringing the nude druid his towel and clothes?" asked Rebecca.

"Hold them out," said Rachel.

The clothes and towel stayed folded but floated to me.

"A bard should not have to do her own chores," she said, and her grin was as wide as ever.

"Where was this power when we were roommates?" asked Nicole, but pride filled her eyes.

"I'm going in," said Rebecca, holding herself. "It's freezing out here."

"Come in for breakfast and a briefing. Everyone is here, and it's crowded inside," said Rachel. She grabbed her shoes and joined the other two inside.

I scrubbed, soaked for a few more seconds, and got out of the luxurious trough. I grabbed the towel from the middle of the air and hurriedly dried and got dressed.

Nathan handed me a plate after I walked in.

I looked at Rebecca sitting next to Nicole. Wow. How could those two have me tied up in knots? I know Rebecca got me back together with Nicole, but it seemed she was insinuating she was back to being available. *Was I crazy?*

Chapter 24—The Threat

I dug into the plate of eggs, potatoes, and sausage. I'd showed up after everyone else either ate or had eaten.

Nathan was already talking. "Corey moved our territory from Grandpa Don's spell to his own spell, which is why there is Fey magic in the Southeast. We are still researching, but all accounts are pointing to only those with attachments to one of the Fey courts can notice it, and it is not enough to cast spells from."

"Corey, I understand it surprised you. The change you made was because of my request from the other day. Since the whole Spring Court is new to us, could you give us a heads up when you are going to cast spells until we learn what to expect?" Preacher Jon sat on the couch with a plate of breakfast with Rebecca and Nicole.

"Yes. It'll be safer. Not every spell has a description of what changed, like Area Ownership." If I was a teammate, I'd have to cooperate and this request made sense for everyone.

Nathan continued. "One surprise effect is beneficial. Magician magic has difficulty in tracking links to those with the Fey Realm now due to all the new noise of Fey magic."

"Damn, you better not be getting ready-to-use it for what I think you are," said Miles. He sat in the kitchen and still had some food in front of him. But he turned and gave a wink.

"Oh, I almost forgot," said Nicole. She walked over to the wall next to the bathroom and pushed in a section of the wall. A cabinet opened, and she pulled out a rifle. "Grandpa Don said you were the only one who knows how to fire Missy." She handed the rifle to Rebecca. "You impressed the hell out of him." Nicole tried to do an impression of Old Donnie. "Can't say much about her choice in fellas, but she knows rifles and can treat Missy right."

"Wow, this is his incredible Model twenty-one Winchester," said Rebecca, and she did gun stuff with the gun she held.

"It's more incredible with these. Fey enhanced ammunition. Double up in hearing protection because they can fire across realms too. When they cross realms, it's like a sonic boom." She handed Rebecca a box. "I'll show you how to make the ammo next week some time."

"Moving on," said Nathan. Nathan must have the same view of guns as I. "The Tribe has a movement of ex Italian Special Forces operating with minor church magicians, two church empaths, and a significant church magician into Chattanooga. We will move out shortly and be ready to intercede immediately to spring the trap before it gets too strong."

"I, um, missed the briefing on the trap," I said.

"Yes, the two most important people were in the Fey Realm during the strategy briefing. I hope whatever you were doing in the Fey Realm was more important than the fight briefing," said Nathan.

Grabbing Rachel's plate, I stood and collected the other plates. "Go on Nathan, I'm going to start some dishes."

"All girls will ride up in Rebecca's car," said Nicole. "No guys."

"No fair," said Miles. He teased, but came over to help with the dishes.

"Where's Trish and Wesley?" I asked, trying to talk about anything else.

Miles rinsed while I washed. "Wesley is helping Trish at the store."

"We will update you two on the plan on the way up," said Nathan. Much louder than we whispered. "Last thing, Corey. Do you have a request for attendees from other territories to ensure we follow all guidelines?"

This got my attention. I only met a few others. "I like Leander, but I think Samantha would be my first choice."

"Samantha who?" asked Nathan.

I turned to stare at Preacher Jon. I wondered if he comprehended who I talked about. "Do you know the last name of who I am talking about?"

He stared at me for a second and nodded. "I will put in the request."

"Okay, then. Let's roll," said Nathan.

I put away the last dish. I grabbed my weapons belt, extra knives, and my waist pack. Putting those on, I walked outside and cast *Create Honeysuckle*, then cast *Mature Plant* on the vine to make a full bush. Using my silver sickle and folding wicker basket, I cut nineteen twigs with trumpets.

Rachel, Nicole, and Rebecca jumped into what must be Rebecca's new car. It was red, sporty, and convertible, although the top was up. Nathan held the front passenger door open for me, then got in back with Miles and Aaron.

PREACHER JON DROVE out and headed toward the highway. Nathan spoke first. The church is planning to sacrifice a young latent woman with the spark. They know you cannot resist the call. They are summoning a Dark Fey from the section that is on fire, something the church refers to as a demon. When you attack the demon, the bishop will erase your circle to kill you, only you sabotaged his plan without his knowledge.

"The plan is we all stay back while Nicole and Rebecca soften up the other side, then we make our push."

"The hell it is," I said.

"What do you mean? This makes perfect sense. We cannot save the girl. The team spends the time to evaluate what each side has, see how the beginning plays out, and if we have an advantage, we press."

"That's sounds like you're planning a guaranteed retreat. We are walking into a trap and Nathan said men who are special forces trained. We will not group together since they will have blast radius attacks and will certainly move to cut off a retreat before we get there." This was all basic Old Donnie training. CJ could have told him this, too.

"So, you're saying we have to play with no ability to fold and the opponent is on the button? In that case, we wouldn't look at our cards and read the opponent."

Miles and Rachel were right, and I could only explain it in one of the two things I understand—loving or fighting. "Can I explain it to you differently? Your terms make no sense."

"Go ahead."

I thought this through and used the analogy Old Donnie used with me. "Have you ever loved?"

"I have kids. Of course, I have."

"No, not like that. Have you ever loved so deeply that it hurt? Have you ever felt the other person's love soak you and realized you couldn't leave?"

He reached into his coat pocket and pulled out a leather case. "I used to use this for checks, but it's perfect to protect pictures." He pulled out an old square picture of a kid in a wide tie with a jacket with wide lapels next to a woman wearing strange make up. "Who's the kid?"

"Look closer."

I looked at the kid, and then I looked at Preacher Jon. "Holy crap, that's you. Are you like twelve?"

"Sixteen. I ran away from home at fourteen. I made a living playing poker while underage and found true love with Mayven. Grandpa Don came and got me when I was eighteen. He convinced me to leave her and come and save the Southeast. It hurts every day."

"My respect for you just grew a thousandfold. When are you going to go find her?" I could change the argument to where he could understand, like Old Donnie made me understand when I was going to ask Rebecca to marry me.

"It's been forty years, and..."

"Shut the hell up." I wasn't about to listen to excuses from him about love.

"What?" It caught him off guard to be spoken to like that.

"You heard me. Today's fight is just like you and Mayven. It should scare us all. If you don't go after Mayven, you lose. You could try to track her down and not find her and you lose. You could find her and she has a life you don't work in and you lose. However, the big prize is out there."

"Wait, you jumped on and lost Nicole, but you still love Rebecca. What is your true love?"

"I'm facing them every day to figure it out, and that's what you should do."

"Mayven and I together rekindling lost love." He looked past the road and I hoped we were safe.

"Exactly. The only way to win is to go for it all. You need to put your heart out there and the possibility of it getting crushed or you looking like a fool is irrelevant. The odds or chances are irrelevant. The only thing that matters is you go after her."

"Skip Mayven for now. How is that a strategy for a fight?"

"CJ will use terms like tactical aggression, strong facing front, and support of the front lines. I won't. I'm going to use terms of love. The full win is what I want. Rekindling the chance with Mayven is all I care about. I'm going to rescue the girl, banish the Dark Fey, and sacrifice the bishop to queen Niamh."

"Yeh, that's the plan," said Miles. "Just like the old days." He pumped his fist in the back seat.

"How will that work?" asked Nathan.

"Send this to the other car. Rachel, Miles, and I will charge. Rachel and Miles support me and try to keep me from fighting. Our first goal is to get the girl. Rebecca and Nicole keep their distance from us and give us tactical support but start separated enough to protect from a blast radius attack. Everyone not doing damage is medical and support."

"There we go," said Miles. "Type that shit out." He pointed to Nathan's phone.

"Once we've cleared the immediate area and rescued the girl, I will make a circle and take on this demon. Miles, you take responsibility for keeping the bishop near me until I deal with the demon. Then I am going to offer the bishop to Queen Niamh. Lastly, this isn't over to you are going after Mayven. I am on this team and not leaving your side until that is done."

Preacher Jon put the picture away and wiped a tear from his eye. "Saving the world didn't interest you, but once I told you about a lost love, you're on board with being by my side."

"Duh." Why wasn't that obvious? The world didn't matter without love in it.

My senses alarmed. "Thirteen vampires just moved into Chattanooga. Also, someone initiated church magic against purple magic."

"I sense it too. Something big is going down in Chattanooga. There is something else there," said Miles.

"Witches," said Preacher Jon.

"The magic is as strong as anything I've ever felt," continued Miles. "Even stronger than Corey's biggest spells."

Nathan interrupted. "Rachel just replied, thank you for listening to Corey. Now we have a chance. She also wants to know how much firepower Nicole can bring."

"As much as she can," I answered. If she had a gun with bigger bullets, more power to her.

We pulled into Lookout field's parking lot and the grassy area between the stadium and the aquarium had a giant column of fire. "Showtime." I pulled off my shirt. It was time for Killer Corey.

Chapter 25—You Done Messed With the Wrong Druid

Preacher Jon power slid the giant SUV into the curb and I jumped out and charged forward. The world turned black and white and sounds became muffled. I ran and pulled a tonfa with my left hand and a throwing knife with my right.

Sensing for animals I found two wounded dogs. I contacted them and they were rescuing their owner. *We are here to save your owner. Pull back.*

I stopped and cast my new *Beast Bond* spell and asked for a Fey creature for combat.

A unicorn, Drisana, showed up. *Wow! Thank you, Spring Court.* I told Drisana. *Collect the two dogs and provide support. Animals are to be kept safe while they help us.*

Miles and Rachel were ahead of me and Drisana charged ahead of them and the dogs harangued the vampire on the right with the unicorn's help. I popped in my mouthpiece.

Charging forward, I threw a knife from my right thigh holder and nailed the back of the vampire on the left, holding the victim. He turned and bared fangs and charged at me with a flash. I made a high block, but it kicked me in the mouth and I slammed into the ground, barely turning in time to land on my front.

Bar fighting vampires aside. I was here, and I came prepared to fight anything. I took ownership of the ground near me with my *Local Nature* spell. The grass turned green and twinkled with sparkles of Fey magic in a one-hundred-foot diameter.

Rachel kicked him in the head and slowed him enough for Miles to join in and tackle him to the ground. Miles grabbed it by its throat before it made it to me and pushed its neck to the ground. Smoke rose from where the vampire touched the ground from my spell as I stood, glad I had in my mouthpiece.

The unnatural creature was as feeble as a baby on the ground with the fey power grabbing it. The other vampire flew towards me and kicked me in the chest. I don't remember being the weakest of the three of us in fights.

Even the heavy rain drops caused the one on the ground to whimper. The victim was the waitress from Mellow Mushroom. My memory came back and her name was Stormy, and she wanted to hike the Appalachian Trail.

Oh, we were saving her.

Stormy ran behind the three of us and held a green bow and arrow. It dissipated the second she saw it, and she screamed. Her two dogs came and stood by her protectively, but gunfire erupted from the other side and the loudest boom I ever heard came from my behind left. It sounded unmuffled, though it must have been. But I didn't have time to help her since the other vampire who kicked me flew towards to do actual damage. Miles stood up with a green two-handed sword and swung at the unnatural creature with his magical sword.

A tremendous blast of shots screamed by me. There must have been thousands of bullets, and I think I peed a little. The special forces along my right retreated from the barrage of bullets.

"They weren't expecting my sister with her M240!" shouted Rachel. "You're the first person ever to let her use a big weapon like that!" Her surujin spun and took the wounded vampire from being attacked by the unicorn. She drew blood as the weighted spike flew into its eye.

Behind me, Nicole was behind a handful of sandbags with a long gun thing sticking out over the top, and she laid down, while a belt churned through the gun.

Miles connected, and the vampire bled from its gut. "Vampire slaying time!" yelled Miles. "Make your circle. We got them."

I told the unicorn to follow the lead of Rachel and Miles.

"We got them," yelled Rachel and flung the chain of her surujin at the one Miles left on the ground, which looked to take me out me and drag it to the ground. The Earth lit up the area with lightning strikes behind the other eleven vampires.

Both undead creatures looked at the six-foot four muscular giant holding a magical sword, next to a master of Shotokan whipping her surujin around her body in a figure eight, and the bloodied horn of a unicorn, and quit going after Stormy and me. They flew as fast as possible toward the fire. Step one done.

Automatic fire from Nicole and vast realm ripping booms from Rebecca made it seem like the world wasn't muffled.

There were eleven vampires lining up, and these two fell into formation. Thirteen vampires and a circle of fire. *Where was the bishop?*

There, behind the circle of fire, someone powerful initiated another circle. Ignoring alter blue warnings from my torc, I created a circle in the pouring rain and muffled thunder. Earth Power already flowed into me, helping me with the pain in my jaw and chest. The well-manicured grass bent, willing me and helped guide my honeysuckle twig.

"What the hell?!" screamed Stormy.

I had to focus on my spell, but Miles tried to calm her. "We protect Corey long enough for him to do his circle stuff and you are going to see who has power. Our boy here can wipe everyone here with a circle. Incoming!"

I appreciated the confidence, but a thirteen-vampire circle, a church circle, and a cauldron next to the witches were new to me. I spilled out the contents of my waist pack. The screams of the undead casting a spell rang through the air, and howls of pain came from that direction. I pulled the mouth guard out and tossed it behind me. It did its job and protected my mouth and kept me from getting knocked out.

I peeked and saw five of the special force guys with the fancy guns and two creatures eight feet tall with faces of dogs charged. The men shot bullets, which deflected off of a Fey shield of Drisana. Boom! From the gun behind me to the left, and a dogman's head exploded. *I never heard Old Donnie's gun sound like that.*

"Two circles, Cor. Two witches are losing the fight to the church, and the vampires are ignoring them."

I couldn't see that far through the pouring rain if I had to, so I focused on what only I could do.

With an extra thirty seconds, I made a twelve-foot diameter circle. I placed nineteen honeysuckle cuttings and used a version of the binding like I had at the donut store and bound to combine all circles. This was the binding that the Earth allowed me to learn after Old Donnie taught me how to banish. With my circle holding nineteen focuses of honeysuckle, I'd never created such a powerful focused circle, but I never experienced vampires creating a circle of fire either.

Nicole's bullets lifted another dogman two feet off the ground with hundreds of bullets as it passed my position until they passed through the creature. It traveled thirty feet by the force of Nicole's bullets before she ripped it to shreds.

Both woman in my heart had saved my life with guns.

My chest hurt from the vampire kick, but the Earth Power surged through me and kept the worst of the pain at bay. Nothing engaged us now, and Miles, Drisana, and Rachel stood in protective stances between my circle and the others.

Neither the church nor the vampires were as practiced with circles. Their circles were feeble. The witch's cauldron was a joke, and I did not even consider worrying about it. The thirteen vampires read the spell from a scroll—pathetic. I was about to be the man.

Then the fire changed and became hellfire and the circle increased in strength to beyond any circle I'd ever used. I was about to be in a fight. But Earth did not grant them power, nor did it like hellfire upon it. My second casting of my binding overwhelmed the circle of the church and made it mine. There was a loud snap when I made it my own.

Gun fire switched directions and Rachel yelled, "you two, go help them, I'll protect Corey!"

Drisana dipped to let Miles ride, and Fey power lit up her horn as it grew for Miles' size—holding an eight-foot-long sword. A shield glowed brightly within ten feet of him and Drisana. The two charged the special forces troops behind us.

Rachel had removed her clothes to her sports bra and skirt, then sang. The beauty of her voice promised a day of love when all evil was vanquished, and my circle emanated green and the power surged through me. Her voice overrode the muffling effect of the black and white realm and penetrated all the way to the Fey Realm. *What was turning green in a land of black and white about? Had we changed realms? Had we overpowered the realm?*

"Priests charging!" Yelled Rachel in song. *She could give commands and sing.*

I kept trying to take over the hellfire circle and came close. Minutes ticked by with me fully engaged, with Earth screaming my binding and linking the two circles, knowing mine would take over the third. Then, the vampires fell back and the hell fire circle exploded, burning them. I had their circle too. Neither group had used focuses, so my nineteen focuses were all I used for the three circles. Power raged through me and though the world was in black and white and sounds were muffled, Earth Power ignited my senses, then tore through my three circles. I strengthened my binding towards its maximum power. If this was a demon or a Dark Fey, or anything. It was going to get me at my strongest, and I was no novice. I was the one scaring the world with my power.

The screams of vampires burning with hellfire of their own summoning were easy to drown out. That's when I saw a demon from biblical paintings caught in the binding of my circle being drawn towards me. It may only have been five feet tall, but it swam in hellfire, had horns, and a tail just like from the medieval paintings.

Old Donnie's memory had my back. *You got this, son. It don't matter what they look like. You learned circles, and he is in yours; don't you fret none about what he could do outside it 'cause he can't get out.*

Earth Power lifted the ground I stood on, and a small hill formed, and I sensed Earth Power seep from my pores. I had the full ten minutes in this binding now, and I controlled and channeled more Earth Power through the three circles that I thought was possible. My torc lit up red to join with the blue. Either this was a real supernatural Fey demon thing or a gargoyle appeared. I'd prefer a gargoyle, but this Dark Fey demon must be the cause.

Stormy screamed. Rachel swung her surujin chain weapon and yelled out words in her song, and the priests all glowed green, and she was messing them up with her weighted chain. I did not recognize. I screamed my Old Gaelic spell as loud as my throat managed and the Earth opened itself to me to combat this foreign invader.

Air a ghlacadh leis an Talamh agus bho rìoghachd eile, fàg am plèana agam no bàsachadh.

Colors came back, but greens were brighter, lightning was white. Blue raindrops caressed me and life forms glowed with a golden light. It wasn't the real world, and it wasn't the Fey world. It was something in between. The sound of gunfire lessened, not in amount, but in volume.

Earth Power coursed through me and my hair stood up from it. My nerves frazzled and my voice shook, but I held on with everything because our lives depended on me holding this. Lightning lit up the area, muffled thunder shook the ground, and rain pelted me, but I continued.

The demon roared and fire came within a few feet of me, and he thrashed against the binding, and the ground shook harder. I focused on my honeysuckle and screamed my binding, and the power of the Earth raged through me back at him. The people inside of the demon's eyes were screaming in pain. *I had to hold this binding.*

The demon fought and howled. Black ichor flew against the binding as it screamed. It alternated between turning into fire and its demon form until it landed on the ground. I kept the circles at my maximum strength as long as I kept repeating the binding. We were in a contest of wills.

The power emanating from me, lifting me along with Miles, Stormy, and Rachel. After the ground brought us up, I saw another plane. The entire scene was even more vibrant, the world was clear, without rain, and four windows opened above me. One window had a snow scene with a woman in it looking at me. Another had an orange window with a different woman yawning at me. A third emerald window had yet another woman, and the last window was regular green and had a fourth woman who looked down at me. She said, "My my. If it isn't my new subjects."

"Huh," said the woman in the white window. "He's real."

The yawning woman in the orange window said, "no wonder you jumped so fast on him. He's the real deal."

"Finally, something interesting," said the woman in the emerald window.

I focused on the circles with the demon, and the tide turned. The demon was tired.

Priests lay on the ground unmoving when one leaped forward holding my magnolia seed pod scream, "Now die pagan!"

He hit my circle with the corrupted seed pod, and nothing happened. Miles and the Unicorn rode back and Rachel worked with them to prevent him from running. Nicole's trap worked.

The witches and vampires cowered from the fight. Nothing they did put out the fire. My three allies landed on the ground and appeared dazed, but I had this, and I smiled at the demon as I screamed out the binding in Gaelic and prepared for the banishing.

Then the demon changed. The supernatural being got on his knees, on the ground in my circle upon Earth I had claimed, and it... cried? "Please." Its throaty voice crackled and barely got out the word of English.

I continued my binding and began the banishment. I had won and I would send it to the Realm of Darkness, where it had no power and was subject to the whims of gargoyles.

"No," crackled the demon. It was begging. "They summoned me. Do not send me to the blackness." Its corrupted, scorched throat barely spoke English, but I was not about to relent. Rachel's voice was the only sound not muffled, and the beauty gave me strength.

I continued. *Was that a broom in the sky?*

The demon summoned hellfire and tried to blast the Earth inside the circle. My binding retaliated, and the Earth threw its power at him through me. The circle exploded along with it and vanished into a giant flame. I landed on the ground in a plop from ten feet high, sweating, and wanting to run home, but knowing I had the bishop and thirteen vampires to account for. Power from my binding vanquished the hellfire. A green swirl circled me, lifted me again above the area where my circle used to be, and flung into my chest. It slammed me to the ground as the green energy filled me. My chest felt like it would explode and four areas of my body, from my forehead to throat, solar plexus, and groin, burned.

When the pain and power dissipated, I took a breath. All three circles boomed out of existence and shook me enough to flip onto my back. Rain pelted my face and a muffled rumble of thunder shook the ground. The falls had not hurt me and I breathed normally except for tiredness. Earth Power rejuvenated me and the calming rain cleansed the battle from the Earth.

I rolled over and crawled to my hands and knees. The man in a leather jacket with a little girl wearing a pink leather jacket and a Hello Kitty helmet landed a broom next to me. "Trust me with the vampires."

I hit the bishop with an uppercut to his jaw and drew a new circle around him. I took my obsidian knife out and stood over his unconscious body.

"Who is that witch, Corey?" Miles stood protectively next to me. Rachel came up and put a hand on Miles' shoulder.

"That's Leander," said Rachel.

I coughed and held up my hand. I gasped out the next words. "He's been an ally, and I'm inclined to trust him."

I prepared the sacrificial ritual, and plunged the obsidian blade into his heart, and issued the end of the spell.

Tha mi le seo a 'tabhann an nàmhaid seo mar urram do mo bhanrigh.

Chapter 26—Queen Niamh

"Well, you certainly jumped on the first task. I granted you ten years, and you completed the task in less than a week. That is impressive," said Queen Niamh.

The circle and our entire team floated from the battle and stood in the Hall of Youth in the palace of the Fey Spring Court. Hundreds of Daoine, faeries, and other creatures stood around us.

The unicorn, Drisana, asked if we were done. I hugged her neck and thanked her. "You were the perfect companion."

She neighed and strutted over to other unicorns, satyrs, swans, and centaurs.

I put my arm around Rachel and I could tell she felt like I did. This was home. The green carpet of grass had moss on either side, with bushes and small trees making the walls. Large trees with branches made a balcony around the entire area, which must be a few thousand square feet. A giant oak tree had a throne grown into it and Queen Niamh wore a dress of flowers and leaves that showed a story of a woman leading the forces of spring to defeat the Unseelie from these lands. Her crown was simple with daisies and her youthful face was all smiles and she beckoned Rachel and I.

The surrounding others didn't seem as comfortable with their twitches and shuffling. I held hands with Rachel and stood in front of my team. "We're still in shorts," whispered Rachel.

I didn't think it mattered here, and I was comfortable as the power of the Fey Realm filled me.

"Approach," said the queen.

I moved my hand to take Rachel's, and we walked forward and even though I had not read the protocol, I knew to kneel on one knee. Rachel and I kneeled in front of the queen.

The queen stood and walked to us. She was Rachel's height and walked with a playful step. "The two of you have been so much more than we could have hoped for. I wish to reward you and your friends."

Rachel squeezed my hand, so I spoke. "Thank you, my queen. The only item I want is the return of Old Donnie, but I realize that's impossible. Otherwise, I have so much, but my team has suffered to bring me the success I've had."

I started calling them out one by one. "Rebecca completely lost her whole life is searching for a new purpose and I sense her loneliness. Due to emulating me, Nicole has made herself lonely and needs help. Nathan has been too busy to attract a mate. Miles is struggling with his new family and responsibilities. Preacher Jon needs to contact his true love, a woman called Mayven." I paused. "Please understand I miss Old Donnie something fierce, but I can never lose my friendship with Rachel." I kept my torn feelings about Nicole and Rebecca to myself. This was going to be my problem.

She turned to Rachel. "Most bards talk more than you. What is it you desire?"

Tears filled her eyes. "My mom, but I could never lose my friendship with Corey."

"Interesting." She walked past Rachel and then went to each of the team members. The queen touched each team member on the forehead.

She called Fionnestra and Verenuala over and whispered to them.

"This is all granted to the extent of Fey magic. Good luck with the next phase of your plan."

We stood back on the battlefield as if nothing happened except the bishop was missing.

"Where did he go?" exclaimed Stormy. She shook. Miles' sales persona took over. "Wait, we talked about ice cream to feel better. I see a shop just past the theater."

"Ice Cream is a great idea," said Rachel.

Nathan held out his hand to Stormy. "Ice cream? And could you two get dressed?"

She grabbed his hand, and all of us looked at me to lead them. Miles tossed my pants in my face and Nicole helped Rachel dress. "So, we have two nudists now. It's like being in your bedroom all over."

"It's a sports bra and short shorts. I'm not nude!"

"I'm in shorts too." They were acting too prudish.

I stood next to Nicole as Miles brought my shirt and shoes to me. "Nicole, now this is past. Please consider if you want me as a teammate or want me as before and what we'd have to do if that's the case."

Nicole took both of my hands. "Corey, look at me." I looked into her eyes. "Our relationship will have drama, and you aren't used to that. You'll have to figure out if drama in your life is worth me." She pulled me in with a surprise jerk and kissed me, then pulled away. "You let me know." She took my hand and started walking.

Rebecca pulled my shirt over my head and held my other hand with my shoes. She pulled me close. "I was serious when I told you that you need to figure out what you want." Then she kissed me.

A smarter man would've known what to do here. Instead, I just looked stupid and thought of the fight. "Did anyone see Suit or Red Shirt?" I asked.

"I put a scope on every human looking for them. Suit is the one who injected chemicals into me and Red Shirt hit me with a stun gun. I promise they were not on the battlefield." Rebecca was sure, and that meant I was sure.

"Crap, that means the monsignor lost the skills of Bishop Pe-drotti, but not his information. Suit is a real professional, and it's worrying me."

I walked holding hands with Rebecca and Nicole, with Rachel right in front of me. I wish it could stay like this forever. We caught up to the others.

Nathan explained things to Stormy. "I'm sorry your introduction is like this. We want to bring people along solely, but Corey changes the lives of women."

Nicole added, "you don't even need to date him."

We walked toward the vampires, and Earth slowly restored my physical strength. The rain was nice now instead of threatening. Even the grass was healing and the scorch marks and hellfire burns were going away.

The biker—witch, Leander, had the vampires arranged into three groups of four, with one on the ground. The heavily burned group, while afraid of the man in the leather jacket, cowered away from me. They didn't dare go into the scorched grass of the circle they created, though it too was healing.

"Unless you want my help with this group, we're going to bring Stormy to get ice cream and calm her."

"I want ice cream," said the little girl.

I pointed at the ice cream shop down the road.

The man looked at me. "Will you take Eliana?" He looked at the little girl and added, "who will behave." Then he looked at the thirteen who summoned a demon, "or shall I take them for ice cream and leave you to the druid who brought a demon to the Fey world and utterly destroyed him? A demon that shook you to your souls."

The vampires, scarred, and some burned beyond recognition, wore burned jeans and shredded business wear, pleaded with the witch for a fair trial.

That's when the world turned back into color.

I was happy to leave and bring Eliana, who regaled us with her favorite flavors on the walk, which calmed Stormy considerably. We walked in and Stormy looked all around the sidewalk and store then whispered, "how are they acting like nothing happened? It was like that in the park. Ten miles away, creatures were screaming and tearing through the woods and I was looking to follow the crowd, but no one helped."

The little girl answered before she skipped to the counter. "It's a dimension thing. Regular people can only see things if they look directly at it and not off by even an itsy bit. Wow! I can get chocolate and rocky road mixed?"

"I have lots of answers and lots of questions myself. Eliana here..."

"She has it right," said Nicole.

The girl called back from the counter. "Call me Ellie. I hate Eliana. I told you we'd get ice cream too. Even my daddy didn't believe me."

"He believed you, dear. He didn't want to." I recognized the voice of Samantha and she stood next to us.

"I figured if you wanted to braid my hair, you'd want to see me doing something I do best."

She laughed. "I hope it's eating ice cream, because watching you battle is as nerve-wracking as one could imagine."

Preacher Jon laughed out loud. Then lost control and had to hold himself on the door frame.

It wasn't that funny.

"What is she talking about?"

"Ellie here can probably answer more than I. Which tells you a lot about me. She told me in New Hampshire we'd get ice cream." I remembered that now, and I hope she has more ice cream predictions, and fewer end of the world predictions.

Ellie looked at Rebecca. "You *are* beautiful. You're the girl he needs to save the world." Ellie was right. She had gun powder blasted onto her face, blood covering her ripped clothes, and gore from Dark Fey—but she was beautiful.

I wondered if Rebecca remembered the conversation on the patio about the ice cream. Rebecca's smile wasn't as large as it usually was.

We all ordered ice cream and I have to admit, the vanilla bean ice cream was fantastic—I don't know if it was seventy dollars for nine people good, but we were between a baseball stadium and an aquarium.

"Your number changed," said Stormy finally. She ate a spoonful of her ice cream.

"I'll need a reference. Everyone who joins this part of the world has unique experiences." But I was relieved she was talking and the ice cream was helping calm her.

"Last year I started seeing numbers over people's heads. When you came in, you had a ten. Now it's yellow and twenty."

"My daddy's is the highest," said Ellie. "Well, except for the lady who liked you in the gondola."

At that point, the biker strode in and Ellie shouted. "I got chocolate and rocky road mixed."

He didn't seem that excited at the thought of his daughter eating a large serving of ice cream, but he smiled and sat with us. "Preacher Jon, it's a pleasure to meet you face to face."

He spoke to Preacher Jon but looked right at me.

"So, thirteen vampires came together to sacrifice one soul to keep the Dark Fey from breaching our world, and you thought the best option was to wade in and stop it."

"Don't forget the bishop who's been tracking him to kill him," added Miles.

I avoided the stares and looked at the biker witch and answered for myself. "Every time. Oh, and by the way, that was a wimpy demon."

"Your number is green and still twenty. It was eleven when you started the fight. That *wimpy* demon was a twenty-four," added Stormy unhelpfully.

"If he was so strong, why did he cry like a little girl?" I looked at Ellie. "Sorry, no offense."

She looked up with chocolate over her face. "Huh?"

The man nodded. "I am Clan Elder Leander, and you've proven to be a good person, and your circle is the most powerful circle we've ever seen, including the ones by Druid Don."

"He made me create thousands of circles before he allowed me to use one."

"You're taking on a lot of responsibility for someone so young."

"If you know anyone else who can stop the church with whatever they are doing with the gargoyles, I'd love to listen. As far as I understand, Old Donnie and I were the only two, and now it's only me. I told Preacher Jon that if no one messed with me and the church stopped trying to bring gargoyles to this world, no one would hear a peep out of me. That is true."

Leander grimaced. "The vampires chose the Southeast because Don had passed and they thought the warning that a more powerful druid had appeared down here was a lie. The church chose the victim."

I stood proud. I was with my team and we kicked it today. "If Preacher Jon is going to go after Mayven, I'm part of a team that's going to save the world."

He looked at Preacher Jon, who gave the thumbs up.

"I hope you live long enough to learn wisdom. But I am rooting for you." He looked at his daughter, who was licking the bottom of the cup. "You ready to go home?"

"Aw. He's around on all my favorite days." Ellie looked at me and added, "don't forget, right before it's darkest, you'll need the blonde lady to save the world. But if both ladies are there, you get to live."

Leander stood up and took his daughter's hand and handed her the Hello Kitty helmet. "She is sleeping through the night. Thank you."

"Wait a second," said Ellie. She pointed to Rachel. "Do you sing?"

"Yes, did you see our performance?"

"She is too young for that, but rest assured, every territory owner has played your performance hoping to learn about the new south and the new members of the Fey Spring Court," answered Leander.

Well, that would not teach them much. I was nothing like that wild eyed southern boy.

"No," said Ellie impatiently. "She sings in my dreams."

That was good. After her comments about me, I doubt I would sleep, but I'm glad Rachel heard something good. The two left and soon, we could see a broom flying in the distance with the two on it.

Nicole handed her ice cream to Rachel and ran her hand over my shoulders. She had gun powder on her face, ripped clothes, scrapes, and cuts like Rebecca. How did those two both become more beautiful in a fight?

She smiled. "Rebecca, we should do our makeup and clothes like this more often. He thinks we both became more beautiful."

"Am I safe now?" Asked Stormy.

"That is a great question," added Miles. They both turned and stared at me with a spoon of vanilla ice cream in my mouth.

"Yes. If Stormy's numbers are right, you are the most powerful druid in nearly one thousand years," said Nathan.

"What's next, great druid leader?" Rachel finished her banana and strawberry-flavored ice cream. She smiled at me as she put the cup down.

"I need a ride to my car. This minor diversion put me behind schedule and I have a gargoyle to banish within ten hours."

"I'll drive you," said Rebecca. "If I'm along for this crazy ride, I might as well know what we do."

"You know I listen to Old Donnie's mix tape music to get in the mood."

She smiled. "I downloaded the new band you like, the Georgia Thunderbolts. How about we listen to that?"

That blew me away, and I smiled. "Nathan, join us. You've never traveled with me and we need to get to know each other, too."

Preacher Jon gathered everyone together. "That is a great idea, Corey. Everyone else, Pile into the SUV. Rebecca, once you all are done, drop Corey off at the love shack, and we'll catch up at the condos."

Don't miss out!

Visit the website below and you can sign up to receive emails whenever Shawn McGee publishes a new book. There's no charge and no obligation.

https://books2read.com/r/B-A-MTXT-VBVHC

BOOKS 2 READ

Connecting independent readers to independent writers.

Did you love *Wild Eyed Southern Boys*? Then you should read *Caught up in You*[1] by Shawn McGee!

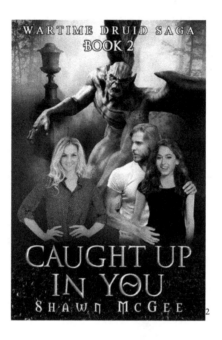

[2]

The world considers Corey to be an unhinged maniac with an uncontrolled libido even though he defeated the lieutenant in control of the gargoyles. His joining the Fey Spring Court, the Court of passion, intimacy, youthful, and fertility has not improved their opinion.

He is dating Nicole to keep her from an arranged marriage. Now she is pregnant and he and Rebecca can't get past they made the worst mistake of their lives not staying together.

The world will end in three weeks at the minute of dark during the winter solstice if Corey can't get his head in the game, train his team, convince Rebecca to give up on them forever to become the

---

1. https://books2read.com/u/4DJveg

2. https://books2read.com/u/4DJveg

Scion of the New Church, so that he can banish the evil back to the Realm of darkness.

Read more at https://WorldofGeoe.com.

Also by Shawn McGee

The World of Geoe
The Herald
The Regnant
The Vanquisher

Wartime Druid Saga
Wild Eyed Southern Boys
Caught up in You
Fantasy Girl

Watch for more at https://WorldofGeoe.com.

About the Author

Shawn McGee writes fantasy and is an IT professional with hobbies in mathematics and gaming. Along with his current series he is writing a new gaming system.

Please this book as reviews are the life blood of independent writers.

You can join Shawn's discord channel, join his email list, and find out all the book information at https://worldofgeoe.com

Read more at https://WorldofGeoe.com.

CPSIA information can be obtained
at www.ICGtesting.com
Printed in the USA
LVHW050917010623
748480LV00008B/517